William Shakespeare, Samuel Butler

Shakespeare's Sonnets Reconsidered

and in part rearranged with introductory chapters, notes, and a reprint of the

original 1609 edition

William Shakespeare, Samuel Butler

Shakespeare's Sonnets Reconsidered
and in part rearranged with introductory chapters, notes, and a reprint of the original 1609 edition

ISBN/EAN: 9783337851309

Printed in Europe, USA, Canada, Australia, Japan

Cover: Foto ©Andreas Hilbeck / pixelio.de

More available books at **www.hansebooks.com**

SHAKESPEARE'S SONNETS

RECONSIDERED, AND IN PART REARRANGED
WITH INTRODUCTORY CHAPTERS,
NOTES, AND A REPRINT
OF THE ORIGINAL 1609 EDITION

BY

SAMUEL BUTLER

AUTHOR OF "EREWHON," "LIFE AND HABIT," "THE AUTHORESS OF THE ODYSSEY,"
"THE WAY OF ALL FLESH," ETC.

> They say best men are moulded out of faults,
> And for the most become much more the better
> For being a little bad.
>
> Measure for Measure, Act V. Sc. i. 444–446.

LONDON : A. C. FIFIELD

PREFACE.

I was led to take up the thorny questions which Shakespeare's Sonnets so abundantly raise, by the appearance of two articles in the *Fortnightly Review* for Dec. 1897 and Feb. 1898. In the first of these, Mr William Archer, inclining to the theory that the Mr W. H. of Thorpe's prefatory address was William Herbert Earl of Pembroke (which involves that the Sonnets were mainly inspired by him), shewed how baseless was the contention that most, or indeed any, of them were addressed to Henry Wriothesley Earl of Southampton. In the second of the articles above referred to, Mr Sidney Lee, inclining to the theory that many of the Sonnets were addressed to Lord Southampton, shewed how baseless was the contention that Mr W. H. could have been Lord Pembroke, and declared him to have been a mere go-between, who procured the copy for Thomas Thorpe the publisher.

Convinced that neither Mr Archer nor Mr Lee had made out a case, except in so far as each of them was destructive of the other, and fired by the success which, I believe, the simple method of studying text much and commentators little, had obtained for me as regards the Odyssey, it occurred to me that the Sonnets offered a problem on which the same method might be hopefully tried. My mind was a blank in respect of them, for it was many years since I had given them any attention; I resolved, therefore, that as soon as my translation of the Iliad was off my hands, I would treat the Sonnets much as I had done the Odyssey, and as a preliminary measure began to commit them all to memory. By September 1898 I had them at my finger's ends, and have daily from that time repeated twenty-five of them, to complete the process of saturation. I may say that there was hardly a sonnet which I did not find that I understood much better after I had learned it by heart than before I had done so.

The first thing that struck me was that the last 29 sonnets of the received editions were out of their proper places, and that many of them belonged to the episode referred to in sonnets 40-42. It was idle to try and understand the Sonnets till they were placed approximately in their original order, I therefore got two copies and cancelled the odd numbers of the one, and the even ones of the other, so as to be able to lay them all face upwards on a large table—as many, that is to say, as raised any suspicion of displacement. Having laid them out, I shifted them again and again tentatively till I had got them into the order in which I have printed them. This turned out to be that of the original Quarto edition, except in the cases of sonnets 35, 121, and 126-154—of course all of the Quarto numbering. lt was some time before I got to understand the displacement of 121, and to see how it had come to be placed after 120 instead of anywhere else, and until I had got hold of this I was aware that the riddle was yet unread. On placing it where I have done I found everything explain itself. The displacement of 35 (of the Quarto) was a simpler matter to catch and to correct.

Though attending to the Sonnets as a bye-work during the first half of 1898, it was not until October that I was free to devote myself wholly to them, and to those so-called editions that appeared before 1780—the year in which Malone's great work was published. As regards these I found myself continually asking,

> Whether we are mended, or whether better they,
> Or whether revolution be the same?

I should be glad if record could with a forward look, even of one hundred courses of the sun, reveal to me what people will then be saying of our boasted criticism, and indeed of our literature as a whole. How, I wonder, shall we stand as compared with Gildon, Sewell, and the ineffable Benson? Perhaps, however, I might find it just as well to have remained contentedly in ignorance.

As for the editions and commentaries that have appeared since 1795, at the close of which year the younger Ireland's forgeries were printed in facsimile, I cannot call to mind a single one from that day to this, with the exception of Mr Aldis Wright's invaluable Cambridge edition, which has not been misled in one direction or another by the direct or indirect consequences of that disastrous fraud.

I am not sanguine about the reception of my conclusions by eminent Shakespearean scholars. One might as well try to convince an anti-Drefusard French general of the innocence of Dreyfus, or an average English or foreign Greek professor that the Odyssey was written at Trapani by Nausicaa, as to make a Herbertite, Southamptonite, Impersonalite, or Baconian devotee give up his own particular heresy. Still even among hot partisans there are always some with minds more open than others, and when a man begins to open his mind at all, the thin end even of a poor wedge, and that but clumsily inserted, will sometimes prise it open altogether. I look hopefully in this respect to Mr Sidney Lee, who, as I shall show in some of the following chapters, has opened his mind so repeatedly, and at such short intervals, that he may well open it again. It will give me great pleasure if I can succeed in inducing him to do so.

Turning now to matters of bibliographical detail in connection with this work, I have followed the usual practice of referring to the original Quarto of 1609, as " Q "—I have, by Mr Tyler's kind permission, reprinted his fac-simile of this edition. The reprint has been compared with the fac-simile, independently by my friend Mr H. Festing Jones (to whom, as in so many others of my books, I am indebted for many valuable suggestions) and by myself ; I heartily hope, therefore, and believe, that misprints, if any, will be few and unimportant. Occasionally it has been impossible to say what a given letter in Q really was ; in these cases I have either had a letter cut to imitate the one in Q as nearly as possible, or if satisfied that it was only a case of ink failing to catch, or of the type being damaged, I have given the letter which I believe to have been set up in Q. In no case, however, has any material question turned upon the doubt.

As regards my own text, I have adhered to all Q's capitals and italics, and have kept Q's Arabic numerals for the sonnets instead of the Roman ones now commonly adopted.

If a departure from the text of Q is more than a mere modernising of spelling or punctuation, I have called attention to it in a note. Small and obvious emendations, such as occasional hyphens, or the addition of inverted commas (none of which are found in Q) I pass over without notice, inasmuch as if the reader is in doubt he can turn to the reprint.

I have endeavoured to select the best variorum readings given in the Cambridge edition (generally referred to as "Camb.") and have added what few emendations occurred to me as likely to bring the text nearer to the actual words of Shakespeare. Those who turn to the Cambridge edition will see that there are comparatively few sonnets in which the text of Q does not require more or less correction. Confident that it would be a mere waste of time to verify Mr Wright's variorum readings, I have refrained from doing so.

I have headed each sonnet with a date, for which I have given my reasons in Chapters X, XI, and also with a short statement indicating the addressee, and epitomising the contents. Some of those which I have headed as addressed to Mr W. H. are not so addressed ostensibly, e.g. sonnets 19 and 146 (123, Q), in which Time is the nominal addressee. If convinced that Mr. W. H. was the person for whom the sonnet was written I have considered it as addressed to him.

In Chapter IX I have justified my retention of the order of the sonnets in Q, with the exceptions already referred to.

I have drawn lines at the end of those sonnets where I consider that there is a break either in time or continuity of thought.

I have said nothing about "Willobie his Avisa." The attempt to suppose that Shakespeare was alluded to in that work rests on the use of the initials W. S.—and that too in a publication so scurrilous that it was suppressed shortly after its appearance. No one should give it a moment's serious consideration. I once had a small object lesson in the danger of trusting to initials, having been repeatedly taxed with writing a poem which appeared in the *Spectator*, I think early in 1882, and was signed S. B. but which I have never seen, much less written. And what an awful object lesson have we not all lately had in France!

October 1, 1899.

CONTENTS.

xii CONTENTS.

CHAPTER XI.

CHAPTER XII.

SHAKESPEARE'S SONNETS

SHAKESPEARE'S SONNETS

ERRATA.

Page 28. I have said that Mr. Sidney Lee in his life of William Shakespeare has not cited Dekker's Satiromastix, as supporting the view that "begetter" in Thorpe's dedicatory address should be taken to mean not "inspirer" but "procurer." On reading Mr. Lee's work again I find that he has done so in his appendix V (p. 405).

Page 67, last line, *for* "two or more years," *read* "three or more years,"

SHAKESPEARE'S SONNETS.

CHAPTER I.

THE ORIGINAL EDITION, AND THE PARTIAL REPUBLICATION
OF 1640.

SHAKESPEARE'S Sonnets were first published, in quarto, together with a poem called "A Lover's Complaint" in 1609. The Title-page of the British Museum copy of this edition (which is generally quoted as Q) is as follows:—

SHAKE - SPEARES
SONNETS.
Neuer before Imprinted.

At London.
By G. Eld for T. T. and are to be solde by John Wright,
dwelling at Christ Church gate.
1609.

Other editions vary the name of the vendor to William Aspley. The prefatory address or dedication reads:—

TO . THE . ONLIE . BEGETTER . OF .
THESE . INSVING . SONNETS .
M^r . W . H . ALL . HAPPINESSE .
AND . THAT . ETERNITIE .
PROMISED .
BY .
OVR . EVER - LIVING . POET .
WISHETH .
THE . WELL - WISHING .
ADVENTVRER . IN .
SETTING .
FORTH .
T .T.

T. T. is identifiable as Thomas Thorpe by means of an entry in the Stationers' Register dated May 20, 1609, which declares that Thomas Thorpe "Entred for his copie vnder th[e h]andes of master WILSON and master LOWNES Warden a Booke called SHAKESPEARES *sonnettes* vj$_d$."[*]

It may be confidently affirmed that Shakespeare had nothing to do with this edition. It is very carelessly printed, and though it has infinite claims on our gratitude, it has none upon our respect. It has, however, every appearance of having intentionally preserved the order in which the Sonnets were written—except as regards those to which attention will be called later. For this mercy we should be grateful, for had the order been irrecoverably disturbed the Sonnets would have been a riddle beyond all reading.

It is surprising that A Lover's Complaint is not mentioned on the title-page of Q. It is only the internal evidence of style (which, however, admits of no doubt) that enables us to ascribe the poem to Shakespeare, but the fact of its having been printed along with sonnets of which Mr W. H. is declared to be the "only begetter," appears to connect it with him, and it is quite possible that T. T. did not mention it as considering it to be a series of sonnets, and as included in the word "insuing." Whether this be so or not it is hard to refrain from surmising that the youth described in stanzas 12—20 is drawn from Mr W. H.—in which case the poem should be associated with the earlier sonnets, and dated not later than 1585. I am glad to find myself here to some extent in agreement with Mr Sidney Lee, who says that if the work is by Shakespeare "it must have been written in very early days."[†]

Two of the Sonnets 46, (138, Q) and 52 (144, Q), had appeared in The Passionate Pilgrim, published by Jaggard in 1599, with some not very important variations from the reading of Q. The remaining 152 were, as stated on the

---

[*] Introduction to Mr Tyler's facsimile of Q p. iii. (Mr Tyler refers to Arber's *Transcript*, Vol. III., p. 183 b.)

[†] "Life of William Shakespeare." Smith, Elder & Co., 1898, p. 91.

title-page of Q, published for the first time in 1609. This unimportant deviation from literal accuracy in a statement that is substantially true leaves us at liberty to hold that though Mr W. H. is declared by Thorpe to be "the only begetter" of the insuing Sonnets, some few of them may not have been directly begotten by him, though he was the begetter of by far the greater number.

We do not know whether the original edition of the Sonnets sold out or no, but no second edition was called for, nor were any of the sonnets reprinted till 1640, when J. Benson published a medley of the Passionate Pilgrim type, but on a more extensive scale. It is entitled "Poems: Written by Will. Shakespeare, Gent." It contains the greater number of the sonnets, but omits seven—probably through sheer inadvertence—for among the omitted is the incomparable "Shall I compare thee to a summer's day" (sonnet 18).* Sonnets 48 (138, Q) and 52 (144, Q) are given in their Passionate Pilgrim form. Venus and Adonis and Lucrece are not included, but A Lover's Complaint is given, and many poems from the Passionate Pilgrim are interspersed among the Sonnets, which are arbitrarily grouped, each group being accorded a heading of its own. The series begins thus:
"The glory of beautie,"
under which head we find sonnets 87, 88, 89 (67, 68, 69, Q);
"Injurious Time,"
sonnets 80, 83—86 (60, 63—66, Q).
Presently we reach :—
"Love's crueltie,"
sonnets 1, 2, 3 ;
"Youthful glory,"
sonnets 13—15 ;
"Quick prevention,"
sonnet 7 ;
and so on, till we come to "Fast and Loose," under which we find "Did not the heavenly Rhetoric of thine eye?" from

---

* The omitted sonnets are 18, 19, 43, 56, 75, 76, 96, 126 of the quarto edition. (Camb.)

Love's Labour's Lost, given in The Passionate Pilgrim; presently we find "A sweet provocation" and "A constant vow," which head "Sweet Cytherea sitting by a brook" and "If love make me forsworn, how shall I swear to love?" both from The Passionate Pilgrim—the second appearing also in Love's Labour's Lost.

These examples shonld be enough to show that Benson was devoid of any kind of literary instinct. It will be incredible to those who do not know Benson's book, how terribly the Sonnets snffer when read under his headings, and in the juxtaposition in which he has seen fit to disarrange them; it is as though some one were to break np an old stained glass window, the story of which conld be determiued sufficiently though not perhaps easily, and present it to us in the form of six or seven dozen of kaleidoscopes. "Cursed be he that moves my bones," indeed! If the Sonnets are not bones of Shakespeare they are nothing.

Not only is The Passionate Pilgrim, or at any rate most of it, interspersed among the Sonnets, but some poems are added which are not Shakespeare's; among these are "The Amorons Epistle of Paris to Helen," and "Helen to Paris," both of them translations from Ovid. Milton's noble epitaph on Shakespeare is reprinted from the preface to the Second Folio, published in 1632, when Milton was only 24 years old, and two other elegies on Shakespeare are added. The medley, as Mr Wyndham justly calls it, concludes with "An addition of some excellent poems, to those precedent, of renowned Shakespeare, by other gentlemen."

Each page is headed "poëms," which word is not infrequently printed "poëmes." Some of the misprints of the 1609 edition are corrected, as for example "Bare rn'wd qniers" in the fourth line of 93 (73, Q), but the greater number are retained as in my Appendix C (146, Q) where the second line still begins as in Q, with a repetition of the "my sinful earth" from the end of the preceding line. The original spelling is generally retained, but is sometimes corrected and sometimes made even worse than it was in Q.

Among other barbarisms is that of sometimes changing

"he" and "his" into "she" and "her," as in sonnet 121 (101, Q), where Benson reads:—

> Because he needs no praise wilt thou be dumb?
> Excuse not silence so, for 't lies in thee
> To make her much outlive a gilded tomb,
> And to be praised of ages still to be.
>> Then do thy office, Muse, I teach thee how
>> To make her seem long hence as she shows now.

Here the "he" of the first line quoted is allowed to stand while the gender is changed in the succeeding lines.

Sonnet 145 (122, Q) is headed "On the receipt of a Table Book from his mistress" when the presumption seems irresistible that the book of tablets had been given to Shakespeare by the male friend to whom the first 126 sonnets of Q appear to have been exclusively addressed. Sonnet 148 (125, Q) is headed "An intreaty for her acceptance," when it should surely have been "for his acceptance," if the sonnet can be called "an intreaty" at all.

Other examples may or may not be found. The above are all that caught my eye, and I did not think it worth while to look for more.

The most interesting thing about the book is the short preface which tells us, firstly, that Shakespeare during his lifetime had "avouched the purity" of the Sonnets, and implies, secondly, that they failed to attract many readers. The preface opens:—

"I here presume (under favour) to present to your view some excellent and sweetely composed Poems of Master William Shakespeare, which in themselves appear of the same purity as the authour himself then living avouched; they had not the fortune by reason of their infancie in his death to have the due accommodation of proportionable glory with the rest of his ever-living Workes, yet the lines themselves will afford you a more authentic approbation than my assurance any way can, to invite your allowance.

     *   *   *   *   *   *"

We do not know where Benson got the statement that Shakespeare had defended the Sonnets, and cannot be certain that the whole story is not an invention; but considering that

Benson was writing only 24 years after Shakespeare's death, when there were many still living who must have known how the publication of the Sonnets had affected him, and considering also that there is no inherent improbability in what Benson tells us, it will be more consonant with the rules of evidence to accept his assertion, under reserve, than to reject it. As regards the implied statement that the Sonnets fell flat, it is probably correct.

The almost universal reproduction of Benson's medley rather than of Q when the Sonnets were wanted—a practice which continued until Malone's Supplement to Johnson's and Steevens' edition of the Plays in 1780—was perhaps due to an impression that the Sonnets wanted Bowdlerising for the public, and that this operation had been sufficiently performed by dislocation, intercalation, and occasional change of sex. As for the omission of seven sonnets, it would remain unknown to all except a very few, for Q appears soon to have become scarce.

I cannot find that there was any other even partial edition of the Sonnets until Lintott published the whole of Shakespeare's Poems, it is believed in 1709, but his edition is undated. The Sonnets are reprinted in the order given in Q, and for the most part with the original spelling. "Bare rn'wd quiers" which became "Bare ruined quires" in Benson's book, is with Lintott "Barren 'wd quiers," and there is no attempt to correct the repetition of "My sinful earth" in line 2 of my Appendix C (146, Q). On the title-page of one of the copies of this edition in the British Museum, the Sonnets are declared to be "all of them" in praise of Shakespeare's Mistress. When, however, we come to them in the book, we find a title-page prefixed to them, "Sonnets to Sundry Notes of Musicke," which seems almost as strange as the statement that they were addressed to a woman. But there are puzzles in connection with the title-pages of this edition with which I need not detain the reader.

CHAPTER II.

CHARLES GILDON [1665—1724], whose name nowhere
appears, but whose connection with the work is made known
to us by Dr Sewell, published in 1710, a seventh volume, supplementary to Rowe's edition of the Plays in six volumes. As
regards Rowe's edition I would remind the reader that we
are hardly less indebted to Rowe than to the editors of the
First Folio. If the Folios snatched Shakespeare as a brand
from the burning, it was Rowe who kindled the smouldering
Folios into that flame of Shakespearian cult which cannot now
be extinguished.

Returning to Gildon, his supplement to Rowe professes
to give "Venus and Adonis, Tarquin and Lucrece, and his
[Shakespeare's] Miscellany Poems," but as regards the
"Miscellany Poems" it is a mere reprint of Benson's medley,
with the same dislocation, barbarous headings, omissions, and
occasional substitutions of "she" and "her" for "he" and
"his." Sometimes he makes a small and very obvious
correction, but it is so very small and so obvious that I am
much inclined to credit the printer's reader with it. I do
not remember to have seen Malone refer to him, though he
occasionally makes a correction which Gildon had already
made. He probably never consulted Gildon at all.

Gildon omits the elegies by Milton, and other poets, and
also the "excellent poems by other gentlemen," but he
includes the translations from Ovid and other pieces which
Benson assigned to Shakespeare. Of these, as well as of
the Sonnets, Gildon declares that they "everyone of them
carry its Author's Mark and Stamp upon it." Whether he

considers the author's mark and stamp to be Shakespeare's does not appear, but there can be no doubt that he means the reader to think that he considers this.

It is plain that Gildon's work is a piece of mere book-making, and I am perhaps dwelling upon it unduly if I give the following extract from the dedication to Charles Mordaunt Earl of Peterborough, which is signed S. N. It will at any rate serve to show into what kind of hands Shakespeare had fallen at the beginning of the eighteenth century. It runs :—

What can I, my Lord, say of your *Generosity*, a heav'nly Quality, and visible in all the Actions of a great Heroe? What, I say, can I speak of it equal to those noble Proofs which are on Record? If I shou'd assert that your Lordship was always liberal of *Your own*, and always frugal of the Treasure of the *Public*, are there not a thousand Instances, as well as Witnesses of so evident a Truth? When you took whole Countries almost without Men, and maintain'd Armies without Money? But, my Lord, what can a Poet? What can all the Art of the best Orator say equal to that unparallel'd Act of Beneficence to the *Public*, when Your Lordship refus'd a Compensation for the Loss of your Baggage at Huete?

Gildon's own work in connection with this volume consists in an Essay some fifty pages long on the Art, Rise, and Progress of the Stage in Greece, Rome, and England, of about 150 pages of Remarks on the Plays, and some 15 pages of Remarks on the Poems.

From the Essay I take the following :—

There is likewise ever a Sprightliness in his [Shakespeare's] Dialogue, and often a Genteelness, especially in his *Much Ado about Nothing*, which is very surprizing for that Age, and what the learned Ben could not attain by all his Industry: and I confess if we make some small allowance for a few Words and Expressions, I question whether any one has since excell'd him in that particular. (pp. iii., iv.)

From the "Remarks on the Poems of Shakespeare" the following passage may suffice :—

All I have to say of the Miscellaneous Poems" [which of course include those of the Sonnets which were published in

Benson's medley] " is that they are generally Epigrams, and those
perfect in their kind according to the best Rules that have been
drawn from the Practice of the *Ancients*, by *Scaliger*, *Lillius
Giraldus*, *Minturnus*, *Robortellus*, *Correas*, *Possovinus*, *Pontatrus*,
Raderus, *Donatus*, *Vossius*, and *Vavasser* the *Jesuit*, at least as far
as they agree, but it is not to be suppos'd that I should give you
here all that has been said of this sort of Poesie by all these
Authors, for that would itself make a Book in Folio, I shall
therefore here only give you some concise Rules for this and some
other Parts of the lesser Poetry on which *Shakespeare* has touched
in these Poems; for he has something Pastoral in some, Elegiac in
others, Lyric in others, and Epigrammatick in most. And when
the general Heads of Art are put down in all these it will be no
hard Matter to form a right Judgment on the several Performances.
(p. 401.)

Gildon's work was republished in 1714 as the ninth and
supplementary volume to an edition of the Plays in eight
Volumes—also edited by Rowe.

The so-called edition of the Poems by Dr Sewell, published
in 1725, a year or so before his death in 1726, as a seventh
and supplementary volume to Pope's Edition of the Plays, is
dedicated to Lord Walpole. From the dedication I take the
following :—

YOUR Lordship knowing his [Shakespeare's] *Excellencies can happily
compare them with the Antients, and have thereby a peculiar Right to
this offering. That Nurse of Arts and Sciences, that Builder and
Refiner of Mankind, (with what Pride I say our common Mother ETON !)
has furnished You with a true Taste of Letters; so that tho
SHAKESPEAR might fear You as a Judge, yet he now prides
himself in courting You as a Patron.*

*IN Your Travels, Your Name, the best Harbinger, prepared for you
at every Court a Reception suitable to the Son of Mr WALPOLE.
You was then the Representative of the English Genius Abroad, dis-
playing that Probity, Integrity, and Openness of Soul that distinguishes
this Nation from all others.*

The reader will know how much to expect from Dr Sewell,
whose work indeed is only a reprint of Gildon's with hardly
any modification, including Gildon's Essay on the Art, Rise,

and Progress of the Stage and his 150 pp. of Remarks on the Plays and Poems of Shakespeare. Speaking of Gildon, Dr Sewell says in his Preface :—

This Gentleman republished these Poems [*i.e.* the whole of Benson's medley] from an old Impression in the Year 1710, at the same time with Mr Rowe's Publication of his Plays. He uses many Arguments to prove them genuine, but the best is the Style, Spirit, and Fancy of SHAKESPEAR, which are not to be mistaken by any tolerable Judge in these Matters.

After showing that Venus and Adonis and Lucrece are indisputably by Shakespeare, Dr Sewell continues :—

IF we allow the rest of these Poems to be genuine (as I think Mr Gildon has prov'd them) the occasional ones [consisting mainly of the Sonnets] will appear to be the first of his Works. A young Muse must have a Mistress to play off the beginnings of Fancy, nothing being so apt to raise and elevate the Soul to a pitch of Poetry as the Passion of Love. We find, to wander no further, that *Spenser*, *Cowley*, and many others paid the First Fruits of Poetry to a real or imaginary Lady.

No weight should be attached to Dr Sewell's opinion here implied that the Sonnets were written before Venus and Adonis. I believe him to be right, but as he is evidently wishing to convey the impression that they were addressed to Shakespeare's Mistress, actual or imaginary, and is only arguing, and arguing insincerely, on this baseless supposition, his opinion cannot be appealed to.

Dr Sewell's preface concludes :—

I HAVE already run this Preface to a great length, otherwise I should have taken Notice of some beautiful Passages in the Poems; but a Reader of Taste cannot miss them.

FOR my own part, as this Revisal of his Works obliged me to look over SHAKESPEARE'S Plays, I can't but think the Pains I have taken in correcting, well recompensed by the Pleasure I have receiv'd in reading: And if after this, I should attempt anything Dramatic in his Vein and Spirit, be it owing to the Flame borrowed from his own Altar!

Dr Sewell had already written one Tragedy, Sir Walter

Raleigh, and two Acts of an unfinished Tragedy, Richard the First, were published after his death, but if he had borrowed flame from Shakespeare's altar, that flame had refused to kindle Dr Sewell's offering.

Lewis Theobald [1688—1744], who in 1733 published an edition of "The Works of Shakespear" in seven volumes, did not include the Poems, and much as he has done for the Plays has left us very little about the Sonnets. It was probably the example of the editors of the First Folio that led so many later editors to treat the Poems as if they were not an integral part of the Works of Shakespeare. That this is so appears from Gildon's Remarks on the Poems of Shakespeare, where he answers some who had contended that the poems were "not valuable enough to be reprinted," and had further urged that the first editors must have been of this opinion or they would have published them along with the Plays. Gildon rejoined, not without a certain amount of truth, firstly that the poems are in reality "much less imperfect in their kind than even the best of the plays," and secondly that "the first editors were Players who had nothing to do with anything but the Dramatic Part" (9th and supplementary volume to the 1714 edition of Shakespeare's Plays by Rowe, p. 392).

The little that Theobald has left us about the Sonnets will be found hidden away in Vol. II. of Jortin's "Miscellaneous Observations upon Authors," to which the Cambridge Edition gives a welcome reference. The textual emendations are only five in number, three of which will be found noted in sonnets 25, 85 (65, Q), and 97 (77, Q). The other two would not have been made at all if Theobald had been working with Q instead of with either Gildon or perhaps more probably Sewell. They are to be found in sonnets 138 (118, Q), and 139 (147, Q) ; in the first case Q has :—

Even so, being full of your nere cloying Sweetnesse,
where " nere " is clearly intended for an abbreviated " never." Benson emended " nere " to " neare," and was followed by Gildon and Sewell, who read " near." Theobald, who had evidently never seen Q, restored the text to that of Q, except as regards modernising the spelling.

In sonnet 147 Q reads :—

"Past cure I am now reason is past care,"

The "a" in "care" is very faulty in Benson's edition, and both Gildon and Sewell have :—

"Past cure I am now reason is past cure."

which will not rhyme with the alternate line.   Theobald again restored the text of Q without knowing that he was doing so.

Malone in his 1780 edition declares Theobald's emendation to be unnecessary, but evidently failed to understand how Theobald came to make it.   In fact his note on the subject in his edition of 1780 is not intelligible, and his omission of part of it in his 1794 edition indicates that by that time he had discovered how it was that Theobald came to make his emendation.

Thomas Tyrwhitt [1730—1786] made many valuable suggestions to Malone—duly acknowledged by him—but I cannot find that he published any work bearing on the Sonnets, and do not suppose that he has left more than Malone has given us.

George Steevens [1736—1800] in 1766 published the text of the Sonnets with their original spelling, errors and all, adhering faithfully to the Quarto edition, but he did not annotate.   He contributed many notes and some emendations —both notes and emendations mostly unsatisfactory—to Malone's edition of the Poems, and Boswell has printed, at the end of the Sonnets in his 1821 edition of Malone's Shakespeare, a discussion concerning them between him and Malone which does him no credit.   I am reminded by Mr Sidney Lee's "Life of W. Shakespeare" that Steevens wrote as follows concerning the Sonnets :—

We have not reprinted the Sonnets, &c. [sic] of Shakspeare because the strongest Act of Parliament that could be framed, would fail to compel readers into their service; notwithstanding these miscellaneous Poems have derived every possible advantage from the literature and judgement of their only intelligent editor, Mr Malone, whose implements of criticism, like the ivory rake and golden spade in Prudentius, are on this occasion disgraced by the objects of their culture.—Had Shakspeare produced no other works than these, his name would have reached us with as little celebrity as time has conferred on Thomas Watson, an older and much more elegant sonetteer.*

Astonishing as the above passage must appear to us, it reflects an estimate of the Sonnets which seems to have been largely held at the close of the last and beginning of the present century. In 1800 a writer in the Monthly Review, reviewing Mr. Chalmers's "Apology" for the believers in the Ireland forgeries, could write:—

It would be much better to admit that there are obscurities in these Pieces [The Sonnets] which cannot be fairly explained, in consequence of their allusion to some private circumstances long since forgotten.—Few persons of good taste will regret those obscurities, in poems so greatly inferior to the other productions of Shakespeare; and for which his name alone can now procure a single reader.

Edward Capell [1713—1781] did not publish anything about the Sonnets, but there can be little doubt that many suggestions and emendations acknowledged by Malone as having been communicated to him by a correspondent C, were Capell's. Among the many books which he gave in his own lifetime to Trinity College Library is a copy of Lintott's edition of the Sonnets. Of this the Cambridge editors say:—

In Capell's Copy with which he evidently intended to go to press, there are many corrections and emendations, which we have referred to as "Capell MS." This volume appears afterwards to have passed through Farmer's hands, as there is a note in his handwriting at the end of the "Advertisement." Possibly, therefore, it may have been seen by Malone, and as many of the alterations proposed by Capell were adopted by Malone or subsequent editors, we have indicated this coincidence by quoting them as "Malone (Capell MS.)" or the like.

This note struck me as likely to suggest to some readers that Malone might have profited by Capell's MS. notes without saying so, I, therefore, called Mr Aldis Wright's attention to it, and he assured me that nothing could be

---

farther from his intention than to convey any such impression. He said that on further consideration he did not think that Farmer had ever owned Capell's copy, but rather that he had written the note after the volume had come into the possession of the College; he added that there was no evidence that Malone ever saw the book in question.

I asked Mr Wright if I was at liberty to say this, and he said he should be very glad if I would do so. In passing I may say that Farmer's note is of no importance; as for Capell's emendations, they are almost always sensible, but there are few, if any, which would not readily suggest themselves to any intelligent reader who was editing the Sonnets, and trying to correct Q's very numerous errors.

Saml. Johnson [1709–1784] in 1771 published his edition of the Plays in 12 vols.—the thirteenth vol. consisting of what professes to be Shakespeare's Poems, but is in reality only a reprint of Benson's medley, with the spelling modernised. No better proof of Johnson's indolence, and, one is tempted to add, of his unfitness to edit Shakespeare at all, can be found than the fact that five years after Steevens had reprinted the text of Q with great fidelity, Johnson should be still content to pass off Benson's medley as Shakespeare's Poems.

In 1774 J. Bell and C. Etherington published an edition of the Plays in 8 vols., with a supplementary vol. containing the Poems. They again content themselves with reprinting Benson's medley. The anonymous writer of the preface to the Poems says :—

If *Shakespeare's* merit as a poet, a philosopher, or a man, was to be estimated from his Poems, though they possess many instances of powerful genius, he would, in every point of view, sink beneath himself in these characters. Many of his subjects are trifling, his versification mostly laboured and quibbling, with too great a degree of licentiousness.

CHAPTER III.

EDMOND MALONE [1741—1812] published in 1780 the Poems of Shakespeare as a supplementary volume to Johnson and Steevens' 1778 edition of the Plays, and with this book, which appears 171 years after the original quarto, we have the first serious attempt at textual emendation and intelligent critical notes. Steevens was quite correct in saying, as already quoted, that Malone was the only intelligent editor of the Poems of Shakespeare; indeed so far as the Sonnets are concerned he might have gone further and said that he was their only editor—for a mere reprint such as those of Lintott and Steevens can hardly claim to be called an edition.

By waiving this, Malone was the first writer to publish an edition of the Sonnets which shows the instincts of a scholar and a gentleman. Granted that he was a shade too conservative, as for example in sonnets 85 (65, Q) line 10, where he rejects the emendation "quest" for "chest," though he tells us that it had occurred to him, and that Theobald had also proposed it. Or again in sonnet 23 line 9, where he retains "Oh let my books be then the eloquence," when "looks" is obviously right. Malone tells us that this emendation has been suggested to him by a correspondent whose suggestions he has marked with the letter C, and who as I have said is generally believed to have been Capell.

He also rejects the emendation "grief's strength" for "grief's length," line 14 of sonnet 28, which he again says had been suggested to him by "an anonymous correspondent, whose favours are distinguished by the letter C." Sometimes he makes an emendation that does not carry conviction, but though I remember to have rejected one or two, I cannot lay my hand on an example; on the whole, however, I find his text preferable to that of the Cambridge editors, who reject many of his emendations, which one would say commend themselves to common sense. Those, however, which they have adopted are enough to establish him as having done more for the text of the Sonnets than anyone (except perhaps Capell, who, however, did not publish) had done before, or than can ever be done again.

He is not always accurate. First class men will sometimes blunder worse than any sloven; it is for the most part only third rate men whose accuracy never fails them. In his original edition of the Poems he wrote:—

Mr Tyrwhitt has pointed out to me a line in the twentieth Sonnet which inclines me to think that the initials W. H. [in the dedication*] stand for William Hughes. Speaking of this person the poet says—
'A man in *hew* all *Hews* in his controlling —'
So the line is exhibited in the old copy. [The name Hughes was formerly written Hews*]. When it is considered that one of these Sonnets is formed entirely on a play on our author's Christian name, this conjecture does not seem improbable. To this person, whoever he was, one hundred and twenty† of the following poems are addressed. The remaining twenty-eight are to a lady.

In this short paragraph, in a preface, too, when people are generally most careful, there are three considerable mistakes, and one considerable omission. There is another matter, also on the same page, to which exception may be justly taken. Malone gives Thorpe's dedicatory preface, but he does not adhere to the punctuation of the original.

In the first place, "the old copy" does not exhibit the line quoted by Malone, in the form he gives. Q does not print the word "hew" in italics. It is the *Hews* which is alone italicised, and the correct form of the Quarto version lends more support to Mr Tyrwhitt's suggestion than the incorrect form in which Malone has given it. The error here noted

---

* The words enclosed in brackets do not appear in the 1780 edition, but are found in that of 1794.

† Corrected to "a hundred and twenty-six" in 1794.

is repeated in the 1794 edition, and in Boswell's edition of 1821.

Secondly, Malone meant to say not that 120, but that 126, of the sonnets were addressed to Mr W. H. 120 and 28 make 148, whereas the Sonnets are 154 in number. This error is corrected in the 1794 edition and in Boswell's edition of 1821 ; I should perhaps say that the Boswell here named is not Johnson's biographer, but his son.

Thirdly, even a cursory examination of the last 28 sonnets should have convinced Malone that some of them were not written to a woman, and that of the others, several, though written to a woman, were not intended to be taken by that woman as coming from Shakespeare.

The omission above referred to consists in the failure to observe what Mr Wyndham has more than once urged. I mean that many of the last 28 sonnets belong to the series 40—42, and are therefore misplaced in Q.

As regards Malone's assertion that the last 28 of the sonnets were written to a woman, 129 Q cannot be so held ; 145 Q is not addressed to a woman, though it has a woman for its subject ; 153, 154 Q, are mere paraphrases, addressed to nobody ; 146 Q is an occasional introspective meditation, priceless, as revealing Shakespeare's truest and most un-clouded mind more certainly and directly than anything else he has left us. It contains nothing to suggest its having been written to or for a woman.

Sonnets 130, 131, 137, 138, 141, 144 (all of them according to the Q numbering) cannot have been intended to be shown to their addressee, and hence can hardly be held as having been addressed to her. Sonnets 135, 136, 151, 152 (all of them Q) were obviously written to a woman, and written by Shakespeare, but I cannot doubt that three at any rate of these four sonnets were written for Mr W. H. to give to Shakespeare's mistress as though he had written them him-self, and if so they cannot be included among sonnets addressed by Shakespeare to a woman.

---

* Wyndham's "Poems of Shakespeare," pp. cx., cxi., and 325.

Sonnets 147–150 (Q) do not on the face of them say whether they are addressed to a man or a woman, but the passionate emotion which they breathe in every line indicates an intensity of feeling which the dark woman does not seem elsewhere able to excite. Assuming, as we may do, that Shakespeare's mistress and the dark woman are one and the same person, Shakespeare tells us that it might "be said" he "loved her dearly" (42 Q), but it is a far cry from this to being "frantic mad with evermore unrest," as he declares himself in sonnet 147 Q. No man can write such a line as this unless he really is what he says he is, but I can find no such pathos in anything written by Shakespeare to the dark woman; nothing, therefore, will persuade me that sonnets 147–150 Q were not addressed to Mr W. H., and that too at a time when Shakespeare was heart-broken at becoming more and more convinced of his idol's utter worthlessness. Of the whole 28, therefore, which Malone includes in his second group, and which he declares to have been addressed to a woman, only 9, *i.e.* 127, 128, 132, 133, 134, 139, 140, 142, 143 (all Q), can be admitted as in reality so addressed.

As regards his failure to see that the last 28 sonnets belong mainly to the episode which is alluded to in sonnets 35, 40, 41, 42 (Q), but nowhere else in the first group, I refer it to the fact that he had too much on his hands to be able to give the Sonnets that long, close, undivided attention which could alone unriddle them.

If he had come after a capable man, who had already done the rough work of textual emendation; if again he had not been also engaged in editing Shakespeare's other Poems, and been anxious to proceed to his own edition of the Plays; if, in fact, he had put everything else on one side and saturated himself with the Sonnets, committing them all to memory, and thus acquiring a mastery over them which nothing else can give so fully—then I cannot doubt that he would not only have seen the point on which Mr Wyndham has so justly insisted, but would have also seen his way to shuffling the Sonnets, at any rate approximately, into their original order.

Lastly (so true is it that Time can kill judges more readily than he can ripen judgements), if the Sonnets had not lien among the pots for near two hundred years—the very Cinderella of literature—at best patted half contemptuously on the back by such men as Gildon and Sewell—if Malone had had the benefit of the additional hundred years of reflection which he did so much to aid, he would have been less apologetic in the discussion with Steevens, already referred to as given by Boswell immediately after the Sonnets themselves.

In that discussion Malone writes :—

I do not feel any great propensity to stand forth as the champion of these compositions. However, as it appears to me that they have been somewhat under-rated, I think it incumbent upon me to do them that justice to which they seem entitled.

He must be a bold man who thinks himself competent to do justice to the Sonnets. The Sonnets may be criticised, studied, elucidated, emended, found fault with—for they are full of faults—but doing justice to them is another and very different thing—one might as well try to do injustice to Benson's medley, or to Gildon and Sewell. A little later Malone writes, concerning the Sonnets :—

When they are described as a mass of affectation, pedantry, circumlocution, and nonsense, the picture appears to me over-charged. Their great defects appear to be a want of variety, and the majority of them not being directed to a female, to whom alone such ardent expressions of esteem could with propriety be addressed. It cannot be denied, too, that they contain some far-fetched conceits ; but are our author's plays entirely free from them ? Many of the thoughts that occur in his dramatic productions are found here likewise; as may appear from the numerous parallels that have been cited from his dramas, chiefly for the purpose of authenticating these poems. Had they therefore no other merit, they are entitled to our attention, as often illustrating obscure passages in the plays.

I do not perceive that the versification of these pieces is less smooth and harmonious than that of Shakespeare's other com-positions. Though many of them are not so simple and clear as they ought to be, yet some of them are written with perspicuity and energy. A few have been already pointed out as deserving this character, and many beautiful lines scattered through these

poems will, it is supposed, strike every reader who is not determined to allow no praise to any species of poetry except blank
verse or heroic couplets.

With the appearance, however, of Malone's 1780 Supplement, it seemed as though the Sonnets were about to emerge
from the slough of both outrage and neglect in which they
had remained so long.   Between 1780 and 1797 there was
no advance made upon Malone save what few corrections
he made in his edition of 1794, but there had been nothing
retrograde or extravagant, and the reception of Malone's
conclusions seems to have been favourable among Shake-
sperean scholars generally.   I can find nothing to indicate
that any doubt existed among literary men as to the
interpretation that should be put upon Thorpe's preface.   We
know what Malone, Tyrwhitt, Farmer, and I think I may
add Steevens and Capell took it to mean.   I can find no trace
of its being even supposed capable of more than one interpretation.   Those who have left any record of their opinion
took it to mean that the Sonnets were all of them, or at
any rate very nearly all of them, inspired by, or in some way
engendered by, a person whose initials were W. H.   Granted
that only a few have expressed any opinion on the subject,
but we may assume confidently that if Malone had known
of any other opinion he would have told us of it.

Again, that Jeroboam the son of Nebat who has made
all subsequent criticism of the Sonnets to sin, I mean
Mr George Chalmers—when in 1799 he first broached the
theory that "begetter" only means "procurer," would have
been only too glad to appeal to any earlier authority had such
authority existed.   So would Dr Drake when in 1817 he
advanced the theory that the Sonnets were addressed to
Lord Southampton.   See how he clutches at such straws as
Gildon and Sewell—misrepresenting both of them, and then
stultifying his appeal by declaring them to have been editors
of "extreme carelessness."

The silence of Malone, Chalmers, and Drake—the first
of whom would have told us in good faith had he known of
any other interpretation of Thorpe's preface than the one

he puts upon it, while the others would have been sure to do so in the interests of their theories—the silence of these men, so placed, will I believe satisfy the reader that the earliest serious students of the Sonnets understood Thorpe's prefatory address to mean, that having undertaken the risk of publishing some Sonnets (which have been stated upon the title-page to be by Shakespeare) he is offering his good wishes to a certain Mr W. H. who, he declares, was the sole cause of the Sonnets having been written, and to whom Shakespeare had promised an eternity of fame.

Looking at the Sonnets apart from the dedicatory address they found them so clearly dominated by one man, that this person, whoever he was, might be justly called their only begetter. They found Shakespeare repeatedly promising him an eternity of fame ; they found what seemed to them, and has seemed to most people ever since, conclusive evidence that his christian name was William, while from another sonnet they gathered that his surname was probably Hughes.

Looking at the preface apart from the Sonnets, they found it appearing to declare that the person who had been the sole cause of the Sonnets having been written was a man whose initials were W. H., and also appearing to declare that Shakespeare had promised this person an eternity of fame. Being reasonable people, and not having any theory as to who Mr W. H. might have been, nor having as yet found anything in the Sonnets to suggest that he was of higher birth than Shakespeare himself, they did not think it an unwarrantable assumption, even though qualifying their acceptance of the name of Hughes with some reserve, to conclude that the addressee of the Sonnets and of the preface were one and the same person.

If the Sonnets had been lost, and nothing had remained to us but the title-page and dedication, who would have doubted that our loss had consisted of certain sonnets by Shakespeare, which were mainly conversant about a Mr W. H. —that is to say, either addressed to him directly or written for his delectation, or in his real or supposed interests ? Admitting the title-page as correct, "only begetter" would have been taken to mean that though Shakespeare's brain was the womb wherein the Sonnets grew, the influence which had fecundated that brain had proceeded solely from Mr W. H. Nor would any one have doubted that the eternity mentioned in the prefatory address as having been promised by Shakespeare was supposed by T. T. to have been promised to Mr W. H. and not to any one else.

Happily the Sonnets have not been lost, and so well do they bear out the statements of the preface, that, as their general tenour is found to be correctly deducible from the prefatory address, so, had the prefatory address been lost, its tenour would have been sufficiently deducible by such men as Malone, Tyrwhitt, Steevens, Farmer, and doubtless Capell, except, of course, in so far as Thorpe and his good-will to Mr W. H. are concerned—these being developments of later date than the writing of the Sonnets.

When the interpretation of words in their most usual sense reveals to us so perfect a correspondence between a collection of poems and its preface, who will doubt, in the absence of conclusive countervailing evidence, that the usual interpretation is the one that ought to be adopted?

CHAPTER IV.

MR GEORGE CHALMERS AND HIS INTERPRETATION OF THE
WORD "BEGETTER" IN THORPE'S PREFACE.

ONE would have thought no man; but the course of true
criticism never did run smooth. In 1795, a year or so after
the second edition of Malone's supplement,* and some 15 years
after his previous edition had been allowed to go unchallenged,
the famous Ireland forgeries threw the Shakespearean world
into confusion.

These forgeries were published in facsimile by the forger's
father, in a volume entitled "Miscellaneous Papers and legal
Instruments under the hand and seal of William Shakespeare";
the volume was published in December 1795, but is dated 1796.
The documents themselves had already been on view for some
months at the house of the elder Ireland, who was completely
taken in by them, as also were many of the best scholars of
the day,—among them Dr. Parr.

One of these forgeries was a letter from Queen Elizabeth
to Shakespeare, which begins :—

Wee didde receive your prettye Verses goode Masterre William
through the hands of oure Lord Chambelayne, ande wee doe
complemente thee onne theyre greate excellence.

Malone, in his "Inquiry into the authenticity of certain
Miscellaneous Papers, &c.," published in 1796, showed how
impossible it was to accept this letter as genuine, and among
other more serious objections, expressed his surprise (pp. 97,
98) that these "pretty verses" should not have been preserved
either by the Queen, or by some of her courtiers.

In 1797 Mr George Chalmers [1742—1825], who was then

---

* This edition, which is in rather smaller type than the first, makes few alterations

Chief Clerk of the Board of Trade, wrote a book of over 600 pages entitled "An Apology for believers in the Shakespeare Papers," the scope of which was to show that though the supposed Shakespearean documents must be admitted to be spurious, yet Malone was wrong in his reasons for rejecting them. This work, according to the *British Critic* (Vol. IX., Lond. 1797, p. 512), was,

a book composed to prove not that the believers of a certain allegation were right, for that is given up, but that they might possibly have been right.

Let us now see how Mr Chalmers meets Malone's surprise that the "pretty verses" mentioned in the forged letter from Queen Elizabeth to Shakespeare were nowhere to be found. With that strange power of having things both ways, which, like conscience, "so greatly boons yet greatly banes" those in whom it is well developed, he declares that, whether they ever existed outside young Ireland's brain or no, they had at any rate not been lost, and if Malone had not been dull of sight he would have detected them. Malone, he says,

has seen them, he has criticised them; but, whatever may be the keenness of his eye, or the acuteness of his criticism, he has not discerned them, though he had the daily help of able coadjutors.

But I will . . . no longer conceal the secret. The *sugr'd sonnets,* of which Meres spoke in 1598,* and which were first printed by Thorpe in 1609 are the *prettye verses* of *honey-tongu'd* Shakspeare. *Impossible!* cries Mr Malone, with the monotonous tongue of his own Pretty Poll. I will now maintain . . . . that the sugr'd sonnets, which were handed about before, and in the year 1598, among Shakspeare's private friends, were the very verses which he addressed to Elizabeth *in his fine filed phrase;* that *the* SONNETS of Shakspeare were addressed, by him, to Elizabeth, although I do not mean to contend for the *spurious performances* of booksellers, the *intermixtures* of critics, nor the interpolations of Mr Malone. In order to see this curious point, in its true light, it will be necessary to advert, with discriminative eye, to the character of Elizabeth, and to the situation of Shakspeare (pp. 41—43).

---

* See "Palladis Tamia," pp. 282, left page (S.B.).

This man's very commas are enough to raise prejudice against him.   See, too, how all these finders of literary mare's nests try to focus the reader's eye, not on the work under consideration, but on something else.   Can there be a doubt that Mr Chalmers had made his theory while still a believer in the Ireland forgeries, and was not going to be balked merely because young Ireland had proved to be forger ?

Malone made no reply, but some one seems to have pointed out to Mr Chalmers that Thorpe's preface declared the Sonnets to have been inspired solely by a Mr W. H., and he must have felt it incumbent upon him to show that this was not the case. In 1799, therefore, he published another 600 pp. entitled "A Supplemental Apology, &c.," and in this he says :—

> Thorpe, the first publisher of them [the Sonnets], dedicated those *Amatory* effusions "to the *only begetter* of these ensuing Sonnets, Mr W. H."   How he was the *begetter* of them, it is not easy to tell; unless we presume, what is not improbable, that he begot a desire in Shakspeare to deliver a copy to the Bookseller, for publication: W. H. was the *getter* of the manuscript, imperfect as it was, from which the Sonnets were printed inaccurately (p. 52).

Later on, on p. 90, he says further to the same purpose :—

> They [the Sonnets] . . . were published . . . by Thorpe, from an imperfect Copy, which may have come into the hands of W. H. who gave it to the Bookseller, without the apparent consent of the author.   But, there was no intimation, to whom they were addressed, except that Thorpe dedicated them to W. H. as the only *begetter* of these sonnets.

In a note on the word "begetter" in the foregoing passage Mr Chalmers writes :—

> See Minsheu, 1616, in vo. *to beget*, signifying in one sense to bring foorth.   W. H. was the bringer forth of the Sonnets. *Beget* is derived by Skinner from the A. S. *begettan*, obtinere. Johnson adopts this derivation and sense; so that *begetter* in the quaint language of Thorpe the Bookseller, Pistol, the *ancient*, and such affected persons, signified the *obtainer*; as to *get*, and *getter*, in the present day, mean *obtain*, and *obtainer*, or *to procure*, and *the procurer*.

Turning to Minsheu I read :—

Beget or *Engender*, a Belg. be et gaeden, i. formáre generándo. G. *Engendrer*. H. *Engendrár*. P. Gérar. I. L. *Generare* à *gignere*, vel genus creáro, *Propagare*, *Procreare*. Gr. γεννάω, à γένος, i. genus, B. Genereren, Wooztbzeugen, i. proferre, Unde Ang. to bring foorth. T. Zeugen, *forte à gr. suprà*. Heb. jaladh, הוליד holidh.

So schoolboys making Latin verses with the help of a gradus, if they find a word with the required quantity at the end of the synonyms, will force it into their line, as hoping that their master will not know, or be too jaded with other like rubbish to remonstrate.

Turning to Johnson I find that he does indeed derive *Beget* from the Anglo-Saxon *Begettan*, to obtain ; but this is not saying that "beget" has meant "obtain" within the last several hundred years. The only uses of the word that he gives are,

1. To generate ; to procreate ; to become the father of, as children.
2. To produce as effects.
3. To produce as accidents.

The only example given of this last sense is,

It is a time for story when each minute Begets a thousand dangers.

There is little difference between the second and third senses ; both mean "engender." As for the substantive "begetter," Johnson simply says that it means "he that procreates or begets." He gives no example of either verb or noun in the sense of "to procure," or "procurer."

It seems, then, that Mr Chalmers has first tampered with plain words, and then with the authorities to whom he appeals in order to show that he had not been tampering.

It is especially incumbent upon me to demolish Mr Chalmers's interpretation of "begetter" inasmuch as to do so kills two birds with one stone ; indeed I should say three, only that the third bird—Mr Chalmers's own theory—is so dead that there is no killing it. The two birds that a reasonable interpretation of "begetter" will kill, are the theory that the Sonnets were most of them addressed to Lord Southampton, and that other even more fatuous supposition, that they were not, or, at any rate not many of them, addressed to or inspired by any one at all. Both these theories are very much alive at the present time. It is obvious, however, that what few and poor pleas for existence either of them can urge may be disallowed at once unless their upholders can make a good case in the outset for setting aside the *primâ facie* interpretation of Thorpe's preface.

I shall waive this point presently and consider what pleas can be urged without regard to the fact that I believe them to have been effectually barred by the words of Thorpe's preface ; but for the present I will harp a little longer on the meaning of the word "begetter."

Doubtless the word "beget" is only "get" with a prefix added, and hence, doubtless, its earliest sense was the same as that of "get." Murray gives "to get, to acquire," as the primary meaning of the word, but the only use of "beget" in this sense which he adduces within a couple of hundred years of Shakespeare's time, is one from Shakespeare himself, to wit, "You must acquire and beget a temperance that may give it smoothness."* Surely, however, Shakespeare meant "You must acquire temperance, aye, and so assimilate it that you may beget it in your speech, and give smoothness to the very torrent of your passion." It is inconceivable that he should have intended his "beget" in this passage to have no further significance than that of the word that he had just used— as though he had written "You must acquire and acquire a temperance, &c." Murray's case, therefore, is not in point.

As for the substantive "begetter," Dr Murray says that it means, "the agent that originates, produces, or occasions," and he quotes Thorpe's preface to the Sonnets ; but whether he meant that Mr W. H. was "the agent that originated" the Sonnets, or "that occasioned them," in which case he is on the

---

* The passage runs :—"for in the very torrent, tempest, and, as I may say, whirlwind of your passion, you must acquire and beget a temperance that may give it smoothness." Hamlet III., ii., 6—9.

side of Malone, or "the agent that produced the Sonnets," in which case he may or may not be on the side of Mr Chalmers and Boswell, I must leave it to the reader to determine. The other three examples of the use of the word which he adduces are incontestably in support of the view that "begetter" means "engenderer."

Boswell, indeed, has trumped up a passage which he pretends bears out his view, though he must have very well known that it cannot equitably be made to do so. In a note on Thorpe's dedicatory address in his 1821 edition of Malone he writes :—

The *begetter* is merely the person who *gets* or *procures* a thing, with the common prefix *be* added to it. So in Decker's Satiromastix : "I have some cousin-germans at Court shall beget you the reversion of master of the king's revels." W. H. was probably one of the friends to whom Shakespeare's sug'red Sonnets, as they are termed by Meres, had been communicated, and who furnished the printer with his copy.

Struck with the fact that Dr Murray has not cited the foregoing passage from Dekker, and has adduced no later example of "beget" being used as "get" or "gain," than one from Gower in 1393—struck also with the fact that Mr Sidney Lee, for whom it is a *sine quâ non* that "begetter" should be misinterpreted, appealed to Dekker in his article on Shakespeare in the "Dictionary of National Biography," but has not done so in his "Life of W. Shakespeare," I turned to Dekker's Satiromastix, and find that the passage in question is put into the mouth of Sir Rees Ap Vaughan, a Welshman, who by way of humour is represented as murdering the English language all through the piece ; I then understood why Dr Murray did not refer to it and why Mr Sidney Lee desisted from doing so ; but I did not and do not understand how Boswell could have adduced it, unless in the hope of hoodwinking unwary readers, who he knew would accept his statement without verifying it. This single factitious example has done duty with Southamptonites and impersonalites for the last 80 years, without anyone's having been able to cap it with another. With

the metaphorical use of the word we are, of course, all familiar
—the use, indeed, is metaphorical in Thorpe's preface—but
the idea behind the metaphor is always that of engendering
from within, not of procuring from without.

Canon Ainger, indeed, in the *Athenæum*, Jan. 28, 1899,
asks leave to "cite yet one more classical example of the use
of 'beget,' in the sense of 'procure,'" as though there were
many such instances already familiar to well-read persons.
He then quotes from *The Critic* a passage in which
Mr Puff proposes to open his piece with the firing of a
morning gun. This, Mr Puff declares, will at once "beget
an awful attention in the audience." Canon Ainger pretends
to have failed to see—for I hold it more polite to suppose
he is pretending—that "beget" in the passage just quoted
is not used "in the sense of 'procure,'" but of "engender."
The gun will not "procure" the required attention *ab extra*,
and present it to the audience; it will breed the attention
within them.

Another consideration of less weight, but one that so far as
I know has not been noted, arises from the prefixing the word
"only" to "begetter" in Thorpe's preface. The fact that the
Sonnets are so almost exclusively conversant, directly or
indirectly, about a single person, suggests that they would all
be in the hands of this person, whoever he may have been.
There is nothing to support the view that copies were circulated
in MS. We have Meres' testimony to the fact that Shakespeare's "private friends" had seen or heard more or fewer of
his "sug'red sonnets"—doubtless the ones we have under
consideration—but if copies had been going about in MS.
they would have reached many another beyond the circle of
Shakespeare's private friends, and Jaggard would have been
able to get hold of more than two of them for his Passionate
Pilgrim. There is no reason, then, for thinking that more
than one person would have to be asked for the copy, and in
this case, supposing "begetter" to mean nothing more than
"procurer," the addition of the word "only" appears too
emphatic for the occasion—"begetter" alone should have been
ample. If on the other hand Mr W. H. was the only cause

of the Sonnets having been written at all, the fact is one of
sufficient interest and importance to make record reasonable
even in a preface so tersely worded as the one in question.
Again the word "only," had, through the Creed, become so in-
separably associated with "begotten," that I cannot imagine
any one's using the words "only begetter" without intending
the verb "beget" to mean metaphorically what it means in
"only begotten."

Lastly I should say a few words about Mr Chalmers's
attempt to make out that Thorpe's preface is couched in
extravagant language such as that of "Pistol, the *ancient*,
and such affected persons," and hence that the word "begetter"
is to be taken in an unusual sense. I see Canon Ainger in
his letter already referred to has endorsed this. He writes :—

I do not suppose that even Mr Lee would plead that the word
"begetter" was a natural word for Thorpe to have used. But the
whole style of the dedication is euphuistic—the vein of Armado or
Osric—and the first thought of euphuists of that calibre was never
to use a common word when an uncommon one would do.

I leave it to the reader to say whether he can find a single
uncommon word, or a single word used in an uncommon sense,
or a single sign of extravagance, in a preface which errs
indeed deplorably on the side of conciseness, but in no other
direction. Have we not here too, as in so much else that
Mr Chalmers has written, all the criteria whereby we may
detect men who are shaping, not theory by fact, but fact by
theory ?

Mr Chalmers and his followers have told equitable presumption to stand aside on no other ground than that of the
exigencies of their own conjectures. Having formed their
conjectures on insufficient grounds, they have taken them for
granted ; on the ground so laid they have built other conjectures ; nor is it easy to say what further folly they will not
commit unless they are effectually dealt with, for men's eyes
are being now focussed upon the Sonnets as they have never
been focussed hitherto, and freedom from extravagance is not
a virtue on which modern theorists can plume themselves.

The little that Mr Chalmers has to say about Tyrwhitt's conjecture, approved by Malone, that "*Hews*," in sonnet 20, is a play on Mr W. H.'s surname, will be found on pp. 53—63 of the Supplemental Apology. His remarks are intended to prove that sonnet 20 was addressed not to a man but to a woman —a supposition so absurd that it is not necessary to do more than refer the reader to Mr Chalmers himself.

CHAPTER V.

But it is not Mr Chalmers's fatuousness that is so deplorable—it is the fatuousness of which he has been the cause in others, and which has vitiated more or less all that has been written about the Sonnets during the last hundred years. His two absurd books unsettled people's minds, and even though it was obvious that the Sonnets were not addressed to Queen Elizabeth, his interpretation of "begetter" opened the door for supposing them to have been addressed to some more interesting person than a plain Mr W. H. whom nobody knew, or was likely to know. The same thing happened to the Sonnets after Mr Chalmers's paradox, as happeued to the Iliad and Odyssey after Wolf had started his multiple-authorship theory on its long and mischievous career: each successive would-be commentator must set out on a new wild-goose chase of his own. It seems as though sound criticism had something of the Prince Rupert's drop about it—once injure it and it shivers into a thousand fragments.

It was some eighteen years before Mr Chalmers's extravagance bore its due fruit, in the form of two large quartos each containing more than 600 pp., entitled "Shakspeare and his Times," by Dr Nathan Drake, M.D. This work appeared in 1817, but its author tells us that he had been engaged upon it for several years—during which if he treated his patients with the recklessness with which he treated the Sonnets, he must have sent many a soul hurrying down to Hades.

Being about to maintain that the Sonnets were maiuly addressed to Lord Southampton, he is of course compelled to adopt Mr Chalmers's interpretation of "begetter." I find I was wrong in my letter to the *Athenæum* of Dec. 24, 1898, in

saying that he had not acknowledged his indebtedness. He
has done so; he quotes, moreover, Mr Chalmers's reference to
Minsheu already given, but gives no more reason than that
gentleman did for adopting an unusual instead of a usual
meaning.*

Dr Drake contends that Gildon must have agreed with him
about the meaning of "begetter," inasmuch as he has said
that all the Sonnets were written in praise of Shakespeare's
Mistress.† There is no trace of any such saying in either of
the editions of the Poems with which we can connect Gildon.
Dr Drake must have been thinking of Lintott's title-page.
He appeals to Sewell as of the same opinion, on the score of a
passage quoted on an earlier page of this book, from which it
is plain that Sewell neither said nor thought what Dr Drake
says he did, though wishing to appear to do so. He then
implies that Mr Chalmers's interpretation of "begetter" had
been universally accepted until 1780, when it was first disturbed
by Malone†—the fact being, as I trust I have made sufficiently
clear, that no one whose opinion is worth the paper it is written
on had published anything or left us any opinion about the
Sonnets. How far Dr Drake himself is competent to discuss
the subject the following extract may suffice to show.

Dr Drake writes :—

We may also very safely affirm of Shakspeare's Sonnets, that if
their style be compared with that of his predecessors and contemporaries, in the same department of poetry, a manifest
superiority must often be awarded him, on the score of force,
dignity, and simplicity of expression ; qualities of which we shall
very soon afford the reader some striking instances.

To a certain extent we must admit the charge of *circumlocution*,
not as applied to individual sonnets, but to the subject on which the
whole series is written. The obscurities of this species of poem
have almost uniformly arisen from density and compression of
style, nor are the compositions of Shakspeare more than usually
free from this style of defect; but when it is considered that
our author has written one hundred and twenty-six sonnets for the
sole purpose of expressing his attachment to his patron, it must

---

* Vol. II., pp. 58, 59.   † p. 59.

necessarily follow that a subject so reiterated would display no small share of circumlocution. Great ingenuity has been exhibited by the poet in varying his phraseology and ideas; but no effort could possibly obviate the monotony, as the result of such a task.[*]

But not to deal with Dr Drake in too cavalier a fashion, let us see whether he may not after all have more reason on his side than we might expect. If he can show strong reasons for thinking that the Sonnets were addressed to Lord Southampton, we may be even compelled to think that Thorpe had used the word "begetter" in an unusual sense. Mr Chalmers's theory was on the face of it so absurd that it was not necessary to refute it, but as regards Dr Drake let us at any rate see what the grounds are on the strength of which he would have us set the ordinary meaning of "begetter" on one side.

They are to be found on pp. 62—72 of Dr Drake's second volume, and rest mainly on a certain, though by no means very remarkable, analogy between sonnet 26 and the dedication of Tarquin and Lucrece to Lord Southampton.

That dedication is as follows :—

The love I dedicate to your lordship is without end; whereof this pamphlet, without beginning, is but a superfluous moiety. The warrant I have of your honourable disposition, not the worth of my untutored lines, makes it assured of acceptance. What I have done is yours, what I have to do is yours; being part in all I have, devoted yours. Were my worth greater, my duty would show greater, mean time as it is, it is bound to your lordship to whom I wish long life, still lengthened with happiness.

Your lordship's in all duty, William Shakspeare.

It may assist the reader to compare the above dedication with sonnet 26, if I repeat the sonnet in this place : —

> Lord of my love, to whom in vassalage
> Thy merit hath my duty strongly knit,
> To thee I send this written ambassage
> To witness duty not to show my wit :

---

[*] "Shakspeare and his Times," by Nathan Drake, M.D., Cadell and Davies. 1817. Vol. II., p. 76.

Duty so great, which wit so poor as mine
May make seem bare, in wanting words to show it,
But that I hope some good conceit of thine
In thy soul's thought, all naked, will bestow it;
Till whatsover star that guides my moving
Points on me graciously with fair aspect,
And puts apparel on my tattered wooing
To show me worthy of thy sweet respect;
    Then may I dare to boast how I do love thee;
    Till then not show my head where thou may'st prove me.

The imagined closeness of analogy between this sonnet and the dedicatory preface to Tarquin and Lucrece was the sheet anchor of those who upheld the Southampton theory until Mr Sidney Lee in his recent " Life of Shakespeare " put forward an argument which I suppose he must consider even stronger, and with which I will deal presently. Granting, however, that the analogy is greater than I am able to find it, it is a bold measure to argue that because there is some analogy between two documents of like purport, and written by the same person, that they must also be written not only by, but to, the same person. This, however, is what Dr Drake insists on :—

Shakspeare [he writes] opens his dedication to his Lordship with the assurance that *his love for him is without end.* In correspondence with this assertion the sonnet commences with this remarkable expression, "Lord of my Love"; while the residue tells us, in exact conformity with the prose address, his high sense of his Lordship's merit and his own unworthiness. (Vol. II., pp. 63, 64.)

We cannot suppose that Dickens had read Dr Drake, but have we not here Serjeant Buzfuz pure and simple, with his " chops and tomato sauce " and his " very very remarkable expression, ' Don't trouble yourself about the warming pan ' " ? Is it not plain that to Dr Drake everything is going so to adhere together that no dram of a scruple, no scruple of a scruple, no obstacle, no incredulous or unsafe circumstance— what can be said? Nothing that can be—can come between him and the conclusion he means to draw.

Dr Drake continues :—

That no doubt may remain of the meaning and direction of this peculiar phraseology, we shall bring forward a few lines from the 110th* sonnet, which uniting the language of both the passages just quoted [i.e., the preface to "Lucrece" and sonnet 26] most incontrovertibly designates the sex, and, at the same time, we think, the individual to whom they are addressed :—

> My best of love,
> Now all is done, *save what shall have no end;*
> Mine appetite I never more will grind
> On newer proof to try an *older friend,*
> *A God in love,* to whom I am confin'd.

Let alone the hardihood of making "My best of love" a vocative beginning, instead of the accusative ending that it really is, how can evidence that these lines were addressed to Lord Southampton be extracted from the foregoing quotation except by one who was predetermined to extract it? I have given all that Dr Drake has said upon this point.

Dr Drake then answers a supposed objector, who has asked how the first seventeen sonnets, which are written for the sole purpose of persuading their object to marry, can have been addressed to Lord Southampton since that nobleman, in 1594, when he was only twenty-one, was madly in love with Elizabeth Vernon. Dr Drake replies that Queen Elizabeth opposed the marriage, and succeeded in delaying it till 1599; during this period Lord Southampton may perhaps have impatiently said that if he could not marry Elizabeth Vernon he would die single. This would alarm Shakespeare, who would immediately set about writing the first seventeen sonnets.

After more rubbish of a like kind, Dr Drake quotes sonnet 121 (101, Q) in full, with much use of Roman Capitals, and declares that it "distinctly marks" "in the most emphatic and explicit terms" "the *sex*, the *dignity*, the *rank*, and the *moral virtue*" of his friend.

To whom [he asks] can this sonnet or indeed all the passages which we have quoted apply, if not to Lord Southampton, the

---

* 120 of my numbering.

bosom friend, the munificent patron of Shakspeare, the noble, the elegant, the brave, the protector of literature and the theme of many a song? And let it be remembered, that if the hundreth [sic] and first sonnet* be justly ascribed to Lord Southampton, or if any one of the passages adduced be fairly applicable to him, the whole of the 126 sonnets must necessarily apply to the same individual, for the poet has more than once affirmed this to have been his plan and object.

Why write I still *all one, ever the same*—

Son. 76 (Q)

*　　*　　*　　*　　*　　*

———— *all alike, my songs and praises be*
To *one*, of *one*, still such and ever so.

Son. 105 (Q)

If the reader on turning to Dr Drake can find any weightier arguments for the view that Shakespeare's Sonnets were mainly addressed to Lord Southampton, he will do more than I can; on the strength, then, of such flimsy stuff as he has alone adduced, we are to set aside the apparently clear statement of the preface that the Sonnets were engendered solely by a Mr W. H. and adopt the interpretation invented when he was in great straits by Mr Chalmers—an interpretation of which it may be said that it was begotten by forgery out of folly, to the breeding of issue wondrously like its parents.

It would not have been necesssary to dwell so long upon Dr Drake, if his theory were not still vigorous—being now, perhaps, more prominently before the public than any other concerning the Sonnets, and having been adopted in the "Dictionary of National Biography," as well as to a considerable extent in Mr Sidney Lee's "Life of William Shakespeare."

Dr Drake, however, deserves credit for having seen that Mr Chalmers was not out of the wood by merely tampering with the meaning of the word "begetter." Thorpe's preface appears to say not only that Mr W. H. was the sole cause of the Sonnets having been written, but also that Shakespeare had promised him an eternity of fame.

Now it is certain that Shakespeare promised the male

---

* No. 121 of this edition.

addressee of the Sonnets an eternity of fame. It might indeed have been better if in sonnet 101 (81, Q) he had said "your initials" (not "your name") "from hence immortal life shall have," but he may have thought he had indicated his friend's name sufficiently clearly in sonnet 20. This, however, is a detail, and *pace* Mr Lee I regard it as certain that all the first 126 sonnets and the greater number of the remaining 28 were so far influenced by the addressee—whoever he was—that but for him not one of them would ever have been written; if, then, Mr W. H. be taken as the addressee, or at any rate engenderer, of all or nearly all the sonnets, Thorpe's seeming statement is obviously true; for Shakespeare repeatedly promises his friend eternal fame. If, on the other hand, Mr W. H. is only the obtainer or procurer of the copy for Thorpe, and none of the sonnets were addressed to him— what becomes of "that eternity promised by our ever-living poet"? We know of no eternity promised to a Mr W. H. by Shakespeare. If such eternity were promised, never has promise of an ever-living poet failed more signally of fulfil- ment, and never was poet so certain not to fail if he had made such a promise.

But Dr Drake is not a man to be non-plussed easily. It seems that we have again misunderstood Thorpe's preface. Thorpe does not say "promised to him," i.e. "promised to Mr W. H." All he says is, "promised." The eternity was not promised to Mr W. H. but

to another, namely to one of the immediate subjects of his sonnets.

That this is the only rational meaning which can be annexed to the word "promised," will appear when we reflect that for Thorpe to have *wished* W. H. the eternity that had been promised *him* by an ever-living poet, would have been not only superfluous but downright nonsense; the *eternity* of an *ever-living poet* must *necessarily ensue*, and was a proper subject of congratulation, but not of wishing or of hope.*

I must leave those readers who feel convinced by the foregoing to think as they will, but for my own part shall

---

* "Shakespeare and His Times," II., p. 59.

still interpret Thorpe as meaning that Shakespeare had promised the eternity to Mr W. H. and in a very terse dedication omitted the word "him."

At the risk of wearying the reader beyond endurance, I will show how Dr Drake meets Tyrwhitt's very plausible conjecture that Mr W. H.'s surname was Hughes, or Hews as the name in Shakespeare's time was very commonly spelt. Dr Drake writes :—

Mr Tyrwhitt, founding his conjecture on a line in the twentieth sonnet, which is thus printed in the old copy,
"A man in *hew* all *Hews* in his controlling,"*
conceives that the letters W. H. were intended to imply *William Hughes*. If we recollect, however, our bard's uncontrollable passion for playing upon words ; that *hew* frequently meant in the language of the time, *mien* and *appearance*, as well as *tint*, and that Daniel who was probably his archetype in these pieces has spelt it in the same way, and once, if not oftener with a capital, see his "Queen's Arcadia," we shall not feel disposed to place much reliance on this supposition.

No one will dispute Shakespeare's love of playing on words ; it is precisely because we admit this that we suspect him of having played upon one in this instance. As for Daniel, whose first sonnets were published in 1592, it will be time enough to argue about him when we have settled whether he did not form his sonnets on Shakespeare's, the last of which I believe to have been written in 1588. But here for once I agree with Mr Chalmers, who in his "Supplemental Apology" declares that there is "between Daniel's sonnets and Shakespeare's no other analogy, than the same construction as Sonnets, and similar topics as amatory verses."†

---

* I have already pointed out that this is not how the line stands in Q.
† pp. 42, 43.

CHAPTER VI.

IT is possible, however, especially when we consider what vitality Dr Drake's theory has proved to have, that he may not have done full justice to it: let us turn, therefore, to its latest exponent Mr Sidney Lee, with whom I regret to find myself in disagreement.

Not only have I heard Mr Lee's recent "Life of William Shakespeare" highly spoken of by men to whose opinion I willingly defer, but like all who dabble in literature I am his daily debtor for the great work over which he has presided so ably for so many years. To whom do I owe the dates of the births and deaths of so many Shakespearean editors that I have given in this book, if not to the staff of writers in the "Dictionary of National Biography"? As bees, wasps, hornets, and all winged insects swarm in mid autumn round some full-flowering ivy-bush, and the air is resonant with the busy buzziness of their flight, even so do readers in the British Museum swarm towards that part of the shelves in which the "Dictionary of National Biography" resides.

A year or two ago I was allowed to take some foreign visitors into the gallery that over-looks the reading-room.

"And why," said one of them, looking towards case No. 2036, "is there a knot of people always forming and reforming at that particular point, though the shelves are nearly empty? And why do they all look so unhappy?"

"That, Madam," I answered, "is where the 'Dictionary of National Biography' would be found, if the volume one wants were not almost always in use, so universal is the demand for it. The people, therefore, have to go away disappointed."

If, then, I use great plainness in dealing with Mr Lee's theories concerning the Sonnets, I must beg both him and the reader to understand that I mean no discourtesy, and shall expect like plainness from himself, if he should think fit to take any notice of my remarks.

My greatest difficulty in dealing with him lies in the determining what his opinions really are. This, indeed, should be no hard matter, for he has had time enough to make up his mind. In the Preface to his recent " Life of William Shakespeare," he writes :—

After studying Elizabethan literature, history, and bibliography for more than eighteen years, I believed that I might, without exposing myself to a charge of presumption, attempt something in the way of filling up this gap, and that I might be able to supply, at least tentatively, a guide-book to Shakespeare's life and work that should be, within its limits, complete and trustworthy. p. vi.

Nothing can be better. We are reminded of the opening paragraph of " The Origin of Species," and feel at once that we are in the hands of one who is both able and willing to inform us; we turn eagerly, therefore, not only to Mr Lee's recent work, but to those earlier ones that have led up to it. The first of these with which I am acquainted was the article on William Herbert Earl of Pembroke, written for the " Dictionary of National Biography " in 1891. Mr Lee, after more than ten years study of Elizabethan literature, then wrote :—

Shakespeare's young friend was doubtless Pembroke himself, and " the dark lady " in all probability was Mary Fitton. Nothing in the sonnets directly contradicts the identification of W. H. their hero and " onlie begetter " with William Herbert, and many minute internal details directly confirm it. (cf. T. Tyler, Shakespeare's Sonnets, 1890, passim, and esp. pp. 44—73).

This is very confident, and proceeding to Mr Lee's article on Shakespeare written for the " Dictionary of National Biography " in 1897, I was surprised to read :—

Some phrases in the dedication to " Lucrece " so clearly resemble expressions that were used in the sonnets to the young friend as to identify the latter with Southampton.

*   *   *   *   *

Other theories of identification rest on wholly erroneous premises.

In a note, again, on p. 406 of Mr. Lee's "Life of W. Shakespeare," published in 1898, we read:—

The Pembroke theory, whose adherents have dwindled of late, will henceforth be relegated, I trust, to the category of popular delusions.

On p. ix. of the preface to the last named work he tells us that he has given in an appendix a review of the facts that seem to him,—

To confute the popular theory that Shakespeare was a friend and *protégé* of William Herbert, third Earl of Pembroke, who has been put forward quite unwarrantably as the hero of the sonnets.

This again is very confident. Granted that in six or seven years a man may modify or even reverse his opinion, but a reader-respecting writer will give prominence to the fact of his own recantation. A certain amount of penance is requisite before the absolution can be given which on moderate penance will very readily be granted. Mr Lee did nothing to warn us, or to explain so complete a change of front, and as a natural consequence he changed his front again in 1898, with the same lightness of heart and absence of apology or explanation. In 1897, after expressing some doubt as to whether we have the Sonnets in exactly the same order as that in which they were written, he wrote:—

But when all allowance is made for internal difficulties, the story the poems tell is, in its general outlines unmistakable. Sonnet 144 (published by Jaggard in 1599) supplies the key.

> Two loves I had of comfort and despair,
> Which like two spirits do suggest [i.e. tempt] me still;
> The better angel is a man right fair,
> The worser spirit a woman coloured ill.

This is very confident, but there is a good deal of difference between "had" and "have" and neither The Passionate Pilgrim nor Q support Mr Lee's reading. They both read "Two loves I have of comfort and despair," not "Two loves I had, &c."—but let this pass. Mr Lee continues:—

A young man and a young woman, both of whom are proved by a variety of touches to be of superior rank to his own, crossed the poet's path. To the former he became devotedly attached; the latter excited in him an overmastering passion. . . . The sonnets divide themselves into two groups corresponding with this two-fold influence. In the first group (1—126) Shakespeare addresses the young man, and traces the fluctuations of an affection which was three years old (104, Q).

*   *   *   *   *

The second group (126—152) narrates the course of the poet's maddening passion for a disdainful and accomplished siren.

Here it is plain Mr Lee holds that the first 126 sonnets of Q were all of them addressed to the same person, who, he tells us later, may be identified as Southampton. In the " Life of W. Shakespeare" written in the following year, we read :

It is usual to divide the sonnets into two groups and to represent that all those numbered i.—cxxvi. by Thorpe, were addressed to a young man, and all those numbered cxxvii.—cliv. were addressed to a woman. This division cannot be literally justified. In the first group some eighty of the sonnets can be proved to be addressed to a man by the use of the masculine pronoun, or some other unequivocal sign ; but among the remaining forty there is no clear indication of the kind. . . . . . And there is no valid objection to the assumption that the poet inscribed the rest of these forty sonnets to a woman (cf. xxi., xlvi., xlvii.). Similarly the sonnets in the second group (cxxvii.—cliv.) have no uniform written super-scription.*

Confidence is the one point in which Mr Lee appears to be consistent. Here we have nearly a third part of those sonnets that had been declared to have been addressed to Lord Southampton taken away from him in one breath. Many, indeed, are still left him, for Mr Lee says :—

I am at one with Mr Massey in identifying the young man to whom many of the sonnets are addressed with the Earl of Southampton. (Note on p. 91).

When, however, we try to discover even approximately how many, and which, these sonnets may be, we are baffled ; but

---

* " Life of W. Shakespeare," p. 97.

as far as we can collect anything at all there cannot be very many, for in Mr Lee's preface we read:—

My conclusion is adverse to the claim of the sonnets to rank as autobiographical documents (p. vii.),

And on the following page he says that in his study of the European sonnet-literature of Shakespeare's time, he has

gone far enough, I think, to justify the conviction that Shakespeare's collection of sonnets has no reasonable title to be regarded as a personal or autobiographical narrative.

So again on p. 109 we learn that "the autobiographic element in his sonnets, although it may not be dismissed altogether, is seen to shrink to very slender proportions."

I will say no more about confidence. If by "auto-biographical" Mr Lee means the intentional and deliberate record of one's own history for the delectation of other people, which we commonly associate with the word "autobiography," all readers will agree with him in holding that Shakespeare's Sonnets are not autobiographical. No one supposes that Shakespeare had any idea of writing his own life. If, on the other hand, Mr Lee means that the Sonnets were not dictated by actual facts and feelings—that they did not grow out of actual occurrences—I prefer the view which he took after only more than seventeen years' study of Elizabethan litera-ture, to the radically different one which a single additional year has, as I will almost immediately show, revealed to him.

The Sonnets are a series of unguarded letters in verse, written as the spirit moved a young poet who had just discovered his own gift, and was glorying in the pride of flight without much either forecast or retrospection. Such letters inevitably record varying phases of the writer's mind, and must occasionally afford a clue to incidents in his life; to this extent, therefore, they are autobiographical, as an invitation to dinner is in some sense autobiographical, as recording the fact that the writer had got a dinner, but this is not the sense in which the word is commonly used. In 1897 Mr Lee recognised this quite correctly, and without contending that the Sonnets were strictly autobiographical, he admitted that they bear to Shakespeare's biography

a relation wholly different from that borne by the rest of his literary work. Attempts have been made to represent them as purely literary exercises, mainly on the ground that a personal interpretation seriously reflects on Shakespeare's moral character (cf. Halliwell-Phillips). But only the two concluding sonnets cliii., cliv.) can be regarded by the unbiassed reader as the artificial product of a poet's fancy. . . . In the rest of the "Sonnets" Shakespeare avows, although in language that is often cryptic, the experiences of his own heart (cf. C. Armitage Brown, "Shakespeare's autobiographical poems," 1838). Their uncontrolled ardour suggests that they came from a youthful pen—from a man not more than thirty.

See how all this changed in 1898; on page 100 of his " Life of Shakespeare," Mr Lee writes :—

In whatever order Shakespeare's sonnets be studied, the claim advanced on their behalf, to rank as autobiographical documents can only be accepted with many qualifications. Elizabethan sonnets were commonly the artificial products of the poet's fancy. (p. 100.)

From which the only reasonable inference is that Mr Lee so regards Shakespeare's Sonnets—with a few exceptions. Again :—

. . . . a vast number of Shakespeare's performances prove to be little more than professional trials of skill, often of superlative merit, to which he deemed himself challenged by the efforts of contemporary practitioners (p. 109),

i.e. " a vast number" of Shakespeare's not very vast number of 154 sonnets are merely academic, and have no heart in them. Again :—

It is likely enough that beneath all the conventional adulation bestowed on Southampton there lay a genuine affection, but his sonnets to the Earl were no involuntary ebullitions of a devoted and disinterested friendship; they were celebrations of a patron's favour in the terminology—often raised by Shakespeare's genius to the loftiest heights of poetry—that was invariably consecrated to such a purpose by a current literary convention. Very few of

Shakespeare's "sugared sonnets" have a substantial right to be regarded as untutored cries of the soul.   p. 151.

Earlier in the same page Mr Lee says :—

The imitative element in his sonnets is large enough to refute the assertion that in them as a whole, he sought to "unlock his heart."

There is, however, according to Mr Lee, "one group, composed of six sonnets scattered throughout the collection," which really do reflect "a love adventure of no normal type." This scattered group he declares to consist of 52 (144, Q), 57, 58, 59 (40, 41, 42, Q), and 60, 61 (133, 134, Q). These six are allowed to remain in 1898, as telling the story which in 1897 was declared to have been unmistakeably told by the whole series. The story (according to Mr Lee) is this :—that a young nobleman to whom Shakespeare is under great obligations has been seduced by, or has seduced, Shakespeare's mistress. Mr Lee does not take a high view of Shakespeare's attitude in this transaction, he writes : —

The sonnetteer's complacent condonation of the young man's offence chiefly suggests the deference that was essential to the maintenance by a dependent of peaceful relations with a self-willed and self-indulgent patron. Southampton's sportive and lascivious temperament might easily impel him to divert to himself the attention of an attractive woman by whom he saw that his poet was fascinated, and he was unlikely to tolerate any outspoken protest on the part of his protégé. (pp. 154, 155).

And again :—

The sole biographical inference deducible from the sonnets is, that at one time in his career Shakespeare disdained no weapon of flattery in an endeavour to monopolise the bountiful patronage of a young man of rank (p. 159).

This amounts to saying that at the no longer immature age of thirty, by which time, indeed, a man's character is well set, Shakespeare would eat any amount of dirt with apparent *gusto*, if mercenary considerations counselled his doing so.

I am confident, however, that Mr Lee does not mean what

he has written; he has been writing in haste; he has been fatigued with having too many irons in the fire; he has been ill; for the moment he has lost count of his words, and of the horrible revulsion of feeling which they must produce in all those to whom the essential nobleness of Shakespeare's character is a well-grounded article of faith.

There is no remorse in the tone with which Mr Lee has written; no appearance as though he had been driven into accepting a theory which has been inexpressibly painful to him. He has adopted a conjecture which, as I have already shown, rests on no foundation but the flimsy stuff which was all that Dr Drake could find in its support. In my next chapter I will show that he adduces no additional arguments which deserve a moment's consideration; nevertheless, like Dr Drake and Mr Chalmers, he settles everything off-hand in his own favour, and then bases upon ground so laid one of the most sordid accusations which it is possible to conceive—and that, too, against the man whose fair fame is no less dear to all right-minded people than is the splendour of that legacy which he has bequeathed us.

Again I repeat my conviction that Mr Lee does not realise the import of his own words.

Roughly, then, to bring this to me most painful chapter to a conclusion, there are three principal views concerning the Sonnets now before the public—The Southampton, the Pembroke, and the Impersonal. Mr Lee began with the Pembroke; he went on to the Southampton, and it is plain that in spite of all he now urges in support of Lord Southampton's claim to be in some way connected with the Sonnets, he has veered round to the Impersonal view, though terribly hampered by his article in the "Dictionary of National Biography." By the time that work reaches Wriothesley I venture to predict that he will have thrown over both Lord Southampton and the Impersonal theory as completely as he has thrown over Lord Pembroke. For his own sake I heartily hope that my prediction may be verified.

CHAPTER VII.

IN the preceding chapter I have shown that no matter
how long Mr Lee may have been learning, he has not come
to any permanent knowledge either of truth or error. His
acquaintance with the thousands of sonnets that teemed from
the French, Spanish, and Italian presses—not to mention the
English—is no doubt both accurate and profound, but I
venture to think that if his judgement had not been impaired
by long companionship with so much that was insincere, he
would have recognised sincerity better when he fell in with it.
I am told that when a new assistant comes to the British
Museum coin-room with his art yet to learn, he is not allowed
to see any of the spurious coins in the collection for several
years, lest they should vitiate his eye. So with the critical
faculty in literature, nothing wrecks it so hopelessly as the
tolerating anything that is written for display. It is impossible
that any man should read Shakespeare in singleness of heart
when he has been living for so many years in an atmosphere
so reeking with affectation as that of the sixteenth century
sonnetteers.

That Mr Lee has read the Sonnets amiss will hardly be
contested. See, for example, how he declares sonnet 143
(119, Q) to be addressed to " benefit of ill ";* is, then, sonnet
115 (95, Q) addressed to " what a mansion," or 129 (109, Q) to
" never say "? A couple of pages further on he says that
in sonnets 131, 132 (111, 112, Q) Shakespeare speaks of
himself as " weary of the profession of acting," that in 91—94
(71—74, Q) he " foretells his approaching death," that sonnets
23, 37, 120, 121, 123, 124 (23, 37, 100, 101, 103, 104, Q) abound

---

* "Life of William Shakespeare," p. 97.

with "obsequious addresses to the youth in his capacity of sole patron of the poet's verse."

See, again, how he says on p. 139 that Shakespeare "assured his friend that he could never grow old." Shakespeare's words are:—

To me, fair friend, you never can be old.*

Is it conceivable that Mr Lee should seriously believe this to be telling a man that he can never grow old?

Impatient, however, as we may well be of such obvious misrepresentation, we must still see whether Mr Lee may not have succeeded in strengthening Dr Drake's position, notwithstanding his very evident desire to retreat from it. What, then, are the grounds on which he asks us to believe that many, at any rate, of the Sonnets are addressed to Lord Southampton?

These will be found on pp. 125—150 of Mr Lee's book. He tells us that twenty sonnets are addressed to one who is declared "without periphrasis and without disguise to be a patron of the poet's verse."† These sonnets are 23, 26, 32, 37, 38, 89 (69, Q), 97—106 (77—86, Q), 120, 121, 123, 124 (100, 101, 103, 104, Q). I have not been able to discover a single passage, neither in the sonnets to which Mr Lee has referred nor in any of the others, which even suggests that, at the time when he was writing the Sonnets, Shakespeare had any patron at all, while in more than one sonnet he intimates that he is poor, friendless, and in disgrace alike with Fortune and men's eyes. Mr Lee, however, quotes one passage from the above-named sonnets in support of his assertion, and it may be assumed that he has selected the strongest in his own favour. Here are the lines; they are from sonnet 98 (78, Q):

So oft have I invoked thee for my Muse
And found such fair assistance in my verse,
As every alien pen hath got my use
And under thee their poesy disperse.

---

* Son. 124 (104, Q).　　　† p. 125.

This is "without periphrasis and without disguise" declaring that the addressee had often been the theme of Shakespeare's verse, and that this theme was so congenial to him as to make him write upon it both well and easily; but if Shakespeare meant to say that the addressee was his patron, in the sense which the word then generally conveyed, the "periphrasis and disguise" have been impenetrably complete.

True, there is the word "assistance." Beggars often say, "Would you be kind enough to assist me with a trifle?" "Assist" is to the necessitous person a euphemism akin to "remove" in the mouth of a dentist, or "punish" in that of a schoolmaster—it means that the man wants money. Shakespeare says that his verse has received "assistance" from the addressee. What can be plainer? Words are written for the use of the reader as well as of the writer; is the writer to have everything his own way? If the writer may write to his liking, may not the reader read to his liking also? Shakespeare's verse, then, has received a "fair" round sum of money from the addressee; therefore the addressee was a patron of Shakespeare's verse; Shakespeare dedicated Venus and Adonis without permission, and Lucrece with permission, to Lord Southampton; we do not know of his having dedicated anything to any other patron; Lord Southampton, therefore, must have been the patron referred to in the lines last quoted. Let me give Mr Lee's own words; he writes:—

The problem presented by the patron is simple. Shakespeare states unequivocally that he has no patron but one.

> Sing [sc. O Muse!] to the ear that doth thy lays esteem,
> And gives thy pen both skill and argument.
>
> 120 (100, Q).
>
> For to no other pass my verses tend
> Than of thy graces and thy gifts to tell.
>
> 123 (103, Q).

The Earl of Southampton, the patron of his narrative poems, is the only patron of Shakespeare that is known to biographical research. No contemporary document or tradition gives the faintest suggestion that Shakespeare was the friend or dependent of any other man of rank. (p. 126.)

Very likely not, but on reading the Sonnets from which Mr
Lee has quoted I cannot find the faintest suggestion that
Shakespeare was in any way the "dependent" of the person
whom he was addressing, if the word "dependent" is taken in
its usual sense. He declares himself to be his friend's vassal,
but what man who is as devotedly attached to another as
Shakespeare evidently was to the worthless fellow whom he
was addressing, does not hold himself the vassal of that friend,
without for a moment considering himself as his dependent?
Indeed I have known cases in which a friend has for years held
himself the vassal of another whom he believed to be
absolutely dependent upon him.

But to return to Mr Lee. That the youth whom Shakespeare was addressing was Shakespeare's theme, goes without
saying; that he was his patron does not appear from any
passage referred to or quoted by Mr Lee. Mr Lee then repeats
in substance Dr Drake's contention that sonnet 26 is but a
poetical rendering of the dedication of Lucrece to Lord
Southampton. In Chapter V I have said what I think of
this contention, and I shall endeavour presently to show that
the sonnet was writtten when Lord Southampton was only
twelve years old, and cannot conceivably be the person to
whom it was addressed.

Every compliment, says Mr Lee,

paid by Shakespeare to the youth, whether it be vaguely or
definitely phrased, applies to Southampton without the least
straining of the words. In real life, beauty, birth, wealth, and
wit, sat "crowned" in the Earl whom poets acclaimed the
handsomest of Elizabethan courtiers, as plainly as in the poet's
verse (pp. 141, 142).

We are not only never told that his friend was richer or
better born than Shakespeare himself, but the general tone of
the Sonnets negatives any such supposition. True we read in
sonnet 37,

> For whether beauty, birth, or wealth, or wit,
> Or any of these all, or all, or more
> Intitled in thy parts do crowned sit,

But there is as much virtue in a "whether" as in an "if."
Shakespeare does not say "you have beauty, birth, wealth,
and wit." He says, "if you have any single one of these four,
or if you even have them all, and others that I have not
named—whatever you may have, I shall graft my love there-
on." Granted that Shakespeare would not name beauty if
his friend was remarkably plain; birth, if he was notoriously
base-born; wealth, if he was necessitous; or wit, if he was
next door to a fool; but if he was good-looking, of the
same social status as Shakespeare himself, not living from
hand to mouth, and not a fool (which by the way I
think he probably was) Shakespeare would be well within
his rights in writing the lines last quoted, nor can I find
clearer proof that nothing in the Sonnets suggests that their
addressee was in a higher social position than Shakespeare's,
than the fact that these lines are the strongest which those
who would have him to have been a great nobleman are able
to bring forward. Mr Lee continues:—

The opening sequence of seventeen sonnets, in which a youth of
rank and wealth is admonished to marry and beget a son so that
his "fair house" may not fall into decay, can only have been
addressed to a young peer like Southampton, who was as yet
unmarried, had vast possessions, and was the sole male representative of his family.

It is indeed true that the word "house" is often used as
meaning not the house itself, but the generations of those who
have lived in it, i.e. a lineage. It is also used metaphorically
for the body, which is held to be the tenement within which the
spirit, or more essential part of a man, resides; so Christians
are held to be temples of the Holy Ghost. It is the context
that can alone decide us as to the meaning a writer may have
chosen to put upon it in any given place.
In Sonnet 10, Shakespeare wrote:—

> For thou art so possessed with murderous hate
> That 'gainst thyself thou stick'st not to conspire,
> Seeking that beauteous roof to ruinate
> Which to repair should be thy chief desire.

The "beauteous roof" here is not his friend's family, nor yet his family mansion. Shakespeare does not mean to say that the roof of his friend's house is very much out of repair, and that unless he has new slates put on to it at once it will become a ruin. The "beauteous roof" is the flesh and blood roof of that particular tenement within which his friend's mind was housed. With this metaphor still fresh in his remembrance, he wrote in sonnet 13 :—

> Who lets so fair a house fall to decay
> Which husbandry in honour might uphold,
> Against the stormy gusts of winter's day
> And barren rage of death's eternal cold
> > O, none but unthrifts ; dear my love you know
> > You had a father ; let your son say so.

Mr Lee says :—

The sonnetteer's exclamation, "you had a father, let your son say so," had pertinence to Southampton at any period between his father's death in his boyhood, and the close of his bachelorhood in 1598. To no other peer of the day are they exactly applicable.

Southampton's father died when Southampton was only eight years old, it is not easy, therefore, to see what pertinence they could have to Southampton for another eight years or so, but let that pass ; when, however, Mr Lee says that Shakespeare's words are exactly applicable to no other peer than to Lord Southampton, he presumes too far on the indolence of his readers. The words are applicable to any male, peer, or not peer, in whom Shakespeare may have taken sufficient interest to wish that he might have children. The only thing required to make them applicable is that the young man, whoever he was, should have been born in the ordinary course of generation.

It is surprising enough that Mr Lee should have ventured on the passage last quoted, but the following is more surprising still. We are now coming to Mr Lee's strongest point, the only one of any even seeming importance that he has added to those of Dr Drake. He writes :—

But the most striking evidence of the identity of the youth of the sonnets of "friendship" with Southampton is found in the likeness of feature and complexion which characterises the poet's description of the youth's outward appearance and the extant pictures of Southampton as a young man (pp. 143, 144).

*   *   *   *   *

The eyes are blue, the cheeks pink, the complexion clear, and the expression sedate; rings are in the ears; beard and moustache are at an incipient stage, and are of the same bright auburn hue as the hair in a picture of Southampton's mother that is also at Welbeck. But, however, scanty is the down on the youth's cheek, the hair on his head is luxuriant. It is worn very long, and falls over and below the shoulder. The colour is now of walnut, but was originally of lighter tint (pp. 145, 146).

*   *   *   *   *

Many times does he tells us that the youth is fair in complexion, and that his eyes are fair. In Sonnet lxviii., when he points to the youth's face as a map of what beauty was " without all ornament itself and true "—before fashion sanctioned the use of artificial " golden tresses," there can be little doubt that he had in mind the wealth of locks that fell about Southampton's neck (p. 146).

Looking at the illustration with which Mr Lee has furnished us, I can see no indication of any natural springing of the hair from the head. I should be as ready to believe that the hair was a wig as that it was natural. I do not suppose there lives the man who can say with even tolerable confidence whether the hair is true or false, and it is just as competent to me to maintain (though heaven forbid that I should do so) that it is but an example of that custom against which Shakespeare had inveighed some eight years earlier in sonnet 88 (68, Q) as it is to Mr Lee to say that "there can be little doubt" about Shakespeare's having alluded to the hair displayed in the portrait given of Lord Southampton. All one can say for certain is that whereas the moustache indicates the spring of hair from flesh in a way which forbids our supposing the moustache false, the hair on the scalp gives no such indication.

"The eyes," says Mr Lee, "are blue." Very likely; but there is nothing in the Sonnets to show that the youth's eyes were also blue—therefore, of course, the addressee must be Lord Southampton. Mr Lee, indeed, says that Shakespeare tells us many times . . . "that the youth is fair in complexion and that his eyes are fair" p. 146.

Let us see how Shakespeare uses the word "fair" in the first twenty-five sonnets—not to fatigue the reader by going through the whole number.

Son. 1. From fairest creatures, &c.

"Fair" here means "beautiful," not "of light complexion," to the exclusion of dark complexion.

Son. 2. This fair child of mine.

Here again "fair" means "beautiful" not "light."

Son. 3. For who is she so fair.

Son. 5. And that unfair, which fairly, &c.

Son. 6. Thou art much too fair to be death's conquest.

Shakespeare does not mean "thou art much too light complexioned," &c.

Son. 10. Shall hate be fairer lodged than gentle love"?

Son. 13. Who lets so fair a house fall to decay?

Son. 18. And every fair from fair sometimes declines,

*   *   *

Nor lose possession of that fair thou owest.

This I presume is one of the many passages in which Shakespeare, according to Mr Lee, declares the youth to have been fair in complexion.

Son. 19. O carve not with thy hours my love's fair brow.

Again no doubt Mr Lee supposes Shakespeare to mean that the youth's forehead was light in complexion.

Son. 21. Who every fair with his fair doth rehearse,

*   *   *

Oh then believe me my love is as fair,

There are no other examples of the word "fair" in the first twenty-five sonnets, nor have I been able to detect the word as used otherwise in any of the remaining sonnets.* The

---

* It occurs (to use the numbers of my own edition only) in sonnets 40, 43, 45, 52, 53, 59, 62, 66, 74, 89, 90, 98, 102, 103, 107, 112, 115, 124, 125, 126, 140, 141, 144.

passage from which Mr Lee gathers that the youth's eyes must have been blue—for this is what his contention comes to—is from sonnet 103 (83, Q) :—

> There lives more life in one of your fair eyes
> Than both your poets can in praise devise.

I can find no passage in the Sonnets that enables us to determine a single feature in the youth's personal appearance, neither will any one else, and yet Mr Lee declares his identification by means of the extant portraits of Southampton as a young man to be "the most striking evidence" that the youth and Southampton were one and the same person. One would think that identification of the Box and Cox order could go no further, were it not for the passage above quoted about the colour of Lord Southampton's hair and that of his mother. Mr Lee there said that the colour of Southampton's hair, as shown in the portrait which he has reproduced, is of "the same bright auburn hue as the hair in a picture of Southampton's mother which is also at Welbeck." He here refers to sonnet 3, in which Shakespeare says that the youth is his mother's glass, and she, in him, calls back the lovely April of her prime; from this we may feel quite certain that mother and son must have had hair of the same shade of colour— which seems according to Mr Lee to be in both cases bright auburn, though in one of them it is not bright auburn, for Mr Lee goes on to say that the colour of the hair in Southampton's portrait is walnut, but that it is darker now than when the picture was painted. One would like to know how Mr Lee has ascertained this. Judging from the illustration given by Mr Lee (the negative for which we may be sure was taken with a lens that had been duly isochromatized) when he says that the hair is "walnut" in colour, he must mean "pickled walnut"—for a pickled walnut really is as black as the hair in the illustration; but how pickled walnut can be called "bright auburn" is one of those puzzles the frequent recurrence of which detracts so seriously from the value of Mr Lee's in many respects most interesting and useful work.

Here I take my leave of Mr Lee's arguments in support of

the view that many of the Sonnets are addressed to Lord Southampton. He has left the nothingness of Dr Drake as nothing as he found it.

So also has Mr Gerald Massey in his "The Secret Drama of Shakespeare's Sonnets unfolded" published in 1872. He refers to Mr Chalmers's attempt to show that the Sonnets were addressed to Queen Elizabeth and says,

It may be mentioned by way of explanation that this preposterous suggestion was hazarded in support of a desperate case—the Ireland forgeries (p. 8).

Readers of my Chapter IV will see how incorrect this statement is. Mr Chalmers admitted in both his books that young Ireland's documents were forged. Mr Massey makes no attempt to justify the attaching an unusual meaning to the word "begetter." All he says on this head is

Drake contended that as a number of the Sonnets were most certainly addressed to a female, it must be evident that "W. H." could not be the only "begetter" of them in the sense which is primarily suggested. He therefore agrees with Chalmers and Boswell that Mr W. H. was the *obtainer* of the Sonnets for Thorpe, and he remarks that the dedication was read in that light by some of the earlier editors.

I have dealt with this last contention earlier, and must decline to follow Mr Massey or any other of the Southamptonites further, being convinced that in dealing with the earliest and latest of them I have shown the reader the strongest points of their argument. Mr Lee may be quite trusted not to have ignored any tolerably effective argument that had been urged by any of his predecessors.

CHAPTER VIII.

THE IMPERSONAL, AND THE WILLIAM HERBERT THEORIES—ON THE SOCIAL STATUS OF MR W. H.

THE reader will observe that the greater part of the three preceding chapters has been occupied in showing that no such case has been made out in support of the opinion that Lord Southampton was the friend addressed in the Sonnets as will justify the attempt to take the words "only begetter" in an unusual sense.

There is, however, another theory concerning the Sonnets which is also based on the supposition that "only begetter" means "only procurer," or "obtainer"; it is to the effect that the Sonnets are merely creations of Shakespeare's fancy, having no reference to actual persons or occurrences. This theory made its first appearance in 1821, in Boswell's edition of Malone's Shakespeare, published nine years after Malone's death; it has since been adopted unreservedly by Staunton, reservedly by Dyce, and in great measure, as we have seen, by Mr Sidney Lee—not to mention others whose names will carry less weight. It is rejected, however, by all the Herbertites, by all thorough-going Southamptonites, by all those who put the only reasonable interpretation on the words of Thorpe's preface, and, I think I may add, by far the greater number of those most competent to form an opinion on the subject.

If such a case had been made out for it as should compel us to set Thorpe's preface aside, we might have had to submit, as we might have had to do if an overwhelming case had been made out in favour of Lord Southampton; but there has been no attempt at making out a case, and if ground for doing so had existed it would have been as easy to state it as regards the other sonnets as it would be, if it were worth while, in regard to five of those that I have excluded from my series. These are obviously impersonal, but no one has attempted to show that any of the others suggest their not having been written to, or for, a real person. The opinion, when advanced, has always been put forward *ex cathedrâ*, as by Boswell, whose gross disingenuousness we have seen, by Staunton, Mr Lee (in so far as he adopts it), and Dyce, which last writer, however, only goes so far as to say that he is " well-nigh convinced " of its truth, and we know what " well-nigh " means.

I credit the upholders of this theory with adopting it mainly because they hope by doing so to free Shakespeare from an odious imputation ; they fail, however, to see what will appear more plainly later on, I mean, that the imputation under which they would thus leave him is far worse than any for which there is a shadow of evidence. To me it is as unthinkable, and as repulsive, as I believe the reader will also find it when he sets himself to consider what it involves ; I therefore dismiss it with no greater display of argument than that adduced by its upholders.

Neither do I propose to spend much time in arguing against the view that the Mr W. H. of Thorpe's preface was William Herbert Earl of Pembroke. This opinion, first put forward in private conversation and letters by Mr Heywood Bright about the year 1819, and advanced publicly some years later by Mr Boaden, was warmly espoused by Hallam, and by several other writers who command respect, but it was refuted, one would have thought sufficiently, by Dyce, in the " Life of Shakespeare " which precedes his edition of Shakespeare's works published in 1864,* and more recently by Mr Sidney Lee in the *Fortnightly Review* for February 1898. Both Dyce and Mr Lee point out how impossible it is to suppose that Thorpe would have ventured to address the Earl of Pembroke as " Mr." Their arguments appear as conclusive against Lord Pembroke's claim to be in any way connected with the Sonnets, as those of Mr Archer

---

* pp 97, 98.

in the preceding number but one of the *Fortnightly* had done against the claims of Lord Southampton; but I will not repeat them here, for I propose to show that there is nothing in the Sonnets which indicates that the friend to whom they were mainly addressed was titled, or even rich, and in a later chapter shall endeavour to establish, that when the last of the Sonnets was written Lord Pembroke was under nine years old, which is an impossible age for the addressee of Shakespeare's Sonnets.

As regards the social status of the youth whom Shakespeare is addressing, almost all who have written about the Sonnets in this century assume that he was a man of exalted rank and great wealth. I have dealt in the preceding chapter with the passage on which they mainly rely for this opinion, but there is another which is also brought forward, I mean the opening line of sonnet 147 (124, Q) : —

If my dear love were but the child of state.

Surely, however, as Mr Archer pointed out in his article in the *Fortnightly* for December 1897, the line that follows,

It might for Fortune's bastard be unfathered,

shows by the word "it" that the "dear love" of the preceding line refers not to the person to whom the sonnet was addressed but to Shakespeare's affection for that person. The lines should be construed, "If my love for you depended only on outward circumstances, it might prove to be no lawfully begotten offspring, but a mere base-born child, subject to the vicissitudes of Fortune"; this line, therefore, fails as completely as the one in sonnet 37 to afford any presumption that Mr W. H. was highly born. No other passages than these two singularly inconclusive ones have ever been, or are ever likely to be, brought forward—for we cannot take seriously Mr Lee's contention that "so fair a house" in sonnet 13 refers to the line of the addressee's ancestry; it would be as easy to believe that Shakespeare referred to an actual roof and an actual house.

Is it conceivable that in the first seventeen sonnets, when

the poet is urging his friend to marry, there should be no plain
indication that he had other and weightier reasons for marrying
than his mere good looks? Is it possible, again, that Shakespeare should apparently regard his own verse as the only
thing that was likely to rescue his friend from oblivion, if that
friend was one before whom a great career presumably lay
open? If the friend is to be remembered after death, it will,
according to the Sonnets, be Shakespeare's doing, not his own ;
but great noblemen are not apt to remain long on intimate
terms with an inferior in rank who harps on such a theme
whether with reason or without it. It is not unnoteworthy
that Shakespeare should have been so elated with his own
compositions as to assert their immortality so repeatedly, even
when addressing one who was socially his equal ; the explanation of this is probably to be found in the newness of his
discovery that he was a poet—a discovery over which he
was as exultant as a father over his first born son ; but if
Shakespeare was addressing a man of exalted rank, and if
he was also the cringing parasite which Mr Lee requires us
to suppose him, would he not rather have congratulated his
own muse at being rescued from oblivion by her connection
with one who was so assured of fame? Even without accepting
Mr Lee's estimate of Shakespeare's conduct, we may admit
that the writer of the dedications to Venus and Adonis
and Lucrece shows himself courtier enough, in the best
sense of the word, to know what he had better say or leave
unsaid when addressing one who was socially far above him.
Great men do, indeed, detest having their wealth and dignity
perpetually paraded, but neither on the other hand do they
quite like seeing it perpetually ignored.

Might we not expect, for example, that sonnet 25 should
have begun,

> Let you who are in favour with your stars
> Of public honour and proud titles boast,

instead of as we find it,

> Let those who are in favour with their stars, &c.

Shakespeare in this same sonnet congratulates himself on

loving and being loved where he may not "remove nor be removed," whereas had he been a great prince's favourite he would have been subject to all the caprices of the great ; but in those days a great nobleman, such as Southampton or Pembroke, was all that was intended by Shakespeare when he speaks of a " great prince." The whole tenor of the sonnet implies that both the writer and his friend lived in a sphere which was far removed from the incidents of rank and greatness.

True, as Dr Drake long since pointed out, in the following sonnet Shakespeare addresses his friend as " Lord of my love "; but it is only Dr Drakes who will insist that this really means " Earl of my love."   When Shakespeare (sonnet 77, 57 Q, line 5) calls his friend his " sovereign," it is only Mr Chalmerses who will hold that the friend was actually on the throne ; I wonder, by the way, that no modern Mr Chalmers has argued on the strength of this line, that the Sonnets were addressed to James the First. So again in sonnet 78 (58, Q) Shakespeare says that he is his friend's " vassal," and " bound to stay his leisure," but sober readers do not take these words literally.

Look again at sonnet 29, which follows very closely after the one just referred to ; if Shakespeare was the familiar friend of a great and wealthy nobleman, it is not to be believed that he would write of himself as " in disgrace with fortune and men's eyes," and as wishing himself like one more rich in hope and less unfriended. What is it that consoles him? His friend's love, but nothing, apparently, except this love. Those who can detect in this sonnet any sign as though patronage or material advantage arising out of his friend's love was present to Shakespeare's mind when he wrote, must have a penetration so far beyond my own that I must leave them to their own opinion ; I can see nothing in the poem but the cry of one who was very poor, and very hopeless, but who was sustained by the confidence that he possessed the love of a friend, who by the mere fact of loving him could comfort him beyond all material comfort.

Look, again, at sonnet 58 (41, Q),

> Those petty wrongs that liberty commits
> When I am sometime absent from thy heart
> Thy beauty and thy years full well permits—

It is the friend's youth and beauty that excuse him; but surely if he had been a great and wealthy nobleman some excuse for him might have been found on the score of his rank and public duties, if not on that of the great social demands upon his time.

Is it conceivable that in sonnet 78 (58, Q) Shakespeare should tell a powerful nobleman that he could not even think of controlling his liberty or requiring him to give an account of his time? Later on he tells this supposed great peer that his hold over him is so great that he may go where he likes and arrange his hours according to his own liking; "I am to wait," he exclaims, "though waiting so be hell, nor blame your pleasure be it ill or well." Shakespeare is evidently very angry; likely enough the friend had been promising to come "if he could," knowing very well all the time that he meant to go elsewhere; and Shakespeare had been waiting hour after hour for his coming. I do not doubt that he was quite justified in being angry, but I find it inconceivable that he should have written as in this and the preceding sonnet to any one who was in a social position much higher than his own. Still more, by the way, inconceivable do I find it that such sonnets as the two just dealt with should have been written as mere literary exercises.

Can we imagine the wise world looking into Lord Southampton's or Lord Pembroke's moan for the death of Shakespeare, and mocking them with him when he was gone? The wise world would take for granted that whatever either of these two personages chose to do was right, but the personages themselves would care very little about what the wise world might or might not say.

Can we fancy Shakespeare telling a great nobleman that though he had been dropping him for some time past in favour of new acquaintances with whom he had become rapidly intimate, yet he was determined not to do so any more, inasmuch as his recent experiences had all been in favour of the great nobleman?

Lastly, to take the sonnet with which the series evidently ended.—How does it conclude?

> No, let me be obsequious in thy heart
> And take thou my oblation, poor but free,
> Which is not mix'd with seconds, knows no art,
> But mutual renders, only me for thee.
>   Hence thou suborned *Informer !* a true soul
>   When most impeached stands least in thy control.

It is impossible to follow the train of thought that was passing in Shakespeare's mind, and which enabled him to offer his friendship frankly if his friend would take it on equal terms, and in the following couplet to call that friend a "suborn'd informer" and to defy him—but it is even more difficult to understand how either the offering or the defiance could be addressed to a man of greatly higher rank than that of the writer.

I have by no means dealt with all the passages which negative the supposition that Mr W. H. was a young man of rank and wealth—but in the first place those who make this assumption have advanced nothing to which I have not already called attention, and in the next, Thorpe's dedication to a plain Mr W. H. ought to be enough to convince all who hold him to have been the engenderer of the Sonnets that whatever else he was, he was not a man of rank. All the other statements in Thorpe's title-page and prefatory inscription are correct. The Sonnets are certainly by Shakespeare; they had never (with two exceptions) been published before; they appear to have been addressed to a young man whose Christian name was certainly William, and whose surname seems to have been Hughes; Shakespeare, as the preface implies, had promised this person an eternity of fame; the names and addresses of the printer and publisher will not be doubted— these are all the statements that can be extracted from the preface and title-page, except the fact that W. H. is styled

Mr.   Why, then, when we find all the rest of Thorpe's statements on title-page and preface to be correct, should we admit of doubt that this last fact also is truly stated?   More especially when it appears to be borne out by the whole tenor of the Sonnets themselves?

This being so we may dismiss the idea that Mr W. H. was William Herbert Earl of Pembroke, as confidently as we have already dismissed the supposition that he was merely the person who procured the Sonnets for Thorpe.   Lord Southampton's claims being also disposed of, and the impersonal theory being ordered out of court, we are left without any theory as to who Mr W. H. may have been, except the very plausible conjecture of Tyrwhitt, endorsed by Malone, that he was a person named William Hughes, or Hewes, or Hews, as the name was very commonly spelt at the close of the sixteenth century.

CHAPTER IX.

ON THE ORDER IN WHICH THE SONNETS WERE WRITTEN, AND ON THE STORY WHICH THEY REVEAL.

A CASUAL reader of the Sonnets as numbered in Q and in almost all modern editions, will be apt to conclude as Malone did, that the first 126 were addressed to a man and the last 28 to a woman; and unless he concentrates his attention on the whole series for a considerable time, he is likely enough to remain, as Malone appears to have done, in this opinion. He will, in fact, divide the Sonnets into two main groups, of (to use the Q numbering) 1—126 and 127—154.

I believe I have shown in Chapter III that only nine sonnets of the second group can be correctly held to have been addressed by Shakespeare to a woman. I believe, moreover, that most readers will agree with me in thinking that 126 Q should be considered not as the last of the first group, but as the first of the second. Let alone its change of form—which seems to forbid its having been an *envoi* to a series of 125 sonnets all of them in another form—it comes after 125 as a May morning after a November afternoon; it is redolent with the spirit in which the earlier sonnets were written, but presents no affinity with the later ones; I imagine, therefore, that it was an occasional piece, written, perhaps, for some one to speak to Mr W. H. when he was playing the part of Cupid, in some mask now lost; but it would by no means necessarily follow from this that Mr W. H. was an actor by profession. Nothing would surprise me less than to find that this sonnet had been originally the first of the whole series, and had been transferred to the beginning of what we should consider as an appendix collection, on the score of its being in a different form from those that follow ; and also less attractive as an opening sonnet.   But whatever may have been the circumstances under which 126 Q was written, and wherever it may have originally stood, it has no connection with the story of the sonnets.

I turn now to the question whether Q gives us the Sonnets in the order in which they were written.   As regards the first 125 (of course, of Q) all of which, I would repeat, appear to have been addressed directly or indirectly to Mr W. H., I can only find two, i.e. 35 and 121, which I believe to have got misplaced.   Of the remaining 29 sonnets, several suggest themselves as written (*inter se*) in the order in which we have them, but some are obviously misplaced, while others are irrelevant to the series. For example, 144 Q, in which Shakespeare cannot determine whether or no Mr W. H. has enjoyed his mistress, cannot come after 134 Q, in which he confesses that Mr W. H. is now his mistress's property. The same holds good with 143 Q, from which it appears that though Shakespeare's mistress is doing her best to catch Mr W. H., she has not yet caught him.   Furthermore, as Mr Wyndham has more than once justly insisted, the greater number of these sonnets should be intercalated among some of the earlier ones. Speaking of the second series (which he opens with 127 Q) Mr Wyndham says :—

Most of the numbers were evidently written at the same time as the numbers of group O (xxxiii.—xlii.) and on the same theme.[*]

I am convinced that those which belong to the series at all belong to 40—42 Q, as also does 35 Q, to which I will return shortly.   Shakespeare would not write 125 sonnets to Mr W. H., four of the earlier of which refer to an intimacy between him and Shakespeare's mistress—which is never in these 125 sonnets touched upon after 42 Q, though the friendship between Mr. W. H. and Shakespeare seems to have been continued for two or more years afterwards—and then after

---

[*] See Mr Wyndham's "Poems of Shakespeare," Methuen, 1897, p. 825, cf. also Mr Wyndham's Preface pp. cx, cxi.

breaking with him, write some 20 additional sonnets, returning with apparent warm interest to this long discarded theme. An explanation, therefore, must be sought for the fact that these and a few other sonnets or so-called sonnets appear where we find them in Q.

I can discover none more simple than to suppose that Thorpe (for Mr W. H. would have known how to avoid some of the misplacements which we find in Q) intended to keep all the sonnets addressed to Mr W. H. in one group, and in the original sequence, in which Mr W. H. had either kept or rearranged them. In a second category he placed, with less care about their due order, the sonnets which I have given as appendices A—F, all the sonnets to or about a woman, all sonnets which were not either directly or indirectly addressed to Mr W. H., and four which, as I have explained in Chapter III, were addressed to Mr W. H., but which reflected upon him so severely that Thorpe determined to place them where they might be taken as having been addressed to Shakespeare's mistress. These four sonnets (147—150 Q) appear to have been taken out *en bloc*, and we may be thankful that they were so taken, for had they been dispersed it would have been impossible to guess what they really were. The not inconsiderable traces of order which can be detected in the last 29 sonnets are probably due not to design but to Thorpe's having never quite lost the original order, even when seriously interfering with it—to luck, in fact, not cunning.

———

I will now go through the first 125 sonnets as they stand in Q, and see how far they bear out the view that we have them, with only two exceptions, in their right order. It would indeed be almost sufficient to refer the reader to the brief headings which I have prefixed to each sonnet, but he will perhaps be glad to have these headings brought together with what few additional remarks may seem likely to assist his judgement.

The first 17 sonnets present every appearance of being in their right order, and have, I believe, been generally considered to be so. They all of them turn upon the same theme, i.e. the urging (obviously *bonâ fide*) Mr W. H. to marry and leave children. After the end of sonnet 17 this theme is abandoned, for good and all, not, I imagine, because Shakespeare had it any the less at heart, but more probably because Mr W. H. showed signs of impatience at being so persistently urged to marry when he had no wish to do so.

I can find nothing in sonnets 18—25 Q, to compel the belief that we have them in their right order, but neither can I find anything to suggest the contrary. Speaking of sonnets 26—32, Mr Wyndham says, as it seems to me quite justly, that they are,

a continuous poem on absence, dispatched it may be in a single letter since it opens with a formal address and ends in a full close (p. cx.).

Of these sonnets, 27 and 28 are certainly in their right order *inter se* ; so also are 30 and 31 ; 26 and 32 appear to be the opening and close of the series ; there is nothing to suggest that the noble sonnet 29 (" When in disgrace," &c.) is out of order; I have no hesitation, therefore, in holding that in these seven sonnets, as in the first 17, the original order has been undisturbed. Surely in the absence of anything to suggest the contrary we must admit a strong presumption that sonnets 18—25 are also in their right order.

Sonnets 1—25 Q seem to have been written while Shakespeare was within easy reach of his friend, whereas 26—32 indicate, as we have seen, a time of absence, and also of deep depression. On his return—we may suppose to London, though there is nothing in the Sonnets which fixes London as the place in which Shakespeare and Mr W. H. were then residing—a trap was laid for him, into which sonnet 23 had shown that he would be only too ready to fall. I think no ill of sonnet 20, considering the conventions of the time, but it is impossible not to see that in sonnet 23 Shakespeare was in a very different frame of mind to that in which he had been when he wrote sonnets 1—17—for there can be no question that " looks " should be read in line 9, and not " books " as given in Q—I find it also impossible to believe that the change in Shakespeare's mental attitude evidenced in sonnet 23 would have been effected unless Mr W. H. had intended to amuse himself by effecting it. Shakespeare's "looks" would never have become "eloquent," unless he had believed Mr W. H.'s to have already been so. Mr W. H. must have lured him on— as we have Shakespeare's word for it that he lured him still more disastrously later. It goes without saying that Shakespeare should not have let himself be lured, but the age was what it was, and I shall show that Shakespeare was very young.

Between sonnets 32, therefore, and 33 Q, I suppose that there has been a catastrophe. The trap referred to in the preceding paragraph I believe to have been a cruel and most disgusting practical joke, devised by Mr W. H. in concert with others, but certainly never intended, much less permitted, to go beyond the raising coarse laughter against Shakespeare. I do not suppose that the trap was laid from any deeper malice than wanton love of so-called sport, and a desire to enjoy the confusion of any one who could be betrayed into being a victim; I cannot, however, doubt that Shakespeare was, to use his own words, made to "travel forth without" that "cloak," which, if he had not been lured, we may be sure that he would not have discarded. Hardly had he laid the cloak aside before he was surprised according to a pre-concerted scheme, and very probably roughly handled, for we find him lame soon afterwards (sonnet 37, lines 3 and 9) and apparently not fully recovered a twelve-month later. Cf. 109 (89, Q) line 3.

The offence above indicated—a sin of very early youth—for which Shakespeare was bitterly penitent, and towards which not a trace of further tendency can be discerned in any subsequent sonnet or work during five and twenty years of later prolific literary activity—this single offence is the utmost that can be brought against Shakespeare with a shadow of evidence in its support.

I cannot pretend to certainty, or even confidence, but am inclined to think that the lines in sonnet 110 (90, Q),

> Ah, do not when my heart hath scaped this sorrow,
> Come in the rearward of a conquered woe,

refer to the matter now in question, as though some eight or nine mouths after the occurrence* Shakespeare had begun to find that people held him to have been more sinned against than sinning. So also in 115 (95, Q) we read,

> That tongue that tells the story of thy days,
> Making lascivious comments on thy sport,
> Cannot dispraise but in a kind of praise,

If the same matter is here referred to it would seem that it was generally regarded as blackguard sport rather than as deliberate malice.

After sonnet 32 I have placed 121 Q, which has no relevancy to its surroundings where it stands in Q, beyond the fact that in 120 Q there are lines which strongly suggest a reference to the catastrophe of 33, 34, Q. When sonnets 126—154 Q were taken out of their original order it is easy to suppose that some few others might get displaced, and assuming 121 Q to have been among these, an editor who did not know exactly how to replace it correctly, but who knew enough of the facts to see that it bore upon a catastrophe then still notorious—an editor, moreover, who, as we shall find when we come to 35 Q, was hasty in forming his opinions—would be more likely to place 121 Q after 120 Q, than anywhere else. This misplacement goes far to convince me that the mischievous division of the sonnets in Q into two groups was the work not of Mr W. H. but of Thorpe. I was in great doubt whether to place 121 Q before sonnets 33, 34 Q, or after them, but I think it should come before, for it suggests a writer who has not yet calmed down after a gross outrage, while in sonnets 33, 34 Q, everything has been forgiven.

That sonnets 33, 34 Q are in their right order *inter se* will not be questioned; not so as regards 35 Q, which I take it was placed where we find it by some one who knew what Shakespeare had been referring to in 33, 34 Q, but did not trouble himself to read more than the opening line of 35 Q, which I must suppose to have got out of its proper place in the

---

* See the dates with which I have headed each Sonnet in my text.

disturbance of the original order occasioned by the formation
of the second group. Knowing that Mr W. H. had done
Shakespeare a great wrong, to which he was referring in
33, 34, Q, and finding a sonnet which began "No more be
grieved at that which thou hast done," he jumped to the
conclusion that the wrong and the sonnet should be connected,
without noting the last lines, which prove that the sonnet
belongs to those in which Shakespeare is condoning Mr
W. H.'s real or supposed enjoyment of his, Shakespeare's,
mistress—to which, indeed, he there declares himself to have
been "accessory."   Had Thorpe read the sonnet, he would
surely have remembered that the words in line 9, "For to thy
sensual fault" &c., could not refer to any sensual fault
committed by Mr W. H. in connection with the events
referred to in 33, 34, Q, for there had been no sensual fault
committed, or even intended, by him ; there had been treachery
and blackguardism on the part both of Mr W. H. and his
confederates, so gross and infamous that nothing viler can
be well conceived ; but there had been nothing that can be
called sensual, and however odious Mr W. H.'s other faults
may have been, sensuality does not appear to have been one of
them.   He was one of those

> Who do not do the thing they most do show,
> Who moving others are themselves as stone,
> Unmoved, cold, and to temptation slow. (Sonnet 94 Q).

The "sensual fault" intended by Shakespeare is the one
which he then supposed Mr W. H. to have committed with his
mistress ; nothing, then, can be more obviously out of place as
coming between 34 and 36, Q, than a sonnet which accuses
Mr W. H. of having committed a "sensual fault" in respect
of the catastrophe of 33 and 34, Q ; on taking out 35 Q, 36 Q
follows 34 Q naturally enough. We cannot demonstrate that
37 Q, is connected either with 36 Q, or 38 Q, but it follows
the first and precedes the second quite smoothly ; 39 Q seems
to flow out of 38 Q, and appears to refer to the separation that
was deemed expedient in 36 Q. As this separation is not
likely to have lasted very long, I think the six sonnets 33, 34,

36, 37, 38, 39, Q, all belong to one another and are presumably in their right order.

Between 39 and 40, Q, I intercalate 16 sonnets from the second group, and after them 35 Q (56 in my text). Being anxious to confine attention for the moment as far as possible to the first 125 sonnets of Q, I must refer the reader to the headings which I have prefixed to the intercalated sonnets, which will sufficiently indicate what I suppose to have taken place between the writing of 39 and 40, Q. Briefly, Shakespeare, unable to induce his friend to marry, and indignant that he should continue to be so unappreciative of the charms of woman, resolved to bring his own mistress and his friend together—believing this (for the age was lax) to be the greatest service that he could render him.

Sonnets 40, 41, 42, Q (57, 58, 59 of my own text) are a sequence, each growing out of the one that precedes it; after these I intercalate 133, 134, and 152, Q, none of them addressed to Mr W. H. The last of these brings the episode to which the preceding 23 sonnets (of my own text) refer to a conclusion; it appears to have been written by Shakespeare for Mr W. H. to give to Shakespeare's mistress as his own composition on breaking off a *liaison* which had lasted but a short time and had given satisfaction to neither party.

As a commentary on the part played by Shakespeare in the story above given, I take the following from a letter signed J. M. S., which appeared in the *Spectator*, Dec. 3, 1898. The writer is quoting from St Evremond, whose mental attitude he contends to be not unlike Shakespeare's as set forth in sonnet 40, 41, 42, Q. The passage runs :—

Peut-être ne savez vous pas, que si je n'ose me plaindre de vous, pour vous aimer trop, je n'oserais me plaindre de lui, pour ne l'aimer guère moins : et s'il faut de nécessité me mettre en colère, apprenez moi contre qui je me dois fâcher davantage ; ou contre lui qui m' enlève une maitresse, ou contre vous qui me volez un ami......j'ai trop de passion pour donner rien au ressentiment ; ma tendresse l'emportera toujours sur vos outrages. J'aime le perfide, j'aime l'infidèle, et crains seulement qu'un ami sincère ne soit mal avec tous les deux.

With 62 (of my text), the last of the three intercalated sonnets above referred to, all trace of anything erotic disappears finally from the sonnets. There is not a word which suggests any further desire on Shakespeare's part to interfere with Mr W. H.'s remaining celibate for as long or as short a time as he might please.

I now return to the question whether Q has preserved the remaining sonnets in the order in which Shakespeare wrote them. There appears to be a lapse between 42 Q, and 43 Q, and when writing this latter sonnet Shakespeare is at a distance from his friend. Sonnets 43—51, Q, appear all of them to belong to this time, and when we examine them, we find 44 and 45 certainly in right order *inter se*, 45 growing out of 44: so again 47 grows out of 46, 49 grows out of the last three lines of 48, and 51 grows out of 50. The right order between each member of the above-named pairs of sonnets having been obviously preserved, and all of them suggesting absence, the presumption is strong that the order between the pairs has been preserved as truly as it has evidently been between the component members of the pairs.

After 51 Q, we must suppose an interval during which Shakespeare has returned to London, for I think we may assume that he was now living in London. Absence has quieted him, and 52 Q is a somewhat lame apology for his not having come to see his friend as often as he used to do; this sonnet, written, as I shall show in a later chapter, about six months after Shakespeare and Mr W. H. had met, marks the beginning of the end. 53 Q deluges Mr W. H. with that praise of which Shakespeare knew him to be more than commonly fond,* and must be looked upon as a peace-offering; 54, which grows out of the last line of 53, is a continuation of the same peace-offering, and 55 grows out of the last line of 54.

Here we must suppose another interval, probably of no very long duration. Mr W. H. having been sufficiently flattered, and having, as he imagined, re-established his ascendancy over Shakespeare, has been neglecting him, so that it becomes

---

* Cf. sonnet 84 Q, line 14.

necessary to tell sweet love to renew its force; there has been a "sad interim" during which the two men have evidently been seeing less of one another, the whole of sonnet 56 Q, though it implies a conviction on Shakespeare's part that Mr W. H. is still very much attached to him, nevertheless betrays a sense that the relations between the writer and his friend are not what they were. Sonnets 57 and 58, Q, which are certainly in right order *inter se*, make it plain that though matters had been set right for a time they had soon got wrong again. Sonnets 59 and 60 Q cannot be shown to be in their right order, but there is nothing to suggest that they are wrongly placed, and it would be exactly like Shakespeare to smooth his friend down after reproaching him as he had done in 57 and 58; 61 Q is written much in the same vein as 57 and 58, and 62 again suggests self-reproach for having been too exacting; 63 Q grows out of the two last lines of 62; 64, 65, 66, Q, all continue the same vein of melancholy reflection upon the effects of time and the wrongs with which the world is filled, 64 and 65 being very closely allied, and 66 appearing to profess weariness and almost despair.

In 67 Q we find Shakespeare remonstrating with Mr W. H. for associating with what Shakespeare evidently considers to be bad company; 68 Q grows out of 67; 69 Q, though not directly growing out of 68, is in the same vein as the two sonnets that have preceded it, and warns Mr W. H. that people are giving him a bad name; 70 Q is certainly in its right order after 69, and is another attempt to soften the effect of sonnets that have gone before it. I cannot doubt that 71—74 Q are in right order *inter se*, but can find nothing to indicate that they grew immediately out of the preceding sonnets; they are all tinged with the deepest melancholy, and with a sense of the growing estrangement which it is plain that Shakespeare deplores and is doing his utmost to conceal; 75, Q, again, appears to stand alone; from it we gather that though Shakespeare is still devoted to Mr W. H. the intercourse between the two has become intermittent.

Between 75 and 76 Q, I suppose a gap of no very long duration, but there is nothing to indicate that 76 is out of order ; the most interesting inference that can be drawn from this sonnet is to the effect that Shakespeare had not yet begun to write plays, nor yet poems other than these sonnets. There is, as I have just said, no sign of any connection between 77 and 76, Q. I shall have more to say about both these sonnets when I come to the dates of the sonnets. For the present I will only say that 77 seems to have accompanied the present of a book of tablets given by Shakespeare to Mr W. H. Jan. 1, 1585-6, i.e. 1586 according to our present reckoning.* Here I suppose another interval.

From 78 Q we learn that Shakespeare, after having set the fashion of sonneteering, is jealous of his imitators, and more particularly of one whom he supposes to have supplanted him in his friend's affections. I do not see how it is possible to doubt that sonnets 78—86, Q, all of them dealing with his jealousy, mainly of a single poet, are in right order *inter se*. From three of these (83, 85, 86) we find that Shakespeare has left off writing, finding his muse tongue-tied by the favour shown to his rival by Mr W. H. We also find from 83 that Mr W. H. has upbraided him for his silence. In 87, Q Shakespeare, convinced, or affecting to be convinced, that all is now over between him and his friend, bids him farewell, and the following six sonnets all of them express a conviction against which he is continually fighting, to the effect that Mr W. H. is trying to "steal himself away," and bring the intimacy to an end ; these six sonnets are, I think I may say certainly, in right order *inter se*, and the whole series 78—93, Q, form a single sequence. All direct reference, indeed, to the rival poet ceases with the last two lines of 86 Q, but the tenor of the following seven sonnets is obviously dictated by jealousy —of which, however, there is no sign in any sonnet later than 93 Q.

I may say in passing that I suspect, though I can find nothing in the words of the jealousy series to bear me out, that it was rather fear lest after all the rival poet's verses should

---

* Some readers may need to be reminded that the official year in Shakespeare's time did not begin till March 26. The first three months, therefore, of what we should call 1586 were then still 1585.

be better than his own, than lest Mr W. H. should become fonder of another friend, that stirred Shakespeare so profoundly. Poor, and almost hopeless as he as yet evidently is, he appears to have felt that he was writing as never man had yet written, and further, that his lines must live for ever. In this last conviction he narrowly escaped proving to have been over-confident, for the Sonnets have been only saved to us by the skin of their teeth, but the conviction would sustain him, and be a more solid satisfaction than he ever probably obtained from Mr W. H. How, then, if his one stay was to be removed? How if he was flattering himself, and the rival poet's verses were as good as, or perhaps better than, his own? Mr W. H. appeared to think so; no doubt other poets made ill-natured remarks. How if they were right? I do not say that we have here the sole cause of Shakespeare's jealousy, but it is impossible that it should not have been enhanced and embittered by some such considerations. No one will probably ever succeed in finding out who the rival poet was, but I should myself incline to Thomas Watson, whose Ἑκατομπαθία or " Passionate Centurie of Love " was published (see Arber's reprint, p. 9), March 31, 1582. Dates exclude Sidney.

Returning to the order in which we find the sonnets in Q, the jealousy series comes to an end with 93 Q. In 94, 95, 96, Q, we have a short sequence which seems to stand alone, but there is nothing to suggest that it is out of order. In 94 Q, Shakespeare again warns his friend of the ill-report in which he is living, and according to his wont in 95 and 96 he gilds the pill of his reproof.

With 97 Q we are in another atmosphere. So great is the difference between the tone of 96 and 97 that we may suppose a lapse of months, in the course of which Shakespeare has probably been travelling in the country with some company, and time, with freedom from provocation, has restored him to his more serene and genial mind. There is now not a trace of either sense of injury or remonstrance. There appears to be an interval of many months between the writing of sonnets 97 and 98, Q, for while 97 implies autumn, 98 and 99, which follow in right order *inter se*, imply spring and early summer.

It is quite likely that sonnets 97, 98, 99, Q, as well, perhaps, as some others written during absence, were enclosed in prose letters which have perished.

We are left in no uncertainty about there having been a long interval between 99 Q and 100 Q, for Shakespeare opens 100 Q by complaining to his Muse that she has forgotten for so long a time to speak of that which gave her all her might, though she has now found time to inspire him to write some worthless songs on other subjects. Sonnets 100—103 all seem to be in their right order *inter se*, the three last of them continuing the theme started in 100. Sonnet 102 admits an apparent falling off in the intensity of the writer's affection. Shakespeare denies that there has been any real falling off, and excuses himself on grounds which, though they leave no doubt that his love was "more weak in seeming," make it hard to believe that it had "been strengthened." The following sonnet (103 Q) shows even more clearly that the outward evidences of his affection were less convincing than formerly; "oh blame me not," he exclaims, "if I no more can write"; but in the old days he found no difficulty in writing when the excuse which he now urges was to the full as valid. The only difficulty he then found was in leaving off writing. "Our love was new," he says in 102 Q,

> . . . and then but in the spring
> When I was wont to greet it with my lays.

In 103 Q, he excuses himself for not writing, on the ground that his friend's looking glass would say all that could be said more effectually than words could do. In 104 we are told that three years had elapsed since he and Mr W. H. met; assuming, as I think we may, that sonnets 100—106 Q, were written much about the same date, the tone of these sonnets as compared with that of the earlier ones fits in well with the statement that there was an interval of three years between them, and hence tends to confirm the opinion that Q gives us the series in their right order—except as regards the formation by Thorpe of an appendix group.

As regards the order *inter se* of sonnets 100—106 Q, 100—103 appear to be a sequence, and though 104—106 are not so closely interpendent, there is nothing to suggest their having been misplaced. They are exactly what one might expect from Shakespeare when he was trying to atone for a long course of silence, by a double dose of affectionate flattery.

We may note that there is not a trace in any of these seven sonnets of the dissatisfaction and remonstrance which from 52—96 Q, had been becoming more and more marked. Furthermore we may suspect both from 100 and 104 (as still more from 108 Q) that Mr W. H.'s good looks were no longer all that they had been, and this would take time to bring about; if, then, this suspicion is held to be well founded, we are again confirmed in accepting the order of Q.

I intend to show in Chapter X that there was an interval of about three or four months between 106 and 107, Q. This last named sonnet does not appear to have been dictated by any thing that had passed between Shakespeare and Mr W. H., nor yet to have been written in his interest; in this respect it stands alone, or nearly so, as it stands also alone in referring to passing events of national importance. It gives expression to a sense of relief, shared by the whole nation, on delivery from what seemed an inevitable national disaster of extreme gravity. Nothing short of a foreboding that England's name and place among nations had been in great jeopardy is large enough for the event that looms behind the words :—

> Not mine own fears, nor the prophetic soul
> Of the wide world dreaming on things to come,
> Can yet the lease of my true love control
> Supposed as forfeit to a confined doom.

When I deal with the dates of the several sonnets I will give my reasons for thinking that the defeat of the Spanish Armada is the event referred to in these lines.

I "imagine," but am shocked to note how frequently I fall back upon this or some kindred word, that Shakespeare was moved by the universal rejoicing to write a sonnet to Mr W. H. to whom he had not written for three or four months. Mr W. H. had been accustomed in the old times to receive a sonnet by Shakespeare, specially written for him on an average two days a week; this would be enough to spoil any man; when the stream of sonnets slackened off so that only two appear to have been written in the year 1587, Mr W. H. would argue that Shakespeare had got tired of him and would naturally enough be piqued; there was a little flow again in the spring of 1588, in the course of which Mr W. H. seems to have reproached Shakespeare with not caring about him now that he had got to look old; Shakespeare met this with sonnets 104–106, Q, but here again the stream ceased to flow, and Shakespeare, knowing that Mr W. H. would be offended, took advantage of the occasion of the defeat of the Armada to write him a friendly sonnet.

The result does not seem to have been satisfactory, for from 108 Q it is tolerably plain that Mr W. H. has been taxing Shakespeare with want of constancy, and has especially galled him by repeating the accusation that Shakespeare had ceased to care for him now that he had got to look old. Hence the asseveration in 108 Q that such a love as his "weighs not the dust and injury of age," and that although "time and outward form" would show that which had at first attracted Shakespeare to be now dead, this had nothing to do with what he still felt, and should ever continue to feel, for Mr W. H.

Shakespeare seems to have been stung to the quick, and sonnets 109–112 Q, are a sequence growing out of 108, and out of the reproach of being "false of heart," which Mr W. H. had brought against him. They are, one would say, certainly in right order *inter se*, and it must be admitted that they do to a certain extent explain how Mr W. H. had come to be nettled. One can have no sympathy with him, but no matter how worthless a man is he resents being dropped, and Shakespeare had been far too fond of him to relish the dropping, or even to admit the fact to himself. The knowledge, indeed, that there was a grain of truth and justice in what Mr W. H. had said would make his words more telling, and Shakespeare's defence more vehement. In 109 Q he admits that absence may have "seemed" his "flame to qualify," and if it had seemed to do so, it had probably done so in reality; 110 is a sequel to 109; 111, 112 Q, are certainly in right order *inter se*, and appear to be a continuation of the penitence already expressed in the three or four immediately preceding sonnets. From all these we gather that Mr W. H. has been accusing Shakespeare of keeping bad company, much as Shakespeare himself had earlier remonstrated with Mr W. H. Shakespeare pleads guilty, but we need not take his self-abasement very literally. No doubt he had his wild oats to sow, and no doubt his frank and fearless nature would lead him in his youth to be hail fellow well met with many a man and many a woman who was utterly unworthy of him. Falstaff, Bardolph, Pistol, Mrs Quickly, and Doll Tearsheet must all have been drawn from life, and if Shakespeare had not been frequent with these people he could not have drawn them as he has. Let us be thankful that he was what he was, and did whatever he did, without asking questions for conscience sake or taking his confessions in 109—112, Q, *au pied de la lettre*.

In 111 Q Shakespeare lays the blame of his misdeeds on his profession. Let any one contrast the tone of this sonnet with that of 29, and he will observe that whereas in 29 Shakespeare does not seem to have anything on his conscience, his fortunes are at a very low ebb. He holds himself as in an "outcast state" with small hope of betterment. In 111 Q he is full of self-reproach on the score of moral delinquencies— real or imaginary—but neither in this, nor in any of the later sonnets is there so much as a hint that he is in an outcast or hopeless state. In 29 Q he appears to be living from hand to mouth ; in 111 Q he has a fixed profession. True he makes this profession a scape-goat for the deterioration of his moral and spiritual nature, but it would be unsafe to argue from this that it was in itself irksome to him.

Sonnets 113, 114, Q, are again in right order *inter se* ; they indicate that Shakespeare is travelling, but there is nothing to connect them with those that immediately precede and follow ; both of them asseverate the strength and permanence of Shakespeare's affection ; so also does 115 Q, but in the old days no such asseveration was needed, and 116 Q implies a recognition of "impediments" to those happy relations between

him and his friend, which he would fain restore, or rather
flatter himself that he was restoring, for in his heart he must
have known that the friendship had been a one-sided affair
from first to last. No one insists when writing to a friend
that love is not love on finding alteration in its object, or
when it meets coldness with coldness, unless he is aware both
of coldness and alteration.

Shakespeare concludes this lovely sonnet by saying that
Love is not Time's fool. If this, he continues,

> . . . be error and upon me proved
> I never writ, nor no man ever loved.

But it was an error; and it was going to be finally proved
upon himself very shortly; and there can be no doubt that he
had written; and many another man has loved as fondly and
as foolishly as he did.

Sonnets 117, 118 Q, follow so naturally on 116 that it is
difficult to question their being in their due order; we saw in
116 that Shakespeare recognised a difference in his friend's
manner towards him; we may infer from the opening line of
117 Q that Mr W. H. has been explaining why and how he
considers himself aggrieved. Shakespeare kisses the rod as
usual, but it must be admitted that his defence is lame. He
says that his having been "frequent with unknown minds"—
which can only mean his having kept low company—was due
to nothing but a desire to prove his friend's constancy. Who
can fail to see that the relations between the two friends,
already strained, are on the point of snapping?

I suppose them to have snapped almost immediately, and
find in sonnets 119, 120 Q—a pair which cannot be separated
and which appear to be in due order *inter se*—an apology
couched in the most affectionate and self-abasing tones for
some unkindness of which Shakespeare confesses himself to
have been guilty. I may be speculating too boldly, but I
imagine that Mr W. H., not too well pleased at the excuses
made in 117, 118, Q, said things to Shakespeare in return
which outraged him not a little, and that Shakespeare in the
heat of anger and passionate regret, wrote the four sonnets

147–150, Q, which Thorpe excluded from the first group, and which I have restored to what I believe to have been their proper place. The two last of these, as usual, offer a golden bridge for his friend's retreat. On the quarrel being again patched up Shakespeare would be almost sure to apologise with a good deal more confession of having been wrong than the occasion warranted. In sonnet 119 Q he is aghast at what he has done, and in 120 Q he refers to a wrong done to him by Mr W. H. a considerable time previously, and appeals to him to set this against his own recent unkindness. This wrong, as I have already said, was no doubt the one not obscurely shadowed forth in 33, 34, Q; the word "once" in line 1 of 120 Q, repeated in line 8, makes it clear that the event referred to was of old date and tends to confirm our opinion that we have the sonnets in right order; if it was what I suppose it to have been, we may be sure that it was one of common notoriety, so that Thorpe would be at no loss to know what Shakespeare was alluding to. Hence, as I have earlier said, his blundering misplacement of 121 Q.

For the moment, then, the ruin'd love between Shakespeare and his friend, was built anew, and Shakespeare, ever sanguine, allowed himself to hope that the reconciliation would be permanent. He declares that he returns rebuk'd to his content and has gained in the restoration of friendship thrice more than he had lost in the quarrel ; but the very next sonnet, i.e. 122 Q, (for 121 Q must not be counted) shows that Mr W. H. has been upbraiding him for having given away a book of tablets of which he had made him a present; Shakespeare excuses himself with much fervour, but in the old days he would never have let those tablets out of his own pocket. In sonnets 123, 124 Q he again insists on the permanence of his devotion to his friend, but there has been another quarrel between 124 and 125 Q. From this last sonnet it is plain that Mr W. H. has been complaining of Shakespeare for having borne, or schemed to bear, a canopy, presumably held over some person of high rank on a great occasion. We cannot gather from the words of the sonnet whether Shakespeare did or did not take any part in the bearing of this canopy, but the two last lines suggest that information given by Mr W. H. may have defeated some hope of advancement which Shakespeare had entertained.

With these two indignant lines,

> Hence thou suborn'd *Informer*, a true soul
> When most impeach'd stands least in thy control,

the Sonnets, as I read them, come to a conclusion, and considering the cat and dog life which, in spite of all Shakespeare's infinite sweetness and forbearance, the two men have evidently long been leading, and considering also how utterly unworthy Mr W. H. was of the affection which Shakespeare lavished so prodigally upon him, there is nothing to regret or be surprised at in the apparent cessation of further intercourse between them.

Having now satisfied myself, and I trust the reader, that the Sonnets were printed in Q in the order in which Shakespeare wrote them with the exception of 35 and 121, Q,—and with the further exception that the last 29 sonnets were taken out of the series, so that they should be replaced as far as possible by one who would read the Sonnets in the order in which Shakespeare left them—I shall assume that sonnet 107 Q is in due order, and shall not argue further on this head. This point being established I can go on to the question of the dates when the Sonnets were written.

But before I do so I would ask the reader to consider whether any other arrangement than the one we find (with the exceptions already noted) in Q could be made to show any thing like so coherent a story as the one indicated in this chapter. Let him take Benson's medley, and see what he can make of that. Let him shuffle the Sonnets into any order he pleases and see whether he can make any story out of them at all. It may be asked why have a story, when the one which Q alone permits is throughout painful and in parts repulsive? Many, indeed say, " Read the Sonnets if you like, but do not go below their surface ; let their music and beauty of expression be enough." I do not write for these good people, nor are they likely to read me; I therefore pass them by at as wide a distance as I can, and confine my attention to those who will not read anything that fell from such a man as Shakespeare without doing their best to fathom it.

No such persons can even begin to read the Sonnets without finding that a story of some sort is staring them in the face. They cannot apprehend it, but they feel that behind some four or five sonnets there is a riddle which more or less taints the series with a vague feeling as though the answer, if found, would be unwholesome. There the Sonnets are; there is no suppressing them; they are being studied yearly more and more, and will continue to be so, in spite, *pace* Steevens, of the strongest act of parliament that can be framed to prevent people from reading them. Therefore they should be faced for better or worse, and until they are restored approximately to the order in which Shakespeare wrote them and until they are approximately dated, it is impossible to face them. Their date is the very essence of the whole matter; for the verdict we are to pass upon some few of them—and these colour the others—depends in great measure on the age of the writer. And furthermore, what we think of Shakespeare himself must depend not a little on what we think of the Sonnets.

If we date them early we suppose a severe wound in youth, but one that was soon healed to perfect wholesomeness. If we date them at any age later than extreme youth, there is no escape from supposing what is morally a malignant cancer. If the evidence points in the direction of the cancer. we must with poignant regret accept it. I submit, however, that it will be found to point with irresistible force in the direction of the mere scar.

It is a pious act to show that it does so; for the man is not dead. The true life of a man is not that which he leads in himself, but the one he leads in others, and of which he knows nothing. Shakespeare is more living in that life of the world to come by virtue of which he entered after death into the lives of millions, than he ever was in that vexed body to which his conscious life was limited. But enough of this.

Those who pass the riddle of the Sonnets over in silence, tacitly convey an impression that the answer would be far more terrible than the facts would show. Those who date the Sonnets as the Southamptonites, and still worse the Herbertites do, cannot escape from leaving Shakespeare suffering as I have said from a leprous or cancerous taint, for they do not even attempt to show that he was lured into a trap, and if they did, he was too old for the excuse to be admitted as much palliation. Those who regard the Sonnets as literary exercises would have us believe that in the naughtiness of his heart, Shakespeare, with a world of subjects to choose from, elected to invent sonnet 23, and to imagine a situation which required the writing of sonnets 33—35 of my numbering. This is the most degrading view of all; but these four ways of treating the Sonnets are the only ones now before the public, and they are all of them alike slovenly and infamous. True, however early the Sonnets are dated a scar must remain; but who under the circumstances will heed it whose moral support is worth a moment's consideration ?

I grant that the story is a very squalid one, but from all we can gather Shakespeare's first few years in London were passed in very squalid surroundings. Furthermore, any one who reads the Sonnets carefully will note that it was not Mr W. H.'s mere good looks which so powerfully attracted Shakespeare. From first to last it is plain that Shakespeare assumed that these were but the outward and visible signs of an inward and spiritual grace. He could not believe that any evil spirit should have so fair a house, and it was the good spirit within, and not the house itself, of which Shakespeare was in truth enamoured; this appears over and over again, and when he has become convinced that his friend's looks are better than his character, he declares the good looks to be like Eve's apple.

Considering, then, Shakespeare's extreme youth, which I shall now proceed to establish, his ardent poetic temperament, and Alas! it is just the poetic temperament which by reason of its very catholicity is least likely to pass scatheless through what he so touchingly describes as "the ambush of young days"; considering also the license of the times, Shakespeare's bitter punishment, and still more bitter remorse—is it likely that there was ever afterwards a day in his life in which the remembrance of that "night of woe" did not at some time or another rise up before him and stab him? nay, is it not quite likely that this great shock may in the end have brought him prematurely to the grave?—Considering, again, the perfect sanity of all his later work; considering further that all of us who read the Sonnets are as men who are looking over another's shoulder and reading a very private letter which was intended for the recipient's eye, and for no one else's; considering all these things—for I will not urge the priceless legacy he has left us, nor the fact that the common heart, brain, and conscience of mankind holds him foremost among all Englishmen as the crowning glory of our race—leaving all this on one side, and considering only youth, the times, penitence, and amendment of life, I believe that those whose judgement we should respect will refuse to take Shakespeare's grave indiscretion more to heart than they do the story of Noah's drunkenness; they will neither blink it nor yet look at it more closely than is necessary in order to prevent men's rank thoughts from taking it to have been more grievous than it was.

Tout savoir, c'est tout comprendre—and in this case surely we may add—*tout pardonner.*

CHAPTER X.

THOSE who believe that Lord Southampton was the friend
to whom Shakespeare addressed the greater number of the
Sonnets can date the beginning of the series approximately—
for the earlier ones are addressed to a smooth-faced youth who
was hardly likely to be more than 18, and may well have
been a few months younger. Lord Southampton was born
in October 1573; adding, say, 18 years to this date, the
earlier sonnets should have been written in the second half
of 1591, when Shakespeare was $27\frac{1}{2}$ years old, while if my
own numbering (which is virtually that of Q) be accepted
as chronological, sonnet 124 (104 Q) should be dated in the
second half of 1594. The remaining 24 sonnets cannot on the
Southampton theory be dated with certainty, but should be
supposed to have followed sonnet 104 at no very distant date.

By a like process of reasoning those who take Mr W. H.
to have been William Herbert Earl of Pembroke, will date
the Sonnets as between 1598 and 1601 or 1602, for Lord
Pembroke was born in April 1580. With the dismissal,
however, of the claims of both these noblemen, all clue to
the date of the Sonnets derivable from their ages disappears,
and we are driven back upon the internal evidence of the
Sonnets, and what few meagre notices of them we can find
elsewhere.

As regards these last they are limited to the fact that
Francis Meres in his "Palladis Tamia," published in 1598,
speaks on p. 282 of Shakespeare's "sugred Sonnets among
his private friends." It is probable that he was alluding
to some, at any rate, of those with which we are familiar.
Again in 1599 Jaggard printed the two sonnets 46 and 52

(138, 144, Q), but this does not prove that any of the later ones had been yet written. Practically, then, we have no evidence for the dates of any of the sonnets but what we can gather from the poems themselves.

Let us go through them as numbered in my own text.

In sonnet 2, we find that the writer holds a man of forty to be "old." Forty years will have dug "deep trenches" in the field of Mr W. H.'s beauty; at forty his eyes will be "deep sunken"; he will feel his blood cold, and must be contented with seeing it warm in the veins of his offspring. In short he is a decrepit old man with one foot in the grave. I cannot think I am forcing a conclusion when I hold that this sonnet can only have been written by one who was still very young. I should say that 21 would be quite old enough for him. I therefore tentatively date this sonnet, and I assume also sonnet 1 as written in the spring of 1585—say, for convenience sake, at the beginning of April, shortly after the beginning of the official year. I dare not lay much stress on the words in sonnet 1 :

> Thou that art now this world's fresh ornament
> And only herald to the gaudy spring,

but they would be less appropriate if written in any other season than that of early or middle spring.

The same opinion as to the senility of a man of forty (or indeed six and thirty) may be gathered from sonnet 3. When Mr W. H.'s son—for Shakespeare never contemplates the possibility of the son's turning out to be a daughter—reaches his father's present age of about 18, Mr W. H., "despite of wrinkles," will be able to look "through windows of his age," and see his present golden time in the person of another. But he will not be over six and thirty, or seven and thirty at the outside, for the baby is to be set on foot at once. The opinion of the writer that a man is broken down and old, say, at 37, is indeed less obviously expressed in sonnet 3, but the unconsciousness with which it has escaped him is even more convincing as to what he really thought than the directer statement of the preceding sonnet. I again infer that 21 years is a reasonable age to give him, of course I mean provisionally. The reader will note that the provisional acceptance of, say, mid-April 1585 as the date of the first three sonnets commits me to the date, say mid-April 1588, as that of sonnet 124 (104, Q), and I am bound to get the intervening ones within these two dates by the light of whatever hints I may gather from the Sonnets themselves.

In sonnet 16 Shakespeare speaks of his "pupil pen." Malone quotes Steevens as thinking this expression to be "some slight proof" that the Sonnets were Shakespeare's earliest compositions. The earliest date commonly assigned to the first 17 sonnets is 1593 or 1594. By this time Shakespeare had written Venus and Adonis, The Rape of Lucrece, and is confidently believed to have written Love's Labour's Lost, Romeo and Juliet, The Two Gentlemen of Verona, and at any rate parts of other plays; all these plays are assigned to 1592 and still earlier years. It is incredible that in 1594 he, being then 30, should speak of his writings as those of a mere beginner. Still more incredible would it be that he should do so at the later date which the Herbertites would assign to the Sonnets. The words "my pupil pen" will, I believe, suggest to most readers more strongly than they seem to have done to Steevens that in the Sonnets we have Shakespeare's first essays in writing. In this case 1585 seems a very reasonable date for the opening sonnets.

Against this must be set the fact that Shakespeare, in his dedication of Venus and Adonis to Lord Southampton, calls it "the first heir of his invention"; he may well, however, have so called it, though aware that he had already written a large number of sonnets. Shakespeare had never seen Shakespeare's Sonnets bound together, and thus made to seem more intentionally articulated than they really are. They prove to be in great measure articulated, but this was the doing of time and circumstance, not of invention: no one considers his occasional letters whether in prose or verse as heirs to his invention; they are determined for him both as regards incident and incidence, and he knows neither the facts nor their grouping *inter se* till time reveals them; they are Fortune's bastards, not begotten in wedlock with a subject chosen beforehand and developed according to the writer's ideas concerning their fittest exposition. The preface, therefore, to Venus and Adonis does not militate against the view that the Sonnets were Shakespeare's first essays in poetry.

Again, as we have just seen, he had written several plays before he published Venus and Adonis, and if he did not hold these as "heirs to his invention," still less would he so hold the sonnets. A concise and formal preface cannot go into details; if Venus and Adonis was Shakespeare's first elaboration of a set subject, and if it was his first published work, this would be enough to justify him in calling it the "first heir of his invention." Of course he ought to have put a parenthesis after these words, in some such precious phrase by all the Muses filed as the following:—

To be strictly accurate, however, I should inform your honour that I have also written a considerable number of Sonnets, and some few Plays, none of which have been published, and which I esteem unworthy of your honour's attention.

Shakespeare perhaps thought that this would be a little long, and that the existence of other unpublished works might be allowed to go without saying. Moreover he knew nothing of eminent Shakespearean scholars.

For reasons which will appear when I reach sonnet 97, I date that sonnet (always provisionally) Jan. 1, 1585-6. I have therefore to date 1—96 as written between April and the end of December 1585. Without, then, having any confidence that the opening line of 18 ("Shall I compare thee to a summer's day?") was actually suggested by the beauty of some day in early June, I will suppose that with this sonnet we have reached, say, early June 1585.

The next apparent clue to Shakespeare's age after those we have deduced from sonnets 2 and 3 and 16 is in 22. Shakespeare here says that his glass shall not persuade him he is old, and this implies that he should have to admit himself old if he believed what his glass told him. Perhaps—but one would like to know exactly what he meant by "old." Shakespeare seems to have regarded male good looks much as Homer, and the writer of the Odyssey did, i. e. to be at their best with the approach of beard and moustaches. Homer makes Mercury appear to Priam in the likeness of a young man "with the down just coming upon his chin, when youth is at its loveliest,"* and the writer of the Odyssey endorses his opinion by taking his line *verbatim*. So Shakespeare writes in his Lover's Complaint :—

> Small show of man was yet upon his chin;
>   His phœnix down began but to appear,
> Like unshorn velvet, on that termless skin,
>   Whose bare outbragg'd the web it seem'd to wear,
>   Yet showed his visage by that coat† more dear;
> And nice affections wavering stood in doubt
> If best were as it was, or best without.

Shakespeare, here, presumably much about the same date as that of the earlier sonnets, is describing ideal youthful beauty in a young man. What fluff—for we may as well call things by their right names—there was, might pass, but had there been more the face would have been better without it; it would have passed its best, and the younger people are, the more apt they are to set down anything that they think past its best, as old, when an older person would give it many another year of youth. Hence from sonnet 46 (138, Q) we may infer that "old," which it seems, from the same sonnet, only means "past the best," may intend nothing more than "past the fluffy stage." Sonnet 22 does indeed show that Shakespeare was older than Mr W. H., but a difference of three or four years would be enough to make him seem old by comparison both to himself and to his friend, especially when we remember that he had married imprudently at 18. Such a marriage as Shakespeare's would age a man early, for there can hardly be a doubt that it was forced upon him, and his wife was 8 years older than he was, to say nothing of other

---

* πρῶτον ὑπηνήτῃ, τοῦ περ χαριεστάτη ἥβη. Il. XXIV., 348. Cf. Od. x. 279.

† Q reads "cost." Malone points out that the line means "Yet his visage showed.........more dear."

evidence that his married life was unhappy, and his youth *orageuse*.

One of my own earlier friends was of the same year as myself at Cambridge, but being three or four years (if so much) older than most of us, we always called him "the old one." He was more active and youthful than many of his juniors, but he accepted his name without demur, and rather gloried in it. It is one of the commonest affectations of youth to think itself old—as it is of age to imagine itself still young. In a note on p. 86 of the second edition of his " Life of W. Shakespeare," Mr Lee quotes Daniel at the age of 29, Barnfield at 20, and Drayton at barely 31, all describing themselves not only as old, but apparently as very old.

Moreover, even the Southamptonites ought not to make Shakespeare older than, say 28, when sonnet 22 was written, and if at this age he could persuade himself into thinking that his glass ought to persuade him he was old, he could so persuade himself at 21. Besides, he repeatedly abases his own appearance by comparison with that of his friend. Seeing, then, how impossible it is that Shakespeare should have been really old, or even elderly, when he wrote sonnet 22, his implying that he was then old points rather in the direction of thinking that he was still very young.

To return for a moment to the preface to Venus and Adonis. Shakespeare speaks of this poem as " unpolished lines," when he must have known that they were the most highly polished that had yet been written in English. He says he fears the world will censure him for having chosen so strong a prop as Lord Southampton, to support so weak a burden. How far, I wonder, did he really believe his poem to be a weak burden ? He continues :—

Only if your honour seem but pleased, I account myself highly praised, and vow to take advantage of all idle hours, till I have honoured you with some graver labour. But if the first heir of my invention prove deformed, I shall be sorry it had so noble a god father, and never after ear so barren a land, for fear it yield me still so bad a harvest.

All very proper, pretty, and polite, but every third word a

lie duer paid to the reader than the Turk's tribute. "If your honour seem but pleased I shall account myself highly praised"; I take it that unless Lord Southampton had declared Venus and Adonis to be the loveliest poem ever written, Shakespeare would have been bitterly disappointed; "honoured you with some graver labour"; surely the labour of writing Venus and Adonis must have been grave enough for any one. And so on to the end of the preface, Shakespeare, meekest of men, is ever ready to disarm criticism by uprearing his hand against himself. I imagine that this is all he is doing when he calls himself old in Sonnet 22, and in others to which I will call attention in due course. Let us, then, hold to our original hypothesis and date the sonnet, summer 1585.

I have said in the preceding chapter that I agree with Mr Wyndham in regarding sonnets 26—32 as written during absence and sent to Mr W. H. "it may be as a single letter." Sonnet 26 will be thus considered not as an *envoi* to the preceding 25, but as a preface to the six that follow. We have no clue to the length of time this absence lasted, but considering that Shakespeare was, on our present hypothesis, in the white heat alike of his infatuation, and of his discovery that he too was a poet, and considering that he only wrote seven sonnets during this absence, I think a month is enough to allow for them. The extreme depression which they betray, especially the hopelessness and friendlessness of his outcast state as depicted in 29, make it impossible to believe that Shakespeare had as yet got his foot even on the lowest rungs of the ladder up which he was to climb to affluence—much less that he had obtained the powerful patronage of Lord Southampton, or had even reached the position which enabled Greene in 1592 to speak of him as "an upstart crow." I see nothing, therefore, to make the hypothesis difficult that he wrote the seven sonnets in question during the summer months of 1585, and returned to London, for want of a more exact date, say, at the end of July.

Another reason for thinking that Shakespeare was still

very young may be gathered from sonnet 32, line 10, where we read in Q:—

Had my friend's Muse grown with this growing age,

Malone evidently meant to read "with his growing age," for he writes :—

We may hence, as well as from other circumstances, infer that these [i.e. the Sonnets] were among our author's earliest compositions.

As I have pointed out in my notes to this sonnet, Malone's words have little force unless he meant to read, not "with this," but "with his"—which is surely right, for the words "with this growing age" add nothing of importance to "had my friend's muse grown," whereas "with his growing age" shows why it might have been expected to do so. I am glad to see that Mr Lee accepts this reading; he writes that Shakespeare's "occasional reference in the Sonnets to his growing age . . . admits of no literal interpretation."* There is no reference in the Sonnets to Shakespeare's "growing age" unless "his" be read in this passage. It is plain, therefore, that Mr Lee is reading "his," not "this."

I suppose the trap already referred to was considered and determined on during Shakespeare's absence and that it was laid for him immediately on his return. Let us then place sonnets 33—37 as written in the first half of August 1585, and 38, 39 in the second half of the month, there or thereabouts, when Shakespeare and Mr W. H. were seeing less of one another by mutual consent.

I cannot say that sonnet 38 compels the inference that Mr W. H. was as yet the sole source of Shakespeare's inspiration, but it suggests this. If the inference is equitable, sonnet 38 must be thrown back to a date earlier than that of the earliest plays, and I will for the present hold to my hypothesis that it was written in the autumn of 1585.

Shakespeare is not likely to have let his newly-found power rust during the time of his separation from his friend, nor is

---

* "Life of W. Shakespeare," p. 85.

he likely to have been long in finding some pretext for bringing the separation to an end. I imagine that no long time would elapse before he conceived the idea of introducing his mistress and Mr W. H. to one another, and can well believe that some of the sonnets addressed to the dark lady were written before he had renewed his full intimacy with his friend. The whole of the episode is comprised between sonnets 40 and 62 of my numbering, and considering how slight some of them are, and that the intimacy between Mr W. H. and the dark woman appears from sonnet 62 to have been soon ended, I can see no great difficulty in thinking that the last of these sonnets may have been written, and Mr W. H. dismissed by the lady, before the end of September.

Sonnets 63—71 (always of my numbering) are written during a second absence from London. We cannot determine how long Shakespeare was away, but let us say a month, and let us then suppose sonnets 72—96 to have been written between Nov. 1 and Dec. 31, 1585.

In sonnet 83 Shakespeare speaks of himself as

> With Time's injurious hand crush'd and o'erworn.

The remarks already made as to Shakespeare's ideas of age apply here, as they also do to the whole of sonnet 93.

It is impossible to believe that sonnet 96 could have been written by one who had even begun to write Venus and Adonis and Lucrece, not to mention the plays of a still earlier time, some of which bear traces of the Sonnets that do not appear nearly so frequently in Shakespeare's later work. The sonnet does not indeed say, "I have never written anything in any other style than that of these sonnets, nor on any other subject than that of yourself, but it does say, 'I never write in any other style than that of these sonnets; I never write of anything but of you, and I have still no other argument than you and my love for you." The word "still" suggests, though I admit that it does not compel, the opinion that the sonnets were Shakespeare's earliest essays.

I will now give my reasons for thinking that sonnet 97 was written to accompany the new year's gift of a book of tablets.

The idea is not mine but Malone's. Steevens had said that the sonnet was probably designed to accompany a present of a book consisting of blank paper. Malone added—

> This suggestion appears to me extremely probable. We learn from the 122nd Sonnet [Q] that Shakespeare received a table-book from his friend. In his age it was customary for all ranks of people to make presents on the first day of the new year.

Jan. 1, not the official new year, is here intended.

My friend Mr H. Festing Jones suggests to me that the book referred to in 97 (77, Q) as having been given by Shakespeare to Mr W. H. was in reality a book of tablets, much like the one referred to in 145 (122, Q) as having been given by Mr W. H. to Shakespeare, and that the two friends probably each made the other a present of a book of tablets on the occasion of a New Year's Day—Shakespeare writing sonnet 97 (77, Q) on the first leaf of the book he gave to Mr W. H.

In a note book started by my grandfather, Dr S. Butler, on New Year's day 1837, I found he began by saying that if Hell was paved with good intentions, a full half of the paving would be found to have been laid on New Year's days. There is a sub-didactic, new-leaf, good resolution tone about sonnet 97 which makes me readily accept Malone's suggestion that it was written to accompany a new year's present, and I not less readily accept Mr H. F. Jones's, that on the occasion of some new year Shakespeare and Mr W. H. determined to set up commonplace-books or diaries, and each made the other a present of the book he was to use. The question then is which new year we are to fix upon?

Adhering to the hypothesis that sonnet 1 was written in mid April 1585, and hence sonnet 124 in mid April 1588, there is only one new year possible, i.e. that of 1585-6. If sonnet 1 is dated April 1585, and Q's order is taken as correct, sonnet 117 should be dated September 1586, and sonnets 118, 119 in the following summer, after an absence which had extended over violet-time and rose-time—these two sonnets, therefore, must be dated summer 1587. Between 119, 120 we are told that there was a long interval, and by 124 we are landed in, say, April 1588. Since, then, sonnet 97 comes before sonnet 117, which cannot have been written later than August or September 1586. Jan. 1, 1585-6, is the only New Year's Day on which we can date it, unless we throw over the conclusion arrived at in the preceding chapter to the effect that the order of the sonnets in Q is substantially chronological.

The jealousy series therefore (sonnets 98—113 of my numbering) must be dated in the spring months of 1585-6, or as we should say 1586. They do not seem necessarily to have been written in rapid succession, for line 5 of sonnet 103,

And therefore have I slept in your report

implies that Shakespeare had let some little time go by without writing. We may, however, provisionally set down sonnets 98—113, and also 114—116, as written before Shakespeare left London in the early summer of 1586. Here practically the intimacy between Shakespeare and Mr W. H. (already much shaken in the autumn of 1585) came to an end. It flickered up brilliantly enough more than once, but it died down again as rapidly as it flickered up. One sonnet, 117, as we have just seen, was written in the autumn of 1586, and two, 118, 119, in the summer of 1587; bearing in mind how Shakespeare tells us that there was a long interval between 119 and 120, and further being bound down to 124 as having been written about April 1588, noting, moreover, that sonnets 120—126 are very kindred in feeling, I will date them provisionally as all of them written between, say, the end of March 1587-8 and the end of April 1588.

In order to establish (provisionally) the date of sonnet 97 as Jan. 1, 1585-6, I have been obliged to pass over the more detailed consideration of sonnets 97—126. I will now return to whatever evidence we can collect from these sonnets to show that they were written very early in Shakespeare's career.

That Mr W. H. was the first to inspire his Muse may be gathered from sonnet 98, where Shakespeare says that Mr W. H.'s eyes had "taught the dumb on high to sing and heavy ignorance aloft to fly." Can there be a doubt that he is alluding to himself, and implying that it was his love for

Mr W. H. that set him on to writing, when heretofore he had written nothing? A few lines lower down he writes ;—

> Yet be most proud of that which I compile,
>   Whose influence is thine and born of thee;
> In other's works thou dost but mend the style,
>   And arts with thy sweet graces graced be;
> But thou art all my art and dost advance
> As high as learning my rude ignorance.

Is not this tantamount to saying that but for Mr W. H. he should never have written at all?

Before Shakespeare had written Venus and Adonis and Lucrece, in moments of self-abasement he might, as he does in sonnet 100, call his poems "a saucy bark inferior far" to the work of able and highly educated poets like Thomas Watson, or Daniel, or Chapman; but it is incredible that he should have done so after Venus and Adonis had assured him of that strength which he had felt at times from the outset, and of which he is so fully aware in 101. He might express himself with excess of modesty in a courtly preface to a great nobleman with whom he was yet slightly, if at all acquainted, but after 1593 he would not do so when writing to an intimate friend of his own rank. Nor would he have been so much afraid of the other poet, as he evidently was, after the publication of Venus and Adonis had assured his own position.

In sonnet 120 we find Shakespeare rebuking his Muse for having so long forgotten to speak of that which gives her all her might—i.e. evidently of Mr W. H.,—and for spending her fury "on some worthless song," which in illumining a base subject darkens her own power. Here, then, we have it that whereas when sonnet 96 was written Shakespeare had no other argument than Mr W. H., he had now found other things to write about, but it was songs and not a play on which his Muse had been expending her fury. Mr Lee says, I have no doubt correctly, that Shakespeare's first essays as a playwright

have been with confidence allotted to 1591. To Love's Labour's Lost may reasonably be assigned priority in point of time, of all Shakespeare's productions ("Life of W. Shakespeare," p. 50).

In a note on p. 52, Mr Lee very justly says that the name Armado for the Spanish pedant in Love's Labour's Lost was doubtless suggested by the Armada—the defeat of which was first publicly proclaimed in London, August 15, 1588, but must have been commonly known a full week earlier. I would remind the reader that in the literature of the time the Armada was generally, if not universally, called the Armado. Love's Labour's Lost, then, which has more affinity with the Sonnets than any other of Shakespeare's plays, though some of the other earliest ones run it close, must have been written between 1588 and 1591, and hence,—if I am right (as I shall argue in my next chapter) in supposing the defeat of the Armada to be referred to in 127, not long after the Sonnets. Probably, therefore, Shakespeare was accurate when in 120 he describes himself as having been occupied with lyrical, not dramatic composition, and the introduction of sonnets into Love's Labour's Lost, as well as of passages which at once recall the Sonnets, must be taken not as a foreshadowing of these poems, but as an overflow from them.

Sonnet 124 throws no direct light upon Shakespeare's age at the date when the earlier sonnets were written, but as I have already insisted, it assures us that that date must be fixed about three years earlier; for we have three recurrences of each of the four seasons, expressly stated as having intervened between sonnet 124 and Shakespeare's first acquaintance with Mr W. H.; therefore, we should be, roughly, at the same part of the year as when we started. The question then is, whether or no I was right in starting with spring for sonnet 1.

I think so. For supposing sonnet 1 to have been written in 1585, Jan. 1, 1585-6, may be taken as a fairly certain date for sonnet 97; and it is impossible to crowd sonnets 1—96, with all the various incidents and absences therein indicated, into a less space than three quarters of a year; furthermore the lines,

> Thou that art now the world's fresh ornament,
> And only herald to the gaudy spring,

do after all suggest spring with some force as the most

appropriate season at which to date sonnet 1 ; I feel fairly confident, therefore, in dating sonnet 124 as written in April, or thereabouts,—but whether the April in question be that of 1588 or no, and hence whether my initial hypothesis of April 1585 for sonnet 1 may stand, will depend on what we think concerning sonnet 127.

I have said in Chapter IX that I take sonnets 120—126 to be closely connected. It is in evidence that there was a long interval between sonnets 119 and 120 ; it is also, as we have just seen, in evidence that sonnet 124 was written about April ; 125 and 126 strongly suggest peace offering as an *amende* after long silence ; I therefore date all the sonnets 120—126 as written in the spring—whenever that spring was—that preceded the writing of 127.

In the following chapter I shall attempt to show that this last-named sonnet was written early in August 1588.

From sonnet 125 we gather that whatever may have been the songs on which his muse had been expending the fury referred to in sonnet 120, they can hardly have been of great importance in Shakespeare's opinion, for in 125 we find him saying that his songs and praises were all alike " To one, of one, still snch and ever so." But these words, it would seem, must be taken *cum grano*.

CHAPTER XI.

I HAVE shown in the preceding chapter that there are many reasons for holding the Sonnets to have been the first poems that Shakespeare wrote; indeed I know of nothing that points in any other direction, except his own attempts to make himself out old—and these I believe I have sufficiently shown to fail. If, then, the Sonnets were Shakespeare's earliest essays in literature, there is nothing strange, when we look at Chatterton whose career ended when he was only 18, in supposing that the first sonnets may have been written when Shakespeare was only 21 years old; for such a prolific genius as his was little likely to be long in finding expression of some sort.

This is the utmost that I can pretend so far to have established. Whether or no the dates which I have provisionally assigned to the various sonnets, or groups of sonnets, may be allowed to stand must depend on what we conclude concerning 127 (107 Q). If we can date this, we can date the whole series, much as I have done; otherwise we can date nothing with precision.

It is agreed on all hands that the sonnet in question refers to an event in contemporary history—and it is the only one in which such reference can be detected. It is surprising, therefore, that neither Malone, nor Steevens, nor any of the earlier students of the Sonnets, should have sought to discover what the event was which so powerfully deflected Shakespeare from

his habitual reticence about current national events.   Let me
repeat the sonnet in full :—

> Not mine own fears, nor the prophetic soul
> Of the wide world dreaming on things to come,
> Can yet the lease of my true love control,
> Supposed as forfeit to a confined doom :
> The mortal moon hath her eclipse endured,
> And the sad augurs mock their own presage ;
> Incertainties now crown themselves assured,
> And peace proclaims ŏlives of endless age.
> Now, with the drops of this most balmy time,
> My love looks frosh, and death to me subscribes,
> Since, spite of him, I'll live in this poor rhyme,
> While he insults o'er dull and speechless tribes ;
>   And thou in this shalt find thy monument,
>   When tyrants' crests and tombs of brass are spent.

Never was time of universal apprehension more graphically
portrayed; who but Shakespeare could have brought so vividly
and concisely before us the relief of a nation on finding its
fears groundless after having delivered itself over to the
gloomiest forebodings?   Not England only, but the whole
civilised world was in suspense; no one knew what might
happen; a shadow overhung the throne, and who could say
whether it would pass away, or prove to be the doom and date
of all things?   Shakespeare feared the worst, and as part of
that worst he and Mr W. H. would probably never see one
another again—and lo! the shadow had passed; the prophets
of evil were now laughing at their own fears; every one was
breathing freely, for security seemed permanently assured;
Shakespeare and his friend were to be drawn together as
closely as in the early days of their acquaintance, and while
death is insulting over dull and speechless tribes, Mr W. H.
will find a monument in Shakespeare's verse which shall
outlive the crests of tyrants.

This is what the sonnet comes to when its substance is
considered in prose.   Is there any event, except the Armada,
that occurred during Shakespeare's youth, to which the above
picture will apply with anything like the same force and

accuracy? I may go even further, and ask whether there is any event between 1585 and 1609, to which the sonnet can apply without both doing violence to the most natural meaning of its words, and arbitrarily dating it many years later than the other sonnets ?

We can see how great a scare had been caused by the Armada from the thanksgiving prayer that was read in all churches after it had been defeated. Stow tells us with what admirable resolution both Queen and nation faced the coming danger, but people may be alarmed though brave, and this naïf prayer does not attempt to conceal from the Almighty that the guilty conscience of the nation had "looked for......the execution of that terrible justice by it so much deserved." The enemy had intended "to destroy us, our cities, towns, countries and peoples, and utterly to root out the memory of our nation from off the earth for ever." Happily, it seems, the Almighty was aware that the Spaniards had "offended and do offend as much or more than we," and therefore he had been pleased

to remember mercy towards us, turning our enemies from us, and that dreadful execution which they intended towards us, into a fatherly and most merciful admonition of us, to the amendment of our lives, and to execute justice upon our cruel enemies ; turning the destruction that they intended against us upon their own heads, &c.*

If this is a true picture Shakespeare might well sketch the general apprehension in such a telling touch as "the prophetic soul of the wide world dreaming on things to come," and might well suppose that the lease of his true love for Mr W. H. was to expire very shortly. But as there is no other such sketch, so neither is any such picture to be found, in prayer nor elsewhere, of any event between 1585 and 1609.

Mr Lee thinks differently ; he says that sonnet 127 (107, Q) is apparently the last of the series, and was

penned almost a decade after the mass of its companions, for it makes references that cannot be mistaken to three events that took

---

* Nichols' "Progresses of Queen Elizabeth," ed. 1823, Vol. II., p. 540.

place in 1603—to Queen Elizabeth's death, to the accession of James I, and to the release of the Earl of Southampton, who had been in prison since he was convicted in 1601 of complicity in the rebellion of the Earl of Essex.

I find it easy to avoid discovering reference to any one of the events mentioned by Mr Lee as being referred to in a way "that cannot be mistaken."

The death of Queen Elizabeth? To me the sonnet suggests that she was not only not dead, but had emerged from a time of apparent peril with splendour all undimmed. "Cynthia, (i.e. the moon)," says Mr Lee, "was the Queen's recognised poetic appellation."* No one will deny that Queen Elizabeth is intended by the words, "The mortal moon," but not many will admit that Shakespeare would have compared her to the moon, and have said that she had endured her eclipse, unless he had meant to say that she had endured it as the moon endures it, and had passed from under the shadow with undiminished brightness.

When Anthony, speaking to Cleopatra, but, I presume, speaking of her at the same time, says

> Alack! our terrene moon is now eclipsed,†

he does not say that she had "endured" her eclipse, for the shadow was still upon her.

Granted that the word "eclipse" is sometimes loosely used for "end"; Shakespeare so used it when he made Talbot say to his son,

> Then here I take my leave of thee, fair son,
> Born to eclipse thy life this afternoon.‡

It is open, therefore, to Mr Lee to urge that Shakespeare has used "endured" loosely first, and "eclipse" loosely afterwards; but there is a difference between using a single word— a mere passing note—loosely when the context admits of no mistake, and the making a lame simile when the simile is fully developed. Moreover it is not open to any one to set aside the *primâ facie* meaning of words, until he has shown that

---

this meaning is impossible or highly improbable; and this, naturally enough, Mr Lee has not attempted. He does indeed write :—

There was hardly a verse-writer who mourned her [Elizabeth's] loss that did not typify it as the eclipse of a heavenly body.*

Perhaps not, but though Mr Lee brings forward several passages to support him, he has not quoted one which looks as though in sonnet 127 (107, Q) the moon's having endured her eclipse should mean that she has not endured it, but has succumbed to it.

———

Let us now see on what grounds Mr Lee bases his conclusion that lines 5—8 of 107 Q can only refer to the accession of James I. If the reasoning contained in the few preceding paragraphs is held as sound these lines cannot refer to the accession of Elizabeth's successor, for the Queen had not died. Is it necessary to say more? Still, let us give Mr Lee a full hearing. After quoting the lines last referred to he says :—

It is in almost identical phrase that every pen in the spring of 1603 was felicitating the nation on the unexpected turn of events, by which Elizabeth's crown had passed, without civil war, to the Scottish King, and thus the revolution which had been foretold as the inevitable consequence of Elizabeth's demise was happily averted.†

Some pens no doubt actually did write as Mr Lee says they did, but he has not quoted, nor have I been able to find, anything written before the accession of James, which suggests any such grave alarm as was felt all over England when the Armada was off Plymouth, or in sight of Dover. There is no reference to any such alarm in Bishop Creighton's admirable work on Queen Elizabeth. Turning to the article on Elizabeth in the " Dictionary of National Biography," I find nothing to indicate that the nation had been seriously afraid of civil war

———

* " Life of W. Shakespeare," p. 148.   † Id. p. 147.

upon the Queen's demise.   Going on to the article on James I,
I read :—

James's eye had for some time been fixed upon the English
succession.   His hereditary right, combined with his protestantism,
gave to his claim a weight which left him the only competitor with
any chance of acceptance   *   *   *   At last on 24 March, 1603
Elizabeth died, and James was at once proclaimed King by the
title James I. King of England.

Any previous apprehensions that may have existed were
not thought sufficiently important by the writer to require
particular attention.

Nevertheless some apprehension there undoubtedly was.
In Howe's continuation of " Stow's Annals " we read that the
princes, peers of the land, and privy councillors of estate,
within six hours after Elizabeth's death, proclaimed James I.
at the court gates—I presume at Richmond where the Queen
died, " knowing above all things delays to be most dangerous."*

But it is not clear from Howes what the danger of delay
was ; there is nothing either of undue haste, or of hesitation in
posting up a notice of the Queen's death and of the accession
of James I. at 8 o'clock in the morning, when the Queen had
died six hours earlier.   There was no rising, nor manifestation
of disapproval in any part of the kingdom, nor yet any sign of
dissentient opinion among the lords of the Council, whose
meeting, considering the nature of the event that had just
happened, was very short.   Everything had been cut and dried
beforehand ; Cecil, indeed, though the Queen had been kept in
ignorance of the fact, had been in correspondence with James
during the last two or three years of her life,† and all those
who would have to take action on the Queen's death knew that
he would be proclaimed at once, and be received gladly by the
nation.   Everything, however, owing to Elizabeth's extreme
jealousy of discussion on this subject, was done with the
utmost secrecy—and it is to this cause that what uneasiness
there was among the people must be assigned.   The following

---

* " Stow's Annals," continued by Howes.   Ed. 1615, p. 816.
† Birch's " Memoirs of the reign of Queen Elizabeth," 1754, II., p. 514.

passage, written, by the way, some thirty-six years after the events with which it deals, brings this most clearly out, and is the strongest on Mr. Lee's side that I have been able to find. It runs:—

But nothing did fill foreign nations more with admiration and expectation of this succession than the wonderfull (and by them unexpected) consent of all estates and subjects of England, for the receiving of the King without the least scruple, pause or question; for it had been generally dispersed by the fugitives beyond the seas * * * * that after Elizabeth's decease there must follow nothing in England but confusions interraignes and perturbations of estate, likely far to exceed the ancient calamities of the civil wars between the house of Lancaster and York, by how much more mortal and bloody, when foreign competition should be added to domestic, and divisions for religion to matter of title to the crown; and in special persons the Jesuit (under a disguised name) had not long before published an express treatise; wherein whether his malice made him believe his own fancies, or whether he thought it the fittest way to move sedition, * * * he laboured to display and give colour to all the vain pretences and dreams of succession he could imagine, and thereby possessed many abroad that knew not the affairs with those his vanities.

Neither wanted there divers persons both wise and well affected, who, though they doubted not the undoubted right, yet setting before themselves the ways of the people's harts, guided no less by sudden and temporary winds, than by the natural course of the waters, were not without fear what might be the event, for Queen Elizabeth being a princess of extreme caution, and yet one that loved admiration above safety, and knowing that the declaration of a successor might, in point of safety, be disputable, but in point of admiration and respect assuredly to her disadvantage, from the beginning set it down as a maxim of state to impose a silence touching succession; neither was it only reserved as a secret of state, but restrained by severe laws, that no man should presume to give opinion and maintain argument touching the same. So though the evidence of right drew all the subjects of the land to think one thought, yet the fear of the danger of the law made no man privy to others thoughts; and therefore it rejoiced all men to see so fair a morning of a kingdom, and to be thoroughly secured of former apprehensions, as a man that awaketh out of a fearful dream.

But so it was, that not only the consent, but the applause and joy was infinite, and not to be expressed throughout the realm of England, upon this succession, whereof the consent (no doubt) may be truly ascribed to the clearness of the right; but the general joy alacrity and gratulation were the effects of differing causes:

> (Genealogical history of the Earldom of Sutherland
> by Sir Robert Gordon Bart. Edinburgh 1813,
> pp. 250, 251.)

Returning to Howes, a little lower than the passage last quoted from him, he writes :—

At about 11 o'clock on the same forenoon, [i.e. Mar. 24] at the West side of the high Cross in Cheapside, where were assembled the most part of the English princes, peers, divers principal prelates, an extraordinary and unexpected number of gallant knights, and brave gentlemen of note well mounted, besides the huge number of common persons, all which with great reverence gave attention to the Proclamation, being most distinctly and audibly read by Mr Secretary Cecil, at the end thereof with one consent cried aloud "God save King James," being not a little glad to see their long feared danger so clearly prevented.

From the passages just quoted it would be easy to infer that the nation was more apprehensive than it really was. Doubtless there had been croakers, and doubtless there was a vague fear that things might not go on so smoothly after the Queen's death as they had done before it, but vague and groundless apprehension is one thing, and the presence of an apparently overwhelming force within sight of the English coast is another; the one may have been a fearful dream; the other was a far more fearful reality. Besides, no matter what laws there may be to the contrary, when all the world is of one opinion every one knows pretty well what that opinion is, and how universally it is held—the dream, therefore, is little likely to have been so very fearful after all. Nevertheless what fearfulness there may have been was sure to be exaggerated by poets and courtiers anxious to ingratiate themselves with the new king, and no doubt a good deal of their exaggeration would in time pass current as history.

I repeat, then, that I can find no evidence in anything written before the Queen's death of such general alarm as is manifested in 127 (107 Q); and so far from thinking with Mr Lee that lines 5—8 of that sonnet make a reference "that cannot be mistaken" to a general sense of relief at the accession of James I, if the reference is indeed there, I find it singularly easy to mistake it for reference to the joy of the nation on learning the defeat of the Armada.

———

I will not argue about Mr Lee's contention that the concluding lines of the sonnet above considered refer to the release of Lord Southampton in 1603. I have already given my reasons for thinking that Lord Southampton was not contemplated by Shakespeare in any one of the Sonnets. Let me then briefly contrast the line taken by Mr Lee and that taken by myself.

Mr Lee, leaning upon the broken reed of Lord Southampton's supposed connection with the sonnets, assumes, with no other ground than this assumption, that the mass of the sonnets were written not later than 1594, nor many of them much earlier. Still leaning on this broken reed, he assumes that the line, "supposed as forfeit to a confin'd doom," can have no other reasonable reference than to Lord Southampton's release from prison in 1603. He confirms himself in this opinion by setting aside the *primâ facie* interpretation of the words "The mortal moon hath her eclipse endured," and making them mean that the mortal moon hath not endured her eclipse.

Intrenched in the above given positions, he separates 127 (107, Q) by about ten years from its fellows, which but for the supposed strength of these positions he could not do. This done he finds it easy to declare that the mocking of their own presage by the sad augurs can have no reference but to the relief of the nation on finding that James succeeded Elizabeth without a disturbance which there was no reasonable ground for anticipating. He does all this with the air of a conjurer, who, on the conclusion of some obvious trick, exclaims

that there is no deception, and says of the concluding lines of
the sonnet :—

It is impossible to resist the inference that Shakespeare thus
saluted his patron on the close of his day of tribulation (p. 149).

I again cannot think that most of my readers will find
resistance so difficult as Mr Lee imagines. My own position
is as follows :—

I have shown, from the internal evidence of the Sonnets, a
strong presumption—for I do not pretend that it is more—in
favour of the opinion that Shakespeare wrote the earliest
sonnets when he was about twenty one, i.e. in the spring
of 1585.

I have shown an equally strong presumption, on the same
evidence, for thinking that 127 (107 Q) was written more than
three years after sonnet 1, i.e. very possibly in August 1588.

It is certain that this sonnet expresses the relief of the
nation at deliverance from a threatened danger of the very
gravest kind.

It is also certain that the defeat of the Armada became
known with the first days of August 1588.

Do not these two certainties harmonise so perfectly with
the two presumptions as to raise them to their own rank, or
at any rate to render them so probable that they should be
accepted in default of any more plausible opinion?

I believe they do; nor do I think that competent judges
will find any other fault with my argument than that I have
developed it at great length when simple statement of the
conclusion arrived at should have been enough to carry conviction. Perhaps it should; but if Shakespeare did not know
anything of eminent Shakespearean scholars, in this respect I
have the disadvantage of him.

What date, then, shall we assign to 148 (125, Q) which I
have supposed to bring the series to a conclusion? There is
nothing in sonnets 128—147 (118—124, Q) which gives any
clue to the dates when they were written, but the signs of
growing estrangement between Shakespeare and his friend are
so numerous as to make it difficult to think that many months

or even weeks elapsed between the writing of 127 (107 Q) and 148 (125, Q). In this last sonnet there is a reference to the bearing of a certain canopy, apparently on some very great occasion, over some great personage : Shakespeare seems either to have had some part in the bearing of this canopy, which had given rise to ill-natured remarks, or else to have been maliciously foiled in an attempt to be included among the bearers ; on the whole, I should say the second interpretation of Shakespeare's words is the more probable. In "Stow's Annals" we read as follows :—

The four and twentieth day of November [1588], being Sunday, her Majesty having attendant upon her the Privy Council and Nobility, and other honourable persons as well spiritual as temporal in great number, the French Ambassador, the Judges of the Realme, the heralds, trumpeters, and all on horseback, did come in a chariot-throne made with four pillars behind, to have a canopy, on the top whereof was made a crown imperial, and two lower pillars before, whereon stood a Lion and a Dragon, supporters of the arms of England, drawn by two white horses from Somerset House to the Cathedral church of St Paul, her footmen and pensioners about her: next after rode the Earl of Essex......

Then follow more particulars of the Queen's progress to St Paul's, and how when she got there she kneeled and "made her hearty prayers unto God."   The account continues—

....which prayers being finished, she was, under a rich canopy brought through the long West aisle to her travers in the quire, the clergy singing the Litany: which being ended she was brought to a closet of purpose made out of the North wall of the Church, towards the pulpit cross, where she heard a sermon made by Dr Pierce Bishop of Salisbury, and then returned through the church to the Bishop's Palace, where she dined ; and returned in like manner, but with great light of torches. Stow's "Annals," Ed. 1615, p. 750.

Here, then, we have two canopies born over a great personage on a great occasion, and it does not seem a very forced supposition to think that the footmen who were about the Queen, had some hand in the bearing one or other or both of them, though the pillars would do the greater part of the bearing in the first mentioned canopy. I know what Mr Lee would do if he were arguing my case ; he would say :—

In 125 Q, we have a reference that cannot be mistaken to the canopy borne over Queen Elizabeth when she went in triumph to St Paul's, Nov. 24, 1588, surrounded by her pensioners and footmen. It is impossible to doubt that the footmen would hold on by tassels to the fringe of the canopy as those who follow a French funeral hold on to the pall, and thus be considered as bearers. This is so absolutely conclusive that no other date than a few days after Nov. 24, 1588, can conceivably be assigned to sonnet 125, Q.

Seriously, without pretending to confidence, except in the opinion that the friendship between Shakespeare and Mr W. H. did not endure for many weeks after the defeat of the Armada, I am inclined to think that if Mr Lee had argued as I have supposed, he would not have been so far wrong as I have sometimes found him.

Roughly, then, I date the Sonnets, adhering to the numbers of my text as follows :—

Sonnets 1—97 (1—77, Q) between April and December 31, 1585, or January 1, 1585-6.

98—116 (78—96, Q) between January 1, 1585-6, and early Summer 1586.

117 (97 Q) Autumn 1586.

118, 119 (98, 99, Q) Summer 1587.

120—126 (100—106, Q) say, March 1587-8 and April 1588.

127 (107 Q) about August 8, 1588.

128—148 (108—125, Q) between, say, August 10 and December 1, 1588.

I can affix no dates to the sonnets which I have placed as appendices, except that A seems to belong to the time of the earliest sonnets.

CHAPTER XII.

I HAVE said in Chapter III that Tyrwhitt and Malone thought it probable that Mr W. H.'s surname was Hughes, or Hewes, or Hews, as the name was then indifferently spelt. That his Christian name was William seems at once so generally received and so self-evident that I shall not follow Mr Lee in his, as it seems to me, singularly inconclusive attempts to show that the 'Will' sonnets (135, 136, 143, Q) öontain no play upon the name of Shakespeare's friend, as well as upon his own.

As regards Mr W. H.'s surname being Hughes, there is considerable presumption that this was so, but no William Hughes can be identified with Mr W. H. unless, *inter alia*, we can date his birth as having taken place in 1567 or 1568; and though we know of many William Hughes's, contemporaries of Shakespeare, there is none, except the well-known Bishop of St Asaph, the year of whose birth we can even approximately ascertain. This prelate is out of the question; for he was between 35 and 40 in 1585, and whatever else Mr W. H. may have been we cannot suppose him to have been a Bishop.

As regards other William Hughes's, seven are mentioned in "Notes and Queries" (5th Series, V, p. 443) not one of them suggesting probable identity with Mr W. H. There was a William Hewes who in 1630 signed a deed of release to Bacon Gawdy,* but we do not know how old he then was, and not to know this is to know nothing. Moreover, I cannot

---

* This deed is in the MS. department of the British Museum. Bacon Gawdy was nephew to Sir Edmund Bacon, who left him a legacy of £300.

think that Mr W. H. was likely in 1630 to be in a position to sign a deed of release to a man so well up in the world as Bacon Gawdy. From "State Papers," domestic series, for 1631–1633, I see there was a William Hughes "guardian of Alexander Ha***n," a ward of King Charles. This man, of age unknown, wanted an allowance from the court to repair the chapel of the church of St Mary Cray, Kent. There is another William Hughes indexed in the same volume. We have no clue to his age; he had denied "christian burial at Burford, Co. Salop, to the body of William Fox, a gentleman of an ancient house"; he had also taken the body out of the grave, carried it to Greet in a cart, and there thrown it "near a swine stye." There was a William Hughes, or Hewes (both forms appearing), who after having been "many years" in the navy and served as steward in the Vanguard, Swiftsure, and Dreadnought, applied in 1633-4 for the post of cook, which I learn was rather more highly paid than that of steward; he was appointed, and died in March 1636-7.* This man is quite as likely to have been Mr W. H. as any of the others. There are other William Hughes's, none of them hopeful to be dug out of "State Papers," and Mr Lee mentions a musician of the name William Hughes,† whose existence, I am now informed, is disbelieved in.

Bearing in mind, then, that for one contemporary William Hughes whose name we know, there must have been many who have left no trace, it is not likely, even though Mr W. H.'s name was Hughes, that we shall learn more about him than what the Sonnets and Thorpe's dedicatory address reveal to us.

How much is this? That in the spring of 1585 he was more boy than man, good looking, of plausible attractive manners, and generally popular, goes without saying. It is also plain that his character developed badly, and that boy as he was, before the end of the year he had got himself a bad name. He was vain, heartless, and I cannot think ever cared two straws for Shakespeare, who no doubt bored him;

---

* See "State Papers," domestic series, for 1633-4 and 1636-7.

† "Life of W. Shakespeare," note on p. 93.

but he dearly loved flattery, and it flattered him to bring Shakespeare to heel; moreover, he had just sense enough to know that Shakespeare laid the praise on thicker and more delectably than any one else did, therefore he would not let him go.

In laying, or abetting the laying, of a trap for Shakespeare, we may charitably suppose that he was too young to fully realise the detestable nature of his own action, and he seems to have been bitterly penitent—at any rate for a time. He was forgiven, but before long the intimacy between him and Shakespeare slackened; if I am held to be as approximately right in my dates as I trust I may be, the high fever of Shakespeare's infatuation did not last beyond mid autumn 1585, if, indeed, so long; from that time onwards, though it again ran high at times, it was intermittent—Mr W. H. playing with him as a cat plays with a mouse. There seems to have been a *redintegratio amoris* during the first few days after the defeat of the Armada had become known, but before many weeks had passed there was a final break. Whether, if the two men met in after time, Shakespeare passed Mr W. H. strangely, and scarcely greeted him with that sun his eye, or whether a *modus vivendi* was established between them, we shall never know, but we may be tolerably sure that Shakespeare's love had cast its utmost sum.

This is as much as we can gather from the Sonnets. From December 1588 to some time not very long before 1609 Mr W. H.'s history is a blank, but—say at the end of 1608 for want of a more exact date—he allowed the Sonnets—and we may assume also that wonderful poem, "A lover's complaint"—to pass into Thorpe's hands—the Sonnets being, probably, for reasons given in Chapter XI, in the order in which Shakespeare wrote them. The question arises why he should have done this.

He must have known that the publication would be exquisitely painful to Shakespeare. Ruined love when it is built anew may sometimes, though not often, grow fairer than at first, but the ruins of a ruined love that after having been loved so well but so unwisely had fallen over its rotten foundations many a long year since, and whose object was like enough now as bald and fleshy as he was disreputable—of a love, too, that had been fraught with such a hideous episode—can any sight be conceived more ghastly for one whose nerves were not of brass or hammered steel? One shudders to think how Shakespeare's gorge must have risen at seeing the skull of his dead folly dug up and tossed about in public. To suppose that he sanctioned the unburying is to deny the commonest instincts of humanity to the most human of all poets, and to suppose that Thorpe and Mr W. H. did not know the pain their action would cause, is to place their intelligence on a par with their brutality.

The wonder, however, is, that well as Mr W. H. must have known how heartless his action was, he must also have known that the eternity conferred upon him by our ever-living poet was of a very unenviable kind. Badly as we must think of him, we must credit him with knowing this much, and it is probably because he knew it, that he had kept the Sonnets for twenty years without parting with them. Why, then, after having held them back so long should he have let a low publisher like Thorpe give to the world so much that reflected so severely upon himself? The only explanation I can think of is that he was in great straits for money, and was glad of the few shillings which were all that Thorpe would be likely to give him for the copy.

If he had been well to do, and anxious on mere literary grounds that the Sonnets should not be lost, a very small sum would have enabled him to print them, and keep the edition under his own control. It is not a large assumption to suppose that he would have omitted the few sonnets from which we have alone collected the infamous trap already too often referred to, and a few others from which it appears that he was generally disesteemed. That he did not withhold these points strongly to the opinion that he could not do so—the bargain being that Thorpe was to have the whole series, and to do what he liked with it. I hardly think, however, that Mr W. H. parted with Shakespeare's original MS.; for while most of the *errata* in Q suggest errors of a printer's eye, many strongly suggest the careless listening of one who was writing from dictation. In Chapter IX I have given my reasons for thinking that the misplacement of sundry sonnets in Q is due, not to Mr W. H. but to Thorpe.

There is no reason to suppose that either Mr W. H. or Thorpe bore any ill-will to Shakespeare; money difficulties on the part of the first, and the hope of making a few pounds on that of the other, will explain their action, though nothing can excuse it. Neither of the two men seem to have prospered. Thorpe ("State Papers," domestic series, 1635) probably ended his days in an almshouse at Ewelme—and let us hope that Mr W. H. died peacefully as cook on board the Vanguard.

The worst of it is that all we who read the Sonnets are accessories after the offence. We are receivers of stolen goods; we are as one who opens and pores over a series of letters addressed to another person, and many of them of a most private nature. Shakespeare's letters—for this is what the Sonnets are—have fallen by stealth into our hands; they are the unguarded expression of the inmost feelings of one whose privacy should have been more especially and particularly sacred. Thorpe's iniquity causes us to set aside every known canon of honourable conduct—and yet is there one of us who could find it in his heart to make an honest man of himself by cancelling that iniquity, and wiping the Sonnets out of existence were it in his power to do so?

The doing of such a right would be a wrong greater than that which it was intended to remove. For after all, the greatness of Mr W. H.'s and of Thorpe's guilt is swallowed up in that of the service they have rendered. Their sin must go scot free by reason of its very enormity—as also must ours in partaking with them. One does not know whether to be more thankful for the righteous deed of Heming and Condell, than for the unrighteous one of Thorpe and Mr W. H. If Heming and Condell had not published the First Folio, we should still have had some twenty of Shakespeare's plays, and among these Hamlet—but if Thorpe and Mr W. H. had not been scoundrels, we should have had nothing of the Sonnets, except the two that were published in The Passionate Pilgrim

—and who could have guessed that these were fragments of such a series as that from which we now know that they were derived?

I cannot see that the Sonnets are in any respect less priceless than the Plays, except in so far as they are less in volume. True, they have something more than their intrinsic worth by reason of our knowledge that they heralded Hamlet and The Tempest, but do not these plays gain in equal measure by our knowledge that they were heralded by the Sonnets? Does not each explain how the other should have been possible? Do we not feel on reading Hamlet that even though the Sonnets had been lost we should have had (as we best could) to presuppose them? and do we not, on reading the Sonnets, cease to wonder that the man who could write them should presently have conceived Hamlet? It is little more than a truism to say, that as it is only the writer of the Plays who could have written the Sonnets, so it is only the writer of the Sonnets who could have written the Plays, and that if there had been no Sonnets going before, so neither would there have been a Hamlet or a Tempest following after.

Moreover in the Plays there is a veil at all times over the face of their author. He looms large behind it as the Armada behind sonnet 107 Q; we feel the mightiness of his presence, but we never see him. In the Sonnets we look upon him face to face; there is no let or hindrance to our gazing on the millions of strange shadows that play round him, nor on the millions of shadows that he can lend. We see the man whom of all others we would most wish to see, in all his beauty, in all his sweetness, in all his strength, and, happily, in all his weakness—for in the very refuse of his deeds there is a strength and warrantise of skill which it were ill to lose.

Of course there is another side to all this; let us take it from Hallam :—

Notwithstanding the frequent beauties of these sonnets . . . it is impossible not to wish that Shakespeare had never written them. There is a weakness and folly in all excessive and misplaced affection, which is not redeemed by the touches of nobler sentiments that abound in this long series of sonnets. But there are also faults of a merely critical nature. The obscurity is often such as only conjecture can penetrate; the strain of tenderness and adoration would be too monotonous, were it less unpleasing; and so many frigid conceits are scattered around, that we might almost fancy the poet to have written without genuine emotion, did not a host of other passages attest the contrary.*

There are few at the present day who will not read the above with something like amazement that it could have been written in this century. Tennyson said well,

> The slow sad hours that bring us all things ill,
> And all good things from evil,†

and it not rarely happens that the lot falls upon the very greatest men to be cursed with that inability to think as every man thinks, which shall balance for ill, at any rate for a time, the greatness of their good endowments. The greater the gifts of the good fairies at a man's birth, the more certainly will a bad fairy step in to mar them; the only comfort is, that without its due proportion of knaves and fools the world would be even more knavish and foolish than it is. It would go mad of its own sanity. And after all, when a man is naturally good, there is no such ἐγκράτεια as that which has been begotten in him by a modicum of μανία.

To regret, moreover, that Shakespeare should have written the Sonnets is to regret that he was Shakespeare; we must not wish to tinker such a man as he was; he must be taken as time and circumstance for better or worse determined him, or let alone: his is indeed a case in which it were sinful,

> . . . . . striving to mend
> To mar the subject that before was well?

Happily neither God nor man can do it, for God cannot alter the past.

A man's style is the essence of the man himself. Never truer saying passed the portals of a man's lips than this of Buffon's—for whatever the exact words he spoke may have been, this is what he meant. It is one of the common-places

---

* "Introduction to the literature of Europe"—Murray 1854, Vol. III, p. 40.
† "Love and Duty."

of modern schoolmen to say that the man and his art—whether literature, painting, music, or what not—are not to be taken as one, but that the corrupt tree may bring forth good fruit, and *vice versâ*. There is no truth in this. The corrupt tree may yield specious fruit which shall be sweet, sweet, poison to the tooth of the corrupt taster, but a healthy appetite will have none of it. If the work is wholesome, genial, and robust, whatever faults the worker may have had were superficial, not structural. No man is without sin;

> . . . . where's the palace whereinto foul things
> Sometimes intrude not? Who has a breast so pure,
> But some uncleanly apprehensions
> Keep leets and law days, and in session sit
> With meditations lawful?

I have repeatedly seen it said in these last few years that Love's Labour's Lost—which, as we have seen, was perhaps the earliest of Shakespeare's Plays—contains more personal notes than any of the others. I think this is true, and believe that I detect one of these notes in the words put into the mouth of Biron,

> For every man with his affects is born,
> Not by might mastered, but by special grace.

It is the old saying—The Lord hath mercy on whom he will have mercy and whom he willeth he hardeneth; but if ever a style carried conviction that the grace which should enable its owner to master his affections had not been withheld from him, that style is Shakespeare's. One of the Bishops said of Handel—quoting from Much Ado about Nothing,

The man doth fear God, howsoever it seems not in him by some large jests he will make.

Much Ado about Nothing is not generally reputed an early play, and the context raises no supposition that a personal note was being consciously or even sub-consciously struck; but no words can be more unconsciously personal as applied to Shakespeare himself, than these which Don Pedro half mockingly applies to Benedick. Let us, then, face the truth, the whole truth, but let not either speech or silence suggest, as is now commonly done, a great deal more than the truth concerning him.

One word more. Fresh from the study of the other great work in which the love that passeth the love of women is portrayed as nowhere else save in the Sonnets, I cannot but be struck with the fact that it is in the two greatest of all poets that we find this subject treated with the greatest intensity of feeling. The marvel, however, is this, that whereas the love of Achilles for Patroclus depicted by the Greek poet is purely English, absolutely without taint or alloy of any kind, the love of the English poet for Mr W. H. was, though only for a short time, more Greek than English. I cannot explain this.

And now, at last, let the Sonnets speak for themselves.

SHAKESPEARE'S SONNETS.

—

1.

1585. Spring.]

To Mr W. H., urging him to marry.

From fairest creatures we desire increase
That thereby beauty's *Rose* might never die,
But as the riper should by time decease
His tender heir might bear his memory:
But thou, contracted to thine own bright eyes,   5
Feed'st thy life's flame with self-substantial fuel,
Making a famine where abundance lies,
Thyself thy foe, to thy sweet self too cruel.
Thou that art now the world's fresh ornament
And only herald to the gaudy spring,   10
Within thine own bud buriest thy content
And, tender churl, makest waste in niggarding.
    Pity the world, or else this glutton be,
    To eat the world's due, by the grave and thee.

line 6. Q reads, "Feed'st thy lights flame." Believing that Q was printed from a copy that had been taken down unintelligently by dictation, I have little hesitation in reading as in my text.

line 12. Boswell cites Venus and Adonis, canto 29;—

    "Upon the earth's increase why should'st thou feed,
    Unless the earth with thy increase be fed,
    By law of nature thou art bound to breed,
    That thine may live when thou thyself art dead :
      And so, in spite of death, thou dost survive,
      In that thy likeness still is left alive."

These lines form an epitome, as it were, of the first 17 sonnets.

cf. also Romeo and Juliet, I, i, 223, 4 :—

    Ben.—"Then she hath sworn that she will still live chaste ?"
    Rom.—"She hath, and in that sparing makes huge waste."

                (Malone, communicated by C[apell].)

2.

1585.　Spring.]

To Mr W. H., urging him to marry.

WHEN forty Winters shall besiege thy brow
And dig deep trenches in thy beauty's field,
Thy youth's proud livéry, so gazed on now,
Will be a tatter'd weed of small worth held:
Then, being ask'd where all thy beauty lies,　　　　5
Where all the treasure of thy lusty days,
To say, within thine own deep-sunken eyes,
Were an all-eating shame and thriftless praise.
How much more praise deserv'd thy beauty's use,
If thou couldst answer 'this fair child of mine　　10
Shall sum my count and make my whole excuse,'
Proving his beauty by succession thine!
　　　　This were to be new made when thou art old,
　　　　And see thy blood warm when thou feel'st it cold.

line 4.　"a tatter'd weed" means "a tatter'd garment."　(MALONE.)

line 11.　Q reads, "and make my old excuse."　I adopt Hazlitt's emendation, given in Camb.

For the reasons which convince me that this sonnet can only have been written when Shakespeare was very young, see Chapter X.

3.

1585. Spring.]

To Mr W. H., urging him to marry.

Look in thy glass, and tell the face thou viewest,
Now is the time that face should form another,
Whose fresh repair if now thou not renewest
Thou dost beguile the world, unbless some mother.
For where is she so fair, whose un-ear'd womb   5
Disdains the tillage of thy husbandry?
Or who is he so fond, will be the tomb
Of his self-love, to stop posterity?
Thou art thy mother's glass, and she in thee
Calls back the lovely April of her prime: 10
So thou through windows of thine age shalt see,
Despite of wrinkles, this thy golden time.
  But if thou list remember'd not to be,
  Die single, and thine Image dies with thee.

line 5. To "ear" land is to till it.   See dedication of Venus and Adonis:—"I shall never after eare so barren a land." (MALONE.)

line 8. Malone cites,

——"beauty starved with her severity,
Cuts beauty off from all posterity."

Romeo and Juliet, I, i, 225, 6.

and

"What is thy body but a swallowing grave,
Seeming to bury that posterity
Which by the rights of time thou needs must have,
If thou destroy them not in their obscurity."

Venus and Adonis, canto 127.

line 10. "Prime" means "Spring."   See sonnets 90 and 117.

line 13. Q reads, "But if thou liue remember'd not to be,"; cf. "Be where you list," Sonnet 78 (58, Q) line 9.

———

In Chapter X, I have given my reasons for thinking that this sonnet can only have been written by a very young man.

4.

1585.   Spring.]

To Mr W. H., urging him to marry.

UNTHRIFTY loveliness, why dost thou spend
Upon thyself thy beauty's legacy?
Nature's bequest gives nothing, but doth lend,
And being frank she lends to those are free.
Then, beauteous niggard, why dost thou abuse   5
The bounteous largess given thee to give?
Profitless usurer, why dost thou use
So great a sum of sums, yet canst not live?
For having traffic with thyself alone,
Thou of thyself thy sweet self dost deceive.   10
Then how, when nature calls thee to be gone,
What acceptable *Audit* canst thou leave?
     Thy unus'd beauty must be tomb'd with thee,
     Which, us'd, lives thy executor to be.

line 3.   Steevens cites Milton's Masque at Ludlow Castle:
     "Why should you be so cruel to yourself,
       And to those dainty limbs which nature lent
       For gentle usage and soft delicacy?
       But you invert the covenants of her trust,
       And harshly deal, like an ill borrower,
       With that which you received on other terms."
It appears certain from this that Milton knew the Sonnets.

line 14.   Q reads "Which vsed liues th' executor to be."   I follow
Malone.

5.

1585.   Spring.]

To Mr W. H., urging him to marry.

THOSE hours that with gentle work did frame
The lovely gaze where every eye doth dwell,
Will play the tyrants to the very same
And that un-fair which fairly doth excel:
For never-resting time leads Summer on   5
To hideons winter and confounds him there;
Sap check'd with frost and lusty leaves quite gone,
Beauty o'ersnow'd and bareness every where:
Then, were not summer's distillation left,
A liquid prisoner pent in walls of glass,   10
Beauty's effect with beauty were bereft,
Nor it, or no remembrance what it was:
    But flowers distill'd, though they with winter meet,
    Leese but their show; their substance still lives sweet.

line 4.   "To *unfair* is, I believe, a word of our author's coinage."
(MALONE.)

line 13.   "This is a thonght with which Shakespeare seems to have been much pleased. We find it again in the 54th sonnet [74 of this edition] and in A Midsummer Night's Dream, I, i, 76." (MALONE.)
The passage referred to by Malone runs "But earthlier happy is the rose distill'd, &c."

line 14.   "Leese = lose, a form constantly used by Chaucer."
(WYNDHAM.)

6.

1585. Spring.]

To Mr W. H., urging him to marry.

THEN let not winter's ragged hand deface
In thee thy summer, ere thou be distill'd:
Make sweet some vial; treasure thou some place
With beauty's treasure ere it be self-kill'd.
That use is not forbidden usury   5
Which happies those that pay the willing loan;
That's for thyself to breed another thee,
Or ten times happier, be it ten for one;
Ten times thyself were happier than thou art;
If ten of thine ten times refigur'd thee,   10
Then what could death do, if thou shouldst depart,
Leaving thee living in posterity?
    Be not self-kill'd, for thou art much too fair
    To be death's conquest and make worms thine heir.

line 13. Q reads, "be not self-will'd." I adopt Delius's conjecture
given in the Cambridge edition. See line 4, " ere it be self-kill'd."

7.

1585. Spring.]

To Mr W. H., urging him to marry.

Lo, in the Orient when the gracious light
Lifts up his burning head, each under eye
Doth homage to his new-appearing sight,
Serving with looks his sacred majesty;
And having climb'd the steep up-heavenly hill,   5
Resembling strong youth in his middle age,
Yet mortal looks adore his beauty still
Attending on his golden pilgrimage;
But when from highmost pitch, with weary car,
Like feeble age he reeleth from the day,   10
The eyes, 'fore duteous, now converted are
From his low tract, and look another way:
     So thou, thyself out-going in thy noon,
     Unlook'd on diest unless thou get a son.

lines 3, 4.   Malone cites from Romeo and Juliet I, i, 125, 6,
     " Madam, an hour before the worshipped sun
       Peered forth the golden window of the east."

line 5.   Modern editions generally follow Malone in reading " steep-up
heavenly hill," Q has no hyphen either after " steep " or " up." I follow
Nicholson and Craig, whose conjecture is given in Camb.

8.

1585. Spring.]

To Mr W. H., urging him to marry.

Music to hear? why hear'st thou music sadly?
Sweets with sweets war not, joy delights in joy;
Why lov'st thou that which thou receiv'st not gladly,
Or else receiv'st with pleasure thine annoy?
If the true concord of well tuned sounds   5
By unions married do offend thine ear,
They do but sweetly chide thee, who confounds
In singleness the parts that thou shouldst bear.
Mark how one string, sweet husband to another,
Strikes each in each by mutual ordering;   10
Resembling sire and child and happy mother,
Who, all in one, one pleasing note do sing:
 Whose speechless song, being many, seeming one,
 Sings this to thee; 'thou single wilt prove none.'

line 1. Q reads,
  " Mvsick to heare, why hear'st thou musick sadly,
   Sweets with sweets, &c."
I have sometimes thought that Shakespeare neither knew nor cared
anything about music. He could say pretty things about it, but I have
known many very unmusical people able to do that. I am told that I ought
not to lay much stress on his explaining that when Helena and Hermia
sang the same tune, they did so in the same key, though what he can have
meant by this the learned must determine, for in Shakespeare's time there
were no "keys" in the sense in which we now use the word; when, however, he talks of music having a " dying fall," do what I may, the Lost Chord
comes into my head at once. As for painting, I believe the only artist—if
he can be called an artist—whom Shakespeare ever mentioned was Giulio
Romano. cf. Note on sonnet 24.

9.

1585. Spring.]

To Mr W. H., urging him to marry.

Is it for fear to wet a widow's eye
That thou consum'st thyself in single life?
Ah! if thou issueless shalt hap to die,
The world will wail thee, like a makeless wife!
The world will be thy widow, and still weep   5
That thou no form of thee hast left behind,
When every private widow well may keep
By children's eyes her husband's shape in mind.
Look, what an unthrift in the world doth spend
Shifts but its place, for still the world enjoys it;   10
But beauty's waste hath in the world an end,
And kept unus'd, the user so destroys it.
  No love toward others in that bosom sits
  That on himself such murd'rous shame commits.

line 4. " a makeless wife." " Make " and " Mate " were formerly synonymous. (MALONE.)

line 10. Q reads "shifts but his place," and it is quite possible that Shakespeare wrote " his," for he is not fastidious about inter-changing " his " and " it "—cf. sonnet 111 (91, Q),

  " And every humour hath his adjunct pleasure,
   Wherein it finds a joy above the rest."

I do not think, however, that there can be much doubt that Shakespeare here means " its," not " his."

IO.

1585.   Spring.]

To Mr W. H., urging him to marry.

For shame deny that thou bear'st love to any
Who for thyself art so unprovident.
Grant, if thou wilt, thou art belov'd of many,
But that thou none lov'st is most evident;
For thou art so possess'd with mard'rous hate   5
That 'gainst thyself thou stick'st not to conspire,
Seeking that beauteous roof to ruinate
Which to repair should be thy chief desire.
O, change thy thought, that I may change my mind!
Shall hate be fairer lodged than gentle love?   10
Be, as thy presence is, gracious and kind,
Or to thyself at least kind-hearted prove:
    Make thee another self for love of me,
    That beauty still may live in thine or thee.

line 7.   Steevens cites,
      " Oh, thou that dost inhabit in my breast,
       Leave not the mansion so long tenantless
       Lest, growing ruinous, the building fall,
         *   *   *
       Repair me with thy presence Silvia."
               Two Gentlemen of Verona, V, iv, 7-11.

11.

1585. Spring.]

To Mr W. H., urging him to marry.

As fast as thou shalt wane, so fast thou grow'st
In one of thine from that which thou departest;
And that fresh blood which youngly thou bestow'st
Thou mayst call thine when thou from youth convertest.
Herein lives wisdom, beauty and increase;   5
Without this, folly, age, and cold decay:
If all were minded so, the times should cease,
And threescore years would make the world away.
Let those whom nature hath not made for store,
Harsh, featureless, and rude, barrenly perish: 10
Look whom she best endow'd, she gave thee more:
Which bounteous gift thou shouldst in bounty cherish:
    She carved thee for her seal, and meant thereby
    Thou shouldst print more, not let that copy die.

line 2. I follow Mr Wyndham in taking the meaning to be " So fast will you grow in the person of a son, offspring of that youth which you will yourself be leaving."

line 8. " Years," Q reads " yeare."

line 11. Q reads, " Looke whom she best indow'd, she gave the more." I adopt Malone's emendation. " Look," here, as in sonnet 37, line 13, means " look at," or " consider."

12,

1585. Spring.]

To Mr W. H., urging him to marry.

WHEN I do count the clock that tells the time,
And see the brave day sunk in hideous night;
When I behold the violet past prime,
And sable curls all silver'd o'er with white;
When lofty trees I see barren of leaves,   5
Which erst from heat did canopy the herd,
And Summer's green all girded up in sheaves,
Borne on the bier with white and bristly beard,
Then of thy beauty do I question make
That thou among the wastes of time must go,   10
Since sweets and beauties do themselves forsake
And die as fast as they see others grow;
  And nothing 'gainst Time's scythe can make defence
  Save breed, to brave him when he takes thee hence.

line 4. Q reads, "curls or silver'd ore." Malone's emendation, given in my text, is generally adopted.

Steevens cites Hamlet I, ii, 241, 2,

> "His beard was as I've seen it in his life,
> A sable silver'd."

13.

1585.   Spring.]

To Mr W. H., urging him to marry.

O, THAT you were yourself! but love, you are
No longer yours than you yourself here live:
Against this coming end you should prepare,
And your sweet semblance to some other give.
So should that beauty which you hold in lease   5
Find no determination; then you were
Yourself again after yourself's decease
When your sweet issue your sweet form should bear.
Who lets so fair a house fall to decay,
Which husbandry in honour might uphold   10
Against the stormy gusts of winter's day
And barren rage of death's eternal cold?
    O, none but unthrifts; dear my love you know
    You had a Father; let your Son say so.

lines 4 to 8.   Malone quotes the lines from Venus and Adonis, already given in a note to sonnet 1.

lines 5, 6.   So Daniel in one of his Sonnets, 1592:—
    "...... in beauty's lease expir'd appears
    The date of age, the calends of our death."   (MALONE.)

lines 9, 10.   cf. note on line 7 of sonnet 10.

14.

1585. Spring.]

To Mr W. H., urging him to marry.

NOT from the stars do I my judgement pluck;
And yet methinks I have Astronomy,
But not to tell of good or evil luck,
Of plagues, of dearths, or seasons' quality;
Nor can I fortune to brief minutes tell,   5
Pointing to each his thunder, rain, and wind,
Or say with Princes if it shall go well,
By oft predict that I in heaven find:
But from thine eyes my knowledge I derive,
And, constant stars, in them I read such art,   10
As truth and beauty shall together thrive
If from thyself to store thou wouldst convert;
    Or else of thee this I prognosticate:
    Thy end is Truth's and Beauty's doom and date.

line 8. "Dr. Sewell reads, perhaps rightly, ' By aught predict.' "
                                 (MALONE.)

"Predict" of course means "prediction." cf. Love's Labour's Lost, I, i, 153,
    "For every man with his affects is born
      Not by might mastered, but by special grace."
Here " affects " of course means " affections."

line 9. Steevens cites,
    " from women's eyes this doctrine I derive."
                        Love's Labour's Lost, IV, iii, 302.

15.

1585. Spring.]

To Mr W. H., urging him to marry.

WHEN I consider every thing that grows
Holds in perfection but a little moment,
That this huge stage presenteth nought but shows
Whereon the Stars in secret influence comment;
When I perceive that men as plants increase,   5
Cheered and check'd even by the self-same sky,
Vaunt in their youthful sap, at height decrease,
And wear their brave state out of memory;
Then the conceit of this inconstant stay
Sets you most rich in youth before my sight,   10
Where wasteful time debateth with decay,
To change your day of youth to sullied night;
   And all in war with Time for love of you,
   As he takes from you I engraft you new.

line 12. Steevens cites K. Richard III, IV, iv, 16,
      " Hath dimm'd your infant morn to aged night."

16.

1585.　Spring.]

To Mr W. H., urging him to marry.

But wherefore do not you a mightier way
Make war upon this bloody tyrant, time?
And fortify yourself in your decay
With meaus more blessed than my barren rhyme?
Now stand you on the top of happy hours,　　　　5
And many maiden gardens yet unset
With virtuous wish would bear you living flowers
Much liker than your painted connterfeit:
So shonld the lines of life that life repair,
Which this time's pencil, nor my pupil pen,　　　　10
Neither in inward worth nor outward fair,
Can make you live yourself in eyes of men.
　　　To give away yourself keeps yourself still,
　　　And you must live, drawn by your own sweet skill.

line 7.　Q reads, "beare your liuing flowers." I adopt Malone's emendation.

line 9.　"The lines of life" perhaps are "living pictures," viz. "children." Anon.　Quoted with approval by Malone.

line 10.　Q reads, "which this (time's pensel or my pupill pen)." I have adopted Hudson's emendation (Camb.), with the addition that I read "nor" instead of "or."　The meaning is, "which neither any painter now living, nor my as yet unpractised pen can &c."

———

In Chapter X, I have urged that we have evidence here that the Sonnets were written very early in Shakespeare's career.

17.

1585. Spring.]

To Mr W. H., urging him to marry.

Who will believe my verse in time to come
If it were fill'd with your most high deserts?
Though yet, heaven knows, it ·is but as a tomb
Which hides your life and shows not half your parts.
If I could write the beauty of your eyes   5
And in fresh numbers number all your graces,
The age to come would say 'this Poet lies,
Such heavenly touches ne'er touch'd earthly faces.'
So should my papers, yellow'd with their age,
Be scorn'd, like old men of less truth than tongue, 10
And your true rights be term'd a Poet's rage
And stretched metre of an Antique song:
    But were some child of yours alive that time,
    You should live twice;—in it and in my rhyme.

Here Shakespeare once for all desists from urging his friend to marry.

———

18.

1585. Say, Early Summer.]

To Mr W. H., promising him an eternity of fame.

SHALL I compare thee to a Summer's day?
Thou art more lovely and more temperate:
Rough winds do shake the darling buds of May
And Summer's lease hath all too short a date:
Sometime too hot the eye of heaven shines   5
And often is his gold complexion dimm'd;
And every fair from fair sometime declines,
By chance or nature's changing course untrimm'd;
But thy eternal Summer shall not fade
Nor lose possession of that fair thou ow'st;   10
Nor shall death brag thou wander'st in his shade
When in eternal lines to time thou grow'st:
    So long as men can breathe or eyes can see,
    So long lives this, and this gives life to thee.

line 8. untrimmed, " i.e. divested of ornament; so in King John
III, i, 209, 'a new untrimmed bride.'"   (MALONE.)

19.

1585. Summer.]

To Mr W. H., forbidding Time to age him.

DEVOURING time, blunt thou the Lion's paws
And make the earth devour her own sweet brood:
Pluck the keen teeth from the fierce Tiger's jaws
And burn the long-lived Phœnix in her blood;
Make glad and sorry seasons as thou fleet'st,   5
And do whate'er thou wilt, swift-footed time,
To the wide world and all her fading sweets,
But I forbid thee one most heinous crime:
O, carve not with thy hours my love's fair brow
Nor draw no lines there with thine antique pen;   10
Him in thy course untainted do allow
For beauty's pattern to succeeding men.
    Yet do thy worst, old Time: despite thy wrong,
    My love shall in my verse ever live young.

20.

1585. Summer.]

To Mr W. H. An extravagant eulogy of his as yet almost
feminine beauty.

A WOMAN'S face with nature's own hand painted
Hast thou, the Master-Mistress of my passion;
A woman's gentle heart, but not acquainted
With shifting change, as is false women's fashion;
An eye more bright than theirs, less false in rolling,   5
Gilding the object whereupon it gazeth;
A man in hue, all *Hues* in his controlling,
Which steals men's eyes and women's souls amazeth.
And for a woman wert thou first created,
Till nature as she wrought thee fell a-doting,   10
And by addition me of thee defeated
By adding one thing to my purpose nothing:
     But since she prick'd thee out for women's pleasure,
     Mine be thy love, and thy love's use their treasure.

line 1. It is plain Mr W. H. has as yet no hair on his face. See also
sonnet 73 line 8.

line 7. Q reads " A man in hew all *Hews* in his controwling." Hue is
here put for " beauty" as " color" is in " formose puer nimium ne crede
colori." cf. 102 line 5, and 124 line 11. I have said in Chapter III that
this line inclined both Tyrwhitt and Malone to think that Mr W. H.'s
surname was Hughes, or Hewes, or Hews, as the name was then
indifferently spelt.

21.

1585. Summer.]

To Mr W. H., extolling his beauty.

So is it not with me as with that Muse
Stirr'd by a painted beauty to his verse,
Who heaven itself for ornament doth use
And every fair with his fair doth rehearse,
Making a couplement of proud compare   5
With Sun and Moon, with earth and sea's rich gems,
With April's first-born flowers, and all things rare
That heaven's air in this huge rondure hems.
O, let me, true in love, but truly write,
And then believe me, my love is as fair   10
As any mother's child, though not so bright
As those gold candles fix'd i' the heavens are.
  Let them say more that like of hearsay well;
  1 will not praise that purpose not to sell.

line 12. Staunton (*Athenæum* Jan. 3, 1874) pointed out that Shakespeare is not likely to have written "heaven's air" here, and thus repeat a combination of words which he had used but four lines earlier. I have, therefore, emended as in my text. "Are" in Shakespeare's time I am told would be a legitimate rhyme for "fair."

line 14. cf. Love's Labour's Lost IV, iii, 240, "To things of sale a seller's praise belongs."   (STEEVENS.)

———

Mr Wyndham thinks that Shakespeare had some particular poet in view when he wrote this sonnet. I do not think he meant more than "I am not one of those poets who &c."

22.

1585.   Summer.]

*To Mr W. H., urging that he and Shakespeare have
exchanged hearts.*

MY glass shall not persuade me I am old,
So long as youth and thou are of one date;
But when in thee time's furrows I behold,
Then look I death my days should expiate.
For all that beauty that doth cover thee   5
Is but the seemly raiment of my heart,
Which in thy breast doth live, as thine in me:
How can I then be elder than thou art?
O, therefore, love, be of thyself so wary
As I, not for myself, but for thee will,   10
Bearing thy heart, which I will keep so chary
As tender nurse her babe from faring ill.
  Presume not on thy heart when mine is slain;
  Thou gav'st me thine, not to give back again.

line 4 "'Then do I expect,' says Shakespeare, 'that death should fill
up the measure of my days.' The word expiate is used nearly in the same
sense in the tragedy of Locrine 1595:—
  'Lives Sabren yet to expiate my wrath,'
i.e. fully to satisfy my wrath."   (MALONE.)

23.

1585.   Summer.]

*To Mr W. H.   Shakespeare's looks must say what
he cannot bring his tongue to speak.*

As an unperfect actor on the stage
Who with his fear is put beside his part,
Or some fierce thing replete with too much rage
Whose strength's abundance weakens his own heart;
So I, for fear of trust, forget to say   5
The perfect ceremony of love's rite,
And in mine own love's strength seem to decay,
O'ercharg'd with burthen of mine own love's might.
O, let my looks be then the eloquence
And dumb presagers of my speaking breast;   10
Who plead for love and look for recompense,
More than that tongue that less hath more express'd,
  O, learn to read what silent love hath writ:
  To hear with eyes belongs to love's fine wit.

line 9.   **Q** reads "Oh let my books be then &c."   Malone mentions the
reading "looks" as suggested to him by C[apell] but rejects it.   Boswell
complains of him justly for having done so.   I note that Camb. passes over
Boswell's and C[apell']s opinion without reference.   All that Camb. says
is "9 *books*] *Looks* Sewell."

line 12.   **Q** reads, "More than that tonge that more hath more
exprest."   Staunton, finding this unintelligible would read "More than that
tongue that love hath more expressed." Bearing in mind Shakespeare's love
of antithesis I venture to read as in my text.   "Less" I take to mean "less
recompense than my eyes are now pleading for."

24.

1585. Summer.]

*To Mr W. H. A Sonnet full of conceits after the
manner of the time.*

MINE eye hath play'd the painter and hath steel'd
Thy beauty's form in table of my heart;
My body is the frame wherein 'tis held,
And perspective it is best Painter's art.
For through the Painter must you see his skill,   5
To find where your true Image pictur'd lies;
Which in my bosom's shop is hanging still,
That hath his windows glazed with thine eyes.
Now see what good turns eyes for eyes have done:
Mine eyes have drawn thy shape, and thine for me 10
Are windows to my breast where-through the Sun
Delights to peep, to gaze therein on thee;
  Yet eyes this cunning want to grace their art,
  They draw but what they see, know not the heart.

line 1.   Q reads, "and hath steeld," which I suppose means "traced
with a steel point."   Camb. reads, "and hath stell'd," with Dyce and Capell
MS.   I know of no verb "to stell," and such rhymes as "steel'd" and
"held" are not uncommon in the Sonnets.   cf. "Noon" and "son,"
sonnet 7; "convertest" and "departest," sonnet 11; "unset" and
"counterfeit," sonnet 16; "come" and "tomb," sonnet 17; "wrong" and
"young," sonnet 19.
 line 4.   cf. Richard II, II, ii, 18.
   " Like perspectives which rightly gazed upon,
    Show nothing but confusion, eyed awry
    Distinguish form."
In Holbein's " Ambassadors " in the National Gallery there is a familiar
example of one of these "perspectives" in the distorted skull which disfigures
the foreground of the picture.   In the time of the Commonwealth, there
were many such "perspectives" painted on tables.   When a silver tankard
was put upon a table so painted the reflection on its round surface showed
a portrait of King Charles.   That Shakespeare should call such a trick as
this "best painter's art" shows that in matters of painting he was profoundly
ignorant.   How could he possibly be anything else?
 line 14.   I am much tempted to read " show not the heart."

25.

1585. Summer.]

To Mr. W. H., rejoicing that Shakespeare, and apparently Mr. W. II. as well, do not move in an exalted sphere.

LET those who are in favour with their stars
Of public honour and proud titles boast,
Whilst I, whom fortune of such triumph bars,
Unhonour'd joy in that I honour most.
Great Princes' favourites their fair leaves spread   5
But as the Marigold at the sun's eye,
And in themselves their pride lies buried
For at a frown they in their glory die.
The painful warrior famoused for fight,
After a thousand victories once foil'd   10
Is from the book of honour razed quite,
And all the rest forgot for which he toil'd:
    Then happy I, that love and am beloved
    Where I may not remove nor be removed.

line 4. Q reads " Vnlookt for ioy." Bearing in mind the carelessness with which this sonnet was printed in line 9, and Shakespeare's great love of antithesis, I have ventured to adopt Staunton's bold conjecture, *Athenæum,* Jan. 3, 1874.

line 9. Q reads " famosed for worth." Considerations of rhyme making this impossible Malone followed Theobald in emending as in my text.

––––––––––––

26.

1585. Summer.]

To Mr W. H. Possibly accompanying a letter containing the
six next following sonnets.

LORD of my love, to whom in vassalage
Thy merit hath my duty strongly knit,
To thee I send this written ambassage
To witness duty, not to show my wit:
Duty so great, which wit so poor as mine   5
May make seem bare, in wanting words to show it,
But that I hope some good conceit of thine
In thy soul's thought, all naked, will bestow it;
Till whatsoever star that guides my moving
Points on me graciously with fair aspect,   10
And puts apparel on my tatter'd loving
To show me worthy of thy sweet respect:
     Then may I dare to boast how I do love thee;
     Till then not show my head where thou mayst prove
     me.

line 12. Q reads " of their sweet respect." Malone, who suggested the
present reading, explains that the abbreviations formerly in use for " their "
and " thy " closely resembled one another. He makes the same correction
repeatedly in other sonnets.

27.

1585. Summer.]

To Mr W. H.   Written during travel.

WEARY with toil, I haste me to my bed,
The dear repose for limbs with travail tir'd;
But then begins a journey in my head,
To work my mind when body's work's expir'd:
For then my thoughts, from far where I abide,   5
Intend a zealous pilgrimage to thee,
And keep my drooping eyelids open wide
Looking on darkness which the blind do see;
Save that my soul's imaginary sight
Presents thy shadow to my sightless view,   10
Which, like a jewel hung in ghastly night,
Makes black night beauteous and her old face new.
  Lo, thus, by day my limbs, by night my mind,
  For thee and for myself no quiet find.

line 2.   Modern editions generally read " with travel tired," but I have kept Q's " trauaill."

line 10.   Q reads " presents their shaddoe."   Malone again emends. See note on preceding sonnet.

line 11.   Malone cites from Romeo and Juliet, I., v., 48,
   " Her beauty hangs upon the cheek of night,
   Like a rich jewel in an Æthiop's ear."

28.

1585.   Summer.]

To Mr W. H.   A sequel to the preceding.

How can I then return in happy plight,
That am debarr'd the benefit of rest?
When day's oppression is not eas'd by night,
But day by night, and night by day, oppress'd?
And each, though enemies to either's reign,   5
Do in consent shake hands to torture me;
The one by toil, the other to complain
How far I toil, still farther off from thee.
I tell the Day, to please him, thou art bright
And dost him grace when clouds do blot the heaven;
So flatter I the swart-complexion'd night,   10
When sparkling stars twire not, thou gild'st the even.
 But day doth daily draw my sorrows longer,
 And night doth nightly make grief's strength seem
  stronger.

line 9.   The sense is " I flatter day by telling him that even when there
is no sun, you are still there to grace him, and so with night when there are
no stars."

line 14.   Q reads " greefe's length seeme stronger."   I follow the
Cambridge edition, which adopts Dyce's emendation.

29.

1585. Summer.]

To Mr W. H. His friend's love is the only solace of his
otherwise almost hopeless state.

WHEN, in disgrace with Fortune and men's eyes
I all alone beweep my outcast state,
And trouble deaf heaven with my bootless cries
And look upon myself and curse my fate,
Wishing me like to one more rich in hope,   5
Featured like him, like him with friends possess'd,
Desiring this man's art and that man's scope,
With what I most enjoy contented least;
Yet in these thoughts myself almost despising,
Haply I think on thee, and then my state   10
Like to the Lark at break of day arising
From sullen earth, sings hymns at Heaven's gate;
    For thy sweet love remember'd, such wealth brings
    That then I scorn to change my state with Kings.

30.

1585.　Summer.]

To Mr W. H.　Written in the same key as the preceding.

WHEN to the Sessions of sweet silent thonght
I summon up remembrance of things past,
I sigh the lack of many a thing I sought
And with old woes new wail my dear time's waste:
Then can I drown an eye, unus'd to flow,　　　5
For precious friends hid in death's dateless night,
And weep afresh love's long since cancell'd woe,
And moan the expense of many a vanish'd sight:
Then can I grieve at grievances foregone,
And heavily from woe to woe tell o'er　　　10
The sad account of fore-bemoaned moan,
Which I new pay as if not paid before.
　　　But if the while I think on thee, dear friend,
　　　All losses are restored and sorrows end.

line 8.　Malone contends that "sight" here means "sigh," which he believes to have been sounded hard in Shakespeare's time.　He adds that by the word "expense," Shakespeare alludes to an old notion that sighing was prejudicial to health.

31.

1585. Summer.]

To Mr W. H.   A sequel to the preceding sonnet.

THY bosom is endeared with all hearts
Which I by lacking have supposed dead;
And there reigns Love, and all Love's loving parts,
And all those friends which I. thought buried.
How many a holy and obsequious tear   5
Hath dear religious love stol'n from mine eye,
As interest of the dead, which now appear
But things remov'd that hidden in thee lie!
Thou art the grave where buried love doth live
Hung with the trophies of my lovers gone,   10
Who all their parts of me to thee did give;
That due of many now is thine alone:
    Their images I lov'd I view in thee,
    And thou, all they, hast all the all of me.

line 8.   Q reads, "hidden in there lie."   The emendation "thee" is by
Gildon.   (CAMB.)

32.

1585.   Summer.]

*To Mr W. H.   Probably a peroration to the preceding five
sonnets.*

IF thou survive my well-contented day,
When that churl death my bones with dust shall cover,
And shalt by fortune once more re-survey
These poor rude lines of thy deceased Lover,
Compare them with the bett'ring of the time,   5
And though they be outstripp'd by every pen
Reserve them for my love, not for their rhyme
Exceeded by the height of happier men.
O, then vouchsafe me but this loving thought:
"Had my friend's Muse grown with his growing age,
A dearer birth than this his love had brought,   11
To march in ranks of better equipage:
    But since he died, and Poets better prove,
    Theirs for their style I'll read, his for his love."

line 7.   "*Reserve* is the same as *preserve*; so in Pericles, 'Reserve that
excellent complexion'" (Malone).   See also sonnet 105 (85, Q) line 2.

line 10.   Q reads, "Had my friend's Muse growne with this growing
age," I see from the Cambridge edition that the emendation "his," adopted
by Hudson, was proposed in MS. by Capell, but erased.   Malone evidently
intended to read "his," though he has not done so.

Between the writing of this sonnet and the next (121, Q), there has been
a catastrophe.   For the nature of this, and for the reasons which have led
me to place 121 Q here, see chapter ix.

33 [121, Q].

1585.   Probably August.]

*To Mr W. H.   Written by Shakespeare before he had calmed
down after the catastrophe referred to in preceding note.*

'TIS better to be vile than vile esteem'd,
When not to be receives reproach of being;
And the just pleasure lost, which is so deem'd
Not by our feeling, but by others' seeing:
For why should others' false adulterate eyes   5
Give salutation to my sportive blood?
Or on my frailties why are frailer spies,
Which in their wills count bad what I think good?
No, I am that I am, and they that level
At my abuses reckon up their own;   10
I may be straight though they themselves be bevel;
By their rank thoughts my deeds must not be shown,
    Unless this general evil they maintain—
    All men are bad and in their badness feign.

lines 1 to 4. ˌThese lines make it clear that Shakespeare's offence never
went beyond intention.

line 14.   Q reads, "and in their badness reign."   But I can make no
sense of this.   The sense I take to be, "I am not to be judged by the rank
thoughts of these men, unless, indeed, they are prepared to admit that all
men are bad, but pretend to be better than they are.   For if they admit this,
it does not matter much what they say."   I am, however, by no means
confident that I understand the passage.

34 [33, Q].

1585.   Probably August.]

To Mr W. H.   Shakespeare forgives his friend.

FULL many a glorions morning have I seen
Flatter the mountain-tops with sovereign eye,
Kissing with golden face the meadows green,
Gilding pale streams with heavenly alchemy;
Anon permit the basest clouds to ride   5
With ugly rack on his celestial face,
And from the forlorn world his visage hide,
Stealing unseen to west with his disgrace:
Even so my Sun one early morn did shine
With all-triumphant splendour on my brow,   10
But, out, alack! he was but one hour mine,
The region cloud hath mask'd him from me now.
       Yet him for this my love no whit disdaineth;
       Suns of the world may stain when heaven's sun
          staineth.

line 6.   "*Rack* is the fleeting motion of clouds."   (MALONE.)

line 8.   Q reads "with this disgrace," I follow Hudson and accept
S. Walker's conjecture (Camb.)

line 12.   Mr Wyndham quotes several passages from Shakespeare in
which the word "region" is used as denoting the air generally.

35 [34, Q].

1585.   Probably August.]

To Mr W. H.   A sequel to the preceding sonnet.

WHY didst thou promise such a beauteous day
And make me travel forth without my cloak,
To let base clouds o'ertake me in my way,
Hiding thy bravery in their rotten smoke?
'Tis not enough that through the cloud thou break   5
To dry the rain on my storm-beaten face,
For no man well of such a salve can speak
That heals the wound and cures not the disgrace:
Nor can thy shame give physic to my grief;
Though thou repent, yet I have still the loss: 10
The offender's sorrow lends but weak relief
To him that bears the strong offence's cross.
    Ah, but those tears are pearl which thy love sheds,
    And they are rich and ransom all ill deeds.

line 12.   Q reads "the strong offenses losse." This would make "loss"
rhyme to "loss"; the emendation "cross" is Malone's.

36.

1585. Probably August.]

To Mr W. II.   A sequel to the preceding sonnets.

LET me confess that we two must be twain
Although our undivided loves are one:
So shall those blots that do with me remain,
Without thy help, by me be borne alone.
In our two loves there is but one respect,   5
Though in our lives a separable spite,
Which, though it alter not love's sole effect,
Yet doth it steal sweet hours from love's delight.
I may not evermore acknowledge thee
Lest my bewailed guilt should do thee shame,   10
Nor thou with public kindness honour me
Unless thou take that honour from thy name:
    But do not so; I love thee in such sort,
    As thou being mine, mine is thy good report.

line 6. " Separable " = " separating." (MALONE.)

lines 13, 14. These two lines occur also as the concluding lines of sonnet 116 (96, Q).

37,

1585. Probably August.]

*To Mr W. H. A sequel to the three preceding sonnets;
Shakespeare appears to be now lame.*

As a decrepit father takes delight
To see his active child do deeds of youth,
So I, made lame by Fortune's dearest spite,
Take all my comfort of thy worth and truth;
For whether beauty, birth, or wealth, or wit, 5
Or any of these all, or all, or more,
Entitl'd in thy parts do crowned sit,
I make my love engrafted to this store:
So then I am not lame, poor, nor despis'd,
Whilst that this shadow doth such substance give 10
That I in thy abundance am suffic'd
And by a part of all thy glory live.
  Look what is best, that best I wish in thee:
  This wish I have; then ten times happy me!

line 3. Malone argues that the lameness spoken of here, and again in
line 9, is metaphorical, as also the poverty and despised state alluded to in
line 9. I accept the lameness, poverty, and contempt as literally true for
this period of Shakespeare's life. It does not follow that he had been lame
long, nor yet that he remained so. He may have been "made lame" by
some accident—possibly in a recent scuffle. Line 3 of sonnet 109 (Q, 89),
("Speak of my lameness, and I straight will halt") indicates that though
Shakespeare did not consider himself lame a year or so later, when we may
suppose sonnet 109 (Q, 89) to have been written, his friends could still see
that he limped occasionally. As for his being poor and despised, I do not
think he would say that he was either of these things, unless they were true.

line 7. Q reads, "their." See note on sonnet 26. "Entitled means, I
think, *ennobled.*" (MALONE.)

38.

1585.   Probably second half of August.]

To Mr W. H.   Apparently closely connected with the
following sonnet.

How can my Muse want subject to invent,
While thou dost breathe, that pour'st into my verse
Thine own sweet argument, too excellent
For every vulgar paper to rehearse?
O, give thyself the thanks if aught in me   5
Worthy perusal stand against thy sight;
For who's so dumb that cannot write to thee,
When thou thyself dost give invention light?
Be thou the tenth Muse, ten times more in worth
Than those old nine which rhymers invocate;   10
And he that calls on thee, let him bring forth
Eternal numbers to outlive long date.
    If my slight Muse do please these curious days,
    The pain be mine, but thine shall be the praise.

line 13. It is plain that some, at any rate, even of these early sonnets
were recited among Shakespeare's friends, and much admired; but I can
find no evidence to suggest that copies were going about in MS.

39.

1585.   Probably second half of August.]

*To Mr W. H.   Apparently a sequel to the preceding sonnet;
the separation referred to in sonnet 36 is still continued.*

O, HOW thy worth with manners may I sing,
When thou art all the better part of me?
What can mine own praise to mine own self bring?
And what is't but mine own when I praise thee?
Even for this let us divided live,   5
And our dear love lose name of single one,
That by this separation I may give
That due to thee which thou deservest alone.
O absence, what a torment wouldst thou prove,
Were it not thy sour leisure gave sweet leave   10
To entertain the time with thoughts of love,
Which time and thought so sweetly doth deceive,
    And that thou teachest how to make one twain,
    By praising him here who doth hence remain!

line 12.   Q reads " which time and thoughts so sweetly dost deceive."
Malone's emendation " doth " has been generally adopted.   Malone adds
" *Thought* in ancient language meant *melancholy*."

    line 13.   cf. The Phœnix and Turtle,
           So they loved as love in twain
           Had the essence but in one;
           Two distincts, division none,
           Number there in love was slain.

40 [127, Q],

1585.   Probably September.]

Concerning Shakespeare's Mistress.

IN the old age black was not counted fair,
Or if it were, it bore not beauty's name;
But now is Black, beauty's successive heir,
And Beauty slander'd with a bastard shame:
For since each hand hath put on Nature's power,   5
Fairing the foul with Art's false borrow'd face,
Sweet beauty hath no home, no holy bower,
But is profan'd, if not lives in disgrace.
Therefore my Mistress' brows are Raven black,
Her eyes so suited, and they mourners seem   10
At such who, not born fair, no beauty lack,
Slandering Creation with a false esteem:
    Yet so they mourn, becoming of their woe,
    That every tongue says beauty should look so,

line 7.   Q reads "Sweet beauty hath no name."

lines 9, 10.   Q reads,
    "Therefore my mistress' eyes are raven black,
      Her eyes so suited............"

Staunton conjectured that "brows" should be read in line 10, but I prefer to read it in line 9 with Sidney Walker and Delius, whose reading I learn from Camb.

Steevens writes:—"The reader will find almost all that is said here on the subject of complexion repeated in Love's Labour's Lost, IV, iii, 258-61,
    'O, if in black my lady's brow be deck'd,
      It mourns that painting and usurping hair
      Should ravish doters with a false aspect;
      And therefore is she born to make black fair.' "

It is the brow that is black here.   Steevens evidently felt that the play was repeating the sonnet, not the sonnet the play.

41 [128, Q].

1585. Probably September.]

To Shakespeare's Mistress.

How oft when thou, my music, music play'st
Upon that blessed wood whose motion sounds
With thy sweet fingers, when thou gently sway'st
The wiry concord that mine ear confounds,
Do I envy those Jacks that nimble leap   5
To kiss the tender inward of thy hand,
Whilst my poor lips, which should that harvest reap,
At the wood's boldness by thee blushing stand!
To be so tickled they would change their state
And situation with those dancing chips   10
O'er whom thy fingers walk with gentle gait,
Making dead wood more blest than living lips.
   Since saucy Jacks so happy are in this,
   Give them thy fingers, me thy lips to kiss.

lines 11 and 14. Malone again corrects Q, which reads " O'er whome
their fingers walke," and " me their lips."

It has been argued from this sonnet that Shakespeare's mistress was
highly accomplished. One would like to have heard whether she could do
more than strum. And one would also like to know how far Shakespeare
was qualified to judge. The sonnet is conventional, and does not suggest
a writer whose ear was likely to be much confounded by either concord or
discord, however wiry.

42 [130, Q].

1585. Probably September.]

Concerning Shakespeare's Mistress—A satire on the amatory sonnets of the time.

My Mistress' eyes are nothing like the Sun;
Coral is far more red than her lips' red:
If snow be white, why then her breasts are dun;
If hairs be wires, black wires grow on her head.
I have seen Roses damask'd, red and white,   5
But no such Roses see I in her cheeks;
And in some perfumes is there more delight
Than in the breath that from my Mistress reeks.
I love to hear her speak, yet well I know
That Music hath a far more pleasing sound: 10
I grant I never saw a goddess go,
My Mistress when she walks treads on the ground:
    And yet, by heaven, I think my love as rare
    As any she belied with false compare.

line 10. Here again we become suspicious about Shakespeare's love of music. He is not discriminating. How often when we ask people whether they like music are we not assured that they adore it, and on enquiring what kind of music they like best, receive the answer " any music."

It was not so with the perfumes in line 7. It was not " any perfumes," but " some perfumes."

43 [131, Q].

1585.   Probably September.]

*Addressed to Shakespeare's Mistress, but not, one would
imagine, shown to her.*

Thou art as tyrannous, so as thou art,
As those whose beauties proudly make them cruel;
For well thou know'st to my dear doting heart
Thou art the fairest and most precious Jewel.
Yet, in good faith, some say that thee behold,   5
Thy face hath not the power to make love groan:
To say they err I dare not be so bold
Although I swear it to myself alone.
And to be sure that is not false I swear,
A thousand groans, but thinking on thy face,   10
One on another's neck do witness bear
Thy black is fairest in my judgement's place.
    In nothing art thou black save in thy deeds,   X
    And thence this slander, as I think, proceeds.

lines 13, 14. The obviously genuine almost fierceness of these two lines
at the conclusion of a conventional sonnet recall the concluding lines
of 45 (137, Q), and also the abrupt changes of tone in the ending of the
highly unconventional sonnets 139, 140, and 148 (147, 148, and 125, Q).

44 [132, Q].

1585.   Probably September.]

*To Shakespeare's Mistress—probably shown to her instead of
the preceding sonnet, which is much the same in substance.*

THINE eyes I love, and they as pitying me,
Knowing thy heart torments me with disdain,
Have put on black and loving mourners be,
Looking with pretty ruth upon my pain.
And truly not the morning Sun of Heaven   5
Better becomes the grey cheeks of the East,
Nor that full Star that ushers in the Even
Doth half that glory to the sober West,
As those two mourning eyes become thy face:
O, let it then as well beseem thy heart   10
To mourn for me, since mourning doth thee grace,
And suit thy pity 'like in every part.
    Then will I swear beanty herself is black,
    And all they foul that thy complexion lack.

line 2.   Q reads " Knowing thy heart torment me with disdaine."
Camb. follows Benson's edition of 1640, which reads as in my text.
Malone reads " knowing thy heart, torment me," &c.

line 12.   Q reads " And sute thy pity like in euery part." I adopt
Allen's conjecture given in Camb.

45 [137, Q].

1585. Probably September.]

An occasional sonnet concerning Shakespeare's Mistress, who has displeased him.

Thou blind fool, love, what dost thou to mine eyes
That they behold and see not what they see?
They know what beauty is, see where it lies,
Yet what the best is, take the worst to be.
If eyes corrupt by over-partial looks   5
Be anchor'd in the bay where all men ride,
Why of eyes' falsehood hast thou forged hooks
Whereto the judgement of my heart is tied?
Why should my heart think that a several plot
Which my heart knows the wide world's common place?
Or mine eyes seeing this, say this is not,   11
To put fair truth upon so foul a face?   X
    In things right true my heart and eyes have erred,
    And to this false plague are they now transferred.

line 9. "a several plot." cf. Love's Labour's Lost, II, i, 223.

    " My lips are no common, though several they be."

See Malone's notes on the meaning of a "several" or "severell" plot as contrasted with a common plot.

46 [138, Q].

1585.   Probably September.]

An occasional sonnet on the subject of Shakespeare's Mistress.

WHEN my love swears that she is made of truth,
I do believe her though I know she lies,   ✕
That she might think me some untutor'd youth
Unlearned in the world's false subtleties.
Thus vainly thinking that she thinks me young   5
Although she knows my days are past the best,
Simply I credit her false-speaking tongue;
On both sides thus is simple truth suppress'd.
But wherefore says she not she is unjust?
And wherefore say not I that I am old?   10
O, love's best habit is in seeming trust,
And age in love loves not to have years told:
    Therefore I lie with her and she with me,
    And in our faults by lies we flatter'd be.

"This sonnet is also found (with some variations) in The Passionate Pilgrim, a collection of verses printed as Shakespeare's in 1599."

(MALONE.)

The version given in **The Passionate Pilgrim** is as follows:

    When my love swears that she is made of truth,
    I do believe her, though I know she lies,
    That she might think me some untutor'd youth,
    Unskilful in the world's false *forgeries*
    Thus vainly thinking that she thinks me young,
    Although *I know* my *years be* past the best,
    I smiling credit her false-speaking tongue,
    Outfacing faults in love with love's ill rest,
    But wherefore says *my love that* she is *young?*
    And wherefore say not I that I am old?
    O, love's best habit is *a soothing tongue,*
    And age in love loves not to have years told.
      Therefore *I'll* lie with *love* and *love* with me,
      Since that our faults *in love thus smother'd* be.

I have italicised the variations as Malone has done.

47 [139, Q].

1585.   Probably September.]

To Shakespeare's Mistress, who is now enamoured of some one
else—presumably of Mr W. H.

O CALL not me to justify the wrong
That thy unkindness lays upon my heart;
Wound me not with thine eye, but with thy tongue;
Use power with power, and slay me not by Art.
Tell me thou lov'st elsewhere, but in my sight,   5
Dear heart, forbear to glance thine eye aside;
What need'st thou wound with cunning, when thy might
Is more than my o'er-press'd defence can bide?
Let me excuse thee; ah, my love well knows
Her pretty looks have been mine enemies;   10
And therefore from my face she turns my foes
That they elsewhere might dart their injuries:
    Yet do not so, but since I am near slain,
    Kill me outright with looks and rid my pain.

line 3.   Malone cites Romeo and Juliet II, iv, 13, 14,
"Alas poor Romeo, he is already dead! Stabbed with a white wench's
black eye."
Steevens cites King Henry VI, Pt. III, V, vi, 26,
    "Ah kill me with thy weapon not with words."

48 [140, Q].

1585.　Probably September.]

*To Shakespeare's Mistress, who is now enamoured of some one
else—presumably of Mr W. H.*

Be wise as thou art cruel, do not press
My tongue-tied patience with too much disdain;
Lest sorrow lend me words, and words express
The manner of my pity-wanting pain.
If I might teach thee wit, better it were　　　　　5
Though not to love, yet, love, to tell me so;
As testy sick men, when their deaths be near,
No news but health from their Physicians know;
For if I should despair I should grow mad,
And in my madness might speak ill of thee;　　　　　10
Now this ill-wresting world is grown so bad,
Mad slanderers by mad ears believed be.
　　That I may not be so, nor thou belied,
　　Bear thine eyes straight, though thy proud heart go
　　wide.

49 [141, Q].

1585.   Probably September.]

*To Shakespeare's mistress, but hardly, one would think, shown
to her.*

In faith, I do not love thee with mine eyes,
For they in thee a thousand errors note;
But 'tis my heart that loves what they despise,
Who, in despite of view, is pleased to dote;
Nor are mine ears with thy tongue's tune delighted,   5
Nor tender feeling to base touch is prone,
Nor taste, nor smell, desire to be iuvited
To any sensual feast with thee alone:
But my five wits nor my five senses can
Dissuade one foolish heart from serving thee,   10
Who leaves unsway'd the likeness of a man
Thy proud heart's slave and vassal wretch to be:
 Only my plague thus far I count my gain,
 That she that makes me sin awards me pain.

line 6.   Q reads " Nor tender feeling to base touches prone."

line 11.   The meaning is—" No argument from wits or senses can
dissuade my heart from serving you; unswayed by anything that either wits
or senses can urge my heart as it were unmans itself, and is contented
to be your drudge."

line 14.   The meaning I take to be—" I shall suffer less for my sin
hereafter, for I get some of the punishment coincidently with the offence."

50 [142, Q].

1585. Probably September.]

To Shakespeare's mistress, who is now enamoured of some else
—presumably of Mr W. H.—who does not respond to
her desires.

Love is my sin, and thy dear virtue hate,
Hate of my sin, grounded on sinful loving:
O, but with mine compare thou thine own state,
And thou shalt find it merits not reproving;
Or, if it do, not from those lips of thine,   5
That have profan'd their scarlet ornaments
And seal'd false bonds of love as oft as mine,
Robb'd others' beds' revenues of their rents.
Be it lawful I love thee, as thou lov'st those
Whom thine eyes woo as mine importune thee: 10
Root pity in thy heart, that, when it grows,
Thy pity may deserve to pitied be.
        If thou dost seek to have what thou dost chide,
        By self-example mayst thou be denied!

lines 1, 2. The sense is, " My sin is love, and your virtue is hatred—
hatred of my sin which is based upon my love for you."

line 13. Q reads " If thou doost seeke to haue what thou doost hide."
The emendation " chide " is by Staunton, and appeared in the *Athenæum,*
Mar. 14, 1874.

51 [143, Q].

1585. Probably September.]

*To Shakespeare's Mistress, who is now enamoured of a young
man named Will—presumably Mr W. H.—who will
have nothing to say to her.*

Lo, as a careful housewife runs to catch
One of her feather'd creatures broke away,
Sets down her babe, and makes all swift dispatch
In pursuit of the thing she would have stay;
Whilst her neglected child holds her iu chase,   5
Cries to catch her whose busy care is bent
To follow that which flies before her face,
Not prizing her poor infant's discontent:
So runn'st thou after that which flies from thee
Whilst I thy babe chase thee afar behind;   10
But if thou catch thy hope, turn back to me
And play the mother's part, kiss me, be kind:
    So will I pray that thou mayst have thy *Will*,
    If thou turn back and my loud crying still.

line 13. I agree with the many commentators who have held that none
other than Mr W. H. is here intended.

52 [144, Q].

1585.　Probably September.]

*An occasional sonnet concerning Mr W. H. and Shakespeare's
Mistress, but not addressed to either of them.*

Two loves I have of comfort and despair
Which like two spirits do suggest me still:
The better angel is a man right fair,
The worser spirit a woman colour'd ill.
To win me soon to hell, my female evil　　　　5
Tempteth my better angel from my side,
And would corrupt my saint to be a devil,
Wooing his purity with her foul pride.
And whether that my angel be turn'd fiend
Suspect I may, yet not directly tell;　　　　10
But being both from me, both to each friend,
I guess one angel in another's hell:
　　Yet this shall I ne'er know, but live in doubt,
　　Till my bad angel fire my good one out.

"This sonnet was printed in The Passionate Pilgrim, 1599, with some
slight variations." (MALONE.)

line 6. The Passionate Pilgrim reads "side" as in my text. Q has
"sight."

line 9. The Passionate Pilgrim reads "feend." Q has "finde."

line 11. The Passionate Pilgrim reads "both to me." Q has "both
from me," as in my text.

line 13. The Passionate Pilgrim reads "The truth I shall not know."
I have retained the text of Q, as most editors have done.

53 [135, Q].

1585. Probably September.]

*Written by Shakespeare for Mr W. H. (who has now changed
his mind) to give to Shakespeare's Mistress (who is now in
her turn coy) as though written by himself.*

WHOEVER hath her wish, thou hast thy *Will*
And *Will* to boot, and *Will* in overplus ;
More than enough am I that vex thee still,
To thy sweet will making addition thus.
Wilt thou, whose will is large and spacious   5
Not once vouchsafe to hide my will in thine ?
Shall will in others seem right gracious,
And on my will no fair acceptance shine ?
The sea, all water, yet receives rain still
And in abundance addeth to his store ;   10
So thou, being rich in *Will*, add to thy *Will*
One will of mine, to make thy large *Will* more.
     Let no unkindness fair beseechers kill ;
     Think all but one, and me in that one *Will*.

line 1. The *Will* here I imagine to be Shakespeare.

line 2. Both the *Wills* I take to be Mr W. H.

line 8. Q reads " in my will."

lines 11 and 12. Each of the three *Wills* in these lines I take to be
Shakespeare.

I suspect the " will " in line 4 to be a printer's error for *Will* i.e. Shakespeare, but cannot build on a suspicion of a printer's error. " Will," without
capital or italics means " desire " all through this sonnet.

line 13. Q reads "Let no vnkinde, no faire beseechers kill." I am told
that the abbreviation " ne," with an elongated e, was in common use for
" nesse " at the close of the 16th century. If this " ne " in the MS. was ever
so little detached from the foregoing part of the word, it would corrupt
readily into the text of Q.

54 [136, Q].

1585.   Probably September.]

*Written by Shakespeare for Mr W. H. to give to his (Shake-
peare's) Mistress, as though written by himself.*

If thy soul check thee that I come so near,
Swear to thy blind soul that I was thy *Will*,
And will, thy soul knows, is admitted there;
Thus far for love, my love-suit, sweet fulfil.
Will will fulfil the treasure of thy love,   5
Ay, fill it full with wills, and my will one.
In things of great receipt with ease we prove
Among a number one is reckon'd none;
Then in the number let me pass untold,
Though in thy store's account I one must be;   10
For nothing hold me, so it please thee hold
That nothing me a some-thing, sweet, to thee:
    Make but my name thy love, and love that still,
    And then thou lov'st me, for my name is *Will*.

line 2.   The *Will* I take to be intended for Shakespeare.   As also the
Will in line 5.

line 6.   Q reads, "I fill it full with wils."   The emendation is Malone's.

line 8.   Steevens cites Romeo and Juliet I, ii, 32,
    "........of many mine being one,
    May stand in numbers, though in reckoning none."

55 [151, Q].

1585.   Probably September.]

*Presumably written by Shakespeare for Mr W. H. to give to
his (Shakespeare's) Mistress, as though written by himself.*

Love is too young to know what conscience is;
Yet who knows not conscience is born of love?
Then, gentle cheater, urge not my amiss,
Lest guilty of my faults thy sweet self prove:
For, thou betraying me, I do betray   5
My nobler part to my gross body's treason;
My soul doth tell my body that he may
Triumph in love; flesh stays no farther reason,
But rising at thy name doth point out thee
As his triumphant prize. Proud of this pride,   10
He is contented thy poor drudge to be,
To stand in thy affairs, fall by thy side.
        No want of conscience hold it that I call
        Her 'love' for whose dear love I rise and fall.

56 [35, Q].

1585.   Probably September.]

To Mr W. H.   Shakespeare affects to consider himself hurt in
that Mr W. H. has been (so he believes) enjoying his
Mistress.   He admits, however, that he has him-
self been accessory to this.

No more be griev'd at that which thou hast done,
Roses have thorns and silver fountains mud;
Clouds and eclipses stain both Moon and Sun,
And loathsome canker lives in sweetest bud.
All men make faults, and even I in this;—   5
Authorizing thy trespass with compare,
Myself corrupting, salving thy amiss,
Excusing thy sins—more than thy sins are;
For to thy sensual fault I bring in sense—
Thy adverse party is thy Advocate—   10
And 'gainst myself a lawful plea commence:
Such civil war is in my love and hate,
    That I an accessory needs must be
    To that sweet thief which sourly robs from me.

line 4.   cf. Two Gentlemen of Verona I, i, 41, 2,
         "..........as in the sweetest bud
        The eating canker dwells,"
and, again, sonnet 90 (70, Q) line 7.

line 8.   Q reads "their" for both the "thy's" in this line.   See note on
sonnet 26.   I understand the meaning to be " All men do wrong sometimes,
as, indeed, I myself am now doing—inasmuch as finding examples that will
justify your act, becoming an accessory to it, glozing it over, and making
excuses for it, are worse sins than any of which you are guilty."

line 9.   "The passage divested of its jingle seems designed to express
this meaning 'Towards thy exculpation I bring in the aid of .... my
sense.' "   (STEEVENS.)

line 13.   I imagine Shakespeare to be referring to the fact that he had
written sonnets for W. H. to give the lady as though they were his own.

57 [40, Q].

1585. Probably September.]

To Mr W. H., condoning everything, but giving him a hint that he may very possibly find the lady not all that he could wish.

TAKE all my loves, my love, yea, take them all;
What hast thou then more than thou hadst before?
No love, my love, that thou mayst true love call;
All mine was thine before thou hadst this more.
Then, if for my love thou my love receivest,   5
I cannot blame thee for my love thou usedst;
But yet be blamed, if thou thyself deceivest
By wilful taste of what thyself refusedst.
I do forgive thy robbery, gentle thief,
Although thou steal thee all my poverty;   10
And yet, love knows, it is a greater grief
To bear love's wrong than hate's known injury.
    Lascivious grace, in whom all ill well shows,
    Kill me with spites, yet we must not be foes.

lines 6 and 8. Q reads "usest" and "refusest." A man cannot "wilfully" taste what at the same time he is "refusing." If my text is admitted the sense will be, "do not blame me if you find this lady troublesome, you refused her for some time, and it is nobody's doing but your own that you now take up with her." The emendation also gets rid of the having four consecutive lines ending in "est."

line 7. Q reads "this selfe." The emendation is given in Camb. as by Gildon.

58 [41, Q].

1585.   Probably September.]

To Mr W. H., excusing him, and at the same time mildly upbraiding him.

THOSE petty wrongs that liberty commits,
When I am sometime absent from thy heart,
Thy beauty and thy years full well befits,
For still temptation follows where thou art.
Gentle thou art, and therefore to be won,   5
Beauteous thou art, therefore to be assailed;
And when a woman woos, what woman's son
Will sourly leave her till she have prevailed?
Ay me! but yet thou mightst, my sweet, forbear,
And chide thy beauty and thy straying youth,   10
Who lead thee in their riot even there
Where thou art forc'd to break a twofold truth,
    Hers, by thy beauty tempting her to thee,
    Thine, by thy beauty being false to me.

line 1. Q reads "pretty wrongs." I take Bell's emendation from Camb.

line 5. Malone cites from I Hen. VI, V, iii, 77,
      " She's beautiful, and therefore to be woo'd;
      She is a woman, therefore to be won."
cf. also, Titus Andronicus II, i, 82, 83,
      " She is a woman, therefore may be woo'd;
      She is a woman, therefore may be won."

line 8. Q reads " he." Malone accepts Tyrwhitt's emendation "she," which is generally adopted.

line 9. Q reads "my seate forbeare." I follow Malone in reading as in my text.

59 [42, Q].

1585.   Probably September.]

To Mr W. H., affecting to be more hurt than he really is.

THAT thou hast her, it is not all my grief,
And yet it may be said I loved her dearly;
That she hath thee is of my wailing chief,
A loss in love that touches me more nearly.
Loving offenders, thus I will excuse ye: 5
Thou dost love her because thou know'st I love her;
And for my sake even so doth she abuse me,
Suffering my friend for my sake to approve her.
If I lose thee, my loss is my love's gain,   \
And losing her, my friend hath found that loss;   10
Both find each other, and I lose both twain,
And both for my sake lay on me this cross:
　　　But here's the joy: my friend and I are one;
　　　Sweet flattery! then she loves but me alone.

As regards this and the two preceding sonnets see quotation from
St Evremond Chap. ix, p 73.

line 2.   One cannot help surmising that with equal truth "it might be
said " that Shakespeare did not love her very dearly.

lines 9, 10.   cf. Two Gentlemen of Verona II, vi, 20, 21,
　　　　　" If I keep them, I needs must lose myself;
　　　　　If I lose them, thus find I by my loss."

60 [134, Q].

1585.   Probably September.]

*To Shakespeare's Mistress, whose conquest of Mr W. H. is
now supposed to have been completed.*

So, now I have confess'd that he is thine
And I myself am mortgag'd to thy will;
Myself I'll forfeit, so that other mine
Thou wilt restore, to be my comfort still:
But thou wilt not, nor he will not be free,   5
For thou art covetous and he is kind;
He learn'd but surety-like to write for me
Under that bond that him as fast doth bind.
The statute of thy beauty thou wilt take,
Thou usurer, that put'st forth all to use,   10
And sue a friend came debtor for my sake;
So him I lose through my unkind abuse.
  Him have I lost; thou hast both him and me:
  He pays the whole, and yet am I not free.

line 9. "'Statute' has here its legal signification—that of a security or
obligation for money." (MALONE.)

61 [133, Q].

1585.   Probably September.]

To Shakespeare's Mistress, who has been found troublesome
both by Mr W. H. and Shakespeare.

BESHREW that heart that makes my heart to groan
For that deep wound it gives my friend and me!
Is't not enough to torture me alone,
But slave to slavery my sweet'st friend must be?
Me from myself thy cruel eye hath taken,   5
And my next self thou harder hast engross'd:
Of him, myself, and thee, I am forsaken—
A torment thrice threefold thus to be cross'd.
Prison my heart in thy steel bosom's ward,
But then my friend's heart let my poor heart bail;   10
Whoe'er keeps me, let my heart be his guard,
Thou canst not then use rigour in my Jail;
   And yet thou wilt; for I, being pent in thee,
   Perforce am thine, and all that is in me.

line 4. "Slave to slavery" I suppose means nothing more than "so
utterly enslaved that he could not be more so though he were slave to
slavery itself."

62 [152, Q].

1585.   Probably September.]

Written by Shakespeare for Mr W. H. to give to Shakespeare's
Mistress (who has dismissed him after a brief experience)
as though written by himself.

In loving thee thou know'st I am forsworn,
But thou art twice forsworn, to me love swearing;
In act thy bed-vow broke, and new faith torn,
In vowing new hate after new love bearing.
But why of two oaths' breach do I accuse thee   5
When I break twenty! I am perjur'd most,
For all my vows are oaths but to misuse thee
And all my honest faith in thee is lost:
For I have sworn deep oaths of thy deep kindness,
Oaths of thy love, thy truth, thy constancy;   10
And, to enlighten thee, gave eyes to blindness
Or made them swear against the thing they see;
   For I have sworn thee fair; more perjur'd I,
   To swear against the truth so foul a lie!

I agree with Mr Wyndham in thinking that the connection between
Mr W. H. and Shakespeare's mistress was of short duration. Her love for
him had been but recent, and already she was hating him. Whether the
disappointment was on her side or on Mr W. H.'s does not appear, but I
suspect it to have been on the lady's, for from sonnet 90 (Q, 70) it appears
that Mr W. H.'s youth has not been stained, and from 114 (Q, 94) we
learn that he does "not do the thing" he "most doth show," and that
though he moves others he is "himself as stone, unmoved, cold, and to
temptation slow."

   line 13. Q reads "more perjurde eye." The emendation "I" is
Malone's.

63 [43, Q].

1585.   Probably September.]

To Mr W. H.   Written during travel.

When most I wink, then do mine eyes best see,
For all the day they view things unrespected;
But when I sleep, in dreams they look on thee,
And, darkly bright, are bright in dark directed.
Then thou, whose shadow shadows doth make bright, 5
How would thy shadow's form form happy show
To the clear day with thy much clearer light,
When to unseeing eyes thy shade shines so!
How would, I say, mine eyes be blessed made
By looking on thee in the living day,   10
When in dead night thy fair imperfect shade
Through heavy sleep on sightless eyes doth stay!
    All days are nights to me, till I see thee,
    And nights bright days when dreams do show thee me.

line 11.   Q reads, "When in dead night their faire imperfect shade."
The emendation "thy" is Malone's—see note on sonnet 26.

line 13.   Q reads "All daies are nights to see."   I have adopted
Malone's suggested emendation "me."

64 [44, Q].

1585.　Probably October.]

To Mr W. H.　Written during travel.

IF the dull substance of my flesh were thought
Injurious distance should not stop my way;
For then, despite of space, I would be brought
From limits far remote, where thou dost stay.
No matter then although my foot did stand　　　5
Upon the farthest earth remov'd from thee;
For nimble thought can jump both sea and land
As soon as think the place where he would be.
But, ah, thought kills me, that I am not thought,
To leap large lengths of miles when thou art gone, 10
But that, so much of earth and water wrought,
I must attend time's leisure with my moan,
　　　Receiving nought by elements so slow
　　　But heavy tears, badges of either's woe.

line 11.　i.e. "being so thoroughly compounded of these two ponderous
elements." (MALONE.)　Malone also cites Hen. V, III, vii, 23, " He is pure
air and fire, and the dull elements of earth and water never appear in him."

65 [45, Q].

1585.   Probably October.]

To Mr W. H.   A continuation of the preceding sonnet.

THE other two, slight air and purging fire,
Are both with thee, wherever I abide;
The first my thought, the other my desire,
These present-absent with swift motion slide.
For when these quicker Elements are gone   5
In tender Embassy of love to thee,
My life, being made of four, with two alone
Sinks down to death, oppress'd with melancholy;
Until life's composition be recur'd
By those swift messengers return'd from thee,   10
Who even but now come back again, assur'd
Of thy fair health, recounting it to me:
   This told, I joy; but then no longer glad,
   I send them back again and straight grow sad.

line 7.   Steevens cites Much Ado About Nothing,
      "Does not our life consist of the four elements?"

line 12.   Q reads "of their faire health."   Malone again corrects.

66 [46, Q].

1585.   Probably October.]

*To Mr W. H.   Apparently still written during a time of
absence.*

MINE eye and heart are at a mortal war
How to divide the conquest of thy sight;
Mine eye my heart thy picture's sight would bar,
My heart mine eye the freedom of that right.
My heart doth plead that thou in him dost lie,   5
A closet never pierc'd with crystal eyes;
But the defendant doth that plea deny
And says in him thy fair appearance lies.
To 'cide this title is impanneled
A quest of thoughts, all tenants to the heart,   10
And by their verdict is determined
The clear eye's moiety and the dear heart's part:
    As thus; mine eye's due is thine outward part
    And my heart's right thine inward love of heart.

In lines 3, 8, Q reads "their" instead of "thy."   See Malone's
explanation as given in note to sonnet 26.

line 9.   Q reads "to side this title."   The emendation "'cide" is
Sewell's.   (Camb.)

67 [47, Q].

1585. Probably October.]

To Mr W. H.   A sequel to the preceding sonnet.

BETWIXT mine eye and heart a league is took,
And each doth good turns now unto the other:
When that mine eye is famish'd for a look,
Or heart in love with sighs himself doth smother,
With my love's picture then my eye doth feast   5
And to the painted banquet bids my heart;
Another time mine eye is my heart's guest
And in his thoughts of love doth share a part:
So, either by thy picture or my love,
Thyself away are present still with me;   10
For thou not farther than my thoughts canst move,
And I am still with them and they with thee;
   Or if they sleep, thy picture in my sight
   Awakes my heart to heart's and eye's delight.

68 [48, Q].

1585.   Probably October.]

To Mr W. H.   Still written during absence.

How careful was I when I took my way,
Each trifle under truest bars to thrust
That to my use it might unused stay
From hands of falsehood, in sure wards of trust!
But thou, to whom my jewels trifles are,   5
Most worthy comfort, now my greatest grief,
Thou, best of dearest and mine only care,
Art left the prey of every vulgar thief.
Thee have I not lock'd up in any chest,
Save where thou art not, though I feel thou art,   10
Within the gentle closure of my breast,
From whence at pleasure thou mayst come and part;
    And even thence thou wilt be stol'n, I fear,
    For truth proves thievish for a prize so dear.

line 11.   Boswell quotes from Venus and Adonis, canto 131,
        " Lest the deceiving harmony should run
        Into the quiet *closure of my breast.*"

69 [49, Q].

1585.   Probably October.]

To Mr W. H.   Growing out of the last three lines of the
preceding sonnet.

AGAINST that time, if ever that time come,
When I shall see thee frown on my defects,
When as thy love hath cast his utmost sum,
Call'd to that audit by advis'd respects;
Against that time when thou shalt strangely pass   5
And scarcely greet me with that sun, thine eye,
When love, converted from the thing it was,
Shall reasons find of settled gravity;
Against that time do I ensconce me here
Within the knowledge of mine own desert,   10
And this my hand against myself uprear,
To guard the lawful reasons on thy part:
    To leave poor me thou hast the strength of laws,
    Since why to love I can allege no cause.

70 [50, Q].

1585.　Probably October.]

*To Mr W. H.　Apparently written while Shakespeare was on
a journey.*

How heavy do I journey on the way,
When what I seek, my weary travel's end,
Doth teach that ease and that repose to say,
'Thus far the miles are measur'd from thy friend!'
The beast that bears me, tired with my woe,　　　5
Plods dully on, to bear that weight in me
As if by some instinct the wretch did know
His rider loved not speed, being made from thee:
The bloody spur cannot provoke him on
That sometimes anger thrusts into his hide;　　　10
Which heavily he answers with a groan,
More sharp to me than spurring to his side;
　　　For that same groan doth put this in my mind;
　　　My grief lies onward, and my joy behind.

line 6.　Q reads "Plods duly on."　The emendation is Malone's.

line 14.　"My grief lies onward."　Is it possible that he was on his way
to Stratford?

71 [51, Q].

1585.   Probably October.]

To Mr W. H.   A continuation of the preceding sonnet.

THUS can my love excuse the slow offence
Of my dull bearer when from thee I speed:
From where thou art why should I haste me thence?
Till I return, of posting is no need.
O, what excuse will my poor beast then find,   5
When swift extremity can seem but slow?
Then should I spur though mounted on the wind,
In winged speed no motion shall I know:
Then can no horse with my desire keep pace,
Therefore desire, of perfect'st love being made,   10
Shall need no dull flesh in his fiery race,
But love, for love, thus shall excuse my jade;
   Since from thee going he went wilful-slow,
   Towards thee I'll run, and give him leave to go.

line 11.   Q reads, "Shall naigh noe dull flesh in his fiery race." Malone
has, "Shall neigh (no dull flesh) in his fiery race," but strongly suspects
corruption.   Camb. reads "Shall neigh—no dull flesh—&c," but gives the
emendation by Kinnear which I have adopted in my text.   I take the
meaning to be:—"My desire to be with you will be so great, that I shall
need no such dull flesh as that of my 'dull bearer' to convey me to you, but
love will find an excuse for my poor beast which he would never have been
able to discover for himself.   Knowing, then, how slow he went when he
was taking me from you, I will excuse him altogether; I will turn him adrift
and will run all the way to you on foot."

72 [52, Q].

1585. Probably late Autumn.]

*To Mr W. H.   Written after Shakespeare's return, and
excusing himself for not coming to see his friend so
frequently as heretofore.*

So am I as the rich, whose blessed key
Can bring him to his sweet up-locked treasure,
The which he will not every hour survey,
For blunting the fine point of seldom pleasure.
Therefore are feasts so solemn and so rare,   5
Since, seldom coming, in the long year set,
Like stones of worth they thinly placed are,
Or captain Jewels in the carcanet.
So is the time that keeps you as my chest,
Or as the wardrobe which the robe doth hide,   10
To make some special instant special blest
By new unfolding his imprison'd pride.
   Blessed are you, whose worthiness gives scope,
   Being had, to triumph, being lack'd, to hope.

line 8. "The carcanet was an ornament worn round the neck."
                              (MALONE.)

73 [53, Q].

1585.   Probably late Autumn.]

To Mr W. H.   A peace-offering of abundant flattery.

WHAT is your substance, whereof are you made,
That millions of strange shadows on you tend?
Since every one, hath every one, one shade.
And you, but one, can every shadow lend.
Describe *Adonis*, and the counterfeit   5
Is poorly imitated after you;
On *Helen's* cheek all art or beauty set,
And you in *Grecian* tires are painted new:
Speak of the spring and foison of the year,
The one doth shadow of your beauty show,   10
The other as your bounty doth appear;
And you in every blessed shape we know.
  In all external grace you have some part,
  But you like none, none you, for constant heart.

line 3.   I keep the punctuation of Q.

line 7.   Q reads " all art of beautie."

line 8.   From this as also from line 1 of sonnet 20 it is plain that
Mr W. H. had still no hair on his face.

74 [54, Q].

1585.   Probably late Autumn.]

To Mr W. H.   Apparently suggested by the last line of the
preceding sonnet.

O, ʜᴏᴡ much more doth beauty beauteous seem
By that sweet ornament which truth doth give!
The Rose looks fair, but fairer we it deem
For that sweet odour which doth in it live.
The Canker-blooms have full as deep a dye   5
As the perfumed tincture of the Roses,
Hang on such thorns, and play as wantonly
When summer's breath their masked buds discloses:
But, for their virtue only is their show,
They live unwoo'd and unrespected fade,   10
Die to themselves. Sweet Roses do not so;
Of their sweet deaths are sweetest odours made:
    And so of you, beauteous and lovely youth,
    When that shall fade, my verse distills your truth.

line 14.   Q reads " When that shall vade, by verse distils your truth."
I follow Malone's reading, and if he had read "When thou shalt fade," I
should have followed him too, despite the "your" later on in the line.
cf. Sonnet 24 for indiscriminate use of " you" and "thou," and the last two
lines of 124 (Q, 104).   At any rate " fade" is indicated by the "fade" at the
end of line 10.

75 [55, Q].

1585.   Probably late Autumn.]

To Mr W. H.   Apparently suggested by the last line of the
preceding sonnet.

NOT marble, nor the gilded monuments
Of Princes, shall outlive this powerful rhyme;
But you shall shine more bright in these contents
Than unswept stone, besmear'd with sluttish time.
When wasteful war shall *Statues* overturn   5
And broils root out the work of masonry,
Nor *Mars* his sword nor war's quick fire shall burn
The living record of your memory.
'Gainst death and all-oblivious enmity
Shall you pace forth; your praise shall still find room
Even in the eyes of all posterity   11
That wear this world out to the ending doom.
   So, till the judgement that yourself arise,
   You live in this, and dwell in lovers' eyes.

line 1.   Q reads " monument."   The emendation is Malone's.

76 [56, Q].

1585.   Probably late Autumn.]

*To Mr W. H., who, satisfied that he has regained his old
ascendency over Shakespeare, is now neglecting him.*

SWEET love, renew thy force; be it not said
Thy edge should blunter be than appetite,
Which but to-day by feeding is allay'd,
To-morrow sharpen'd in his former might:
So, love, be thou; although to-day thou fill   5
Thy hungry eyes even till they wink with fulness,
To-morrow see again, and do not kill
The spirit of Love with a perpetual dulness.
Let this sad *Interim* like the Ocean be
Which parts the shore where two contracted new   10
Come daily to the banks, that when they see
Return of love, more blest may be the view;
   Or call it Winter, which, being full of care,
   Makes Summer's welcome thrice more wish'd, more
     rare.

line 13.   Q reads "As cal it Winter." I follow Malone in reading " or "
for " as," on Tyrwhitt's suggestion.

77 [57, Q].

1585. Probably late Autumn.]

To Mr W. H., who has again been trifling with the writer.

BEING your slave, what should I do but tend
Upon the hours and times of your desire?
I have no precious time at all to spend,
Nor services to do, till you require.
Nor dare I chide the world-without-end hour   5
Whilst I, my sovereign, watch the clock for you,
Nor think the bitterness of absence sour
When you have bid your servant once adieu;
Nor dare I question with my jealous thought
Where you may be, or your affairs suppose,   10
But, like a sad slave, stay and think of nought
Save, where you are, how happy you make those.
So true a fool is love, that in your Will,
(Though you do any thing) he thinks no ill.

line 5. Malone cites from Love's Labour's Lost, V, ii, 799,
" .... a time methinks too short
To make a world-without-end bargain in."

line 13. I keep the punctuation of Q. The capital W is perhaps a printer's error. If not, this passage again suggests a play on Shakespeare's Christian name. I read as in Q, but suspect that " Will " should have been in italics, as I see from Camb. that Mr Massey has conjectured.

line 14. I keep the brackets of Q.

78 [58, Q].

1585.   Probably late Autumn.]

To Mr W. H.   A sequel to the preceding sonnet.

THAT God forbid that made me first your slave,
I should in thought control your times of pleasure,
Or at your hand the account of hours to crave,
Being your vassal, bound to stay your leisure!
O, let me suffer, being at your beck,   5
The imprison'd absence of your liberty;
And patience, tame to sufferance, bide each check,
Without accusing you of injury.
Be where you list, your charter is so strong
That you yourself may privilege your time;   10
Do what you will, to you it doth belong
Yourself to pardon of self-doing crime.
      I am to wait, though waiting so be hell,
      Not blame your pleasure, be it ill or well.

line 6.   The meaning is "Let me suffer the imprisonment of being kept at home waiting for you while you take your liberty and absent yourself [after having promised to come to see me]."

lines 10, 11.   Q reads
            "That you your selfe may priuiledge your time
            To what you will."
I have adopted Malone's emendation.

79 [59, Q].

1585.   Probably late Autumn.]

To Mr W. H.   A peace-offering of abundant flattery.

IF there be nothing new, but that which is
Hath been before, how are our brains beguil'd,
Which, labouring for invention, bear amiss
The second burthen of a former child!
O, that record could with a backward look   5
Even of five hundred courses of the Sun,
Show me your image in some antique book,
Since mind at first in character was done;
That I might see what the old world could say
To this composed wonder of your frame,   10
Whether we are mended, or whether better they,
Or whether revolution be the same.
    O, sure I am, the wits of former days
    To subjects worse have given admiring praise.

line 8.   " Would that I could read a description of you in the earliest manuscript that appeared after the first use of letters."   (MALONE.)

" This may allude to the ancient custom of inserting real portraits among the ornaments of illuminated manuscripts, with inscriptions under them."
    (STEEVENS.)

80 [60, Q].

1585.　Probably late Autumn.]

To Mr W. H.　Another peace-offering.

LIKE as the waves make towards the pebbl'd shore,
So do our minutes hasten to their end;
Each changing place with that which goes before,
In sequent toil all forwards do contend.
Nativity, once in the main of light,　　　　　　　5
Crawls to maturity, wherewith being crown'd,
Crooked eclipses 'gainst his glory fight,
And Time that gave, doth now his gift confound.
Time doth transfix the flourish set on youth
And delves the parallels in beauty's brow,　　　　10
Feeds on the rarities of nature's truth,
And nothing stands but for his scythe to mow:
　　And yet to times in hope my verse shall stand,
　　Praising thy worth, despite his cruel hand.

line 5.　Malone points out that the "main of light" means "the great
body of light," as we call the sea "the main" of waters.

81 [61, Q].

1585. Probably late Autumn.]

To Mr W. H.   Again affectionately reproachful.

Is it thy will thy Image should keep open
My heavy eyelids to the weary night?
Dost thou desire my slumber should be broken,
While shadows like to thee do mock my sight?
Is it thy spirit that thou send'st from thee   5
So far from home into my deeds to pry,
To find out shames and idle hours in me,
The scope and tenour of thy Jealousy?
O, no! thy love, though much, is not so great;
It is my love that keeps mine eye awake;   10
Mine own true love that doth my rest defeat,
To play the watchman ever for thy sake:
> For thee watch I whilst thou doth wake elsewhere,
> From me far off, with others all too near.

82 [62, Q].

1585.   Probably late Autumn.]

To Mr W. H.   A sonnet of peace-offering and self-abasement.

Sin of self-love possesseth all mine eye
Aud all my soul and all my every part;
And for this sin there is no remedy,
It is so grounded inward in my heart.
Methinks no face so gracious is as mine,   5
No shape so true, no truth of such account;
And for myself mine own worth do define,
As I all other in all worth surmount.
But when my glass shows me myself indeed,
Beated and chopp'd with tann'd antiquity,   10
Mine own self-love quite contrary I read;
Self so self-loving were iniquity.
    'Tis thee, myself, that for myself I praise,
    Painting my age with beauty of thy days.

line 8.   Q reads " in all worths."
line 10.   " *Beated* was perhaps a misprint for *'bated*. *'Bated* is properly, *overthrown, laid low, abated ;* from *abbattre*."   (MALONE.)

———

For the reasons why I hold that Shakespeare was still very young see Chap. X.

83 [63, Q].

1585. Probably late Autumn.]

To Mr W. H.   Growing out of the last six lines of the preceding sonnet.

AGAINST my love shall be as I am now
With Time's injurious hand crush'd and o'erworn,
When hours have drain'd his blood and fill'd his brow
With lines and wrinkles, when his youthful morn
Hath travell'd on to Age's steepy night,   5
And all those beauties whereof now he's King
Are vanishing or vanish'd out of sight,
Stealing away the treasure of his Spring;
For such a time do I now fortify
Against confounding Age's cruel knife,   10
That he shall never cut from memory
My sweet love's beauty, though my lover's life:
   His beauty shall in these black lines be seen,
   And they shall live, and he in them still green.

lines 1, 2.   Again I must refer the reader to Chap. X for the reasons why I hold that Shakespeare was still very young.

line 5.   Malone was at one time inclined to read "age's sleepy night," but on consideration rejected this emendation.

84 [64, Q].

1585.   Probably late Autumn.]

To Mr W. H.   Continuing the train of thought that pervades
the preceding sonnet.

WHEN I have seen by Time's fell hand defac'd
The rich-proud cost of outworn buried age ;
When sometime lofty towers I see down-raz'd,
And brass eternal slave to mortal rage ;
When I have seen the hungry Ocean gain   5
Advantage on the Kingdom of the shore,
And the firm soil win of the watery main,
Increasing store with loss and loss with store ;
When I have seen such interchange of state,
Or state itself confounded to decay ;   10
Ruin hath taught me thus to ruminate,
That Time will come and take my love away.
    This thought is as a death, which cannot choose
    But weep to have that which it fears to lose.

lines 5—10. Malone acknowledges the citation of C[apell] from
Henry IV, Pt. II, III, i, 45—53,

    " O heaven ! that one might read the book of fate,
      And see the revolution of the times,
      Make mountains level, and the continent
      Weary of solid firmness, melt itself
      Into the sea, and, other times, to see
      The beachy girdle of the ocean
      Too wide for Neptune's hips ; how chances mock,
      And changes fill the cup of alteration
      With diverse liquors."

85 [65, Q].

1585. Probably late Autumn.]

*To Mr W. H. Still continuing the same train of melancholy
reflection.*

SINCE brass, nor stone, nor earth, nor boundless sea,
But sad mortality o'er-sways their power,
How with his rage shall beauty hold a plea
Whose action is no stronger than a flower?
O, how shall summer's honey breath hold out   5
Against the wreckful siege of battering days,
When rocks impregnable are not so stout,
Nor gates of steel so strong, but Time decays?
O fearful meditation! where, alack,
Shall Time's best Jewel from Time's quest lie hid?   10
O what strong hand can hold his swift foot back,
Or who his spoil of beauty can forbid?
   O, none, unless this miracle have might,
   That in black ink my love may still shine bright.

line 3. Q reads "How with this rage." Malone says, "Shakespeare, I
believe, wrote 'How with *his* rage,' i.e. with the rage of Mortality." He
reads "this," however, in his text.

line 10. Q reads "from Time's chest lie hid?" Malone was at one
time inclined to read "quest," as Theobald had also conjectured. He points
out that a jewel does not lie hid "from" the chest in which it is kept.
Alarmed probably by Steevens's rejection of the emendation, he withdrew
his approval. But Theobald is surely right, for the following line shows
that Time is supposed to be going about in quest of this or that.

line 11. Q reads "Or what strong hand."

line 12. Q reads "Or who his spoile or beautie." The emendation is
Malone's.

8ᵹ [66, Q].

1585.   Probably late Autumn.]

To Mr W. H.   A cry of pain.

Tir'd with all these, for restful death I cry,
As, to behold desert a beggar born,
And needy Nothing trimm'd in jollity,
And purest faith unhappily forsworn,
And gilded honour shamefully misplac'd,   5
And maiden virtue rudely strumpeted,
And right perfection wrongfully disgrac'd,
And strength by limping sway disabled,
And art made tongue-tied by authority,
And Folly, Doctor-like, controlling skill,   10
And simple Truth miscall'd Simplicity,
And captive good attending Captain ill:
     Tir'd with all these, from these would I be gone,
     Save that, to die, I leave my love alone.

---

87 [67, Q].

1585.   Probably late Autumn.]

To Mr W. H., who has been keeping company of which
Shakespeare did not approve.

Ah, wherefore with infection should he live
And with his presence grace impiety,
That sin by him advantage should achieve
And lace itself with his society?
Why should false painting imitate his cheek,   5
And steal dead seeming of his living hue?
Why should poor beauty indirectly seek
Roses of shadow, since his Rose is true?
Why should he live, now Nature bankrupt is,
Beggar'd of blood to blush through lively veins?   10
For she hath no exchequer now but his,
And, prov'd of many, lives upon his gains.
   O, him she stores, to show what wealth she had
   In days long since, before these last so bad.

line 4.   "'Lace itself with his society.' i.e. embellished itself.   So
Romeo and Juliet III, v, 7, 8,
               '..... . what envious streaks
               Do lace the severing clouds.'"   (STEEVENS.)

line 6.   Q reads "Steale dead seeing of his lining hew?"   I see from
Camb. that the emendation "seeming" was conjectured by Dr Farmer and
Capell.   Malone mentions it but does not adopt it.

line 12.   Q reads "proud of many."   cf. Appendix B (129, Q), line 11.
The reading "prov'd" is due to Capell (Camb.).   I cannot say that I understand exactly what Shakespeare meant.

88 [68, Q].

1585.   Probably late Autumn.]

To Mr W. H.   A sequel to the preceding sonnet.

Thus is his cheek the map of days outworn,
When beauty liv'd and died as flowers do now,
Before these bastard signs of fair were born,
Or durst inhabit on a living brow;
Before the golden tresses of the dead,   5
The right of sepulchres, were shorn away
To live a second life on second head;
Ere beauty's dead fleece made another gay:
In him those holy antique hours are seen,
Without all ornament himself and true,   10
Making no summer of another's green,
Robbing no old to dress his beauty new;
    And him as for a map doth Nature store,
    To show false Art what beauty was of yore.

line 10.   Q reads " Without all ornament itselfe and true."   Malone
conjectured " himself and true " as the correct reading, but did not venture
to adopt it in his text.

89 [69, Q].

1585.   Probably late Autumn.]

To Mr W. H.   Warning him that he is being much
ill-spoken of.

Those parts of thee that the world's eye doth view
Want nothing that the thought of hearts can mend;
All tongues, the voice of souls, give thee that due,
Uttering bare truth, even so as foes Commend.
Thy outward thus with outward praise is crown'd;   5
But those same tongues, that give thee so thine own,
In other accents do this praise confound
By seeing farther than the eye hath shown.
They look into the beauty of thy mind,
And that, in guess, they measure by thy deeds;   10
Then, churls, their thoughts, although their eyes were
    kind,
To thy fair flower add the rank smell of weeds:
    But why thy odour matcheth not thy show,
    The soil is this—that thou dost common grow.

line 3.   Q reads "give thee that end."   Tyrwhitt suggested the emendation "due," and Malone adopted it.   Malone adds "The letters that compose the word 'due' were probably transposed in the press, and the u inverted."

line 5.   Q reads "their outward thus, &c."   Malone has again emended.

line 14.   Q reads "The solye is this."   The edition of 1640 reads "soyle" for "solye." (Camb.)   Malone declaring himself at fault reads "solve."

90 [70, Q].

1585. Probably late Autumn.]

*To Mr W. H.   A sequel to the preceding sonnet, softening
its effect.*

THAT thou art blam'd shall not be thy defect,
For slander's mark was ever yet the fair;
The ornament of beauty is suspect,
A Crow that flies in heaven's sweetest air.
So thou be good, slander doth but approve　　　　5
Thy worth the greater, being woo'd oftime;
For Canker vice the sweetest buds doth love
And thou present'st a pure unstained prime.
Thou hast pass'd by the ambush of young days,
Either not assail'd, or victor being charg'd;　　　10
Yet this thy praise cannot be so thy praise,
To tie up envy evermore enlarg'd:
　　　If some suspect of ill mask'd not thy show,
　　　Then thou alone kingdoms of hearts shouldst owe.

line 3. " Suspect" means "suspicion," as it also does in line 13.

line 6. Q reads, "Their worth the greater beeing woo'd of time."
Malone corrects the " their " as usual.

I see from the Cambridge edition that the emendation " oftime" for
" of time " has been suggested, but no one seems to have adopted it and at
the same time kept " woo'd." The sense is :—" If you are good now, slander
only shows how confirmed your goodness is; for you have been often
woo'd; vice, moreover, generally confines its attacks to the immature, and
you have now passed victoriously through your most trying time."

line 7. Malone refers to C[apell] as citing Two Gentlemen of
Verona, III, i, 41, 2,
　　　　　　　" .... as in the sweetest bud
　　　　　　　The loathsome canker dwells."

line 8. " Prime " means " spring." cf. Sonnets 3 and 117.

91 [71, Q].

1585.   Probably early Winter.]

To Mr W. H.   Written in great dejection.

No Longer mourn for me when I am dead,
Than you shall hear the surly sullen bell
Give warning to the world that I am fled
From this vile world, with vilest worms to dwell:
Nay, if you read this line remember not,   5
The hand that writ it: for I love you so
That I in your sweet thoughts would be forgot
If thinking on me then should make you woe.
O, if, I say, you look upon this verse
When I perhaps compounded am with clay,   10
Do not so much as my poor name rehearse,
But let your love even with my life decay;
    Lest the wise world should look into your moan
    And mock you with me after I am gone.

line 2.   Malone cites Henry IV, Pt. II, I, i, 101−103,
        " ...... and his tongue
    Sounds ever after as a sullen bell,
    Remember'd knolling a departed friend."

92 [72, Q].

1585.   Probably early Winter.]

To Mr W. H.   A sequel to the preceding sonnet.

O, LEST the world should task you to recite
What merit lived in me, that you should love,
After my death, dear love, forget me quite,
For you in me can nothing worthy prove;
Unless you would devise some virtuous lie,   5
To do more for me than mine own desert,
And hang more praise upon deceased I
Than niggard truth would willingly impart:
O, lest your true love may seem false in this,
That you for love speak well of me untrue,   10
My name be buried where my body is
And live no more to shame nor me nor you.
  For I am sham'd by that which I bring forth,
  And so should you, to love things nothing worth.

line 7.   This line (as well as line 14, and many another in the Sonnets) makes it idle to maintain that Shakespeare was a purist in the matter of grammar.

line 10.   " Untrue " here = " untruly."

93 [73, Q].

1585.   Probably early Winter.]

To Mr W. H.   A sequel to the two preceding sonnets.

THAT time of year thou mayst in me behold
When yellow leaves, or none, or few, do hang
Upon those boughs which shake against the cold,
Bare ruin'd choirs where late the sweet birds sang.
In me thou see'st the twilight of such day   5
As after Sunset fadeth in the West;
Which by and by black night doth take away
Death's second self, that seals up all in rest.
In me thou see'st the glowing of such fire,
That on the ashes of his youth doth lie,   10
As the death-bed whereon it must expire,
Consum'd with that which it was nourish'd by.
  This thou perceiv'st, which makes thy love more
   strong,
  To love that well which thou must leave ere long.

line 4.   "The quarto has 'rn'wd quiers,' from which the reader must extract what meaning he can—the edition of 1640 has ' ruined.' "
               (MALONE.)

line 7.   Steevens quotes from Two Gentlemen of Verona, I, iii, 87,
    "And by and by a cloud takes all away."

line 14.   Q reads as in my text, but I think it probable that Shakespeare wrote " which thou must leese ere long."   See line 14 of sonnet 5.

94 [74, Q].

1585.　Probably early Winter.]

To Mr W. H.　A sequel to the three preceding sonnets.

BUT be contented: when that fell arrest
Without all bail shall carry me away,
My life hath in this line some interest,
Which for memorial still with thee shall stay.
When thou reviewest this thou dost review　　　　5
The very part was consecrate to thee;
The earth can have but earth, which is his due;
My spirit is thine, the better part of me:
So then thou hast but lost the dregs of life,
The prey of worms, my body being dead,　　　　10
The coward conquest of a wretch's knife,
Too base of thee to be remembered.
　　　　The worth of that is that which it contains,
　　　　And that is this, and this with thee remains.

line 1.　Malone refers to C [apell] as citing Hamlet V, ii, 347,
　　　　"Had I but time (as this fell serjeant, death,
　　　　　Is strict in his arrest,) O I could tell you—
　　　　　But let it be."

line 12.　I presume it is the "body," not the "wretch," that is "too
base" &c.

95 [75, Q].

1585. Probably early Winter.]

*To Mr W. H., whose intercourse with Shakespeare is now
evidently intermittent.*

So are you to my thoughts as food to life,
Or as sweet-season'd showers are to the ground;
And for the prize of you I hold such strife
As 'twixt a miser and his wealth is found;
Now proud as an enjoyer, and anon   5
Doubting the filching age will steal his treasure;
Now counting best to be with you alone,
Then better'd that the world may see my pleasure:
Sometime all full with feasting on your sight,
And by and by clean starved for a look;   10
Possessing or pursuing no delight,
Save what is had or must from you be took.
    Thus do I pine and surfeit day by day,
    Or gluttoning on all, or all away.

line 3. Q reads, "And for the peace of you." Staunton (*Athenæum*,
Dec. 6, 1873) conjectured "prize." Malone says that the context seems to
require "price" or "sake"; he adheres, however, to the reading of Q,
believing that an antithesis was intended between "peace" and "strife." I
have preferred to follow Staunton.

96 [76, Q].

1585.   Probably December.]

To Mr W. H.   Declaring (so it would seem) that these sonnets
are the only things the writer has yet written.

WHY is my verse so barren of new pride,
So far from variation or quick change?
Why with the time do I not glance aside
To new-found methods and to compounds strange?
Why write I still all one, ever the same,   5
And keep invention in a noted weed,
That every word doth almost tell my name,
Showing their birth and whence they did proceed?
O, know, sweet love, I always write of you,
And you and love are still my argument;   10
So all my best is dressing old words new,
Spending again what is already spent:
　　For as the Sun is daily new and old,
　　So is my love still telling what is told.

line 6. The meaning is that the invention is clothed in a weed, or
garment, by which it is easily recognised.

line 7. Q reads, "doth almost fel my name." The emendation is
Malone's.

line 8. Q reads, "and where they did proceed," I have adopted Capell's
suggested emendation. (Camb.)

97 [77, Q].

1585-6.   Probably Jan. 1.]

*To Mr W. H.   Apparently accompanying a new year's
present of a book of tablets.*

THY glass will show thee how thy beauties wear,
Thy dial how thy precious minutes waste;
These vacant leaves thy mind's imprint will bear,
And of this book this learning mayst thou taste.
The wrinkles which thy glass will truly show   5
Of mouthed graves will give thee memory;
Thou by thy dial's shady stealth mayst know
Time's thievish progress to eternity.
Look, what thy memory cannot contain
Commit to these waste blanks, and thou shalt find 10
Those children nursed, deliver'd from thy brain
To take a new acquaintance of thy mind.
　　　These offices, so oft as thou wilt look,
　　　Shall profit thee and much enrich thy book.

line 3.   Q reads "The vacant leaues." Malone suggested the emendation
"these," but did not adopt it; he refers, however, to line 10, where we read,
"commit to these waste blanks."

line 10.   Q reads "commit to these waste blacks." The emendation is
Theobald's.

———

For the reasons which lead me to date this sonnet as I have done see
pp. 96, 97.

98 [78, Q].

1586.   Probably Spring of 1585-6.]

To Mr W. H.   Shakespeare having set the fashion of writing
sonnets to Mr W. H. is now jealous of other poets,
and more particularly of one.

So oft have I invok'd thee for my Muse
And found such fair assistauce in my verse
As every *Alien* pen hath got my use
And under thee their poesy disperse.
Thine eyes, that taught the dumb on high to sing   5
And heavy ignorance aloft to fly,
Have added feathers to the learned's wing
And given grace a double Majesty.
Yet be most proud of that which I compile,
Whose influence is thine and born of thee: 10
In others' works thou dost but mend the style,
And Arts with thy sweet graces graced be;
    But thou art all my art, and dost advance
    As high as learning my rude ignorance.

line 5.   Surely these lines afford considerable ground for thinking that
Shakespeare had not written at all before falling in with Mr W. H.   cf. " By
heaven I do love ; and it hath taught me to rhyme."   Love's Labour's
Lost, IV, iii—the opening speech.

99 [79, Q].

1586.   Probably Spring of 1585-6.]

To Mr W. H.   On the same subject as the preceding sonnet.

WHILST I alone did call upon thy aid
My verse alone had all thy gentle grace;
But now my gracious numbers are decay'd
And my sick Muse doth give another place.
I grant, sweet love, thy lovely argument   5
Deserves the travail of a worthier pen,
Yet what of thee thy Poet doth invent
He robs thee of, and pays it thee again.
He lends thee virtue, and he stole that word
From thy behaviour; beauty doth he give,   10
And found it in thy cheek: he can afford
No praise to thee but what in thee doth live;
    Then thank him not for that which he doth say,
    Since what he owes thee thou thyself dost pay.

line 7.   I shall not attempt to discover who the poet here referred to is;
it is quite likely that he was some one whose very name has been lost to us.
Of known poets Thomas Watson was the best then writing, except of course
Spenser, who was in Ireland during the whole time covered by the sonnets,
and need not, therefore, be considered.   As for Sir Philip Sidney, he too
was out of England, having left for Flushing in November 1585.

100 [80, Q].

1586.   Probably Spring of 1585-6.]

*To Mr W. H.   On the same subject as the two preceding
sonnets.*

O, HOW I faint when I of you do write,
Knowing a better spirit doth use your name,
And in the praise thereof spends all his might
To make me tongue-tied, speaking of your fame!
But since your worth, wide as the Ocean is,
The humble as the proudest sail doth bear,
My saucy bark, inferior far to his,
On your broad main doth wilfully appear.
Your shallowest help will hold me up afloat,
Whilst he upon your soundless deep doth ride;   10
Or, being wreck'd, I am a worthless boat,
He of tall building and of goodly pride:
     Then if he thrive and I be cast away,
     The worst was this;—my love was my decay.

lines 5—8.   Steevens cites Troilus and Cressida, I, iii, 34 &c,
        " . . . . The sea being smooth
      How many shallow bauble boats dare sail
      Upon her patient breast, making their way
      With those of nobler bulk?
        *   *   *   *

     . . . . Where's then the saucy boat?"

101 [81, Q].

1586.   Probably Spring of 1585-6.]

To Mr W. H.   Shakespeare consoles himself with the reflection that, come what may, his verse has immortalised Mr W. H.

Oʀ I shall live your Epitaph to make,
Or you survive when I in earth am rotten ;
From hence your memory death cannot take,
Although in me each part will be forgotten.
Your name from hence immortal life shall have,   5
Though I, once gone, to all the world must die :
The earth can yield me but a common grave,
When you entombed in men's eyes shall lie.
Your monument shall be my gentle verse,
Which eyes not yet created shall o'er-read,   10
And tongues to be your being shall rehearse,
When all the breathers of this world are dead,
   You still shall live—such virtue hath my Pen—
   Where breath most breathes—even in the mouths of
   men.

line 1.   "Or" has here the sense of "whether."

lines 10, 11, 12.   I have kept the punctuation of Q, leaving the reader to decide whether to put (as Malone and the Cambridge edition do) a semicolon at the end of line 12, or to have the semicolon at the end of line 11, and no stop after "dead" in line 12.

102 [82, Q].

1586. Probably Spring of 1585-6.]

*To Mr W. H. Contending that his praises were better worth
having than those of the other poets whom his example
had fired.*

I GRANT thou wert not married to my Muse,
And therefore mayst without attaint o'erlook
The dedicated words which writers use
Of their fair subject, blessing every book.
Thou art as fair in knowledge as in hue,   5
Finding thy worth a limit past my praise,
And therefore art enforc'd to seek anew,
Some fresher stamp of the time-bettering days.
And do so, love; yet when they have devis'd
What strained touches Rhetoric can lend,   10
Thou truly fair wert truly sympathiz'd
In true plain words by thy true-telling friend;
    And their gross painting might be better us'd
    Where cheeks need blood; in thee it is abus'd.

In lines 5, 6, 7, 8, I have kept the punctuation of Q. The intention of
the passage would be more evident if line 6 were treated as a parenthesis.

103 [83, Q].

1586.   Perhaps April.]

To Mr W. H.   Shakespeare's jealousy has led him to leave off
writing.   Mr W. H., however, being "fond on praise,"
has again cajoled him.

I NEVER saw that you did painting need
And therefore to your fair no painting set:
I found, or thought I found, you did exceed
The barren tender of a Poet's debt:
And therefore have I slept in your report,   5
That you yourself, being extant, well might show
How far a modern quill doth come too short,
Speaking of worth, what worth in you doth grow.
This silence for my sin you did impute,
Which shall be most my glory, being dumb;   10
For I impair not beauty being mute,
When others would give life and bring a tomb:
   There lives more life in one of your fair eyes
   Than both your Poets can in praise devise.

Without any confidence that it is safe to date sonnets 98–116 (78–96, Q)
more closely than as between Jan. 1, 1585-6, and the beginning of the
following summer, I take advantage of the interval of silence implied in
line 5, to suggest April 1586 as a possible date.

104 [84, Q].

1586, Perhaps April.]

To Mr W. H.   Shakespeare is mollified, but reproaches
Mr W. H. with being "fond on praise."

Who is it that says most? which can say more
Than this rich praise, that you alone are you?
In whose confine immured is the store
Which should example where your equal grew?
Lean penury within that Pen doth dwell   5
That to his subject lends not some small glory;
But he that writes of you, if he can tell
That you are you, so dignifies his story.
Let him but copy what in you is writ,
Not making gross what nature made so clear,   10
And such a counterpart shall fame his wit,
Making his style admired every where.
    You to your beauteous blessings add a curse,
    Being fond on praise, which makes your praises
    worse,

lines 1—4.   Q has no note of interrogation in any of the first four lines
of this sonnet.   Malone introduced them in the first two lines, and Staunton
(*Athenæum*, Jan. 31, 1874), whom I have followed, suggested that there
should be one at the end of line 4.

line 10.   Q reads "Not making worse" &c.   I adopt Staunton's
conjecture from *The Athenæum* Jan. 31, 1874.

105 [85, Q].

1586.   Perhaps between April and June.]

*To Mr W. H.   Shakespeare declares that as long as the other
poet keeps on writing, his own tongue is tied.*

My tongue-ti'd Muse in manners holds her still,
While comments of your praise, richly compil'd,
Reserve thy Character with golden quill,
And precious phrase by all the Muses fil'd.
I think good thoughts, whilst other write good words,
And, like unletter'd clerk, still cry 'Amen'   6
To every Hymn that able spirit affords,
In polish'd form of well refined pen.
Hearing you prais'd, I say ''tis so, 'tis true,'
And to the most of praise add something more;   10
But that is in my thought, whose love to you,
Though words come hindmost, holds his rank before.
   Then others for the breath of words respect,
   Me for my dumb thoughts, speaking in effect.

line 3.   Q reads "Reserne their Character." Malone here again emends
by reading "thy," regardless of the "your" in the preceding line.
"Reserne" is an obvious misprint for "Reserue," i.e. reserve.   Malone says
"'Reserve,' here, as in line 7 of sonnet 32, is equivalent to 'preserve.'"   I
see from Camb. that "rehearse" has been proposed as an emendation.

106 [86, Q].

1586.   Perhaps between April and June.]

To Mr W. H.   Shakespeare declares that his silence is only due to the countenance given by Mr W. H. to the rival poet.

WAS it the proud full sail of his great verse,
Bound for the prize of all too precious you,
That did my ripe thoughts in my brain inhearse,
Making their tomb the womb wherein they grew?
Was it his spirit, by spirits taught to write   5
Above a mortal pitch, that struck me dead?
No, neither he, nor his compeers by night
Giving him aid, my verse astonished.
He, nor that affable familiar ghost
Which nightly gulls him with intelligence,   10
As victors, of my silence cannot boast;
I was not sick of any fear from thence:
  But when your countenance fil'd up his line,
  Then lack'd I matter; that enfeebl'd mine.

line 4.   Malone cites Romeo and Juliet II, iii, 9, 10,
   "The earth that's nature's mother is her tomb;
   What is her burying grave, that is her womb."

line 13.   Q reads "fild vp his line"; Malone reads "fil'd"; the Cambridge edition has "fill'd."   In favour of "fil'd," we find this word in line 4 of the preceding sonnet.

107 [87, Q].

1586.   Perhaps between April and June.]

To Mr W. H.   Shakespeare convinced, or affecting to be con-
vinced, that all is over between him and his friend, bids
him farewell.

FAREWELL! thou art too dear for my possessing,
And like enough thou know'st thy estimate:
The Charter of thy worth gives thee releasing;
My bonds in thee are all determinate.
For how do I hold thee but by thy granting?   5
And for that riches where is my deserving?
The cause of this fair gift in me is wanting,
And so my patent back again is swerving.
Thyself thou gav'st, thy own worth then not knowing,
Or me, to whom thou gav'st it, else mistaking;   10
So thy great gift, upon misprision growing,
Comes home again on better judgement making.
    Thus have I had thee as a dream doth flatter,
    In sleep a King, but waking no such matter.

108 [88, Q].

1586. Perhaps between April and June.]

To Mr W. H.   If Mr W. H. is determined so to have it,
Shakespeare will attack himself, in order to justify
his friend's estrangement.

WHEN thou shalt be dispos'd to set me light,
And place my merit in the eye of scorn,
Upon thy side against myself I'll fight
And prove thee virtuous though thou art forsworn.
With mine own weakness being best acquainted,   5
Upon thy part I can set down a story
Of faults conceal'd wherein I am attainted,
That thou in losing me shalt win much glory:
And I by this will be a gainer too;
For bending all my loving thoughts on thee,   10
The injuries that to myself I do,
Doing thee vantage, double-vantage me.
       Such is my love, to thee I so belong,
       That for thy right myself will bear all wrong.

109 [89, Q].

1586.   Perhaps between April and June.]

To Mr W. H.   A sequel to the preceding sonnet.

SAY that thou didst forsake me for some fault
And I will comment upon that offence:
Speak of my lameness and I straight will halt,
Against thy reasons making no defence.
Thou canst not, love, disgrace me half so ill,   5
To set a form upon desired change,
As I'll myself disgrace; knowing thy will
I will acquaintauce strangle aud look strauge;
Be absent from thy walks; and in my tongue
Thy sweet beloved name no more shall dwell,   10
Lest I, too much profane, should do it wrong
And haply of our old acquaintance tell.
    For thee against myself I'll vow debate,
    For I must ne'er love him whom thou dost hate.

line 3.   This line seems to imply that the lameness of which Shakespeare spoke in sonnet 37 had not entirely left him.   It suggests, "I am no longer lame, but if you choose to say that I still go more or less halt, I will halt at once."   Probably he still halted a little sometimes.

110 [90, Q].

1586.   Perhaps between April and June.]

*To Mr W. H.   If his friend is determined to break with him,
Shakespeare implores him to let him know the worst at once.*

THEN hate me when thou wilt; if ever, now ;
Now, while the world is bent my deeds to cross,
Join with the spite of fortune, make me bow,
And do not drop in for an after-loss :
Ah, do not, when my heart hath 'scap'd this sorrow 5
Come in the rearward of a conquer'd woe ;
Give not a windy night a rainy morrow
To linger out a purpos'd overthrow.
If thou wilt leave me, do not leave me last,
When other petty griefs have done their spite,   10
But in the onset come: so shall I taste
At first the very worst of fortune's might ;
    And other strains of woe, which now seem woe,
    Compared with loss of thee will not seem so.

lines 5—8. I incline to think that these lines refer to the subject of
sonnets 33-35, and not to the " spite of fortune " mentioned in line 3. It is
impossible, however, to be confident, for the words " this sorrow " seem to
apply to a still recent " spite of fortune."

111 [91, Q].

1586. Perhaps between April and June.]

*To Mr W. H. Shakespeare declares that the fear lest his
friend should break with him mars his enjoyment of all else.*

Some glory in their birth, some in their skill,
Some in their wealth, some in their body's force;
Some in their garments, though new-fangled ill;
Some in their Hawks and Hounds, some in their Horse;
And every humour hath his adjunct pleasure   5
Wherein it finds a joy above the rest:
But these particulars are not my measure,
All these I better in one general best.
Thy love is better than high birth to me,
Richer than wealth, prouder than garments' cost,   10
Of more delight than Hawks or Horses be;
And having thee, of all men's pride I boast:
    Wretched in this alone, that thou mayst take
    All this away and me most wretched make.

112 [92, Q].

1586.   Perhaps between April and June.]

To Mr W. H.   A sequel to the preceding sonnet.

BUT do thy worst to steal thyself away,
For term of life thou art assured mine;
And life no longer than thy love will stay,
For it depends upon that love of thine.
Then need I not to fear the worst of wrongs,   5
When in the last of them my life hath end.
I see a better state to me belongs
Than that which on thy humour doth depend:
Thou canst not vex me with inconstant mind,
Since that my life on thy revolt doth lie,   10
O, what a happy title do I find,
Happy to have thy love, happy to die!
    But what's so blessed-fair that fears no blot?
    Thou mayst be false and yet I know it not.

line 6.   Q reads " when in the least of them." But surely Shakespeare
cannot consider Mr W. H.'s leaving him as " the least" of wrongs. It
would be the culminating, and hence the last misfortune; it would
immediately kill Shakespeare, and, therefore, this wrong, at any rate, has no
terrors for him.

113 [93, Q].

1586.   Perhaps between April and June.]

To Mr W. H.   A sequel to the two preceding sonnets.

So shall I live supposing thou art true,
Like a deceived husband; so love's face
May still seem love to me, though alter'd new—
Thy looks with me, thy heart in other place.
For there can live no hatred in thine eye, 5
Therefore in that I cannot know thy change;
In many's looks the false heart's history
Is writ in moods and frowns and wrinkles strange,
But heaven in thy creation did decree
That in thy face sweet love should ever dwell; 10
Whate'er thy thoughts or thy heart's workings be
Thy looks should nothing thence but sweetness tell.
 How like *Eve's* apple doth thy beauty grow,
 If thy sweet virtue answer not thy show.

lines 13, 14. Here, again, as in some few other sonnets, the two
concluding lines are somewhat sterner than the tone of the preceding ones
would lead us to expect.

114 [94, Q].

1586. Perhaps early Summer.]

To Mr W. H. A word of warning very affectionately couched.

THEY that have power to hurt and will do none,
That do not do the thing they most do show,
Who, moving others, are themselves as stone,
Unmoved, cold and to temptation slow—
They rightly do inherit heaven's graces   5
And husband nature's riches from expense;
They are the Lords and owners of their faces,
Others but stewards of their excellence.
The summer's flower is to the summer sweet
Though to itself it only live and die;   10
But if that flower with base infection meet
The basest weed outbraves his dignity:
    For sweetest things turn sourest by their deeds;
    Lilies that fester smell far worse than weeds.

line 14. Steevens pointed out that this line is likewise found in the anonymous play of King Edward III. I see from the Temple edition of the Sonnets that this play was entered on the books of the Stationers' Register Dec. 1, 1595.

115 [95, Q].

1586. Perhaps early Summer.]

*To Mr W. H. Again very affectionately chiding with him for
the ill report in which he is obviously living.*

How sweet and lovely dost thou make the shame
Which, like a canker in the fragrant Rose,
Doth spot the beauty of thy budding name!
O, in what sweets dost thou thy sins inclose!
That tongue that tells the story of thy days,   5
Making lascivious comments on thy sport,
Cannot dispraise but in a kiud of praise;
Naming thy name blesses an ill report.
O, what a mausion have those vices got
Which for their habitation chose out thee,   10
Where beauty's veil doth cover every blot
And all things turn to fair that eyes can see!
    Take heed, dear heart, of this large privilege;
    The hardest knife ill us'd doth lose his edge.

line 6. It is probable, though by no means certain, that the "sport"
here alluded to is to be connected with the subject of sonnets 33-35.

116 [96, Q].

1586.　Perhaps early Summer.]

To Mr W. H.　A continuation of the same affectionate chiding.

SOME say thy fault is youth, some wantonness;
Some say thy grace is youth and gentle sport;
Both grace and faults are loved of more and less;
Thou mak'st faults graces that to thee resort.
As on the finger of a throned Queen　　　　　5
The basest Jewel will be well esteem'd,
So are those errors that in thee are seen
To truths translated and for true things deem'd.
How many Lambs might the stern Wolf betray
If like a Lamb he could his looks translate!　　　10
How many gazers mightst thou lead away
If thou wouldst use the strength of all thy state!
　　　But do not so; I love thee in such sort,
　　　As thou being mine, mine is thy good report.

lines 13, 14.　These lines are also found as the last two lines of
sonnet 36.

117 [97, Q].

1586. Autumn.]

To Mr W. H.   Perhaps accompanying a letter in prose.

How like a Winter hath my abseuce been
From thee, the pleasure of the fleetiug year!
What freezings have I felt, what dark days seen!
What old December's bareuess every where!
And yet this time remov'd was summer's time;   5
The teeming Autumn, big with rich increase,
Bearing the wanton burthen of the prime,
Like widow'd wombs after their Lords' decease:
Yet this abundant issue seem'd to me
But crop of Orphans and unfather'd fruit;   10
For Summer and his pleasures wait on thee,
And, thou away, the very birds are mute;
    Or, if they sing, 'tis with so dull a cheer
    That leaves look pale, dreading the Winter's near.

line 5. Malone explains that "this time remov'd" means "this time when I was remote, or absent, from you."

line 7. "The prime is the spring." (MALONE.)   cf. sonnets 3 and 90.

line 10. Q reads "But hope of orphans." The emendation "crop" is by Staunton. (*Athenæum*, Jan. 31, 1874.)

118 [98, Q].

1587.   Summer.]

To Mr W. H.   Again perhaps accompanying a letter in prose.

FROM you have I been absent in the spring,
When proud-pied April, dress'd in all his trim,
Had put a spirit of youth in every thing,
That heavy *Saturn* laugh'd and leap'd with him.
Yet nor the lays of birds, nor the sweet smell   5
Of different flowers in odour and in hue,
Could make me any summer's story tell
Or from their proud lap pluck them where they grew:
Nor did I wonder at the Lily's white,
Nor praise the deep vermilion in the Rose;   10
They were but, sweet, but figures of delight
Drawn after you, you pattern of all those.
  Yet seem'd it Winter still, and, you away,
  As with your shadow I with these did play.

line 2.   Malone cites Romeo and Juliet I, ii, 27,
   " Where well-apparell'd April on the heel
    Of limping winter treads."

line 3.   Q reads " Hath put a spirit," but seeing that all the rest of the
sonnet is in past time it seems more likely that Shakespeare wrote " had."

line 11.   Q reads " They were but sweet," Malone suggested the
reading " They were, my sweet," finding an anticlimax in the assertion that
flowers were nothing more than sweet, and suspecting that the compositor
caught the word " but " from a later part of the line.   He did not, however,
introduce the emendation into his text.   A comma after the first "but"
would get rid of the anticlimax.

119 [99, Q].

1587. Summer.]

To Mr W. H.   A sequel to the preceding sonnet.

THE forward violet thus did I chide:
Sweet thief, whence didst thou steal thy sweet that smells,
If not from my love's breath?   The purple pride
Which on thy soft cheek for complexion dwells
In my love's veins thou hast too grossly dy'd.   5
The Lily I condemned for thy hand,
And buds of marjoram had stol'n thy hair;
The Roses fearfully on thorns did stand,
One blushing shame, another white despair;
A third, nor red nor white, had stol'n of both,   10
And to his robbery had annex'd thy breath;
But, for his theft, in pride of all his growth
A vengeful canker ate him up to death.
    More flowers I noted, yet I none could see
    But sweet or colour it had stol'n from thee.   15

lines 1—5.   This quatrain has a *coda* by way of a fifth line.
Q reads line 4 thus:—
    " Which on thy soft cheeke for complexion dwells?"
This is what Shakespeare doubtless wrote in the first instance—intending
the quatrain to end with a question.   He probably cancelled the query—or
forgot to cancel it—and added the fifth line, because until he did so the
query remained unanswered, unless by bringing the answer to the preceding
query over, and so making the violet steal its complexion from Mr W. H.'s
breath; it may have further occurred to him that he had not chidden the
violet directly.   The slovenliness of Q which has retained the original query
after " dwells " has here stood us in good stead.

line 9.   Q reads "Our blushing shame."   Malone corrected, as I see
from Camb. that Sewell had also done.

120 [100, Q].

1588.   Probably Spring.]

*To Mr W. H.   After a considerable interval during which
Shakespeare has found other things to write about, but has
not yet (so it would seem) become a playwright.*

WHERE art thou, Muse, that thou forget'st so long
To speak of that which gives thee all thy might?
Spend'st thou thy fury on some worthless song,
Darkening thy power to lend base subjects light!
Return, forgetful Muse, and straight redeem   5
In gentle numbers time so idly spent;
Sing to the ear that doth thy lays esteem
And gives thy pen both skill and argument.
Rise, resty Muse, my love's sweet face survey,
If time have any wrinkle graven there;   10
If any, be a *Satire* to decay,
And make time's spoils despised every where.
        Give my love fame faster than Time wastes life;
        So thou prevent'st his scythe and crooked knife.

line 9.   Malone reads, " Rise restive Muse."   Q has "resty."   Perhaps
Shakespeare meant, or even wrote, " rested."

lines 10, 11.   These lines suggest that Mr W. H.'s good looks were
beginning to go off, though not so strongly as the opening lines of
sonnet 124, nor the concluding ones of 128.

121 [101, Q].

1588. Probably Spring.]

To Mr W. H.   A sequel to the preceding sonnet.

O TRUANT Muse, what shall be thy amends
For thy neglect of truth in beauty dy'd?
Both truth and beauty on my love depends;
So dost thou too, and therein dignified.
Make answer, Muse: wilt thou not haply say,   5
Truth needs no colour with his colour mix'd,
Beauty no pencil beauty's truth to lay,
But best is best if never intermix'd?
Because he needs no praise, wilt thou be dumb?
Excuse not silence so, for 't lies in thee   10
To make him much outlive a gilded tomb
And to be praised of ages yet to be.
     Then do thy office, Muse; I teach thee how
     To make him seem long hence as he shows now.

line 6.   Q reads " with his collour fixt."

Shakespeare makes "use" rhyme to "abuse" (sonnet 4 lines 5, 7);
"abus'd" rhyme to "us'd" (sonnet 102 [82, Q] lines 13, 14); "express"
rhyme to "press" (sonnet 48 [140, Q] lines 1, 3); and "decrease" rhyme
to "increase" (sonnet 15, lines 5, 7); and "commend" rhyme to "mend"
(sonnet 89 [69, Q] lines 2, 4).   I think it most likely that he made " mixt"
and "intermixt" rhyme, and that "fixt" is the correction of some clever
printer.

122 [102, Q].

1588.   Probably Spring.]

*To Mr W. H., who has been upbraiding Shakespeare for
having lost his old affection for him.*

My love is strengthen'd, though more weak in seeming,
I love not less, though less the show appear:
That love is merchandiz'd whose rich esteeming
The owner's tongue doth publish every where.
Our love was new and then but in the spring	5
When I was wont to greet it with my lays;
As *Philomel* in summer's front doth sing,
And stops his pipe in growth of riper days:
Not that the summer is less pleasant now
Than when her mournful hymns did hush the night, 10
But that wild music burthens every bough,
And sweets grown common lose their dear delight.
    Therefore, like her, I sometime hold my tongue,
    Because I would not dull you with my song.

line 7.   Malone cites A Winter's Tale IV, iv, 2, 3,
    " .... no shepherdess but Flora
      Peering in April's front."
Again, Coriolanus II, i, 57, " .... one that converses more with the
buttock of the night than the forehead of the morning."
Again, King Henry IV, pt. 2, IV, iv, 91–93,
    " .... thou art a summer bird,
      Which ever in the haunch of winter sings
      The lifting up of day."

line 8.   Q reads as in my text. The Cambridge edition adopting
Mr Housman's emendation reads "her," which seems preferable, but
Shakespeare is quite capable of writing "his" in one line and "her" two
lines later, about the same object. Seeing that Malone keeps to the text
of Q, I do also.

123 [103, Q].

1588. Probably Spring.]

*To Mr W. H. Excusing himself, and plying his friend with
the flattery which he knows to be so dear to him.*

ALACK, what poverty my Muse brings forth,
That having snch a scope to show her pride,
The argument, all bare, is of more worth
Than when it hath my added praise beside !
O, blame me not if I no more can write !   5
Look in your glass, and there appears a face
That over-goes my blunt invention quite,
Dulling my lines and doing me disgrace.
Were it not sinful then, striving to mend,
To mar the subject that before was well?   10
For to no other pass my verses tend
Than of your graces and your gifts to tell;
    And more, much more, than in my verse can sit,
    Your own glass shows you when you look in it.

lines 9, 10. Malone cites King Lear I, iv, 369,
    " Striving to better oft we mar what's well."

124 [104, Q]

1588.   Probably Spring.]

*To Mr W. H., asseverating that his good looks are not
leaving him.*

To me, fair friend, you never can be old,
For as you were when first your eye I eyed,
Such seems your beauty still. Three Winters cold
Have from the forests shook three summers' pride,
Three beauteous springs to yellow *Autumn* turn'd   5
In process of the seasons have I seen,
Three April perfumes in three hot Junes burn'd,
Since first I saw you fresh, which yet are green.
Ah, yet doth beauty, like a Dial-hand,
Steal from his figure and no pace perceiv'd ;   10
So your sweet hue, which methinks still doth stand,
Hath motion, and mine eye may be deceiv'd :
  For fear of which, hear this, thou age unbred ;
  Ere you were born was beauty's summer dead.

line 1.   It would seem as though Mr W. H. had been saying something
to Shakespeare about his looking old.   Shakespeare asseverates that to him
be can never seem old, however much he may do so to other people.
" Such seems your beauty still," gives an uncertain sound ; so also do the
last six lines.   See notes on sonnets 120 lines 10, 11, and 128 lines 9-14.

lines 3-7.   We have three of each of the four seasons, and should be
now at the same part of the year as that in which the series began, but
three years later.   For the reasons which convince me that this should be
spring, see Chapter **X**.

125 [105, Q].

1588.   Probably Spring.]

To Mr W. H.   Plying him with affectionate flattery.

LET not my love be call'd Idolatry,
Nor my beloved as an Idol show,
Since all alike my songs and praises be
To one, of one, still such, and ever so.
Kind is my love to-day, to-morrow kind,   5
Still constant in a wondrous excellence;
Therefore my verse to constancy confin'd,
One thing expressing, leaves out difference.
Fair, kind, and true, is all my argument,
Fair, kind, and true, varying to other words;   10
And in this change is my invention spent,
Three themes in one, which wondrous scope affords.
   Fair, kind, and true, have often liv'd alone,
   Which three till now never kept seat in one.

126 [106, Q].

1588.   Probably Spring.

To Mr W. H.   Again plying him with affectionate flattery.

When in the Chronicle of wasted time
I see descriptions of the fairest wights,
And beauty making beautiful old rhyme
In praise of Ladies dead and lovely Knights,
Then, in the blazon of sweet beauty's best,   5
Of hand, of foot, of lip, of eye, of brow,
I see their antique Pen would have express'd
Even such a beauty as you master now.
So all their praises are but prophecies
Of this our time, all you prefiguring;   10
And, for they look'd but with divining eyes,
They had not skill enough your worth to sing:
    For we, which now behold these present days,
    Have eyes to wonder, but lack tongues to praise.

line 12.   Q reads "They had not still enough." Malone adopts the emendation suggested to him by Tyrwhitt. The sense is "The ancients were labouring to express such beauty as your's, but could not praise you inasmuch as they could not see you well enough. We on the other hand can see you but cannot praise you, for our tongues fail us, as their eyes failed the ancients."

Mr Wyndham adheres to the reading of Q. I agree with his interpretation of the passage, but cannot see how it can be got quite equitably out of either the Quarto or the amended version.

127 [107, Q].

1588.   About Aug. 8.]

*To Mr W. H.   Reflecting the relief of the nation on having
passed safely through a time of great peril.   Probably
an advance on Shakespeare's part, after an interval
of coldness.*

Not mine own fears, nor the prophetic soul
Of the wide world dreaming on things to come,
Can yet the lease of my true love control,
Suppos'd as forfeit to a confin'd doom.
The mortal Moon hath her eclipse endur'd,   5
And the sad Augurs mock their own presage;
Incertainties now crown themselves assur'd,
And peace proclaims Olives of endless age.
Now with the drops of this most balmy time
My love looks fresh, and Death to me subscribes, 10
Since, spite of him, I'll live in this poor rhyme,
While he insults o'er dull and speechless tribes:
    And thou in this shalt find thy monument,
    When tyrants' crests and tombs of brass are spent.

In Chapter XI I have given my reasons for holding that this sonnet
refers to the defeat of the Spanish Armada.

128 [108, Q].

1588.　Between Aug. 8 and Dec. 1.]

To Mr W. H., who has not accepted Shakespeare's advance and has been upbraiding him for want of constancy.

WHAT'S in the brain, that Iuk may character,
Which hath not figur'd to thee my true spirit?
What's new to speak, what new to register,
That may express my love, or thy dear merit?
Nothing, sweet boy; but yet, like prayers divine,　　5
I must each day say o'er the very same;
Counting no old thing old, thou mine, I thine,
Even as when first I hallow'd thy fair name.
So that eternal love in love's fresh case
Weighs not the dust and injury of age,　　　　　10
Nor gives to necessary wrinkles place,
But makes antiquity for aye his page;
　　Finding the first conceit of love there bred
　　Where time and outward form would show it dead.

line 3. Q reads, "What now to register." The emendation "new" is Malone's.

The last six lines of this sonnet, as also the passages already noted in 120 and 124, suggest with some force that Mr W. H. was losing his good looks. Mr Wyndham says, "I am convinced that the Poet does *not* refer to any change in the outward beauty of the Friend." I think that if Mr Wyndham was as fully convinced of this as he believes himself to be, he would not have put his "*not*" in italics.

129 [109, Q].

1588. Between Aug. 8 and Dec. 1.]

To Mr W. H.   A sequel to the preceding sonnet.

O, NEVER say that I was false of heart,
Though absence seem'd my flame to qualify.
As easy might I from myself depart
As from my soul, which in thy breast doth lie:
That is my home of love ; if I have rang'd   5
Like him that travels I return again
Just to the time, not with the time exchang'd,
So that myself bring water for my stain.
Never believe, though in my nature reign'd
All frailties that besiege all kinds of blood,   10
That it could so preposterously be strain'd,
To leave for nothing all thy sum of good ;
  For nothing this wide Universe I call,
  Save thou, my Rose ; in it thou art my all.

line 4. Malone cites Love's Labour's Lost, V, ii, 826,
  " Hence ever, then, my heart is in thy breast."
And Venus and Adonis canto 97,
  " Bids him farewell and look well to her heart,
  The which.........
  He carries thence incaged in his breast."

line 11. Q reads "so preposterouslie be stain'd." I have adopted
Staunton's (*Athenæum*, Jan. 31, 1874) emendation; the meaning is "Never
believe that the strain of my blood is so abnormal," &c.

130 [110, Q].

1588.   Between Aug. 8 and Dec. 1.]

*To Mr W. H.   Continuing to express penitence for the
inconstancy with which Mr W. H. has been
reproaching him.*

ALAS, 'tis true I have gone here and there
And made myself a motley to the view,
Gor'd mine own thoughts, sold cheap what is most dear,
Made old offences of affections new;
Most true it is that I have look'd on truth   5
Askance and strangely: But, by all above,
These blenches gave my heart another youth,
And worse essays prov'd thee my best of love.
Now all is done save what shall have no end:
Mine appetite I never more will grind   10
On newer proof, to try an older friend,
A God in love, to whom I am confin'd.
    Then give me welcome, next my heaven the best,
    Even to thy pure and most, most loving breast.

line 9.   Q reads, "Now all is done, haue what shall haue no end."
Malone adopted Tyrwhitt's conjectural emendation "save what shall
have," &c.

131 [111, Q].

1588. Between Aug. 8 and Dec. 1.]

To Mr W. H.   Still continuing the same vein of penitence.

O, FOR my sake do you with fortune chide,
The guilty goddess of my harmful deeds,
That did not better for my life provide
Than public means which public manners breeds.
Thence comes it that my name receives a brand,   5
And almost thence my nature is subdu'd
To what it works in, like the Dyer's hand;
Pity me then and wish I were renew'd,
Whilst, like a willing patient, I will drink
Potions of Eisel 'gainst my strong infection;   10
Nor bitterness that I will bitter think,
Nor double penance, to correct correction.
      Pity me then, dear friend, and I assure ye
      Even that your pity is enough to cure me.

line 1.   Q reads " doe you wish fortune chide."   The Cambridge edition quotes Gildon as the emendator.   Malone also made the same emendation.

line 10.   Eisel is vinegar.   "Vinegar is esteemed very efficacious in preventing the communication of plague and other contagious distempers."
                                      (MALONE.)

132 [112, Q].

1588.   Between Aug. 8 and Dec. 1.]

To Mr W. H.   A sequel to the preceding sonnet.

YOUR love and pity doth the impression fill
Which vulgar scandal stamp'd upon my brow;
For what care I who calls me well or ill,
So you o'er-green my bad, my good allow?
You are my All the world, and I must strive   5
To know my shames and praises from your tongue;
None else to me, nor I to none alive,
That my steel'd sense or changes right or wrong.
In so profound *Abism* I throw all care
Of others' voices, that my Adder's sense   10
To critic and to flatterer stopped are.
Mark how with my neglect I do dispense:
   You are so strongly in my purpose bred
   That all the world beside methinks are dead.

line 14.   Q reads "That all the world besides me thinkes y'are dead."
Malone in his edition of 1780 reads as in my text, which is the one
generally adopted.   This reading was also conjectured by Capell and
Steevens.   In his latest edition Malone reads "methinks they are dead,"
adding "Y'are was, I suppose, an abbreviation for 'they are' or 'th' are.'
Such unpleasing contractions are often found in our old poets."

133 [113, Q].

1588. Between, say, Sep. 1 and Dec. 1.]

To Mr W. H.   Written during travel.

Since I left you mine eye is in my mind,
And that which governs me to go about
Doth part his function and is partly blind,
Seems seeing, but effectually is out;
For it no form delivers to the heart   5
Of bird, of flower, or shape which it doth latch:
Of his quick objects hath the mind no part,
Nor his own vision holds what it doth catch;
For if it see the rud'st or gentlest sight,
The most sweet favour or deformed'st creature,   10
The mountain or the sea, the day or night,
The Crow or Dove, it shapes them to your feature:
   Incapable of more, replete with you,
   My most true mind thus maketh mine untrue.

line 3. i.e. "partly performs his office." (Malone).

line 6. Q reads "which it doth lack." The emendation is Malone's.
He explains that "to latch" formerly meant "to lay hold of." Mr Wyndham
says "'Latch' in old English meant a 'crossbow,' also a 'snare,' akin
perhaps to 'leash,' French *laisse*."

line 11. One wonders whether Shakespeare had as yet ever seen a
mountain, and if so what mountain? Hampstead Heath might do.

line 14. "Untrue" is here, as Malone pointed out, a substantive,
i.e. "untruth." The sense is "The untruthfulness of my perceptions is
caused by the truthfulness of my affection for you."

134 [114, Q].

1588.   Between, say, Sep. 1 and Dec. 1.]

To Mr W. H.   A sequel to the preceding sonnet.

OR whether doth my mind being crown'd with you
Drink up the monarch's plague, this flattery?
Or whether shall I say, mine eye seeth true,
And that your love taught it this *Alchemy*,
To make of monsters and things indigest   5
Such cherubins as your sweet self resemble,
Creating every bad a perfect best
As fast as objects to his beams assemble?
O, 'tis the first; 'tis flattery in my seeing,
And my great mind most kingly drinks it up;   10
Mine eye well knows what with his gust is 'greeing
And to his palate doth prepare the cup;
    If it be poison'd, 'tis the lesser sin
    That mine eye loves it and doth first begin.

line 3.   Q reads "saith."   The emendation (which I learn from Camb.)
is anonymous.

135 [115, Q].

1588. Between, say, Sep. 1 and Dec. 1.]

*To Mr W. H. Protesting that the writer's affection for him is
not decreasing, but on the contrary still growing.*

THOSE lines that I before have writ do lie,
Even those that said I could not love you dearer:
Yet then my judgement knew no reason why
My most full flame should afterwards burn clearer.
But reckoning time, whose millon'd accidents   5
Creep in 'twixt vows and change decrees of Kings,
Tan sacred beauty, blunt the sharp'st intents,
Divert strong minds to the course of altering things,
Alas, why, fearing of Time's tyranny,
Might I not then say 'Now I love you best,'   10
When I was certain o'er incertainty,
Crowning the present, doubting of the rest?
    Love is a Babe, then might I not say so,
    To give full growth to that which still doth grow.

lines 13, 14. I have followed Mr Wyndham in keeping to the punctuation
of Q. The sense is "I ought not to have said I loved you best, then; for I
should have remembered that Love is a babe, and I should have allowed for
his growing."

136 [116, Q].

1588.   Between, say, Sep. 1 and Dec. 1.]

*To Mr. W. H., who has been again upbraiding the writer and
making a continuation of the old friendship difficult.*

LET me not to the marriage of true minds
Admit impediments; love is not love
Which alters when it alteration finds,
Or bends with the remover to remove:
O, no! it is an ever-fixed mark,   5
That looks on tempests and is never shaken;
It is the star to every wandering bark,
Whose worth's unknown, although his height be taken.
Love's not Time's fool, though rosy lips and cheeks
Within his bending sickle's compass come;   10
Love alters not with his brief hours and weeks,
But bears it out even to the edge of doom.
    If this be error and upon me prov'd,
    I never writ, nor no man ever lov'd.

line 5.   Malone cites Coriolanus V, iii, 74, 5,
         " Like a great sea-mark, standing every flow
           And saving those that eye thee."

line 8.   Kinnear (Camb.) suggests " whose orb's unknown although," &c.
It is difficult not to suspect corruption in the text, but, I fear, impossible to
emend satisfactorily.

line 9.   Malone cites King Henry IV, Pt. I, V, iv, 81,
         " But thought's the slave of life, and life Time's fool."

137 [117, Q].

1588.   Between, say, Sep. 1 and Dec. 1.]

*To Mr W. H. A continuation of the same vein of apology and
self-abasement.*

ACCUSE me thus: that I have scanted all
Wherein I should your great deserts repay,
Forgot upon your dearest love to call,
Whereto all bonds do tie me day by day;
That I have frequent been with unknown minds   5
And given to them your own dear-purchas'd right;
That I have hoisted sail to all the winds
Which should transport me farthest from your sight.
Book both my wilfulness and errors down,
And on just proof surmise accumulate;   10
Bring me within the level of your frown,
But shoot not at me in your waken'd hate;
   Since my appeal says I did strive to prove
   The constancy and virtue of your love.

line 6.   Q reads "and given to time."   I have no hesitation in adopting
Staunton's emendation from the *Athenæum*, Jan. 31, 1874.

138 [118, Q].

1588.   Between, say, Sep. 1 and Dec. 1.]

To Mr W. H.   A sequel to the preceding sonnet.

LIKE as, to make our appetites more keen
With eager compounds we our palate urge;
As, to prevent our maladies unseen,
We sicken to shun sickness when we purge;
Even so, being full of your ne'er-cloying sweetness,   5
To bitter sauces did I frame my feeding;
And sick of welfare found a kind of meetness
To be diseas'd ere that there was true needing.
Thus policy in love, to anticipate
The ills that were not, grew to faults assur'd,   10
And brought to medicine a healthful state,
Which, rank of goodness, would by ill be cur'd:
    But thence I learn, and find the lesson true,
    Drugs poison him that so fell sick of you.

139 [147, Q].

1588.   Between, say, Sep. 1 and Dec. 1.]

*Probably to Mr W. H., after an open rupture between him and
Shakespeare.*

My love is as a fever, longing still
For that which longer nurseth the disease;
Feeding on that which doth preserve the ill,
The uncertain sickly appetite to please.
My reason, the Physician to my love,   5
Angry that his prescriptions are not kept
Hath left me, and I desperate now approve
Desire is death, which Physic did except.
Past cure I am, now Reason is past care,
And frantic-mad with evermore unrest   10
My thoughts and my discourse as madmen's are,
At random from the truth vainly express'd;
   For I have sworn thee fair, and thought thee bright,
   Who art as black as hell, as dark as night.

line 8.   "The sense is, 'I being in despair, now recognise that desire to
be fatal which took exception to the teaching of physic.'" (WYNDHAM.)

line 9.   Malone quotes Love's Labour's Lost, V, ii, 38,
       "Great reason, for past cure is still past care."

lines 13, 14.   I have already called attention to the fierceness of these
two lines as compared with the rest of the sonnet.

———

On pp. 18, 82, 83, I have given my reasons for intercalating here this
and the three following sonnets.

140 [148, Q].

1588.   Between, say, Sep. 1 and Dec. 1.]

Probably sent to Mr W. H. along with the preceding sonnet.

O ME, what eyes hath love put in my head,
Which have no correspondence with true sight!
Or if they have, where is my judgement fled,
That censures falsely what they see aright?
If that be fair whereon my false eyes dote,   5
What means the world to say it is not so?
If it be not, then love doth well denote
Love's eye is not so true as all men's: no,
How can it? O, how can love's eye be true,
That is so vex'd with watching and with tears?   10
No marvel then, though I mistake my view;
The sun itself sees not till heaven clears.
    O cunning love! with tears thou keep'st me blind,
    Lest eyes well-seeing thy foul faults should find.

line 4. " That censures falsely."   Malone points out that " censures "
here means " estimates."

lines 13, 14.   See note on the two last lines of the preceding sonnet.

141 [149, Q].

1588.   Between, say, Sep. 1 and Dec. 1.]

*Probably sent to Mr W. H. along with the two preceding
sonnets.*

CANST thou, O cruel! say I love thee not,
When I against myself with thee partake?
Do I not think on thee, when I forgot
Am of myself all tyrant for thy sake?
Who hateth thee that I do call my friend?   5
On whom frown'st thou that I do fawn upon?
Nay, if thou lour'st on me do I not spend
Revenge upon myself with present moan?
What merit do I in myself respect
That is so proud thy service to despise,   10
When all my best doth worship thy defect,
Commanded by the motion of thine eyes?
    But, love, hate on, for now I know thy mind;
    Those that can see thou lov'st, and I am blind.

line 2. " A 'partaker' was in Shakespeare's time the term for an
associate or confederate in any business." (MALONE.)

lines 3, 4. i.e. " When I, quite forgetful of self, tyrannise over myself
for your sake."

line 10. i.e. " That is too proud to stoop in order to do you service."

142 [150, Q].

1588.   Between, say, Sep. 1 and Dec. 1.]

*Probably sent to Mr W. H. along with the three preceding
sonnets.*

O, FROM what power hast thou this powerful might
With insufficiency my heart to sway?
To make me give the lie to my true sight
And swear that brightness doth not grace the day?
Whence hast thou this becoming of things ill,   5
That in the very refuse of thy deeds
There is such strength and warrantise of skill,
That in my mind thy worst all best exceeds?
Who taught thee how to make me love thee more
The more I hear and see just cause of hate?   10
O, though I love what others do abhor,
With others thou shouldst not abhor my state:
    If thy unworthiness rais'd love in me
    More worthy I to be belov'd of thee.

line 4.   Steevens cites Romeo and Juliet, III, v, 17, 18,
    "I am content, so thou wilt have it so.
    I'll say yon grey is not the morning's eye."

143 [119, Q].

1588. Between, say, Sep. 1 and Dec. 1.]

To Mr W. H.   On reconciliation.

WHAT potions have I drunk of *Siren* tears,
Distill'd from Limbecks foul as hell within,
Applying fears to hopes and hopes to fears,
Still losing when I saw myself to win!
What wretched errors hath my heart committed   5
Whilst it hath thought itself so blessed never!
How have mine eyes out of their Spheres been fitted
In the distraction of this madding fever!
O benefit of ill! now I find true
That better is by evil still made better;   10
And ruin'd love when it is built anew
Grows fairer than at first, more strong, far greater.
　　So I return rebuk'd to my content,
　　And gain by ill thrice more than I have spent.

line 2. " Limbecks," i.e. alembics; an alembic is the cap of a still; this is here used for the still as a whole.

line 7. i.e. " How have my eyes been convulsed during the frantic fits of my feverous love." (MALONE.)

144 [120, Q].

1588.   Between, say, Sep. 1 and Dec. 1.]

To Mr W. H.   On reconciliation; a sequel to the preceding
sonnet.

THAT you were once unkind befriends me now
And for that sorrow which I then did feel
Needs must I under my transgression bow,
Unless my Nerves were brass or hammer'd steel.
For if you were by my unkindness shaken   5
As I by yours, you've pass'd a hell of Time,
And I, a tyrant, have no leisure taken
To weigh how once I suffer'd in your crime.
O, that our night of woe might have remember'd
My deepest sense, how hard true sorrow hits,   10
And soon to you, as you to me then, tender'd
The humble salve which wounded bosoms fits!
     But that your trespass now becomes a fee;
     Mine ransoms yours, and yours must ransom me.

line 5. The unkindness on Shakespeare's part I take to be the bitterness of sonnets 140–143 (Q, 147–150) which I suppose Shakespeare to have
sent to Mr W. H. With the unkindness " once " received by Shakespeare
at the hands of Mr W. H. I have dealt fully in Chapter IX.

line 11. I have adopted the punctuation of Dyce, conjectured also by
Staunton and S. Walker. (Camb.)

145 [122, Q].

1588.   Between, say, Sep. 1 and Dec. 1.]

*To Mr W. H., who has upbraided the writer for having given
away a present which Mr W. H. had made him.**

THY gift, thy tables, are within my brain
Full character'd with lasting memory,
Which shall above that idle rank remain,
Beyond all date even to eternity,
Or, at the least, so long as brain and heart   5
Have faculty by nature to subsist;
Till each to raz'd oblivion yield his part
Of thee, thy record never can be miss'd.
That poor retention could not so much hold,
Nor need I tallies thy dear love to score,   10
Therefore to give them from me was I bold,
To trust those tables that receive thee more:
    To keep an adjunct to remember thee
    Were to import forgetfulness in me.

* See pp. 96, 97.

line 11. It is not possible to say that the tables had not been given
away recently, but the impression is left that it was some little time since
Shakespeare had parted with them.

146 [123, Q].

1588.   Between, say, Sep. 1 and Dec. 1.]

To Mr W. H. Asseverating that his affection will never alter.

No, Time, thou shalt not boast that I do change:
Thy pyramids built up with newer might
To me are nothing novel, nothing strange,
They are but dressings of a former sight:
Our dates are brief, and therefore we admire   5
What thou dost foist upon us that is old,
And rather make them born to our desire
Than think that we before have heard them told.
Thy registers and thee I both defy,
Not wondering at the present nor the past,   10
For thy records and what we see doth lie,
Made more or less by thy continual haste.
   This I do vow, and this shall ever be,
   I will be true despite thy scythe and thee.

line 7.   Q reads "borne to our desire," which I see Mr Wyndham
interprets as "bourne" or "limit." I follow the Cambridge edition and
Malone in reading "born." The meaning is, "We prefer to think of them
as something quite new that has been made expressly for ourselves, than to
see them as a mere revival of an old performance."

147 [124, Q].

1588.   Between, say, Sep. 1 and Dec. 1.]

A sequel to the preceding sonnet, and to the same effect.

IF my dear love were but the child of state,
It might for fortune's bastard be unfather'd,
As subject to time's love or to time's hate,
Weeds among weeds, or flowers with flowers gather'd.
No, it was builded far from accident;   5
It suffers not in smiling pomp, nor falls
Under the blow of thralled discontent,
Whereto the inviting time or fashion calls:
It fears not policy, that *Heretic*,
Which works on leases of short-number'd hours,   10
But all alone stands hugely politic,
That it nor grows with heat nor drowns with showers
    To this I witness call the souls oftime
    Which die for goodness, who have liv'd for crime.

lines 1—4.   i.e. "If my affection for you were but a creature of circumstance, or the environment of the moment, it might prove no lawful issue, but a base child of Fortune—weed or flower as it might happen."

line 8.   Q reads "our fashion calls."   I adopt Capell's conjecture given in Camb.

lines 13, 14.   Q reads ".... the foles of time," modern editions read "fools."   But Shakespeare would never call a man a fool for dying well after living ill, and there is no relevancy in calling such persons to bear witness to the fact that Shakespeare's love for Mr W. H. was not subject to vicissitudes.   I suppose "foles" to be a misprint for "foles," and take the emended passage to mean, "If I have been inconstant, nothing can shake me further, in witness whereof I call the souls of them whose repentance even after a life of crime has been often genuine."

148 [125, Q].

1588.   Probably about Nov. 24.]

To Mr W. H.   After another and probably final rupture.

WERE 't aught to me I bore the canopy,
With my extern the outward honouring,
Or laid great bases for eternity,
Which proves more short than waste or ruining?
Have I not seen dwellers on form and favour   5
Lose all, and more, by paying too much rent?
For compound sweet Forgoing simple savour,
Pitiful thrivers, in their gaining spent?
No, let me be obsequious in thy heart,
And take thou my oblation, poor but free,   10
Which is not mix'd with seconds, knows no art
But mutual renders, only me for thee.
  Hence, thou suborn'd *Informer*! a true soul
  When most impeach'd stands least in thy control.

line 1.   Canopy,] see end of Chapter XI.

line 6.   Q reads
  " Lose all, and more by paying too much rent
   For compound sweet; Forgoing simple sauor."
The present pointing is Malone's.

line 8.   Q reads "in their gazing spent." The emendation is Staunton's,
given in the *Athenæum*, Dec. 6, 1873.

line 12.   Q reads "but mutuall render."

lines 13, 14.   I can see no way of reconciling the fierceness of these two
with the desire for reconciliation expressed in the preceding lines. The
transition, however, is almost as abrupt in the closing lines of sonnets
139, 140.

APPENDIX A [126, Q].

1585. Probably Spring.]

*To Mr W. H.   Written under some special circumstances, the
clue to which is lost.   Perhaps to be spoken to Mr W. H.
when acting the part of Cupid in some Masque.*

O THOU, my lovely Boy, who in thy power
Dost hold time's sickle, glass, his fickle hour;
Who hast by waning grown, and therein show'st
Thy hours withering as thy sweet self grow'st;
If Nature, sovereign mistress over wrack,   5
As thou goest onwards still will pluck thee back,
She keeps thee to this purpose, that her skill
May time disgrace, and wretched minutes kill.
Yet fear her, O thou minion of her pleasure!
She may detain, but not still keep, her treasure: 10
Her *Audit*, though delay'd, answer'd must be,
And her *Quietus* is to render thee.
   (   )
   (   )

line 2.   Q reads,
 "Doest hould times fickle glasse, his sickle, hower."
I see from the Cambridge edition that many emendations to this obviously
corrupt line have been proposed, but cannot find that the line has ever been
read exactly as in my text.

line 4.   Q reads "Thy louers withering."

The brackets.   These appear in Q as in my text, but it is not likely that
any lines are missing.   Lines 11 and 12 have every appearance of being a
full close.

APPENDIX B [129, Q].

*An occasional sonnet, probably given, but not addressed to
Mr W. H., nor in any way referring to him.*

THE expense of Spirit in a waste of shame
Is lust in action; and till action, lust
Is perjured, murderous, bloody, full of blame,
Savage, extreme, rude, cruel, not to trust;
Enjoy'd no sooner but despised straight;   5
Past reason hunted; and no sooner had,
Past reason hated, as a swallow'd bait,
On purpose laid to make the taker mad:
Mad In pursuit, and in possession so;
Had, having, and in quest to have, extreme;   10
A bliss in proof, and prov'd, a very woe;
Before, a joy propos'd; behind, a dream.
　　All this the world well knows, yet none knows well
　　To shun the heaven that leads men to this hell.

line 11.　Q reads, " and proud and very woe."　(cf. 87 [Q, 67] line 12.)
The emendation " prov'd " was first made by Sewell (Camb.)　The rest of
the emendation is Malone's.

Appendix C [145, Q].

*Possibly a translation, made by request, for some occasion;
but without any connection with the sonnets.*

Those lips that Love's own hand did make
Breath'd forth the sound that said 'I hate,'
To me that languish'd for her sake:
But when she saw my woeful state,
Straight in her heart did mercy come,   5
Chiding that tongue that ever sweet
Was used in giving gentle doom;
And taught it thus anew to greet;
'I hate' she alter'd with an end,
That follow'd it as gentle day   10
Doth follow night, who, like a fiend,
From heaven to hell is flown away;
  'I hate' from hate away she threw,
  And saved my life, saying 'not you.'

Appendix D [146, Q].

*An occasional sonnet, probably shown and given to Mr W. H.,
but not having any reference to him.*

Poor soul, the centre of my sinful earth,
Starv'd by these rebel powers that thee array,
Why dost thou pine within and suffer dearth,
Painting thy outward walls so costly gay?
Why so large cost, having so short a lease,   5
Dost thou upon thy fading mansion spend?
Shall worms, inheritors of this excess,
Eat up thy charge? is this thy body's end?
Then, soul, live thou upon thy servant's loss,
And let that pine to aggravate thy store;   10
Buy terms divine in selling hours of dross;
Within be fed, without be rich no more:
    So shalt thou feed on death, that feeds on men,
    And death once dead, there's no more dying then.

lines 1, 2. Q reads,
    " Poore soule the center of my sinfull earth,
      My sinfull earth these rebbel powers that thee array."
I adopt Steevens' conjectural emendation.

line 10. cf. Love's Labour's Lost, I, i. 25.
    " The mind shall banquet, though the body pine."

APPENDIX E [153, Q].

A sonnet probably based on a Latin version of a Greek
*Epigram by Byzantine Marianus.**

CUPID laid by his brand and fell asleep:
A maid of *Dian's* this advantage found,
And his love-kindling fire did quickly steep
In a cold valley-fountain of that ground;
Which borrow'd from this holy fire of Love   5
A dateless lively heat, still to endure,
And grew a seething bath, which yet men prove
Against strange maladies a sovereign cure.
But at my mistress' eye love's brand new-fired,
The boy for trial needs would touch my breast;   10
I, sick withal, the help of bath desired,
And thither hied, a sad distemper'd guest,
    But found no cure: the bath for my help lies
    Where *Cupid* got new fire, my mistress' eyes.

* See Preface to Mr Gollancz's Temple edition.

Appendix F [154, Q].

Alternative and improved version of the preceding.

The little Love-God lying once asleep
Laid by his side his heart-inflaming brand,
Whilst many Nymphs that vow'd chaste life to keep
Came tripping by; but in her maiden hand
The fairest votary took up that fire   5
Which many Legions of true hearts had warm'd;
And so the General of hot desire
Was sleeping by a Virgin hand disarm'd.
This brand she quenched in a cool Well by,
Which from Love's fire took heat perpetual,   10
Growing a bath and healthful remedy
For men diseased; but I, my Mistress' thrall,
　　　Came there for cure, and this by that I prove,
　　　Love's fire heats water, water cools not love.

SHAKESPEARE'S SONNETS,

*Reprinted by kind permission of T. Tyler, Esq., from his fac-simile
of the text of the original edition.*

[The numbers within the brackets refer to the numbering of the Sonnets
in my own text. For the title-page and prefatory inscription,
see page 1 of this volume.]

1

FRom faireſt creatures we deſire increaſe,
  That thereby beauties *Roſe* might neuer die,
But as the riper ſhould by time deceaſe,
His tender heire might beare his memory:
But thou contracted to thine owne bright eyes,
Feed'ſt thy light's flame with ſelfe ſubſtantiall ſewell,
Making a famine where aboundance lies,
Thy ſelfe thy foe, to thy ſweet ſelfe too cruell:
Thou that art now the worlds freſh ornament,
And only herauld to the gaudy ſpring,
Within thine owne bud burieſt thy content,
And tender chorle makſt waſt in niggarding:
    Pitty the world, or elſe this glutton be,
    To eate the worlds due, by the graue and thee.

2

VVHen fortie Winters ſhall beſeige thy brow,
  And digge deep trenches in thy beauties field,
Thy youthes proud liuery ſo gaz'd on now,
Wil be a totter'd weed of ſmal worth held:
Then being askt, where all thy beautie lies,
Where all the treaſure of thy luſty daies;
To ſay within thine owne deepe ſunken eyes,
Were an all-eating ſhame, and thriftleſſe praiſe.
How much more praiſe deſeru'd thy beauties vſe,
If thou couldſt anſwere this faire child of mine
Shall ſum my count, and make my old excuſe
Proouing his beautie by ſucceſſion thine.
    This were to be new made when thou art ould,
    And ſee thy blood warme when thou feel'ſt it could.

3

LOoke in thy glaſſe and tell the face thou veweſt,
Now is the time that face ſhould forme an other,
Whoſe freſh repaire if now thou not reneweſt,
Thou doo'ſt beguile the world, vnbleſſe ſome mother.
For where is ſhe ſo faire whoſe vn-eard wombe
Diſdaines the tillage of thy husbandry?
Or who is he ſo fond will be the tombe,
Of his ſelfe loue to ſtop poſterity?
Thou art thy mothers glaſſe and ſhe in thee
Calls backe the louely Aprill of her prime,
So thou through windowes of thine age ſhalt ſee,
Diſpight of wrinkles this thy goulden time.
    But if thou liue remembred not to be,
    Die ſingle and thine Image dies with thee.

4

VNthrifty louelineſſe why doſt thou ſpend,
Vpon thy ſelfe thy beauties legacy?
Natures bequeſt giues nothing but doth lend,
And being franck ſhe lends to thoſe are free:
Then beautious nigard why dooſt thou abuſe,
The bountious largeſſe giuen thee to giue?
Profitles vferer why dooſt thou vſe
So great a ſumme of ſummes yet can'ſt not liue?
For hauing traffike with thy ſelfe alone,
Thou of thy ſelfe thy ſweet ſelfe doſt deceaue,
Then how when nature calls thee to be gone,
What acceptable *Audit* can'ſt thou leaue?
    Thy vnuf'd beauty muſt be tomb'd with thee,
    Which vſed liues th' executor to be.

5

THoſe howers that with gentle worke did frame,
The louely gaze where euery eye doth dwell
Will play the tirants to the very ſame,
And that vnfaire which fairely doth excell:
For neuer reſting time leads Summer on,
To hidious winter and confounds him there,
Sap checkt with froſt and luſtie leau's quite gon.
Beauty ore-ſnow'd and barenes euery where,
Then were not ſummers diſtillation left
A liquid priſoner pent in walls of glaſſe,
Beauties effect with beauty were bereft,
Nor it nor noe remembrance what it was.
    But flowers diſtil'd though they with winter meete,
    Leeſe but their ſhow, their ſubſtance ſtill liues ſweet.

6

THen let not winters wragged hand deface,
In thee thy fummer ere thou be diftil'd:
Make fweet fome viall; treafure thou fome place,
With beautits treafure ere it be felfe kil'd:
That vfe is not forbidden vfery,
Which happies thofe that pay the willing lone;
That's for thy felfe to breed an other thee,
Or ten times happier be it ten for one,
Ten times thy felfe were happier then thou art,
If ten of thine ten times refigur'd thee,
Then what could death doe if thou fhould'ft depart,
Leauing thee liuing in pofterity?
  Be not felfe-wild for thou art much too faire,
  To be deaths conqueft and make wormes thine heire.

7

LOe in the Orient when the gracious light,
Lifts vp his burning head, each vnder eye
Doth homage to his new appearing fight,
Seruing with lookes his facred maiefty,
And hauing climb'd the fteepe vp heauenly hill,
Refembling ftrong youth in his middle age,
Yet mortall lookes adore his beauty ftill,
Attending on his goulden pilgrimage:
But when from high-moft pich with wery car,
Like feeble age he reeleth from the day,
The eyes (fore dutious) now conuerted are
From his low tract and looke an other way:
  So thou, thy felfe out-going in thy noon:
  Vnlok'd on dieft vnleffe thou get a fonne.

8

MVfick to heare, why hear'ft thou mufick fadly,
Sweets with fweets warre not, ioy delights in ioy:
Why lou'ft thou that which thou receauft not gladly,
Or elfe receau'ft with pleafure thine annoy?
If the true concord of well tuned founds,
By vnions married do offend thine eare,
They do but fweetly chide thee, who confounds
In fingleneffe the parts that thou fhould'ft beare:
Marke how one ftring fweet husband to an other,
Strike each in each by mutuall ordering;
Refembling fier, and child, and happy mother,
Who all in one, one pleafing note do fing:
  Whofe fpeechleffe fong being many, feeming one,
  Sings this to thee thou fingle wilt proue none.

9

IS it for feare to wet a widdowes eye,
That thou confum'ft thy felfe in fingle life ?
Ah ; if thou iffuleffe fhalt hap to die,
The world will waile thee like a makeleffe wife,
The world wilbe thy widdow and ftill weepe,
That thou no forme of thee haft left behind,
When euery priuat widdow well may keepe,
By childrens eyes, her husbands fhape in minde :
Looke what an vnthrift in the world doth fpend
Shifts but his place, for ftill the world inioyes it
But beauties wafte, hath in the world an end,
And kept vnvfde the vfer fo deftroyes it :
    No loue toward others in that bofome fits
    That on himfelfe fuch murdrous fhame commits.

10

FOr fhame deny that thou bear'ft loue to any
Who for thy felfe art fo vnprouident
Graunt if thou wilt, thou art belou'd of many,
But that thou none lou'ft is moft euident :
For thou art fo poffeft with murdrous hate,
That gainft thy felfe thou ftickft not to confpire,
Seeking that beautious roofe to ruinate
Which to repaire fhould be thy chiefe defire :
O change thy thought, that I may change my minde,
Shall hate be fairer log'd then gentle loue ?
Be as thy prefence is gracious and kind,
Or to thy felfe at leaft kind harted proue,
    Make thee an other felfe for loue of me,
    That beauty ftill may liue in thine or thee.

11

AS faft as thou fhalt wane fo faft thou grow'ft
In one of thine, from that which thou departeft,
And that frefh bloud which yongly thou beftow'ft,
Thou maift call thine, when thou from youth conuerteft,
Herein liues wifdome, beauty, and increafe,
Without this follie, age, and could decay,
If all were minded fo, the times fhould ceafe,
And threefcoore yeare would make the world away :
Let thofe whom nature hath not made for ftore,
Harfh, featureleffe, and rude, barrenly perrifh,
Looke whom fhe beft indow'd, fhe gaue the more ;
Which bountious guift thou fhouldft in bounty cherrifh,
    She caru'd thee for her feale, and ment therby,
    Thou fhouldft print more, not let that coppy die.

12

VVHen I doe count the clock that tels the time,
And fee the braue day funck in hidious night,
When I behold the violet paft prime,
And fable curls or filuer'd ore with white:
When lofty trees I fee barren of leaues,
Which erft from heat did canopie the herd
And Sommers greene all girded vp in fheaues
Borne on the beare with white and briftly beard:
Then of thy beauty do I queftion make
That thou among the waftes of time muft goe,
Since fwcets and beauties do them-felues forfake,
And die as faft as they fee others grow,
   And nothing gainft Times fieth can make defence
   Saue breed to braue him, when he takes thee hence.

13

OThat you were your felfe, but loue you are
No longer yours, then you your felfe here liue,
Againft this cumming end you fhould prepare,
And your fweet femblance to fome other giue.
So fhould that beauty which you hold in leafe
Find no determination, then you were
You felfe again after your felfes deceafe,
When your fweet iffue your fweet forme fhould beare.
Who lets fo faire a houfe fall to decay,
Which husbandry in honour might vphold,
Againft the ftormy gufts of winters day
And barren rage of deaths eternall cold?
   O none but vnthrifts, deare my loue you know,
   You had a Father, let your Son fay fo.

14

NOt from the ftars do I my iudgement plucke,
And yet me thinkes I haue Aftronomy,
But not to tell of good, or euil lucke,
Of plagues, of dearths, or feafons quallity,
Nor can I fortune to breefe mynuits tell;
Pointing to each his thunder, raine and winde,
Or fay with Princes if it fhal go wel
By oft predict that I in heauen finde.
But from thine eies my knowledge I deriue,
And conftant ftars in them I read fuch art
As truth and beautie fhal together thriue
If from thy felfe, to ftore thou wouldft conuert:
   Or elfe of thee this I prognofticate,
   Thy end is Truthes and Beauties doome and date.

15

WHen I confider euery thing that growes
Holds in perfection but a little moment.
That this huge ftage prefenteth nought but fhowes
Whereon the Stars in fecret influence comment,
When I perceiue that men as plants increafe,
Cheared and checkt euen by the felfe-fame skie :
Vaunt in their youthfull fap, at height decreafe,
And were their braue ftate out of memory.
Then the conceit of this inconftant ftay,
Sets you moft rich in youth before my fight,
Where waftfull time debateth with decay
To change your day of youth to fullied night,
    And all in war with Time for loue of you
    As he takes from you, I ingraft you new.

16

BVt wherefore do not you a mightier waie
Make warre vppon this bloudie tirant time ?
And fortifie your felfe in your decay
With meanes more bleffed then my barren rime ?
Now ftand you on the top of happie houres,
And many maiden gardens yet vnfet,
With vertuous wifh would beare your liuing flowers,
Much liker then your painted counterfeit :
So fhould the lines of life that life repaire
Which this (Times penfel or my pupill pen)
Neither in inward worth nor outward faire
Can make you liue your felfe in eies of men,
    To giue away your felfe, keeps your felfe ftill,
    And you muft liue drawne by your owne fweet skill,

17

VVHo will beleeue my verfe in time to come
If it were fild with your moft high deferts ?
Though yet heauen knowes it is but as a tombe
Which hides your life, and fhewes not halfe your parts :
If I could write the beauty of your eyes,
And in frefh numbers number all your graces,
The age to come would fay this Poet lies,
Such heauenly touches nere toucht earthly faces.
So fhould my papers (yellowed with their age)
Be fcorn'd, like old men of leffe truth then tongue,
And your true rights be termd a Poets rage,
And ftretched miter of an Antique fong.
    But were fome childe of yours aliue that time,
    You fhould liue twife in it, and in my rime.

18

SHall I compare thee to a Summers day?
Thou art more louely and more temperate:
Rough windes do fhake the darling buds of Maie,
And Sommers leafe hath all too fhort a date:
Sometime too hot the eye of heauen fhines,
And often is his gold complexion dimn'd,
And euery faire from faire fome-time declines,
By chance, or natures changing courfe vntrim'd:
But thy eternall Sommer fhall not fade,
Nor loofe poffeffion of that faire thou ow'ft,
Nor fhall death brag thou wandr'ft in his fhade,
When in eternall lines to time thou grow'ft,
   So long as men can breath or eyes can fee,
   So long liues this, and this giues life to thee,

19

DEuouring time blunt thou the Lyons pawes,
And make the earth deuoure her owne fweet brood,
Plucke the keene teeth from the fierce Tygers yawes,
And burne the long liu'd Phænix in her blood,
Make glad and forry feafons as thou fleet'ft,
And do what ere thou wilt fwift-footed time
To the wide world and all her fading fweets:
But I forbid thee one moft hainous crime,
O carue not with thy howers my loues faire brow,
Nor draw noe lines there with thine antique pen,
Him in thy courfe vntainted doe allow,
For beauties patterne to fucceding men.
   Yet doe thy worft ould Time difpight thy wrong,
   My loue fhall in my verfe euer liue young.

20

A Womans face with natures owne hand painted,
Hafte thou the Mafter Miftris of my paffion,
A womans gentle hart but not acquainted
With fhifting change as is falfe womens fafhion,
An eye more bright then theirs, leffe falfe in rowling:
Gilding the obiect where-vpon it gazeth,
A man in hew all *Hews* in his controwling,
Which fteales mens eyes and womens foules amafeth,
And for a woman wert thou firft created,
Till nature as fhe wrought thee fell a dotinge,
And by addition me of thee defeated,
By adding one thing to my purpofe nothing.
   But fince fhe prickt thee out for womens pleafure,
   Mine be thy loue and thy loues vfe their treafure.

21

SO is it not with me as with that Mufe,
Stird by a painted beauty to his verfe,
Who heauen it felfe for ornament doth vfe,
And euery faire with his faire doth reherfe,
Making a coopelment of proud compare
With Sunne and Moone, with earth and feas rich gems :
With Aprills firft borne flowers and all things rare,
That heauens ayre in this huge rondure hems,
O let me true in loue but truly write,
And then beleeue me, my loue is as faire,
As any mothers childe, though not fo bright
As thofe gould candells fixt in heauens ayer :
     Let them fay more that like of heare-fay well,
     I will not prayfe that purpofe not to fell.

22

MY glaffe fhall not perfwade me I am ould,
So long as youth and thou are of one date,
But when in thee times forrwes I behould,
Then look I death my daies fhould expiate.
For all that beauty that doth couer thee,
Is but the feemely rayment of my heart,
Which in thy breft doth liue, as thine in me,
How can I then be elder then thou art ?
O therefore loue be of thy felfe fo wary,
As I not for my felfe, but for thee will,
Bearing thy heart which I will keepe fo chary
As tender nurfe her babe from faring ill,
     Prefume not on thy heart when mine is flaine,
     Thou gau'ft me thine not to giue backe againe.

23

AS an vnperfect actor on the ftage,
Who with his feare is put befides his part,
Or fome fierce thing repleat with too much rage,
Whofe ftrengths abondance weakens his owne heart ;
So I for feare of truft, forget to fay,
The perfect ceremony of loues right,
And in mine owne loues ftrength feeme to decay,
Ore-charg'd with burthen of mine owne loues might :
O let my books be then the eloquence,
And domb prefagers of my fpeaking breft,
Who pleade for loue, and look for recompence,
More then that tonge that more hath more expreft.
     O learne to read what filent loue hath writ,
     To heare wit eies belongs to loues fine wiht.

24

Mine eye hath play'd the painter and hath ſteeld,
   Thy beauties forme in table of my heart,
My body is the frame wherein ti's held,
And perſpectiue it is beſt Painters art.
For through the Painter muſt you ſee his skill,
To finde where your true Image pictur'd lies,
Which in my boſomes ſhop is hanging ſtil,
That hath his windowes glazed with thine eyes:
Now ſee what good-turnes eyes for eies haue done,
Mine eyes haue drawne thy ſhape, and thine for me
Are windowes to my breſt, where-through the Sun
Delights to peepe, to gaze therein on thee
   Yet eyes this cunning want to grace their art
   They draw but what they ſee, know not the hart.

25

Let thoſe who are in fauor with their ſtars,
   Of publike honour and proud titles boſt,
Whilſt I whome fortune of ſuch tryumph bars
Vnlookt for ioy in that I honour moſt;
Great Princes fauorites their faire leaues ſpread,
But as the Marygold at the ſuns eye,
And in them-ſelues their pride lies buried,
For at a frowne they in their glory die.
The painefull warrier famoſed for worth,
After a thouſand victories once foild,
Is from the booke of honour raſed quite,
And all the reſt forgot for which he toild:
   Then happy I that loue and am beloued
   Where I may not remoue, nor be remoued.

26

Lord of my loue, to whome in vaſſalage
   Thy merrit hath my dutie ſtrongly knit;
To thee I ſend this written ambaſſage
To witneſſe duty, not to ſhew my wit.
Duty ſo great, which wit ſo poore as mine
May make ſeeme bare, in wanting words to ſhew it;
But that I hope ſome good conceipt of thine
In thy ſoules thought (all naked) will beſtow it:
Til whatſoeuer ſtar that guides my mouing,
Points on me gratiouſly with faire aſpect,
And puts apparrell on my tottered louing,
To ſhow me worthy of their ſweet reſpect,
   Then may I dare to boaſt how I doe loue thee,
   Til then, not ſhow my head where thou maiſt proue me.

27

WEary with toyle, I haſt me to my bed,
  The deare repoſe for lims with trauaill tired,
But then begins a iourny in my head
To worke my mind, when boddies work's expired.
For then my thoughts (from far where I abide)
Intend a zelous pilgrimage to thee;
And keepe my drooping eye-lids open wide,
Looking on darknes which the blind doe ſee.
Saue that my ſoules imaginary ſight
Preſents their ſhaddoe to my ſightles view,
Which like a iewell (hunge in gaſtly night)
Makes blacke night beautious, and her old face new.
    Loe thus by day my lims, by night by mind,
    For thee, and for my ſelfe, noe quiet finde.

28

HOw can I then returne in happy plight
  That am debard the benifit of reſt?
When daies oppreſſion is not eazd by night,
But day by night and night by day opreſt.
And each (though enimes to ethers raigne)
Doe in conſent ſhake hands to torture me,
The one by toyle, the other to complaine
How far I toyle, ſtill farther off from thee.
I tell the Day to pleaſe him thou art bright,
And do'ſt him grace when clouds doe blot the heauen:
So flatter I the ſwart complexiond night,
When ſparkling ſtars twire not thou guil'ſt th' eauen,
    But day doth daily draw my ſorrowes longer, (ſtronger
    And night doth nightly make greefes length ſeeme

29

VVHen in diſgrace with Fortune and mens eyes,
  I all alone beweepe my out-caſt ſtate,
And trouble deafe heauen with my bootleſſe cries,
And looke vpon my ſelfe and curſe my fate.
Wiſhing me like to one more rich in hope,
Featur'd like him, like him with friends poſſeſt,
Deſiring this mans art, and that mans skope,
With what I moſt inioy contented leaſt,
Yet in theſe thoughts my ſelfe almoſt deſpiſing,
Haplye I thinke on thee, and then my ſtate,
(Like to the Larke at breake of daye ariſing)
From ſullen earth ſings himns at Heauens gate,
    For thy ſweet loue remembred ſuch welth brings,
    That then I skorne to change my ſtate with Kings.

30

VVHen to the Seffions of fweet filent thought,
I fommon vp remembrance of things paft,
I figh the lacke of many a thing I fought,
And with old woes new waile my deare times wafte:
Then can I drowne an eye (vn-vf'd to flow)
For precious friends hid in deaths dateles night,
And weepe a frefh loues long fince canceld woe,
And mone th'expence of many a vannifht fight.
Then can I greeue at greeuances fore-gon,
And heauily from woe to woe tell ore
The fad account of fore-bemoned mone,
Which I new pay, as if not payd before.
  But if the while I thinke on thee (deare friend)
  All loffes are reftord, and forrowes end.

31

Thy bofome is indeared with all hearts,
Which I by lacking haue fuppofed dead,
And there raignes Loue and all Loues louing parts,
And all thofe friends which I thought buried.
How many a holy and obfequious teare
Hath deare religious loue ftolne from mine eye,
As intereft of the dead, which now appeare,
But things remou'd that hidden in there lie.
Thou art the graue where buried loue doth liue,
Hung with the tropheis of my louers gon,
Who all their parts of me to thee did giue,
That due of many, now is thine alone.
  Their images I lou'd, I view in thee,
  And thou (all they) haft all the all of me.

32

IF thou furuiue my well contented daie,
When that churle death my bones with duft fhall couer
And fhalt by fortune once more re-furuay:
Thefe poore rude lines of thy deceafed Louer:
Compare them with the bett'ring of the time,
And though they be out-ftript by euery pen,
Referue them for my loue, not for their rime,
Exceeded by the hight of happier men.
Oh then voutfafe me but this louing thought,
Had my friends Mufe growne with this growing age,
A dearer birth then this bis loue had brought
To march inranckes of better equipage:
  But fince he died and Poets better proue,
  Theirs for their ftile ile read, his for his loue.

33 [34]

FVll many a glorious morning haue I feene,
  Flatter the mountaine tops with foueraine eie,
Kiffing with golden face the meddowes greene;
Guilding pale ftreames with heauenly alcumy:
Anon permit the bafeft cloudes to ride,
With ougly rack on his celeftiall face,
And from the for-lorne world his vifage hide
Stealing vnfeene to weft with this difgrace:
Euen fo my Sunne one early morne did fhine,
With all triumphant fplendor on my brow,
But out alack, he was but one houre mine,
The region cloude hath mask'd him from me now.
   Yet him for this, my loue no whit difdaineth,
   Suns of the world may ftaine, whē heauens fun ftainteh.

34 [35]

VVHy didft thou promife fuch a beautious day,
  And make me trauaile forth without my cloake,
To let bace cloudes ore-take me in my way,
Hiding thy brau'ry in their rotten fmoke.
Tis not enough that through the cloude thou breake,
To dry the raine on my ftorme-beaten face,
For no man well of fuch a falue can fpeake,
That heales the wound, and cures not the difgrace :
Nor can thy fhame giue phificke to my griefe,
Though thou repent, yet I haue ftill the loffe,
Th' offenders forrow lends but weake reliefe
To him that beares the ftrong offenfes loffe.
   Ah but thofe teares are pearle which thy loue fheeds,
   And they are ritch, and ranfome all ill deeds.

35 [56]

NO more bee greeu'd at that which thou haft done,
  Rofes haue thornes, and filuer fountaines mud,
Cloudes and eclipfes ftaine both Moone and Sunne,
And loathfome canker liues in fweeteft bud.
All men make faults, and euen I in this,
Authorizing thy trefpas with compare,
My felfe corrupting faluing thy amiffe,
Excufing their fins more then their fins are ;
For to thy fenfuall fault I bring in fence,
Thy aduerfe party is thy Aduocate,
And gainft my felfe a lawfull plea commence,
Such ciuill war is in my loue and hate,
   That I an acceffary needs muft be,
   To that fweet theefe which fourely robs from me.

36

LEt me confeffe that we two muft be twaine,
Although our vndeuided loues are one:
So fhall thofe blots that do with me remaine,
Without thy helpe, by me be borne alone.
In our two loues there is but one refpect,
Though in our liues a feperable fpight,
Which though it alter not loues fole effect,
Yet doth it fteale fweet houres from loues delight,
I may not euer-more acknowledge thee,
Leaft my bewailed guilt fhould do thee shame,
Nor thou with publike kindneffe honour me,
Vnleffe thou take that honour from thy name:
 But doe not fo, I loue thee in fuch fort.
 As thou being mine, mine is thy good report.

37

AS a decrepit father takes delight,
To fee his actiue childe do deeds of youth,
So I, made lame by Fortunes deareft fpight
Take all my comfort of thy worth and truth.
For whether beauty, birth, or wealth, or wit,
Or any of thefe all, or all, or more
Intitled in their parts, do crowned fit,
I make my loue ingrafted to this ftore:
So then I am not lame, poore, nor difpif'd,
Whilft that this fhadow doth fuch fubftance giue,
That I in thy abundance am fuffic'd,
And by a part of all thy glory liue:
 Looke what is beft, that beft I wifh in thee,
 This wifh I haue, then ten times happy me.

38

HOw can my Mufe want fubiect to inuent
While thou doft breath that poor'ft into my verfe,
Thine owne fweet argument, to excellent,
For euery vulgar paper to rehearfe:
Oh giue thy felfe the thankes if ought in me,
Worthy perufal ftand againft thy fight,
For who's fo dumbe that cannot write to thee,
When thou thy felfe doft giue inuention light?
Be thou the tenth Mufe, ten times more in worth
Then thofe old nine which rimers innocate,
And he that calls on thee, let him bring forth
Eternal numbers to out-liue long date.
 If my flight Mufe doe pleafe thefe curious daies,
 The paine be mine, but thine fhal be the praife.

U

39

OH how thy worth with manners may I finge,
When thou art all the better part of me?
What can mine owne praife to mine owne felfe bring;
And what is't but mine owne when I praife thee,
Euen for this, let vs deuided liue,
And our deare loue loofe name of fingle one
That by this feperation I may giue:
That due to thee which thou deferu'ft alone:
Oh abfence what a torment wouldft thou proue,
Were it not thy foure leifure gaue fweet leaue,
To entertaine the time with thoughts of loue,
VVhich time and thoughts fo fweetly doft deceiue.
　　And that thou teacheft how to make one twaine,
　　By praifing him here who doth hence remaine.

40 [57]

TAke all my loues, my loue, yea take them all,
What haft thou then more then thou hadft before?
No loue, my loue, that thou maift true loue call.
All mine was thine, before thou hadft this more:
Then if for my loue, thou my loue receiueft,
I cannot blame thee, for my loue thou vfeft,
But yet be blam'd, if thou this felfe deceaueft
By wilfull tafte of what thy felfe refufeft.
I doe forgiue thy robb'rie gentle theefe
Although thou fteale thee all my pouerty:
And yet loue knowes it is a greater griefe
To beare loues wrong, then hates knowne iniury.
　　Lafciuious grace in whom all il wel fhowes,
　　Kill me with fpights yet we muft not be foes.

41 [58]

THofe pretty wrongs that liberty commits,
When I am fome-time abfent from thy heart,
Thy beautie, and thy yeares full well befits,
For ftill temptation followes where thou art.
Gentle thou art, and therefore to be wonne,
Beautious thou art, therefore to be affailed.
And when a woman woes, what womans fonne,
Will fourely leaue her till he haue preuailed.
Aye me, but yet thou mighft my feate forbeare,
And chide thy beauty, and thy ftraying youth,
Who lead thee in their ryot euen there
Where thou art forft to breake a two fold truth:
　　Hers by thy beauty tempting her·to thee,
　　Thine by thy beautie beeing falfe to me.

42 [59]

THat thou haft her it is not all my griefe,
  And yet it may be faid I lou'd her deerely,
That fhe hath thee is of my wayling cheefe,
A loffe in loue that touches me more neerely.
Louing offendors thus I will excufe yee,
Thou dooft loue her, becaufe thou knowft I loue her,
And for my fake euen fo doth fhe abufe me,
Suffring my friend for my fake to approoue her,
If I loofe thee, my loffe is my loues gaine,
And loofing her, my friend hath found that loffe,
Both finde each other, and I loofe both twaine,
And both for my fake lay on me this croffe,
  But here's the ioy, my friend and I are one,
  Sweete flattery, then fhe loues but me alone.

43 [63]

WHen moft I winke then doe mine eyes beft fee,
  For all the day they view things vnrefpected,
But when I fleepe, in dreames they looke on thee,
And darkely bright, are bright in darke directed.
Then thou whofe fhaddow fhaddowes doth make bright,
How would thy fhadowes forme, forme happy fhow,
To the cleere day with thy much cleerer light,
When to vn-feeing eyes thy fhade fhines fo ?
How would (I fay) mine eyes be bleffed made,
By looking on thee in the liuing day ?
When in dead night their faire imperfect fhade,
Through heauy fleepe on fightleffe eyes doth ftay ?
  All dayes are nights to fee till I fee thee,
  And nights bright daies when dreams do fhew thee me.

44 [64]

IF the dull fubftance of my flefh were thought,
  Iniurious diftance fhould not ftop my way,
For then difpight of fpace I would be brought,
From limits farre remote, where thou dooft ftay,
No matter then although my foote did ftand
Vpon the fartheft earth remoou'd from thee,
For nimble thought can iumpe both fea and land,
As foone as thinke the place where he would be.
But ah, thought kills me that I am not thought
To leape large lengths of miles when thou art gone,
But that fo much of earth and water wrought,
I muft attend, times leafure with my mone.
  Receiuing naughts by elements fo floe,
  But heauie teares, badges of eithers woe.

45 [65]

THe other two, flight ayre, and purging fire,
  Are both with thee, where euer I abide,
The firft my thought, the other my defire,
Thefe prefent abfent with fwift motion flide,
For when thefe quicker Elements are gone
In tender Embaffie of loue to thee,
My life being made of foure, with two alone,
Sinkes downe to death, oppreft with melancholie,
Vntill liues compofition be recured,
By thofe fwift meffengers return'd from thee,
Who euen but now come back againe affured,
Of their faire health, recounting it to me.
  This told, I ioy, but then no longer glad,
  I fend them back againe and ftraight grow fad.

46 [66]

MIne eye and heart are at a mortall warre,
  How to deuide the conqueft of thy fight,
Mine eye, my heart their pictures fight would barre,
My heart, mine eye the freeedome of that right,
My heart doth plead that thou in him dooft lye,
(A clofet neuer peaift with chriftall eyes)
But the defendant doth that plea deny,
And fayes in him their faire appearance lyes,
To fide this title is impannelled
A queft of thoughts, all tennants to the heart,
And by their verdict is determined
The cleere eyes moyitie, and he deare hearts part.
  As thus, mine eyes due is their outward part,
  And my hearts right, their inward loue of heart.

47 [67]

BEtwixt mine eye and heart a league is tooke,
  And each doth good turnes now vnto the other,
When that mine eye is famifht for a looke,
Or heart in loue with fighes himfelfe doth fmother;
With my loues picture then my eye doth feaft,
And to the painted banquet bids my heart:
An other time mine eye is my hearts gueft,
And in his thoughts of loue doth fhare a part.
So either by thy picture or my loue,
Thy feife away, are prefent ftill with me,
For thou nor farther then my thoughts canft moue,
And I am ftill with them, and they with thee.
  Or if they fleepe, thy picture in my fight
  Awakes my heart, to hearts and eyes delight.

48 [68]

HOw carefull was I when I tooke my way,
Each trifle vnder trueſt barres to thruſt,
That to my vſe it might vn-vſed ſtay
From hands of falſehood, in ſure wards of truſt?
But thou, to whom my iewels trifles are,
Moſt worthy comfort, now my greateſt griefe,
Thou beſt of deereſt, and mine onely care,
Art left the prey of euery vulgar theefe.
Thee haue I not lockt vp in any cheſt,
Saue where thou art not, though I feele thou art,
Within the gentle cloſure of my breſt,
From whence at pleaſure thou maiſt come and part,
    And euen thence thou wilt be ſtolne I feare,
    For truth prooues theeuiſh for a prize ſo deare.

49 [69]

AGainſt that time (if euer that time come)
When I ſhall ſee thee frowne on my defects,
When as thy loue hath caſt his vtmoſt ſumme,
Cauld to that audite by aduiſ'd reſpects,
Againſt that time when thou ſhalt ſtrangely paſſe,
And ſcarcely greete me with that ſunne thine eye,
When loue conuerted from the thing it was
Shall reaſons finde of ſetled grauitie.
Againſt that time do I inſconce me here
Within the knowledge of mine owne deſart,
And this my hand, againſt my ſelfe vpreare,
To guard the lawfull reaſons on thy part,
    To leaue poore me, thou haſt the ſtrength of lawes,
    Since why to loue, I can alledge no cauſe.

50 [70]

HOw heauie doe I iourney on the way,
When what I ſeeke (my wearie trauels end)
Doth teach that eaſe and that repoſe to ſay
Thus farre the miles are meaſurde from thy friend.
The beaſt that beares me, tired with my woe,
Plods duly on, to beare that waight in me,
As if by ſome inſtinct the wretch did know
His rider lou'd not ſpeed being made from thee:
The bloody ſpurre cannot prouoke him on,
That ſome-times anger thruſts into his hide,
Which heauily he anſwers with a grone,
More ſharpe to me then ſpurring to his ſide,
    For that ſame grone doth put this in my mind,
    My greefe lies onward and my ioy behind.

51 [71]

THus can my loue excufe the flow offence,
Of my dull bearer, when from thee I fpeed,
From where thou art, why fhoulld I haft me thence,
Till I returne of pofting is noe need.
O what excufe will my poore beaft then find,
When fwift extremity can feeme but flow,
Then fhould I fpurre though mounted on the wind,
In winged fpeed no motion fhall I know,
Then can no horfe with my defire keepe pace,
Therefore defire (of perfects loue being made)
Shall naigh noe dull flefh in his fiery race,
But loue, for loue, thus fhall excufe my iade,
　Since from thee going, he went wilfull flow,
　Towards thee ile run, and giue him leaue to goe.

52 [72]

SO am I as the rich whofe bleffed key,
Can bring him to his fweet vp-locked treafure,
The which he will not eu'ry hower furuay,
For blunting the fine point of feldome pleafure.
Therefore are feafts fo follemne and fo rare,
Since fildom comming in the long yeare fet,
Like ftones of worth they thinly placed are,
Or captaine Iewells in the carconet.
So is the time that keepes you as my cheft,
Or as the ward-robe which the robe doth hide,
To make fome fpeciall inftant fpeciall bleft,
By new vnfoulding his imprifon'd pride,
　Bleffed are you whofe worthineffe giues skope,
　Being had to tryumph, being lackt to hope.

53 [73]

VVHat is your fubftance, whereof are you made,
That millions of ftrange fhaddowes on you tend ?
Since euery one, hath euery one, one fhade,
And you but one, can euery fhaddow lend :
Defcribe *Adonis* and the counterfet,
Is poorely immitated after you,
On *Hellens* cheeke all art of beautie fet,
And you in *Grecian* tires are painted new :
Speake of the fpring, and foyzon of the yeare,
The one doth fhaddow of your beautie fhow,
The other as your bountie doth appeare,
And you in euery bleffed fhape we know.
　In all externall grace you haue fome part,
　But you like none, none you for conftant heart.

54 [74]

OH how much more doth beautie beantious feeme,
By that fweet ornament which truth doth giue,
The Rofe lookes faire, but fairer we it deeme
For that fweet odor, which doth in it liue:
The Canker bloomes haue full as deepe a die,
As the perfumed tincture of the Rofes,
Hang on fuch thornes, and play as wantonly,
When fommers breath their masked buds difclofes:
But for their virtue only is their fhow,
They liue vnwoo'd, and vnrefpected fade,
Die to themfelues. Sweet Rofes doe not fo,
Of their fweet deathes, are fweeteft odors made:
 And fo of you, beautious and louely youth,
 When that fhall vade, by verfe diftils your truth.

55 [75]

NOt marble, nor the guilded monument,
Of Princes fhall out-liue this powrefull rime,
But you fhall fhine more bright in thefe contents
Then vnfwept ftone, befmeer'd with fluttifh time.
When waftefull warre fhall *Statues* ouer-turne,
And broiles roote out the worke of mafonry,
Nor *Mars* his fword, nor warres quick fire fhall burne:
The liuing record of your memory.
Gainft death, and all obliuious emnity
Shall you pace forth, your praife fhall ftil finde roome,
Euen in the eyes of all pofterity
That weare this world out to the ending doome.
 So til the iudgement that your felfe arife,
 You liue in this, and dwell in louers eies.

56 [76]

Sweet loue renew thy force, be it not faid
Thy edge fhould blunter be then apetite,
Which but too daie by feeding is alaied,
To morrow fharpned in his former might.
So loue be thou, although too daie thou fill
Thy hungrie eies, euen till they winck with fulneffe,
Too morrow fee againe, and doe not kill
The fpirit of Loue, with a perpetual dulneffe:
Let this fad *Intrim* like the Ocean be
Which parts the fhore, where two contracted new,
Come daily to the banckes, that when they fee:
Returne of loue, more bleft may be the view.
 As cal it Winter, which being ful of care,
 Makes Somers welcome, thrice more wifh'd, more rare.

57 [77]

BEing your flaue what fhould I doe but tend,
Vpon the houres, and times of your defire ?
I haue no precious time at al to fpend;
Nor feruices to doe til you require.
Nor dare I chide the world without end houre,
Whilft I (my foueraine) watch the clock for you,
Nor thinke the bitterneffe of abfence fowre,
VVhen you haue bid your feruant once adieue.
Nor dare I queftion with my iealious thought,
VVhere you may be, or your affaires fuppofe,
But like a fad flaue ftay and thinke of nought
Saue where you are, how happy you make thofe.
  So true a foole is loue, that in your Will,
  (Though you doe any thing) he thinkes no ill.

58 [78]

THat God forbid, that made me firft your flaue,
  I fhould in thought controule your times of pleafure,
Or at your hand th' account of houres to craue,
Being your vaffail bound to ftaie your leifure.
Oh let me fuffer (being at your beck)
Th' imprifon'd abfence of your libertie,
And patience tame, to fufferance bide each check,
Without accufing you of iniury.
Be where you lift, your charter is fo ftrong,
That you your felfe may priuiledge your time
To what you will, to you it doth belong,
Your felfe to pardon of felfe-doing crime.
  I am to waite though waiting fo be hell,
  Not blame your pleafure be it ill or well.

59 [79]

IF their bee nothing new, but that which is,
Hath beene before, how are our braines beguild,
Which laboring for inuention beare amiffe
The fecond burthen of a former child ?
Oh that record could with a back-ward looke,
Euen of fiue hundreth courfes of the Sunne,
Show me your image in fome antique booke,
Since minde at firft in carrecter was done.
That I might fee what the old world could fay,
To this compofed wonder of your frame,
Whether we are mended, or where better they,
Or whether reuolution be the fame.
  Oh fure I am the wits of former daies,
  To fubiects worfe haue giuen admiring praife.

60 [80]

Like as the waues make towards the pibled fhore,
So do our minuites haften to their end,
Each changing place with that which goes before,
In fequent toile all forwards do contend.
Natiuity once in the maine of light.
Crawies to maturity, wherewith being crown'd,
Crooked eclipfes gainft his glory fight,
And time that gaue, doth now his gift confound.
Time doth tranffixe the florifh fet on youth,
And delues the paralels in beauties brow,
Feedes on the rarities of natures truth,
And nothing ftands but for his fieth to mow.
   And yet to times in hope, my verfe fhall ftand
   Praifing thy worth, difpight his cruell hand.

61 [81]

Is it thy wil; thy Image fhould keepe open
My heauy eielids to the weary night?
Doft thou defire my flumbers fhould be broken,
While fhadowes like to thee do mocke my fight?
Is it thy fpirit that thou fend'ft from thee
So farre from home into my deeds to prye,
To find out fhames and idle houres in me,
The skope and tenure of thy Ieloufie?
O no, thy loue though much, is not fo great,
It is my loue that keepes mine eie awake,
Mine owne true loue that doth my reft defeat,
To plaie the watch-man euer for thy fake.
   For thee watch I, whilft thou doft wake elfewhere,
   From me farre of, with others all to neere.

62 [82]

Sinne of felfe-loue poffeffeth al mine eie,
And all my foule, and al my euery part;
And for this finne there is no remedie,
It is fo grounded inward in my heart.
Me thinkes no face fo gratious is as mine,
No fhape fo true, no truth of fuch account,
And for my felfe mine owne worth do define,
As I all other in all worths furmount.
But when my glaffe fhewes me my felfe indeed
Beated and chopt with tand antiquitie,
Mine owne felfe loue quite contrary I read
Selfe, fo felfe louing were iniquity,
   T'is thee (my felfe) that for my felfe I praife,
   Painting my age with beauty of thy daies,

63 [83]

AGainſt my loue ſhall be as I am now
   With times iniurious hand chruſht and ore-worne,
When houres haue dreind his blood and fild his brow
With lines and wrincles, when his youthfull morne
Hath trauaild on to Ages ſteepie night,
And all thoſe beauties whereof now he's King
Are vaniſhing, or vaniſht out of ſight,
Stealing away the treaſure of his Spring.
For ſuch a time do I now fortifie
Againſt confounding Ages cruell knife,
That he ſhall neuer cut from memory
My ſweet loues beauty, though my louers life.
   His beautie ſhall in theſe blacke lines be ſeene,
   And they ſhall liue, and he in them ſtill greene.

64 [84]

VVHen I haue ſeene by times fell hand defaced
   The rich proud coſt of outworne buried age,
When ſometime loftie towers I ſee downe raſed,
And braſſe eternall ſlaue to mortall rage.
When I haue ſeene the hungry Ocean gaine
Aduantage on the Kingdome of the ſhoare,
And the firme foile win of the watry maine,
Increaſing ſtore with loſſe, and loſſe with ſtore,
When I haue ſeene ſuch interchange of ſtate,
Or ſtate it ſelfe confounded, to decay,
Ruine hath taught me thus to ruminate
That Time will come and take my loue away.
   This thought is as a death which cannot chooſe
   But weepe to haue, that which it feares to looſe.

65 [85]

SInce braſſe, nor ſtone, nor earth, nor boundleſſe ſea,
   But ſad mortallity ore-ſwaies their power,
How with this rage ſhall beautie hold a plea,
Whoſe action is no ſtronger then a flower?
O how ſhall ſummers hunny breath hold out,
Againſt the wrackfull ſiedge of battring dayes,
When rocks impregnable are not ſo ſtoute,
Nor gates of ſteele ſo ſtrong but time decayes?
O fearefull meditation, where alack,
Shall times beſt Iewell from times cheſt lie hid?
Or what ſtrong hand can hold his ſwift foote back,
Or who his ſpoile or beautie can forbid?
   O none, vnleſſe this miracle haue might,
   That in black inck my loue may ſtill ſhine bright.

66 [86]

TYr'd with all thefe for reftfull death I cry,
 As to behold defert a begger borne,
And needie Nothing trimd in iollitie,
And pureft faith vnhappily forfworne,
And gilded honor fhamefully mifplaft,
And maiden vertue rudely ftrumpeted,
And right perfection wrongfully difgrac'd,
And ftrength by limping fway difabled,
And arte made tung-tide by authoritie,
And Folly (Doctor-like) controuling skill,
And fimple-Truth mifcalde Simplicitie,
And captiue-good attending Captaine ill.
  Tyr'd with all thefe, from thefe would I be gone,
  Saue that to dye, I leaue my loue alone.

67 [87]

AH wherefore with infection fhould he liue,
 And with his prefence grace impietie,
That finne by him aduantage fhould atchiue,
And lace it felfe with his focietie ?
Why fhould falfe painting immitate his cheeke,
And fteale dead feeing of his liuing hew ?
Why fhould poore beautie indirectly feeke
Rofes of fhaddow, fince his Rofe is true ?
Why fhould he liue, now nature banckrout is,
Beggerd of blood to blufh through liuely vaines,
For fhe hath no exchecker now but his,
And proud of many, liues vpon his gaines ?
  O him fhe ftores, to fhow what welth fhe had,
  In daies long fince, before thefe laft fo bad.

68 [88]

THus is his cheeke the map of daies out-worne,
 When beauty liu'd and dy'ed as flowers do now,
Before thefe baftard fignes of faire were borne,
Or durft inhabit on a liuing brow :
Before the goulden treffes of the dead,
The right of fepulchers, were fhorne away,
To liue a fcond life on fecond head,
Ere beauties dead fleece made another gay :
In him thofe holy antique howers are feene,
Without all ornament, it felfe and true,
Making no fummer of an others greene,
Robbing no ould to dreffe his beauty new,
  And him as for a map doth Nature ftore,
  To fhew faulfe Art what beauty was of yore,

69 [89]

THofe parts of thee that the worlds eye doth view,
  Want nothing that the thought of hearts can mend:
All toungs (the voice of foules) giue thee that end,
Vttring bare truth, euen fo as foes Commend.
Their outward thus with outward praife is crownd,
But thofe fame tongues that giue thee fo thine owne,
In other accents doe this praife confound
By feeing farther then the eye hath fhowne.
They looke into the beauty of thy mind,
And that in gueffe they meafure by thy deeds,
Then churls their thoughts (although their eies were kind)
To thy faire flower ad the rancke fmell of weeds,
  But why thy odor matcheth not thy fhow,
  The folye is this, that thou doeft common grow.

70 [90]

THat thou art blam'd fhall not be thy defe&ct,
  For flanders marke was euer yet the faire,
The ornament of beauty is fufpe&ct,
A Crow that flies in heauens fweeteft ayre.
So thou be good, flander doth but approue,
Their worth the greater being woo'd of time,
For Canker vice the fweeteft buds doth loue,
And thou prefent'ft a pure vnftayined prime.
Thou haft paft by the ambufh of young daies,
Either not affayld, or vi&ctor beeing charg'd,
Yet this thy praife cannot be foe thy praife,
To tye vp enuy, euermore inlarged,
  If fome fufpe&ct of ill maskt not thy fhow,
  Then thou alone kingdomes of hearts fhouldft owe.

71 [91]

NOe Longer mourne for me when I am dead,
  Then you fhall heare the furly fullen bell
Giue warning to the world that I am fled
From this vile world with vildeft wormes to dwell :
Nay if you read this line, remember not,
The hand that writ it, for I loue you fo,
That I in your fweet thoughts would be forgot,
If thinking on me then fhould make you woe.
O if (I fay) you looke vpon this verfe,
When I (perhaps) compounded am with clay,
Do not fo much as my poore name reherfe ;
But let your loue euen with my life decay.
  Leaft the wife world fhould looke into your mone,
  And mocke you with me after I am gon.

72 [92]

OLeaft the world fhould taske you to recite,
What merit liu'd in me that you fhould loue
After my death (deare loue) for get me quite,
For you in me can nothing worthy proue.
Vnleffe you would deuife fome vertuous lye,
To doe more for me then mine owne defert,
And hang more praife vpon deceafed I,
Then nigard truth would willingly impart :
O leaft your true loue may feeme falce in this,
That you for loue fpeake well of me vntrue,
My name be buried where my body is,
And liue no more to fhame nor me, nor you.
  For I am fhamd by that which I bring forth,
  And fo fhould you, to loue things nothing worth.

73 [93]

THat time of yeeare thou maift in me behold,
When yellow leaues, or none, or few doe hange
Vpon thofe boughes which fhake againft the could,
Bare rn'wd quiers, where late the fweet birds fang.
In me thou feeft the twi-light of fuch day,
As after Sun-fet fadeth in the Weft,
Which by and by blacke night doth take away,
Deaths fecond felfe that feals vp all in reft.
In me thou feeft the glowing of fuch fire,
That on the afhes of his youth doth lye,
As the death bed, whereon it muft expire,
Confum'd with that which it was nurrifht by.
  This thou perceu'ft, which makes thy loue more ftrong,
  To loue that well, which thou muft leaue ere long.

74 [94]

BVt be contented when that fell areft,
With out all bayle fhall carry me away,
My life hath in this line fome intereft,
Which for memoriall ftill with thee fhall ftay.
When thou reueweft this, thou doeft reuew,
The very part was confecrate to thee,
The earth can haue but earth, which is his due,
My fpirit is thine the better part of me,
So then thou haft but loft the dregs of life,
The pray of wormes, my body being dead,
The coward conqueft of a wretches knife,
To bafe of thee to be remembred,
  The worth of that, is that which it containes,
  And that is this, and this with thee remaines.

75 [95]

SO are you to my thoughts as food to life,
Or as fweet feafon'd fhewers are to the ground ;
And for the peace of you I hold fuch ftrife,
As twixt a mifer and his wealth is found.
Now proud as an inioyer, and anon
Doubting the filching age will fteale his treafure,
Now counting beft to be with you alone,
Then betterd that the world may fee my pleafure,
Some-time all ful with feafting on your fight,
And by and by cleane ftarued for a looke,
Poffeffing or purfuing no delight
Saue what is had, or muft from you be tooke.
 Thus do I pine and furfet day by day,
 Or gluttoning on all, or all away,

76 [96]

VVHy is my verfe fo barren of new pride ?
So far from variation or quicke change ?
Why with the time do I not glance afide
To new found methods, and to compounds ftrange ?
Why write I ftill all one, euer the fame,
And keepe inuention in a noted weed,
That euery word doth almoft fel my name,
Shewing their birth, and where they did proceed ?
O know fweet loue I alwaies write of you,
And you and loue are ftill my argument:
So all my beft is dreffing old words new,
Spending againe what is already fpent:
 For as the Sun is daily new and old,
 So is my loue ftill telling what is told,

77 [97]

THy glaffe will fhew thee how thy beauties were,
Thy dyall how thy pretious mynuits wafte,
The vacant leaues thy mindes imprint will beare.
And of this booke, this learning maift thou tafte.
The wrinckles which thy glaffe will truly fhow,
Of mouthed graues will giue thee memorie,
Thou by thy dyals fhady ftealth maift know,
Times theeuifh progreffe to eternitie.
Looke what thy memorie cannot containe,
Commit to thefe wafte blacks, and thou fhalt finde
Thofe children nurft, deliuerd from thy braine,
To take a new acquaintance of thy minde.
 Thefe offices, fo oft as thou wilt looke,
 Shall profit thee, and much inrich thy booke.

78 [98]

SO oft haue I inuok'd thee for my Mufe,
And found fuch faire affiftance in my verfe,
As euery *Alien* pen hath got my vfe,
And vnder thee their poefie difperfe.
Thine eyes, that taught the dumbe on high to fing,
And heauie ignorance aloft to flie,
Haue added fethers to the learneds wing,
And giuen grace a double Maieftie.
Yet be moft proud of that which I compile,
Whofe influence is thine, and borne of thee,
In others workes thou dooft but mend the ftile,
And Arts with thy fweete graces graced be.
　　But thou art all my art, and dooft aduance
　　As high as learning, my rude ignorance.

79 [99]

WHilft I alone did call vpon thy ayde,
My verfe alone had all thy gentle grace,
But now my gracious numbers are decayde,
And my fick Mufe doth giue an other place.
I grant (fweet loue) thy louely argument
Deferues the trauaile of a worthier pen,
Yet what of thee thy Poet doth inuent,
He robs thee of, and payes it thee againe,
He lends thee vertue, and he ftole that word,
From thy behauiour, beautie doth he giue
And found it in thy cheeke: he can affoord
No praife to thee, but what in thee doth liue.
　　Then thanke him not for that which he doth fay,
　　Since what he owes thee, thou thy felfe dooft pay,

80 [100]

OHow I faint when I of you do write,
Knowing a better fpirit doth vfe your name,
And in the praife thereof fpends all his might,
To make me toung-tide fpeaking of your fame.
But fince your worth (wide as the Ocean is)
The humble as the proudeft faile doth beare,
My fawfie barke (inferior farre to his)
On your broad maine doth wilfully appeare.
Your fhalloweft helpe will hold me vp a floate,
Whilft he vpon your foundleffe deepe doth ride,
Or (being wrackt) I am a worthleffe bote,
He of tall building, and of goodly pride.
　　Then If he thriue and I be caft away,
　　The worft was this, my loue was my decay.

81 [101]

OR I fhall liue your Epitaph to make,
Or you furuiue when I in earth am rotten,
From hence your memory death cannot take,
Although in me each part will be forgotten.
Your name from hence immortall life fhall haue,
Though I (once gone) to all the world muft dye,
The earth can yeeld me but a common graue,
When you intombed in mens eyes fhall lye,
Your monument fhall be my gentle verfe,
Which eyes not yet created fhall ore-read,
And toungs to be, your beeing fhall rehearfe,
When all the breathers of this world are dead,
  You ftill fhall liue (fuch vertue hath my Pen)
  Where breath moft breaths, euen in the mouths of men.

82 [102]

I Grant thou wert not married to my Mufe,
And therefore maieft without attaint ore-looke
The dedicated words which writers vfe
Of their faire fubiect, bleffing euery booke.
Thou art as faire in knowledge as in hew,
Finding thy worth a limmit paft my praife,
And therefore art inforc'd to feeke anew,
Some frefher ftampe of the time bettering dayes,
And do fo loue, yet when they haue deuifde,
What ftrained touches Rhethorick can lend,
Thou truly faire, wert truly fimpathizde,
In true plaine words, by thy true telling friend.
  And their groffe painting might be better vf'd,
  Where cheekes need blood, in thee it is abuf d.

83 [103]

I Neuer faw that you did painting need,
And therefore to your faire no painting fet,
I found (or thought I found) you did exceed,
The barren tender of a Poets debt :
And therefore haue I flept in your report,
That you your felfe being extant well might fhow,
How farre a moderne quill doth come to fhort,
Speaking of worth, what worth in you doth grow,
This filence for my finne you did impute,
Which fhall be moft my glory being dombe,
For I impaire not beautie being mute,
When others would giue life, and bring a tombe.
  There liues more life in one of your faire eyes,
  Then both your Poets can in praife deuife.

84 [104]

WHO is it that fayes moft, which can fay more,
Then this rich praife, that you alone, are you,
In whofe confine immured is the ftore,
Which fhould example where your equall grew,
Leane penurie within that Pen doth dwell,
That to his fubiect lends not fome fmall glory,
But he that writes of you, if he can tell,
That you are you, fo dignifies his ftory.
Let him but coppy what in you is writ,
Not making worfe what nature made fo cleere.
And fuch a counter-part fhall fame his wit,
Making his ftile admired euery where.
 You to your beautious bleffings adde a curfe,
 Being fond on praife, which makes your praifes worfe.

85 [105]

MY toung-tide Mufe in manners holds her ftill,
While comments of your praife richly compil'd,
Referne their Character with goulden quill,
And precious phrafe by all the Mufes fil'd,
I thinke good thoughts, whilft other write good wordes,
And like vnlettered clarke ftill crie Amen,
To euery Himne that able fpirit affords,
In polifht for ne of well refined pen.
Hearing you praifd, I fay 'tis fo, 'tis true,
And to the moft of praife adde fome-thing more,
But that is in my thought, whofe loue to you
(Though words come hind-moft) holds his ranke before,
 Then others, for the breath of words refpect,
 Me for my dombe thoughts, fpeaking in effect.

86 [106]

VVAs it the proud full faile of his great verfe,
Bound for the prize of (all to precious) you,
That did my ripe thoughts in my braine inhearce,
Making their tombe the wombe wherein they grew?
Was it his fpirit, by fpirits taught to write,
Aboue a mortall pitch, that ftruck me dead?
No, neither he, nor his compiers by night
Giuing him ayde, my verfe aftonifhed.
He nor that affable familiar ghoft
Which nightly gulls him with intelligence,
As victors of my filence cannot boaft,
I was not fick of any feare from thence,
 But when your countinance fild vp his line,
 Then lackt I matter, that infeebled mine.

87 [107]

FArewell thou art too deare for my poffeffing,
    And like enough thou knowſt thy eſtimate,
The Cha.ter of thy worth giues thee releaſing :
My bonds in thee are all determinate.
For how do I hold thee but by thy granting,
And for that ritches where is my deſeruing ?
The cauſe of this faire guift in me is wanting,
And ſo my patlent back againe is ſwcruing.
Thy ſelfe thou gau'ſt, thy owne worth then not knowing,
Or mee to whom thou gau'ſt it, elſe miſtaking,
So thy great guift vpon miſpriſion growing,
Comes home againe, on better iudgement making.
    Thus haue I had thee as a dreame doth flatter,
    In ſleepe a King, but waking no ſuch matter.

88 [108]

VVHen thou ſhalt be difpode to ſet me light,
    And place my merrit in the eie of skorne,
Vpon thy ſide, againſt my ſelfe ile ûght,
And proue thee virtuous, though thou art forſworne :
With mine owne weakeneſſe being beſt acquainted,
Vpon thy part I can ſet downe a ſtory
Of faults conceald, wherein I am attainted :
That thou in looſing me, ſhall win much glory :
And I by this wil be a gainer too,
For bending all my louing thoughts on thee,
The iniuries that to my ſelfe I doe,
Doing thee vantage, duble vantage me,
    Such is my loue, to thee I ſo belong,
    That for thy right, my ſelfe will beare all wrong.

89 [109]

SAy that thou didſt forſake mee for ſome falt,
    And I will comment vpon that offence,
Speake of my lameneſſe, and I ſtraight will halt :
Againſt thy reaſons making no defence.
Thou canſt not (loue) difgrace me halfe ſo ill,
To ſet a forme vpon deſired change,
As ile my ſelfe difgrace, knowing thy wil,
I will acquaintance ſtrangle and looke ſtrange :
Be abſent from thy walkes and in my tongue,
Thy ſweet beloued name no more ſhall dwell,
Leaſt I (too much prophane) ſhould do it wronge :
And haplie of our old acquaintance tell.
    For thee, againſt my ſelfe ile vow debate,
    For I muſt nere loue him whom thou doſt hate.

90 [110]

THen hate me when thou wilt, if euer, now,
Now while the world is bent my deeds to croffe,
Ioyne with the fpight of fortune, make me bow.
And doe not drop in for an after loffe:
Ah doe not, when my heart hath fcapte this forrow,
Come in the rereward of a conquerd woe,
Giue not a windy night a rainie morrow,
To linger out a purpofd ouer-throw.
If thou wilt leaue me, do not leaue me laft,
When other pettie griefes haue done their fpight,
But in the onfet come, fo ftall I tafte
At firft the very worft of fortunes might.
  And other ftraines of woe, which now feeme woe,
  Compar'd with loffe of thee, will not feeme fo.

91 [111]

SOme glory in their birth, fome in their skill,
Some in their wealth, fome in their bodies force,
Some in their garments though new-fangled ill:
Some in their Hawkes and Hounds, fome in their Horfe.
And euery humor hath his adiunct pleafure,
Wherein it findes a ioy aboue the reft,
But thefe perticulers are not my meafure,
All thefe I better in one generall beft.
Thy loue is bitter then high birth to me,
Richer then wealth, prouder then garments coft,
Of more delight then Hawkes or Horfes bee:
And hauing thee, of all mens pride I boaft.
  Wretched in this alone, that thou maift take,
  All this away, and me moft wretched make.

92 [112]

BVt doe thy worft to fteale thy felfe away,
For tearme of life thou art affured mine,
And life no longer then thy loue will ftay,
For it depends vpon that loue of thine.
Then need I not to feare the worft of wrongs,
When in the leaft of them my life hath end,
I fee, a better ftate to me belongs
Then that, which on thy humor doth depend.
Thou canft not vex me with inconftant minde,
Since that my life on thy reuolt doth lie,
Oh what a happy title do I finde,
Happy to haue thy loue, happy to die!
  But whats fo bleffed faire that feares no blot,
  Thou maift be falce, and yet I know it not.

93 [113]

SO fhall I liue, fuppofing thou art true,
Like a deceiued husband, fo loues face,
May ftill feeme loue to me, though alter'd new:
Thy lookes with me, thy heart in other place.
For their can liue no hatred in thine eye,
Therefore in that I cannot know thy change,
In manies lookes, the falce hearts hiftory
Is writ in moods and frounes and wrinckles ftrange,
But heauen in thy creation did decree,
That in thy face fweet loue fhould euer dwell,
What ere thy thoughts, or thy hearts workings be,
Thy lookes fhould nothing thence, but fweetneffe tell.
   How like *Eaues* apple doth thy beauty grow,
   If thy fweet vertue anfwere not thy fhow.

94 [114]

THey that haue powre to hurt, and will doe none,
That doe not do the thing, they moft do fhowe,
Who mouing others, are themfelues as ftone,
Vnmooued, could, and to temptation flow:
They rightly do inherrit heauens graces,
And husband natures ritches from expence,
They are the Lords and owners of their faces,
Others, but ftewards of their excellence:
The fommers flowre is to the fommer fweet,
Though to it felfe, it onely liue and die,
But if that flowre with bafe infection meete,
The bafeft weed out-braues his dignity:
   For fweeteft things turne fowreft by their deedes,
   Lillies that fefter, fmell far worfe then weeds.

95 [115]

HOw fweet and louely doft thou make the fhame,
Which like a canker in the fragrant Rofe,
Doth fpot the beautie of thy budding name?
Oh in what fweets doeft thou thy finnes inclofe!
That tongue that tells the ftory of thy daies,
(Making lafciuious comments on thy fport)
Cannot difpraife, but in a kinde of praife,
Naming thy name, bleffes an ill report.
Oh what a manfion haue thofe vices got,
Which for their habitation chofe out thee,
Where beauties vaile doth couer euery blot,
And all things turnes to faire, that eies can fee!
   Take heed (deare heart) of this large priuiledge,
   The hardeft knife ill vf'd doth loofe his edge.

96 [116]

SOme fay thy fault is youth, fome wantoneffe,
Some fay thy grace is youth and gentle fport,
Both grace and faults are lou'd of more and leffe:
Thou makft faults graces, that to thee refort:
As on the finger of a throned Queene,
The bafeft Iewell will be well efteem'd:
So are thofe errors that in thee are feene,
To truths tranflated, and for true things deem'd.
How many Lambs might the fterne Wolfe betray,
If like a Lambe he could his lookes tranflate.
How many gazers mighft thou lead away,
If thou wouldft vfe the ftrength of all thy ftate?
  But doe not fo, I loue thee in fuch fort,
  As thou being mine, mine is thy good report.

97 [117]

HOw like a Winter hath my abfence beene
From thee, the pleafure of the fleeting yeare?
What freezings haue I felt, what darke daies feene?
What old Decembers bareneffe euery where?
And yet this time remou'd was fommers time,
The teeming Autumne big with ritch increafe,
Bearing the wanton burthen of the prime,
Like widdowed wombes after their Lords deceafe:
Yet this aboundant iffue feem'd to me,
But hope of Orphans, and vn-fathered fruite,
For Sommer and his pleafures waite on thee,
And thou away, the very birds are mute.
  Or if they fing, tis with fo dull a cheere,
  That leaues looke pale, dreading the Winters neere

98 [118]

FRom you haue I beene abfent in the fpring,
When proud pide Aprill (dreft in all his trim)
Hath put a fpirit of youth in euery thing:
That heauie *Saturne* laught and leapt with him.
Yet nor the laies of birds, nor the fweet fmell
Of different flowers in odor and in hew,
Could make me any fummers ftory tell:
Or from their proud lap pluck them where they grew
Nor did I wonder at the Lillies white,
Nor praife the deepe vermillion in the Rofe,
They weare but fweet, but figures of delight:
Drawne after you, you patterne of all thofe.
  Yet feem'd it Winter ftill, and you away,
  As with your fhaddow I with thefe did play.

99 [119]

THe forward violet thus did I chide,
  Sweet theefe whence didſt thou ſteale thy ſweet that
If not from my loues breath, the purple pride,   (ſmels
Which on thy ſoft cheeke for complexion dwells ?
In my loues veines thou haſt too groſely died ;
The Lillie I condemned for thy hand,
And buds of marierom had ſtolne thy haire,
The Roſes fearefully on thornes did ſtand,
Our bluſhing ſhame, an other white diſpaire :
A third nor red, nor white, had ſtolne of both,
And to his robbry had annext thy breath,
But for his theft in pride of all his growth
A vengſull canker eate him vp to death.
    More flowers I noted, yet I none could ſee,
    But ſweet, or culler it had ſtolne from thee.

100 [120]

VVHere art thou Muſe that thou forgetſt ſo long,
  To ſpeake of that which giues thee all thy might ?
Spendſt thou thy furie on ſome worthleſſe ſonge,
Darkning thy powre to lend baſe ſubiects light.
Returne forgetfull Muſe, and ſtraight redeeme,
In gentle numbers time ſo idely ſpent,
Sing to the eare that doth thy laies eſteeme,
And giues thy pen both skill and argument.
Riſe reſty Muſe, my loues ſweet face ſuruay,
If time haue any wrincle grauen there,
If any, be a *Satire* to decay,
And make times ſpoiles diſpiſed euery where.
    Giue my loue fame faſter then time waſts life,
    So thou preuenſt his ſieth, and crooked knife.

101 [121]

OH truant Muſe what ſhalbe thy amends,
  For thy neglect of truth in beauty di'd ?
Both truth and beauty on my loue depends :
So doſt thou too, and therein dignifi'd :
Make anſwere Muſe, wilt thou not haply ſaie,
Truth needs no collour with his collour fixt,
Beautie no penſell, beauties truth to lay :
But beſt is beſt, if neuer intermixt.
Becauſe he needs no praiſe, wilt thou be dumb ?
Excuſe not ſilence ſo, for't lies in thee,
To make him much out-liue a gilded tombe :
And to be praiſd of ages yet to be.
    Then do thy office Muſe, I teach thee how,
    To make him ſeeme long hence, as he ſhowes now.

102 [122]

MY loue is ftrengthned though more weake in fee-
I loue not leffe, thogh leffe the fhow appeare,   (ming
That loue is marchandiz'd, whofe ritch efteeming,
The owners tongue doth publifh euery where.
Our loue was new, and then but in the fpring,
When I was wont to greet it with my laies,
As *Philomell* in fummers front doth finge,
And ftops his pipe in growth of riper daies:
Not that the fummer is leffe pleafant now
Then when her mournefull himns did hufh the night,
But that wild muſick burthens euery bow,
And fweets growne common loofe their deare delight.
 Therefore like her, I fome-time hold my tongue:
 Becaufe I would not dull you with my fonge.

103 [123]

ALack what pouerty my Mufe brings forth,
That hauing fuch a skope to fhow her pride,
The argument all bare is of more worth
Then when it hath my added praife befide.
Oh blame me not if I no more can write!
Looke in your glaffe and there appeares a face,
That ouer-goes my blunt inuention quite,
Dulling my lines, and doing me difgrace.
Were it not finfull then ftriuing to mend,
To marre the fubiect that before was well,
For to no other paffe my verfes tend,
Then of your graces and your gifts to tell.
 And more, much more then in my verfe can fit,
 Your owne glaffe fhowes you, when you looke in it.

104 [124]

TO me faire friend you neuer can be old,
For as you were when firft your eye I eyde,
Such feemes your beautie ftill: Three Winters colde,
Haue from the forrefts fhooke three fummers pride,
Three beautious fprings to yellow *Autumne* turn'd,
In proceffe of the feafons haue I feene,
Three Aprill perfumes in three hot Iunes burn'd,
Since firft I faw you frefh which yet are greene.
Ah yet doth beauty like a Dyall hand,
Steale from his figure, and no pace perceiu'd,
So your fweete hew, which me thinkes ftill doth ftand
Hath motion, and mine eye may be deccaued.
 For feare of which, heare this thou age vnbred,
 Ere you were borne was beauties fummer dead.

105 [125]

LEt not my loue be cal'd Idolatrie,
Nor my beloued as an Idoll fhow,
Since all alike my fongs and praifes be
To one, of one, ftill fuch, and euer fo.
Kinde is my loue to day, to morrow kinde,
Still conftant in a wondrous excellence,
Therefore my verfe to conftancie confin'de,
One thing expreffing, leaues out difference.
Faire, kinde, and true, is all my argument,
Faire, kinde and true, varrying to other words,
And in this change is my inuention fpent,
Three theams in one, which wondrous fcope affords,
　Faire, kinde, and true, haue often liu'd alone.
　Which three till now, neuer kept feate in one.

106 [126]

WHen in the Chronicle of wafted time,
I fee difcriptions of the faireft wights,
And beautie making beautifull old rime,
In praife of Ladies dead, and louely Knights,
Then in the blazon of fweet beauties beft,
Of hand, of foote, of lip, of eye, of brow,
I fee their antique Pen would haue expreft
Euen fuch a beauty as you maifter now.
So all their praifes are but prophefies
Of this our time, all you prefiguring,
And for they look'd but with deuining eyes,
They had not ftill enough your worth to fing:
　For we which now behold thefe prefent dayes,
　Haue eyes to wonder, but lack toungs to praife.

107 [127]

NOt mine owne feares, nor the prophetick foule,
Of the wide world, dreaming on things to come,
Can yet the leafe of my true loue controule,
Suppofde as forfeit to a confin'd doome.
The mortall Moone hath her eclipfe indur'de,
And the fad Augurs mock their owne prefage,
Incertenties now crowne them-felues affur'de,
And peace proclaimes Oliues of endleffe age,
Now with the drops of this moft balmie time,
My loue lookes frefh, and death to me fubfcribes,
Since fpight of him Ile liue in this poore rime,
While he infults ore dull and fpeachleife tribes.
　And thou in this fhalt finde thy monument,
　When tyrants crefts and tombs of braffe are fpent.

108 [128]

VVHat's in the braine that Inck may charačter,
   Which hath not figur'd to thee my true fpirit,
What's new to fpeake, what now to regifter,
That may expreffe my loue, or thy deare merit?
Nothing fweet boy, but yet like prayers diuine,
I muft each day fay ore the very fame,
Counting no old thing old, thou mine, I thine,
Euen as when firft I hallowed thy faire name.
So that eternall loue in loues frefh cafe,
Waighes not the duft and iniury of age,
Nor giues to neceffary wrinckles place,
But makes antiquitie for aye his page,
   Finding the firft conceit of loue there bred,
   Where time and outward forme would fhew it dead.

109 [129]

ONeuer fay that I was falfe of heart,
   Though abfence feem'd my flame to quallifie,
As eafie might I from my felfe depart,
As from my foule which in thy breft doth lye:
That is my home of loue, if I haue rang'd,
Like him that trauels I returne againe,
Iuft to the time, not with the time exchang'd,
So that my felfe bring water for my ftaine,
Neuer beleeue though in my nature raign'd,
All frailties that befiege all kindes of blood,
That it could fo prepofterouflie be ftain'd,
To leaue for nothing all thy fumme of good;
   For nothing this wide Vniuerfe I call,
   Saue thou my Rofe, in it thou art my all.

110 [130]

ALas 'tis true, I haue gone here and there,
   And make my felfe a motley to the view,
Gor'd mine own thoughts, fold cheap what is moft deare,
Made old offences of affečtions new.
Moft true it is, that I haue lookt on truth
Afconce and ftrangely: But by all aboue,
Thefe blenches gaue my heart an other youth,
And worfe effaies prou'd thee my beft of loue,
Now all is done, haue what fhall haue no end,
Mine appetite I neuermore will grin'de
On newer proofe, to trie an older friend,
A God in loue, to whom I am confin'd.
   Then giue me welcome, next my heauen the beft,
   Euen to thy pure and moft moft louing breft.

111 [131]

OFor my fake doe you wifh fortune chide,
 The guiltie goddeffe of my harmfull deeds,
That did not better for my life prouide,
Then publick meanes which publick manners breeds.
Thence comes it that my name receiues a brand,
And almoft thence my nature is fubdu'd
To what it workes in, like the Dyers hand,
Pitty me then, and wifh I were renu'de,
Whilft like a willing pacient I will drinke,
Potions of Eyfell gainft my ftrong infection,
No bitterneffe that I will bitter thinke,
Nor double pennance to correct correction.
  Pittie me then deare friend, and I affure yee,
  Euen that your pittie is enough to cure mee.

112 [132]

YOur loue and pittie doth th' impreffion fill,
 Which vulgar fcandall ftampt vpon my brow,
For what care I who calls me well or ill,
So you ore-greene my bad, my good alow?
You are my All the world, and I muft ftriue,
To know my fhames and praifes from your tounge,
None elfe to me, nor I to none aliue,
That my fteel'd fence or changes right or wrong,
In fo profound *Abifme* I throw all care
Of others voyces, that my Adders fence,
To cryttick and to flatterer ftopped are :
Marke how with my neglect I doe difpence.
  You are fo ftrongly in my purpofe bred,
  That all the world befides me thinkes y'are dead.

113 [133]

SInce I left you, mine eye is in my minde,
 And that which gouernes me to goe about,
Doth part his function, and is partly blind,
Seemes feeing, but effectually is out :
For it no forme deliuers to the heart
Of bird, of flowre, or fhape which it doth lack,
Of his quick obiects hath the minde no part,
Nor his owne vifion houlds what it doth catch :
For if it fee the rud'ft or gentleft fight,
The moft fweet-fauor or deformedft creature,
The mountaine, or the fea, the day, or night :
The Croe, or Doue, it fhapes them to your feature.
  Incapable of more repleat, with you,
  My moft true minde thus maketh mine vntrue.

114 [134]

OR whether doth my minde being crown'd with you
Drinke vp the monarks plague this flattery ?
Or whether fhall I fay mine eie faith true,
And that your loue taught it this *Alcumie?*
To make of monfters, and things indigeft,
Such cherubines as your fweet felfe refemble,
Creating euery bad a perfect beft
As faft as obiects to his beames affemble :
Oh tis the firft, tis flatry in my feeing,
And my great minde moft kingly drinkes it vp,
Mine eie well knowes what with his guft is greeing,
And to his pallat doth prepare the cup.
    If it be poifon'd, tis the leffer finne,
    That mine eye loues it and doth firft beginne.

115 [135]

THofe lines that I before haue writ doe lie,
Euen thofe that faid I could not loue you deerer,
Yet then my iudgement knew no reafon why,
My moft full flame fhould afterwards burne cleerer,
But reckening time, whofe milliond accidents
Creepe in twixt vowes, and change decrees of Kings,
Tan facred beautie, blunt the fharp'ft intents,
Diuert ftrong mindes to th' courfe of altring things :
Alas why fearing of times tiranie,
Might I not then fay now I loue you beft,
When I was certaine ore in-certainty,
Crowning the prefent, doubting of the reft :
    Loue is a Babe, then might I not fay fo
    To giue full growth to that which ftill doth grow.

116 [136]

LEt me not to the marriage of true mindes
Admit impediments, loue is not loue
Which alters when it alteration findes,
Or bends with the remouer to remoue.
O no, it is an euer fixed marke
That lookes on tempefts and is neuer fhaken ;
It is the ftar to euery wandring barke,
Whofe worths vnknowne, although his higth be taken.
Lou's not Times foole, though rofie lips and cheeks
Within his bending fickles compaffe come,
Loue alters not with his breefe houres and weekes,
But beares it out euen to the edge of doome :
    If this be error and vpon me proued,
    I neuer writ, nor no man euer loued.

117 [137]

ACcuſe me thus, that I haue ſcanted all,
Wherein I ſhould your great deſerts repay,
Forgot vpon your deareſt loue to call,
Whereto al bonds do tie me day by day,
That I haue frequent binne with vnknown mindes,
And giuen to time your owne dear purchaſ'd right,
That I haue hoyſted ſaile to al the windes
Which ſhould tranſport me fartheſt from your ſight.
Booke both my wilfulneſſe and errors downe,
And on iuſt proofe ſurmiſe, accumilate,
Bring me within the leuel of your frowne,
But ſhoote not at me in your wakened hate:
   Since my appeale ſaies I did ſtriue to prooue
   The conſtancy and virtue of your loue

118 [138]

LIke as to make our appetites more keene
With eager compounds we our pallat vrge,
As to preuent our malladies vnſeene,
We ſicken to ſhun ſickneſſe when we purge.
Euen ſo being full of your nere cloying ſweetneſſe,
To bitter ſawces did I frame my feeding;
And ſicke of wel-fare found a kind of meetneſſe,
To be diſeaſ'd ere that there was true needing.
Thus pollicie in loue t'anticipate
The ills that were, not grew to faults aſſured,
And brought to medicine a healthfull ſtate
Which rancke of goodneſſe would by ill be cured.
   But thence I learne and find the leſſon true,
   Drugs poyſon him that ſo fell ſicke of you.

119 [143]

WHat potions haue I drunke of *Syren* teares
Diſtil'd from Lymbecks foule as hell within,
Applying feares to hopes, and hopes to feares,
Still looſing when I ſaw my ſelfe to win?
What wretched errors hath my heart committed,
Whilſt it hath thought it ſelfe ſo bleſſed neuer?
How haue mine eies out of their Spheares bene fitted
In the diſtraction of this madding feuer?
O benefit of ill, now I find true
That better is, by euil ſtill made better.
And ruin'd loue when it is built anew
Growes fairer then at firſt, more ſtrong, far greater.
   So I returne rebukt to my content,
   And gaine by ills thriſe more then I haue ſpent.

120 [144]

THat you were once vnkind be-friends mee now,
  And for that forrow , which I then didde feele,
Needes muft I vnder my tranfgreffion bow,
Vnleffe my Nerues were braffe or hammered fteele.
For if you were by my vnkindneffe fhaken
As I by yours , y'haue paft a hell of Time,
And I a tyrant haue no leafure taken
To waigh how once I fuffered in your crime.
O that our night of wo might haue remembred
My deepeft fence, how hard true forrow hits,
And foone to you, as you to me then tendred
The humble falue, which wounded bofomes fits !
    But that your trefpaffe now becomes a fee,
    Mine ranfoms yours, and yours muft ranfome mee.

121 [33]

TIS better to be vile then vile efteemed,
  When not to be, receiues reproach of being,
And the iuft pleafure loft, which is fo deemed,
Not by our feeling, but by others feeing.
For why fhould others falfe adulterat eyes
Giue falutation to my fportiue blood ?
Or on my frailties why are frailer fpies ;
Which in their wils count bad what I think good ?
Noe, I am that I am, and they that leuell
At my abufes, reckon vp their owne,
I may be ftraight though they them-felues be beuel
By their rancke thoughtes, my deedes muft not be fhown
    Vnleffe this generall euill they maintaine,
    All men are bad and in their badneffe raigne.

122 [145]

TThy guift,, thy tables, are within my braine
  Full characterd with lafting memory,
Which fhall aboue that idle rancke remaine
Beyond all date euen to eternity.
Or at the leaft, fo long as braine and heart
Haue facultie by nature to fubfift,
Til each to raz'd obliuion yeeld his part
Of thee, thy record neuer can be mift :
That poore retention could not fo much hold,
Nor need I tallies thy deare loue to skore,
Therefore to giue them from me was I bold,
To truft thofe tables that receaue thee more,
    To keepe an adiunckt to remember thee,
    Were to import forgetfulneffe in mee.

123 [146]

NO! Time, thou fhalt not boft that I doe change,
Thy pyramyds buylt vp with newer might
To me are nothing nouell, nothing ftrange,
They are but dreffings of a former fight:
Our dates are breefe, and therefor we admire,
What thou doft foyft vpon vs that is ould,
And rather make them borne to our defire,
Then thinke that we before haue heard them tould:
Thy regifters and thee I both defie,
Not wondring at the prefent, nor the paft,
For thy records, and what we fee doth lye,
Made more or les by thy continuall haft:
   This I doe vow and this fhall euer be,
   I will be true difpight thy fyeth and thee.

124 [147]

YF my deare loue were but the childe of ftate,
It might for fortunes bafterd be vnfathered,
As fubiect to times loue, or to times hate,
Weeds among weeds, or flowers with flowers gatherd,
No it was buylded far from accident,
It fuffers not in fmilinge pomp, nor falls
Vnder the blow of thralled difcontent,
Whereto th'inuiting time our fafhion calls:
It feares not policy that *Heriticke*,
Which workes on leafes of fhort numbred howers,
But all alone ftands hugely pollitick,
That it nor growes with heat, nor drownes with fhowres.
   To this I witnes call the foles of time,
   Which die for goodnes, who haue liu'd for crime.

125 [148]

VVEr't ought to me I bore the canopy,
With my extern the outward honoring,
Or layd great bafes for eternity,
Which proues more fhort then waft or ruining?
Haue I not feene dwellers on forme and fauor
Lofe all, and more by paying too much rent
For compound fweet; Forgoing fimple fauor,
Pittifull thriuors in their gazing fpent.
Noe, let me be obfequious in thy heart,
And take thou my oblacion, poore but free,
Which is not mixt with feconds, knows no art,
But mutuall render onely me for thee.
   Hence, thou fubbornd *Informer*, a trew foule
   When moft impeacht, ftands leaft in thy controule.

126 [APPENDIX A]

OThou my louely Boy who in thy power,
  Doeſt hould times fickle glaſſe, his fickle, hower:
Who haſt by wayning growne, and therein ſhou'ſt,
Thy louers withering, as thy ſweet ſelfe grow'ſt.
If Nature (ſoueraine miſteres ouer wrack)
As thou goeſt onwards ſtill will plucke thee backe,
She keepes thee to this purpoſe, that her skill.
May time diſgrace, and wretched mynuit kill.
Yet feare her O thou minnion of her pleaſure,
She may detaine, but not ſtill keepe her treſure!
Her *Andite* (though delayd) anſwer'd muſt be,
And her *Quietus* is to render thee.
               (   )
               (   )

127 [40]

IN the ould age blacke was not counted faire,
  Or if it weare it bore not beauties name:
But now is blacke beauties ſucceſſive heire,
And Beautie ſlanderd with a baſtard ſhame,
For ſince each hand hath put on Natures power,
Fairing the foule with Arts faulſe borrow'd face,
Sweet beauty hath no name no holy boure,
But is prophan'd, if not liues in diſgrace.
Therefore my Miſterſſe eyes are Rauen blacke,
Her eyes ſo ſuted, and they mourners ſeeme,
At ſuch who not borne faire no beauty lack,
Slandring Creation with a falſe eſteeme,
    Yet ſo they mourne becomming of their woe,
    That euery toung ſaies beauty ſhould looke ſo.

128 [41]

HOw oft when thou my muſike muſike playſt,
  Vpon that bleſſed wood whoſe motion ſounds
With thy ſweet fingers when thou gently ſwayſt,
The wiry concord that mine eare confounds,
Do I enuie thoſe Iackes that nimble leape,
To kiſſe the tender inward of thy hand,
Whilſt my poore lips which ſhould that harueſt reape,
At the woods bouldnes by thee bluſhing ſtand.
To be ſo tikled they would change their ſtate,
And ſituation with thoſe dancing chips,
Ore whome their fingers walke with gentle gate,
Making dead wood more bleſt then liuing lips,
    Since fauſie Iackes ſo happy are in this,
    Giue them their fingers, me thy lips to kiſſe.

129 [APPENDIX B]

TH' expence of Spirit in a wafte of fhame
  Is luft in action, and till action, luft
Is periurd, murdrous, blouddy full of blame,
Sauage, extreame, rude, cruell, not to truft,
Inioyd no fooner but difpifed ftraight,
Paft reafon hunted, and no fooner had
Paft reafon hated as a fwollowed bayt,
On purpofe layd to make the taker mad.
Made In purfut and in poffeffion fo,
Had, hauing, and in queft, to haue extreame,
A bliffe in proofe and proud and very wo,
Before a ioy propofd behind a dreame,
  All this the world well knowes yet none knowes well,
  To fhun the heauen that leads men to this hell.

130 [42]

MY Miftres eyes are nothing like the Sunne,
  Currall is farre more red, then her lips red,
If fnow be white, why then her brefts are dun :
If haires be wiers, black wiers grow on her head :
I haue feene Rofes damaskt, red and white,
But no fuch Rofes fee I in her cheekes,
And in fome perfumes is there more delight,
Then in the breath that from my Miftres reekes.
I loue to hear her fpeake, yet well I know,
That Muficke hath a farre more pleafing found :
I graunt I neuer faw a goddeffe goe,
My Miftres when fhee walkes treads on the ground,
  And yet by heauen I thinke my loue as rare,
  As any fhe beli'd with falfe compare.

131 [43]

THou art as tiranous, fo as thou art,
  As thofe whofe beauties proudly make them cruell ;
For well thou know'ft to my deare doting hart
Thou art the faireft and moft precious Iewell.
Yet in good faith fome fay that thee behold,
Thy face hath not the power to make loue grone ;
To fay they erre, I dare not be fo bold,
Although I fweare it to my felfe alone.
And to be fure that is not falfe I fweare
A thoufand grones but thinking on thy face,
One on anothers necke do witneffe beare
Thy blacke is faireft in my iudgements place.
  In nothing art thou blacke faue in thy deeds,
And thence this flaunder as I thinke proceeds.

132 [44]

THine eies I loue, and they as pittying me,
  Knowing thy heart torment me with difdaine,
Haue put on black, and louing mourners bee,
Looking with pretty ruth vpon my paine,
And truly not the morning Sun of Heauen
Better becomes the gray cheeks of th' Eaft,
Nor that full Starre that vfhers in the Eauen
Doth halfe that glory to the fober Weft
As thofe two morning eyes become thy face :
O let it then as well befeeme thy heart
To mourne for me fince mourning doth thee grace,
And fute thy pitty like in euery part.
  Then will I fweare beauty her felfe is blacke,
  And all they foule that thy complexion lacke.

133 [61]

BEfhrew that heart that makes my heart to groane
  For that deepe wound it giues my friend and me ;
I'ft not ynough to torture me alone,
But flaue to flauery my fweet'ft friend muft be.
Me from my felfe thy cruell eye hath taken,
And my next felfe thou harder haft ingroffed,
Of him, my felfe, and thee I am forfaken,
A torment thrice three-fold thus to be croffed :
Prifon my heart in thy fteele bofomes warde,
But then my friends heart let my poore heart bale,
Who ere keepes me, let my heart be his garde,
Thou canft not then vfe rigor in my Iaile.
  And yet thou wilt, for I being pent in thee,
  Perforce am thine and all that is in me.

134 [60]

SO now I haue confeft that he is thine,
  And I my felfe am morgag'd to thy will,
My felfe Ile forfeit, fo that other mine,
Thou wilt reftore to be my comfort ftill :
But thou wilt not, nor he will not be free,
For thou art couetous, and he is kinde,
He learnd but furetie-like to write for me,
Vnder that bond that him as faft doth binde.
The ftatute of thy beauty thou wilt take,
Thou vfurer that put'ft forth all to vfe,
And fue a friend, came debter for my fake,
So him I loofe through my vnkinde abufe.
  Him haue I loft, thou haft both him and me,
  He paies the whole, and yet am I not free.

135 [53]

WHo euer hath her wifh, thou haft thy *Will*,
   And *Will* too boote, and *Will* in ouer-plus,
More then enough am I that vexe thee ftill,
To thy fweet will making addition thus.
Wilt thou whofe will is large and fpatious,
Not once vouchfafe to hide my will in thine,
Shall will in others feeme right gracious,
And in my will no faire acceptance fhine:
The fea all water, yet receiues raine ftill,
And in aboundance addeth to his ftore,
So thou beeing rich in *Will* adde to thy *Will*,
One will of mine to make thy large *Will* more.
   Let no vnkinde, no faire befeechers kill,
    Thinke all but one, and me in that one *Will*.

136 [54]

IF thy foule check thee that I come fo neere,
   Sweare to thy blind foule that I was thy *Will*,
And will thy foule knowes is admitted there,
Thus farre for loue, my loue-fute fweet fullfill.
Will, will fulfill the treafure of thy loue,
I fill it full with wils, and my will one,
In things of great receit with eafe we prooue,
Among a number one is reckon'd none.
Then in the number let me paffe vntold,
Though in thy ftores account I one muft be,
For nothing hold me fo it pleafe thee hold,
That nothing me, a fome-thing fweet to thee.
   Make but my name thy loue, and loue that ftill,
    And then thou loueft me for my name is *Will*.

137 [45]

THou blinde foole loue, what dooft thou to mine eyes,
   That they behold and fee not what they fee:
They know what beautie is, fee where it lyes,
Yet what the beft is, take the worft to be:
If eyes corrupt by ouer-partiall lookes,
Be anchord in the baye where all men ride,
Why of eyes falfehood haft thou forged hookes,
Whereto the iudgement of my heart is tide?
Why fhould my heart thinke that a feuerall plot,
Which my heart knowes the wide worlds common place?
Or mine eyes feeing this, fay this is not
To put faire truth vpon fo foule a face,
   In things right true my heart and eyes haue erred,
    And to this falfe plague are they now tranfferred.

138 [46]

WHen my loue fweares that fhe is made of truth,
  I do beleeue her though I know fhe lyes,
That fhe might thinke me fome vntuterd youth,
Vnlearned in the worlds falfe fubtilties.
Thus vainely thinking that fhe thinkes me young,
Although fhe knowes my dayes are paft the beft,
Simply I credit her falfe fpeaking tongue,
On both fides thus is fimple truth fuppreft :
But wherefore faves fhe not fhe is vniuft ?
And wherefore fay not I that I am old ?
O loues beft habit is in feeming truft,
And age in loue, loues not t'haue yeares told.
   Therefore I lye with her, and fhe with me,
   And in our faults by lyes we flattered be.

139 [47]

OCall not me to iuftifie the wrong,
  That thy vnkindneffe layes vpon my heart,
Wound me not with thine eye but with thy toung,
Vfe power with power, and flay me not by Art,
Tell me thou lou'ft elfe-where ; but in my fight,
Deare heart forbeare to glance thine eye afide,
What needft thou wound with cunning when thy might
Is more then my ore-preft defence can bide ?
Let me excufe thee ah my loue well knowes,
Her prettie lookes haue beene mine enemies,
And therefore from my face fhe turnes my foes,
That they elfe-where might dart their iniuries :
   Yet do not fo, but fince I am neere flaine,
   Kill me out-right with lookes, and rid my paine.

140 [48]

BE wife as thou art cruell, do not preffe
  My toung tide patience with too much difdaine :
Leaft forrow lend me words and words expreffe,
The manner of my pittie wanting paine.
If I might teach thee witte better it weare,
Though not to loue, yet loue to tell me fo,
As teftie fick-men when their deaths be neere,
No newes but health from their Phifitions know.
For if I fhould difpaire I fhould grow madde,
And in my madneffe might fpeake ill of thee,
Now this ill wrefting world is growne fo bad,
Madde flanderers by madde eares beleeued be.
   That I may not be fo, nor thou be lyde,   (wide.
   Beare thine eyes ftraight, though thy proud heart goe

141 [49]

IN faith I doe not loue thee with mine eyes,
For they in thee a thoufand errors note,
But 'tis my heart that loues what they difpife,
Who in difpight of view is pleafd to dote.
Nor are mine eares with thy toungs tune delighted,
Nor tender feeling to bafe touches prone,
Nor tafte, nor fmell, defire to be inuited
To any fenfuall feaft with thee alone :
But my fiue wits, nor my fiue fences can
Difwade one foolifh heart from feruing thee,
Who leaues vnfwai'd the likeneffe of a man,
Thy proud hearts flaue and vaffall wretch to be :
 Onely my plague thus farre I count my gaine,
 That fhe that makes me finne, awards me paine.

142 [50]

LOue is my finne, and thy deare vertue hate,
Hate of my finne, grounded on finfull louing,
O but with mine, compare thou thine owne ftate,
And thou fhalt finde it merrits not reproouing,
Or if it do, not from thofe lips of thine,
That haue prophan'd their fcarlet ornaments,
And feald falfe bonds of loue as oft as mine,
Robd others beds reuenues of their rents.
Be it lawfull I loue thee as thou lou'ft thofe,
Whome thine eyes wooe as mine importune thee,
Roote pittie in thy heart that when it growes,
Thy pitty may deferue to pittied bee.
 If thou dooft feeke to haue what thou dooft hide,
 By felfe example mai'ft thou be denide.

143 [51]

LOe as a carefull hufwife runnes to catch,
One of her fethered creatures broake away,
Sets downe her babe and makes all fwift difpatch
In purfuit of the thing fhe would haue ftay :
Whilft her neglected child holds her in chace,
Cries to catch her whofe bufie care is bent,
To follow that which flies before her face :
Not prizing her poore infants difcontent,
So runft thou after that which flies from thee,
Whilft I thy babe chace thee a farre behind,
But if thou catch thy hope turne back to me :
And play the mothers part kiffe me, be kind.
 So will I pray that thou maift haue thy *Will*,
 If thou turne back and my loude crying ftill.

144 [52]

TWo loues I haue of comfort and difpaire,
    Which like two fpirits do fugieft me ftill,
The better angell is a man right faire :
The worfer fpirit a woman collour'd il.
To win me foone to hell my femall euill,
Tempteth my better angel from my fight,
And would corrupt my faint to be a diuel :
Wooing his purity with her fowle pride.
And whether that my angel be turn'd finde,
Sufpeċt I may yet not directly tell,
But being both from me both to each friend,
I geffe one angel in an others hel.
    Yet this fhal I nere know but liue in doubt,
    Till my bad angel fire my good one out.

145 [APPENDIX C]

THofe lips that Loues owne hand did make,
    Breath'd forth the found that faid I hate,
To me that languifht for her fake :
But when fhe faw my wofull ftate,
Straight in her heart did mercie come,
Chiding that tongue that euer fweet,
Was vfde in giuing gentle dome :
And tought it thus a new to greete :
I hate fhe alterd with an end,
That follow'd it as gentle day,
Doth follow night who like a fiend
From heauen to hell is flowne away.
    I hate, from hate away fhe threw,
    And fau'd my life faying 'not you.'

146 [APPENDIX D]

POore foule the center of my finfull earth,
    My finfull earth thefe rebbell powres that thee array,
Why doft thou pine within and fuffer dearth
Painting thy outward walls fo coftlie gay ?
Why fo large coft hauing fo fhort a leafe,
Doft thou vpon thy fading manfion fpend ?
Shall wormes inheritors of this exceffe
Eate vp thy charge ? is this thy bodies end ?
Then foule liue thou vpon thy feruants loffe,
And let that pine to aggrauat thy ftore ;
Buy tearmes diuine in felling houres of droffe :
Within be fed, without be rich no more,
    So fhalt thou feed on death, that feeds on men,
    And death once dead, ther's no more dying then.

147 [139]

MY loue is as a feauer longing ftill,
For that which longer nurfeth the difeafe,
Feeding on that which doth preferue the ill,
Th'vncertaine ficklie appetite to pleafe:
My reafon the Phifition to my loue,
Angry that his prefcriptions are not kept
Hath left me, and I defperate now approoue,
Defire is death, which Phifick did except.
Paft cure I am, now Reafon is paft care,
And frantick madde with euer-more vnreft,
My thoughts and my difcourfe as mad mens are,
At randon from the truth vainely expreft.
    For I haue fworne thee faire, and thought thee bright,
    Who art as black as hell, as darke as night.

148 [140]

O Me! what eyes hath loue put in my head,
Which haue no correfpondence with true fight,
Or if they haue, where is my iudgment fled,
That cenfures falfely what they fee aright?
If that be faire whereon my falfe eyes dote,
What meanes the world to fay it is not fo?
If it be not, then loue doth well denote,
Loues eye is not fo true as all mens: no,
How can it? O how can loues eye be true,
That is fo vext with watching and with teares?
No maruaile then though I miftake my view,
The funne it felfe fees not, till heaucn cleeres.
    O cunning loue, with teares thou keepft me blinde,
    Leaft eyes well feeing thy foule faults fhould finde.

149 [141]

CAnft thou O cruell, fay I loue thee not,
When I againft my felfe with thee pertake:
Doe I not thinke on thee when I forgot
Am of my felfe, all tirant for thy fake?
Who hateth thee that I doe call my friend,
On whom froun'ft thou that I doe faune vpon,
Nay if thou lowrft on me doe I not fpend
Reuenge vpon my felfe with prefent mone?
What merrit do I in my felfe refpect,
That is fo proude thy feruice to difpife,
When all my beft doth worfhip thy defect,
Commanded by the motion of thine eyes.
    But loue hate on for now I know thy minde,
    Thofe that can fee thou lou'ft, and I am blind.

150 [142]

OH from what powre haft thou this powrefull might,
VVith infufficiency my heart to fway,
To make me giue the lie to my true fight,
And fwere that brightneffe doth not grace the day?
Whence haft thou this becomming of things il,
That in the very refufe of thy deeds,
There is fuch ftrength and warrantife of skill,
That in my minde thy worft all beft exceeds?
Who taught thee how to make me loue thee more,
The more I heare and fee iuft caufe of hate,
Oh though I loue what others doe abhor,
VVith others thou fhouldft not abhor my ftate.
   If thy vnworthineffe raifd loue in me,
   More worthy I to be belou'd of thee.

151 [55]

LOue is too young to know what confcience is,
Yet who knowes not confcience is borne of loue,
Then gentle cheater vrge not my amiffe,
Leaft guilty of my faults thy fweet felfe proue.
For thou betraying me, I doe betray
My nobler part to my grofe bodies treafon,
My foule doth tell my body that he may,
Triumph in loue, flefh ftaies no farther reafon,
But ryfing at thy name doth point out thee,
As his triumphant prize, proud of this pride,
He is contented thy poore drudge to be
To ftand in thy affaires, fall by thy fide.
   No want of confcience hold it that I call,
   Her loue, for whofe deare loue I rife and fall.

152 [62]

IN louing thee thou know'ft I am forfworne,
But thou art twice forfworne to me loue fwearing,
In act thy bed-vow broake and new faith torne,
In vowing new hate after new loue bearing:
But why of two othes breach doe I accufe thee,
When I breake twenty: I am periur'd moft,
For all my vowes are othes but to mifufe thee:
And all my honeft faith in thee is loft.
For I haue fworne deepe othes of thy deepe kindneffe:
Othes of thy loue, thy truth, thy conftancie,
And to inlighten thee gaue eyes to blindneffe,
Or made them fwere againft the thing they fee.
   For I haue fworne thee faire: more periurde eye,
   To fwere againft the truth fo foule a lie.

153 [APPENDIX E]

C*Vpid* laid by his brand and fell a fleepe,
A maide of *Dyans* this aduantage found,
And his loue-kindling fire did quickly fteepe
In a could vallie-fountaine of that ground :
Which borrowd from this holie fire of loue,
A dateleffe liuely heat ftill to indure,
And grew a feething bath which yet men proue,
Againft ftrang malladies a foueraigne cure :
But at my miftres eie loues brand new fired,
The boy for triall needes would touch my breft,
I fick withall the helpe of bath defired,
And thether hied a fad diftemperd gueft.
　　But found no cure, the bath for my helpe lies,
　　Where *Cupid* got new fire ; my miftres eye.

154 [APPENDIX F]

THe little Loue-God lying once a fleepe,
Laid by his fide his heart inflaming brand,
Whilft many Nymphes that vou'd chaft life to keep,
Came tripping by, but in her maiden hand,
The fayreft votary tooke vp that fire,
Which many Legions of true hearts had warm'd,
And fo the Generall of hot defire,
Was fleeping by a Virgin hand difarm'd.
This brand fhe quenched in a coole Well by,
Which from loues fire tooke heat perpetuall,
Growing a bath and healthfull remedy,
For men difeafd, but I my Miftriffe thrall,
　　Came there for cure and this by that I proue,
　　Loues fire heates water, water cooles not loue.

FINIS.

www.ingramcontent.com/pod-product-compliance
Lightning Source LLC
Chambersburg PA
CBHW031140120726
47905CB00006B/1760